THE ALBATROSS RUN

Ben remained rooted to the spot, tense and more than a little unnerved by that silent stare. He let out his breath in a sigh: unaware that he had been holding it, as if the act of daring to breathe would have caused some cataclysm. He felt emotionally drained, torn between an anxious compassion for Taggart and a fear-filled foreboding.

For the briefest of moments, he had glimpsed once more into the troubled heart of the master of the Kildare Glen and sensed a loneliness that was dark with a confusion of feelings. But what they were he could only begin to guess. Because he had sensed, too, a rage of such torment bottled within the man that it chilled his own heart with fear. Taggart was denying an outlet to the fury of emotions that bubbled within him and, in so doing, was compounding the dangerously volatile nature of that something mix.

Ben could not dispel the sudden fear that Taggart — as admirable and brave as he was — had the stability of a landmine with a trembler fuse.

Also in Arrow by Douglas Scott

**CHAINS
DIE FOR THE QUEEN
EAGLES BLOOD
THE HANGED MAN
IN THE FACE OF THE ENEMY**

THE ALBATROSS RUN

Douglas Scott

ARROW BOOKS

Arrow Books Limited
62–65 Chandos Place, London WC2N 4NW

An imprint of Century Hutchinson Limited

London Melbourne Sydney Auckland
Johannesburg and agencies throughout
the world

First published by Martin Secker & Warburg Limited 1986

Arrow edition 1988

© 1986 by Douglas Scott

This book is sold subject to the condition that it shall not, by way of trade or otherwise, be lent, resold, hired out, or otherwise circulated without the publisher's prior consent in any form of binding or cover other than that in which it is published and without a similar condition including this condition being imposed on the subsequent purchaser

Phototypeset by Input Typesetting Ltd

Printed and bound in Great Britain by
Anchor Brendon Limited, Tiptree, Essex

ISBN 0 09 951100 2

CONTENTS

One	Living Legend	7
Two	Sister Hewson	35
Three	The Party	58
Four	Outward Bound	77
Five	Storms	100
Six	Ocean without End	130
Seven	After the Storm	159
Eight	Durban	188
Nine	Ship of Hate	209
Ten	The Finding	237
Eleven	Confessions	252
Twelve	Detour	274
Thirteen	Revelation	300
Fourteen	Landfall	324

CHAPTER 1

Living Legend

Ben Darby had no recollection of landing in Bombay. All he remembered was that the Dakota seemed to be coming down sideways. A wing-tip had hit the runway, there had been a thundering crash like the end of the world, and he had experienced the sensation of hurtling through space into a black void.

When he opened his eyes, it was to stare up into the serene faces of five misty figures clothed in white. The last thing he had expected to encounter after shedding his earthly existence was a welcome from the angelic band, so it was almost with exploding relief that he realised that, in place of harps, his 'angels' were equipped with more practical accoutrements. One carried a stainless-steel tray, on which sat a bottle, a dish and hypodermic needles. Another held what looked like a temperature chart on a board. A third had a stethoscope protruding from a breast pocket.

'I'm alive,' Ben murmured, and there was as much question as statement in the soft utterance. So much so that the figure with the stethoscope —a doctor — felt obliged to confirm that he was indeed alive. Alive and lucky. The crew of the Dakota on which Ben had hitched a ride had not survived the crash.

'Now we're going to put you to sleep again,' the doctor said, and made a signal to the nurse with the tray. She handed him the hypodermic.

It was some time later that Ben fully regained

consciousness and learned that the damage he had suffered could have been worse. He had a broken arm, a broken leg, two cracked ribs and a multiplicity of contusions that had required stitching and patching.

'We'll have you out of here before Christmas,' the doctor promised him, and Ben was relieved to find that he meant Christmas 1943. It was then September 1943.

On a morning in December, Ben held the doctor to his word and insisted on being discharged.

'You really need a longer convalescence,' the doctor warned him. 'If it were peacetime, I would recommend a holiday at a hill station or a long relaxing sea cruise.' Ben would remember his words about the sea cruise but, at the time, he scoffed at the idea of not getting straight back to work. All he needed was a typewriter and he was back in business.

The doctor nodded knowingly, undeceived. He had heard, of course, about Ben's last assignment – in China with Stillwell's forces – and how he had come out overland, on foot.

'The way I hear it,' the doctor said, 'you war correspondents get into some pretty hairy places. You won't be doing yourself any favours if you go charging off to war again before you've got your strength back. Will you be working in Bombay?'

'That really depends on the Washington office. Actually, I was just passing through when that Dakota came to grief. Bombay was only going to be a stop-over. I was on my way to Sierra Leone.'

The doctor made a face. 'That bloody hell-hole? The White Man's Grave. The mind boggles at contemplating how the devil you hoped to get there from here. But may I ask why? Why Sierra Leone, for God's sake?'

Ben smiled. 'You can't have read any of my stuff.'

'No . . . I'm sorry. I've never had the pleasure.

Ben grinned broadly. 'It's no great pleasure, Doc. I'm no Hemingway. Just a hard-working hack who's gotten

8

himself type-cast. I write about the Forgotten Man's war – the little guy who is fighting a lonely battle, where there's precious little glamour and no glory. That's what took me over the Hump into China . . . That's why I'm heading for Sierra Leone. The guys there don't get many medals, because they don't have Panzer attacks to beat off or little yellow men to shoot. They've got to fight boredom and going out of their minds. . . Their enemies are insects that poison their blood and foul up their systems with fevers that can turn healthy men into physical wrecks overnight. They don't rate the headlines, Doc . . . Unless somebody like me happens along and says his little hooray for them.'

'The unsung hero's champion?' said the doctor with a smile. 'Well, if you gotta go, Mr Darby, you gotta go. We'll miss you. You're our first American and our very first war correspondent. I must say that makes a change from squaddies with syph and matelots with malaria.' He smiled again. 'You know, if it's tropical diseases that interest you, you don't need to go traipsing off to West Africa. Bombay's got just about every variety known to man, and a few more besides.'

'I'll take your word for it,' Ben said.

He moved out from the hospital and got a room at the Taj Hotel. It was at the Taj that he first saw Taggart. It would have been impossible to miss him. Taggart was a big man and he was a loud man. When he couldn't be seen, he could be heard, with his voice like rolling thunder. When he could be seen, the rest of humanity seemed to shrink to insignificance before his giant presence.

Ben was drinking tea in the lounge with Harris, an acquaintance from Associated Press, when Taggart boomed on to the scene. He had an RNR three-ringer in tow and was lecturing the strained-looking navyman on the follies of architects.

'Take this hotel,' he invited the commander in a voice

that could have been heard two miles out at sea. 'The silly sod who designed it wasn't very original, was he? He copied the Taj-ma-hal – a bloody tomb, for God's sake! As if there weren't enough hotels like tombs, he's got to go and build another one. And what do the builders do with his masterpiece? They build the bloody thing arse-to-front, don't they? It looks bloody marvellous from the deck of a dhow out in the bay, but the people who use the place and pay through the nose for the privilege have to come and go by the back door!'

Ben found himself smiling at the fog-horn comments of the big man. 'He's got a point, hasn't he?' he said to Harris. 'Who is he?'

'Steer clear of him, Ben,' Harris warned, keeping his voice low. 'If he finds out you're a pressman, he'll be on to you like a hawk and telling you his life story. He's a glutton for publicity... But his story's been done to death. He doesn't seem to realise that what made news in 1940 isn't exactly an earth-shattering scoop in 1943.'

'Who is he?' Ben repeated.

'Haven't you heard of Taggart of the *Kildare Cape*? Taggart, the scourge of Hitler's Navy? Big Bill Taggart, the Buccaneer with the Bulldog Spirit? He was international news once, Ben. He was plastered across the front pages all over the world. You couldn't open a magazine without his face staring out at you... He was on every blessed newsreel for weeks...'

'What did he do?'

'He took on a U-boat single-handed and sank it. He was a hero when the British Empire was badly in need of heroes – the British captain who turned and fought a U-boat with an obsolete twelve-pounder gun. Oh, don't get me wrong, it was a brave thing he did. And he was worth his weight in gold to our propaganda machine. But he developed a taste for being in the limelight. Now he's a bit of a bloody menace. He expects brass bands and red carpets everywhere he goes because he's *the famous Captain Taggart*! A living legend. The trouble is that people have short memories – and Taggart just can't come to terms with the fact that the spotlight has moved on. He wants to keep reminding people who he is and what he did, with the result that he's becoming a monumental bore.'

'You're getting a bit sour in your old age,' Ben said to Harris. The accusation was accompanied by a smile. 'He seems quite a character.'

Harris shrugged. 'I won't argue about that. I was just giving you a friendly warning. He's a resident here . . . Has been for about a month. You may find it hard to keep out of his way if you're going to be holed up here for any time.'

'He's a dry-land sailor now then?'

'Not quite. The Japs got his ship off Colombo and he's hanging around here for another one, or so I gather. His crew were shipped home in a trooper, but he didn't go with them. Look, Ben, let's get the hell out of here. If he spots me, he'll be over like a shot and I'm in no mood to be talked at until my ears bleed!'

Ben deferred to Harris and they made their escape, but it was only to be a matter of time before Taggart loomed into the American's life once more.

The gharry-driver accepted the ten-rupee note and blinked with surprise when Ben told him to keep the change. The bearded Indian had been pushing his luck when he had suggested five rupees as the cost of the fare, and the munificence of Ben's tip took his breath away.

'Thank you, Sahib. You are most generous, Sahib,' the driver trilled in a sing-song voice, trying not to betray chagrin at perhaps having pitched his asking price too modestly. 'May the most excellent spirits of Christmas be with you, Sahib.'

'And with you, too,' Ben replied, without hinting that he was in any way taken in by the false heartiness of the other's tone. The American was in no doubt that the sentiment embodied in a greeting that somersaulted so casually over a wide chasm in religious philosophies was one of commercial nicety. He frowned at the driver. 'Perhaps I have been too generous . . .'

The driver's face fell. 'Too generous, Sahib?'

'You asked me for five rupees and I gave you ten. Maybe six would have been enough . . .?'

'But Sahib . . .'

'OK, OK,' Ben relented, putting the man out of his misery. 'You keep the ten rupees. But do something for me, will you? Just save some of those rupees to buy feed for your horse, eh? Goddammit, look at the poor beast!'

'Sahib, I am a poor man. I have many mouths to feed . . .'

'Sure you do,' Ben agreed, 'But if you don't give that animal of yours some nourishment pretty soon, he's sure as hell going to drop dead between the shafts and you could find yourself in the rickshaw business.'

He stood watching as the driver cracked his whip and urged his emaciated horse forward at a shambling trot. There remained with Ben a gnawing disgust at the sight of the animal's frailty – a xylophonist could have played medleys on its protruding ribs – but he was already regretting the rather petty attitude he had adopted with the driver. He probably was as poor as he said he was, and who the hell was Ben Darby to castigate him if, as was probably the case, he had to choose between feeding his children and his worn-out horse? It was the kind of choice that Ben Darby had never had to make.

Ben was still unsure quite what he had hoped to achieve by getting riled over the welfare of one halfstarved horse. Some quixotic impulse had prompted his remonstrance with the gharry-driver – but it had been as stupid as it was futile. What was the use of getting worked up over one wretched animal in a city where a million human beings scavenged in the gutters for food? A week exploring the sights and sounds of Bombay had left Ben feeling degraded and despairing for mankind.

All big cities had deprived areas but no other, in Ben's experience, paraded its stinking squalor with the aggression of Bombay's assault upon the senses. Its poverty and suffering were thrust at the visitor like a street-vendor's wares: numbing spontaneous pity and inducing only nausea. It was as if the scale of human deprivation was here so vast that hope of correcting the condition had long-since vanished and ceased to matter. The only sure thing about the condition was that it was incurable.

Since he had come out of hospital, Ben had used his freedom to explore Bombay, not in the manner of a tourist but with the relentless curiosity of a reporter in an unfamiliar land. From the forbidding Towers of Silence, where vultures purified the remains of the departed Zoroastrian devout by stripping their bones of corrupt flesh, to the red-light districts – where corruption of the flesh was a way of life – Ben had roamed until he could stomach no more. Degradation clung to him like a smell that would not wash off. To see was to be contaminated and scarred by the thrusting misery: the begging children, maimed at birth in the interests of their allotted calling; the spectre-like lepers, without noses, without ears, and without hope; the abandoned old, all skin and bone and festering sores.

Even the street entertainments were grotesque. In Times Square, the gully-gully men with their ascetic mysticism and repertoires of gruesome magic would have brought the traffic to a halt. Here, their acolytes had to accost the hurrying crowds like hectoring magpies to fill a cap with annas enough to underwrite the master's performance. Ben found it morbidly fascinating, once, to watch a holy man impale himself on swords and display his pierced body. But wonder gave way to revulsion and novelty diminished as other exponents reproduced similar acts on the next street corner and on the next. Novelty wore thin, too, at the staged spectacle of mammal pitted against reptile in a fight to the death. The lively mongoose triumphed inevitably over the snake but often – perhaps too often – the snake had to be prodded from torpidity to take more than a languid interest in its own demise.

It was to escape the uproar and milling throngs of the city streets that Ben had bidden the gharry-driver to drop him off at the *maidan*. Here, as the afternoon cooled into evening, it was possible to walk – as the doctor had recommended – and feel the fan of air from any breeze that was going. Here, in the wide open acres of the *maidan*, the squalid aspects of Bombay could be kept at arm's length. Half a dozen football matches were in progress and Ben – as he made his way across the broad parkland – paused to admire the skills and enthusiasm of the bare-footed players.

There was something ironic in the spectacle. British rule had given India superb railway communications, a legal system and a bureaucracy of civil servants and it was possible that all would survive the days of Empire – but would any of these things be more durable than the love of ball sports and attitudes of fair play that the British had brought in with the military baggage train, as it were, and which had caught the imagination of the natives more readily than concepts imposed by law?

Ben savoured the thought and decided he would write an article on the subject sometime: the power of the pastime as opposed to the musket. The musket could command obedience from a subject people but could not win their hearts. What made more impression was what the soldier carried in his pack and which he produced when the musket was laid aside: a ball to bat or kick around; a musical instrument to play; a sketchbook and pencil to draw.

It amused Ben to let the ideas tumble and churn in his mind as he crossed the *maidan*. In a corner, beyond the football pitches, a small crowd had gathered around the tail-gate of a ramshackle blue truck. He gravitated towards the assembly, drawn by curiosity. From the back of the truck, an ample-figured Hindu in a caftan-collared blackjacket was haranguing an audience of about fifty. Ben drifted on to the fringe of the onlookers where, at first, his presence went unnoticed by the speaker. The Urdu rhetoric was lost on Ben. It took on a different tone, however, when the orator spotted the American and launched into passionate invective which was accompanied by flourishes in Ben's direction.

Dark faces turned to stare at him and the stares were nakedly hostile. Ignorant of why his innocent interest should provoke such animosity, and just a little resentful of it, Ben decided nevertheless that a dignified withdrawal would be prudent. The speaker's voice halted him as he edged away. It was directed unmistakably at him and it challenged.

'Do you run from the truth?' the voice mocked in English. 'Is the Sahib deaf to what he is not wanting to hear?'

Ben smiled and held up his hands, a gesture that indicated the wish not to be involved. 'I was just passing by. I'm not running anywhere . . . Just minding my own business. Please don't take any notice of me . . .'

He turned to move off, not hurrying, but again the voice followed him.

'Blood-sucker! Violator of our sacred soil! Despoiler of our holy earth! See how he flees from the truth I am telling you!'

Ben suddenly found himself surrounded and jostled by angry gesticulating Indians. Retreating from flailing fists, he stumbled before a sea of brown faces deeper into the crowd. All but engulfed, the tide of bodies ejected him below the tail-gate of the ramshackle lorry, where he fell full length. Scrambling to a sitting position he waited, shaking with fear and anger, for the mob to fall on him. But they held back as the orator's high-pitched voice rang out.

'Wait, brethren ... Let the imperialist dog tremble before your wrath. Let him be answering with his evil tongue the truths I am proclaiming.' The man on the truck had struck a dramatic pose, his left arm raised like a policeman's halting traffic, his right pointed accusingly at Ben. His eyes bulged, indignant and emotion-filled, in his flabby well-fed face. He waited for the American to answer.

Ben scrambled to his feet and looked uneasily at the speaker and then at the intense worked-up faces of his followers. He raised his hands, palms outward in a signal of peace, and stared up at his accuser.

'You've got the wrong guy.... Look, Mister, I don't know what it is you're selling or why you've picked on me.... But politics is not my line of country. I'm American ...'

'Hah!' scoffed the man on the truck. 'Do you hear that, brethren? He says that he is American! He is not a British imperialist ... He is a British imperialist lackey ...'

'I am nobody's lackey,' Ben interrupted stoutly.

Again, there was a scoffing response.

'Hear him!' cried the Hindu orator. 'He says he is not being the lackey of the filthy British who suck our blood! But are not the Americans licking imperialist boots with their tongues? Are they not giving lakhs of their almighty dollars to Churchill to be fighting his imperialist wars?' He glared accusingly at Ben. 'Can you be telling me that you are not a keeper of nigger slaves who work on your plantations, so that you are growing rich on the breaking of their backs?'

The sudden question was so unexpected and absurd that it took Ben a moment to recover from his surprise. When he did, he stared up at the Indian's petulant face without being able to keep his own straight. He laughed: a strange despairing laugh. The sound was somehow a lament for the other's unanswerable ignorance and an alternative to tears of dismay. A situation that had the trappings of tragedy was being enacted with the dialogue of farce. The animosity in the dark faces around him no longer seemed real. He grinned at the nearest face and found that the mask of hatred slipped and was replaced with the puzzled beginnings of an answering smile.

Ben pointed at the speaker on the truck and then, for his neighbour's benefit, tapped his temple with a forefinger.

'Him up there, crazy. You *mallum?*' he said, rolling his eyes.

The neighbour frowned. Anger flashed in the dark face. It was matched by the fury of the indignant Hindu on the truck.

'Sucker of our blood!' he screamed at the American. 'Defiler of Mother India!'

His words dispelled Ben's last illusion that levity or persuasion were to be of any assistance to him. There was a surge of bodies towards him and he went down as scrawny brown hands clawed at him. He curled up, foetus-like, as the mob closed in. Jabbering cries echoed in his ears as he was trampled and kicked. Like a drowning man confronted with the imminence of the end, he began to fight with thrashing limbs against the forces overwhelming him: rolling, kicking, lashing out in any direction he could move. A sense of futility intensified rather than calmed the frenzy of his struggles.

From somewhere beyond the heat and fury of his resistance, sounds intruded meaninglessly. He heard the roar of the ramshackle truck's engine and the squeal of tyres as it was driven off at speed. Without comprehending, he also heard the bellow of a human voice above the general bedlam, a voice that had the deep resonance of a charging elephant's trumpeted rage.

It took Ben a few bewildered moments to associate the voice with the sudden relaxation of the press of bodies around him. The kicking brown legs, wrapped in dhotis, suddenly retreated, leaving a clearing amid the forest of dark limbs in his immediate vicinity. Then the trumpeting voice roared again and the ring of legs widened, making an avenue through which the owner of the voice strode.

'Stand back, you heathen bastards!' rang the uncompromising command. The mob parted like the Red Sea before Moses as the titanic figure of Captain William Taggart barged to its centre. One defiant Indian did not move out of Taggart's way. A sweep of one mighty arm sent the unfortunate spinning head over heels into the crowd. Six men went down like skittles before he came to rest.

The space around Ben suddenly increased from ten to twenty feet as belligerence melted and discretion spread through the mob like a contagious infection.

Ben – aching in a thousand places and his clothes hanging in tatters from his body – hauled himself to his feet, agreeably surprised that he was able to do so. He could only stare in awe at the commanding presence of his rescuer. The sea-captain was magisterial in his arrogance: well over six feet tall and his imposing stature augmented by the tall crest of naval cap on his head. His ox-like shoulders and massive chest bristled power in the way they strained against the cloth of his white tunic jacket, threatening to pop the gold buttons.

Taggart bent towards the American, granite jaw thrust out and his face clouded in the frown that had opened a way through the mob.

'Have these heathens hurt you?'

'I'm OK. Just sore.'

'Let's get the hell out of here then. Don't hurry and don't look scared. Look the bastards straight in the eye.'

Taggart turned to lead the way but, even as he did so, restive elements at the back of the crowd began to bay and push. The ring around the sea-captain and the American tightened untidily. The rear ranks of the mob were more vocal and more courageous than those at the front. The latter showed a marked reluctance to get any closer to Taggart than they already were, and they dug in their heels. But they could not stem the pushing from behind. Taggart smiled grimly as the avenue of escape closed. He pushed up his cuffs and the light in his eyes seemed to indicate relish at the prospect of breaking Hindu heads with his fists.

Ben was tripped and went sprawling. Taggart immediately took up a stance astride him and met the sudden surge of engulfing bodies by using his fists and forearms like clubs. He kept the area around Ben clear by flailing at anyone who came within range, and was aided in this by the determination of the Indians nearest him to exchange places with the less cautious elements howling in the rear. Those seeking to escape blunted the momentum of the more adventurous and the attack had already stalled when it suddenly disintegrated. The signal, at which the pressing ranks broke in disorder, was a series of piercing whistle blasts from the direction of the road.

Advancing in open line and at a steady trot came a squad of Indian police. Fewer than a dozen in number, the fresh arrivals descended on the breaking mob with their lathis twirling like windmills. The crowd scattered in all directions: running and leaping to escape the dexterous manipulation of the flashing canes. Within the space of two minutes, the rout was complete. The unruly throng had evaporated and the only evidence that it had ever existed was in the limping retreat of isolated stragglers, hurrying from the scene.

A grinning moustached sergeant – his uniform unruffled and his puggaree undisturbed by his recent exertions – presented himself to Taggart.

'These Congress wallahs are one damned nuisance, Sahib,' he commented nonchalantly. 'They will not be making more trouble for you now.' He eyed Ben. 'Is the Sahib injured?'

'I'm OK,' Ben replied, as Taggart helped him upright. His lopsided smile of gratitude took in both Taggart and the policeman. 'It looks like I owe a vote of thanks all round. You gentlemen saved my life.'

He explained how he had been an innocent bystander and had been picked on by the soap-box politician.

'I saw the fellow,' Taggart confirmed. 'Made off in his wagon like a bat out of hell.'

'We are knowing the blighter jolly well,' the sergeant said in his jovial manner. 'He is one Banarjee and he is making trouble wherever he goes. But he will not be escaping next time. He is very naughty fellow who is belonging in jail.'

When it was discovered that Ben was staying at the Taj, Taggart took control of the situation. What Ben needed, he declared, was a *burra* peg, a bath and a change of clothes – in that order. The police sergeant was more than happy to relinquish the dishevelled American to Taggart's care.

The sea-captain led the way towards a grey-painted jeep parked close to the road that bisected the *maidan*. Hovering close to it was the RNR commander, whom Ben had seen previously in Taggart's company. The navyman came to meet them.

'You're a bloody madman!' he greeted Taggart heatedly. 'You could have got yourself killed!'

'And where the hell were you?' Taggart rebuked him in reply. 'Scared of some Indian rabble, were you?'

'It was me who flagged down the constabulary,' the other snapped. 'You can thank me for the fact that you're still in one piece. Hell's bloody-teeth, Bill, you should have more sense than interfere with these quit-India wallaha. They'd cut you up for dogmeat as soon as look at you.'

'And what would have happened to our American friend here if I hadn't interfered?' Taggart demanded. 'Goddamnit, those Hindu savages would have torn him limb from limb!'

'That would have been his bad luck!' The navyman glanced at Ben and said in a less heated tone: 'I'm sorry, friend, but you must know it's asking for trouble to go anywhere near those rabble-rousing demonstrations. If anything had happened to you, it would have been on your own head. I certainly don't intend to apologise for not charging into that mob . . . We saw you go down and I, for one, thought you were a goner.'

'You and me both!' Ben agreed warmly. Now that the excitement was over, a reaction was setting in. He could feel sweat running down his back in rivulets and his hands were trembling. He turned to Taggart. 'I think I could use that drink you talked about.'

Taggart pushed the bottle of whisky across the table to the American and invited him to finish it off. Ben waved the bottle away.

'Thanks, but I've still got plenty.' He displayed his half-full tumbler before taking a sip. 'Cheers.'

Taggart emptied the bottle into his own glass.

'Can't let it go to waste,' he said. He topped the drink with soda from the syphon on the table and settled back into the cane armchair. 'What time is it?'

Ben focused his eyes on the Ingersoll on his wrist. The watch had miraculously survived the fracas on the *maidan* some ten hours earlier.

'Twenty-three minutes after two,' he announced. 'Long past my bedtime.'

'The night is young,' said Taggart. 'Shall I pop along to my room for more hooch? There's plenty more where that bottle came from.'

Ben held up his hands in supplication.

'I think I've had what is known as an elegant sufficiency,' he demurred. 'I'm ready to sleep the sleep of the just.'

'Then you're a very lucky man,' said Taggart. It was a strangely wistful remark. Ben eyed him with curiosity.

'An insomniac, are you? Is what what you are, Captain?'

Taggart did not reply immediately. He stared thoughtfully at his glass, gently twirling the contents. Then he downed the drink and put the empty glass on the table. He continued to stare at it.

'I remember a time when I used to sleep...' He shook his head, as if shedding a pleasant memory with regret. 'Now, I hate the night,' he said, with a bitterness and finality that surprised Ben. He stood up and, glimpsing the American's expression, laughed.

'I won't keep you from your beauty sleep... I don't need any! I shall retire to my boudoir, pour myself a large peg to poison any mosquitoes who fancy a diet of English beef... and read a few more chapters of a very dirty book that cost me fourteen rupees in Patel's Bazaar.'

When Taggart had gone, Ben did not go to bed. He remained in his chair, staring up thoughtfully at the slow mesmeric spin of the big-bladed ceiling fan. Taggart's remark, about hating the night, kept revolving in his mind with the same nagging monotony as the sweeping blades.

The remark had been dropped in an unguarded moment and was strangely at odds with the Taggart that was normally on show to the world. It gave the hint of a hidden inner dimension of some complexity that was not displayed by the seemingly indestructible exterior of the man. As an observer of his fellow men, with an almost obsessive interest in the mechanics of the human mind, Ben was gripped by an intense curiosity to know more about Taggart. The man was an original, cast from an heroic mould – but what unknown metals had gone into the casting? It had been Ben's first impression that the Captain had been fashioned from some steely compound of far greater toughness than in his own mortal make-up. But now he sensed, if not a flaw in the heroic figure, at least the tiniest of signs of hidden vulnerability. The discovery fascinated him.

Ben regretted now that Harris had clouded his first image of Taggart. A living legend, Harris had called him, cynically. A publicity-seeker. A bore. Well, so far, Ben had found Taggart anything but a bore. The man was a walking volume of adventure stories, with surprises on every page. And the captain had not struck Ben as a publicity-seeker. He had shown a lively and intelligent interest in Ben's work as a journalist but had displayed no ulterior motive in the process.

No, Harris had got a very superficial picture of Taggart. Ben had been given a much more accurate impression of the man from his actions, not his words. Up there on the *maidan*, Taggart had been under no necessity to get himself involved in the predicament of a total stranger. Yet he had involved himself. Demonstrating a courage and a fearlessness that was rare among men, he had saved his life. That was what set William Taggart apart from lesser men: the deeds that spoke louder than any words. You could forgive a man a hell of a lot of idiosyncracies if, behind them all, the genuine substance was there.

That Taggart was loud and domineering, Ben would not dispute. But these were attributes that could be tolerated in a colossus. And when these same attributes were used in the protection of a weaker vessel – as Ben saw himself – they took on the very gloss of virtue.

Ben could not forget that it was Taggart who had brought him safely back to the Taj; Taggart, who had chased the gaping onlookers, drawn like bees to honey at his tatterdemalion appearance and obvious distress; Taggart, who had summoned the fussy little Indian doctor to minister to him; Taggart, who had bullied the hotel staff into preparing a bath with unguents and, in general, attending to his comforts.

The Samaritans, whose kindness to a stranger had become a byword, had done no more for the man who had fallen among thieves than Taggart had done for Ben.

Later – it had been nearly midnight – Ben had been lying, sleepless, inside his mosquito net when Taggart had come to his room to check on the welfare of his new-found protégé. Finding the American awake and restless, he had prescribed a night-cap and had gone off to his room to fetch a bottle.

Ben smiled to himself as he recalled Taggart's estimate of what constituted a night-cap. Brooking no argument, the big man had settled down to kill the bottle with the journalist's help, as if the act of recorking it would have been an unpardonable breach of etiquette.

It was as he sat alone, recollecting Taggart's capacity to drink and talk, that Ben realised, with hindsight, another unadvertised aspect of the Taggart phenomenon. Taggart was a *lonely* man.

Of course! It was something he should have recognised instantly. Because, all his life, the lonely and the troubled of this world had homed on him like missiles guided by radar. It was as if they perceived in Ben a ready and sympathetic listener. He did not know whether his capacity to listen was a gift or a curse – but he *was* a good listener. It stemmed from what he thought of as his Dorothy Dix syndrome: an inbuilt tolerance to let people unburden themselves of their anxieties by just talking to him.

Others, less tolerant, would have run a mile when button-holed in bars or on train journeys by complete strangers who wanted to talk – but Ben never ran. He always listened. He listened because he recognised, in someone's need to talk, a need that he could not deny. The compulsion to talk, the desperate need for an audience was often the outward manifestation of an unarticulated cry for help.

In the two and a half hours after midnight, Taggart had done a great deal of talking and Ben had done a great deal of listening. For all that, it seemed just a mite ludicrous to construe the sea-captain's loquacity as a veiled cry for help. He was a big exuberant fellow, tough as a rhinoceros, and with the self-confidence of ten other men. The thought that he was beset by dark inner anxieties was surely a figment of Ben's overactive imagination.

But the thought persisted. The idea took firm root in the American's brain that Captain William Taggart desperately *needed* a friend and that, by a curious mixture of circumstances, he, Ben Darby, had been selected.

He went to sleep with the notion still turning in his mind but assuaged by the belief that, come morning, it would have evaporated without trace. The opposite occurred. The notion was not given time to evaporate.

Ben was wakened from a deep sleep by a persistent knocking on his door. Bleary-eyed, he staggered to the door to be confronted by Taggart: a Taggart resplendent in newly laundered whites and with the groomed freshness of someone who had bathed and shaved fastidiously.

'Rise and shine,' he exhorted the American. 'I've got a boat ordered for seven.'

'Boat?' Ben stared at his watch. It was twenty minutes after six.

'Boat,' confirmed Taggart, and beamed a craggy smile. 'I thought you might like a little trip to blow away the cobwebs. So let's be having you. You get yourself dressed and presentable and I'll organise some tea and toast from what passes for a galley in this hotel. We're going out to meet my new ship. She's due in the Roads from Karachi at eight.'

There was something about the ship that awakened old excitements in Ben. From the moment he had followed Taggart up the Jacob's ladder against the rust-stained hull, he had felt a strangely bittersweet enthralment. A heady pleasure was tinged with regret for what might have been.

Taggart had gone off to introduce himself to the officers of his new command and Ben, pleased with her captain's sanction to take a look around, had wandered about the newly anchored ship with the fascination of a child. He explored the weather-beaten freighter with all the wonder of a small boy who had been given the opportunity to taste at first hand the substance of his dreams.

He found his senses fired with the forgotten images and desires of a younger and more innocent Ben Darby: the Ben Darby who had spent the first ten years of his life in New Bedford, when the Acushnet's estuary teemed with tall-masted ships, homing to Massachusetts after voyages to polar seas. What ambitions of adventure those ships had evoked!

They came back with a startling reality and vividness now. Ben's senses thrilled to the ring of his leather shoes on the steel deck, the tangy ship smell of anti-corrosive paint and tarry rope, the distant mysterious hum of the engine-room generator. He remembered how much he had wanted to go to sea: lured by the spume-tossed wastes that beckoned from beyond Nantucket. The sound of a ship's siren in the fog-enshrouded estuary had been enough to intoxicate him with visions of exotic palm-clad islands in the sun and ice-fringed seas where the sperm whales played.

But the small-boy dreams had been lost somewhere along the path of growing up. His family had moved from New Bedford: first to Boston and then to New York City. New horizons had awakened new dreams and new ambitions. By the time Ben was sixteen and realising unsuspected talents as editors of his highschool magazine, fresh goals were beckoning and a new dream had taken the place of the old.

But now, it seemed, the old dream had only lain dormant all these years. It came bursting into new life as Ben roamed the *Kildare Glen* from bow to poop: filling him as he stared down into the immensity of the holds as they were stripped of the hatch-boards; exciting him as he peered down into the steamy cavern of the engine-room, where the great metal arms of the tripleexpansion steam engine were temporarily silent from their labours.

The seamen, as they went about their work, were friendly and disposed to stop and talk to Ben; unaware of the feelings they provoked in him. He felt a strange envy for them, these men of the sea: members of an exclusive band of brethren from whose ranks and rites he was shut out because he was not one of them. His lot was the lot of the outsider, always looking in: the observer, the interpreter, the recorder. Always detached, never belonging.

As he returned to the midships area, Ben was hailed from the lower bridge by Taggart. He climbed the ladder to be introduced to Mr Fowler, the Chief Officer. Fowler had held temporary command of the *Kildare Glen* for two months, ever since the hospitalisation of the previous master in Aden. Ben got the distinct impression that Fowler was less than overjoyed at having to relinquish the post that he had been looking after for Taggart. Perhaps he had thought that he would have been able to keep it. Certainly, his manner was sullen and he used the pretext of work to be done as a reason for excusing himself and departing.

'Well, what do you think of the *Kildare Glen*?' Taggart asked the American as Fowler disappeared below.

'I wish she was mine and not yours,' Ben said enviously. 'She's a fine ship.'

'A fine ship, is she? Is that what you think? It shows how bloody little you know.'

Ben was unprepared for the rudeness of Taggart's tone. He stared at the Captain, perplexed.

'Look at her!' Taggart invited him. 'She's a bloody disgrace! Dirty as a cattle-boat! She needs chipping and painting from truck to keel. I've never seen a scruffier tub!'

Ben flushed with embarrassment. 'You should know. You're the expert,' he said lamely. But Taggart had not finished.

'... As for the shower running her, you won't find a more idle bunch of lead-swingers this side of Suez. And ...' He paused to draw breath and glower at the American with scowling ferocity. 'And there are going to be some changes made. I promise you!'

Ben shrugged. 'I guess I'm just a sucker for ships. I get a kick out of just being on one. The guys I spoke to seemed OK, too. Just talking to them made me feel I'd like to be one of them ... I wanted to up the anchor and just sail away ...'

Taggart laughed, his fierce scowl vanishing as quickly as it had come.

'Sailing in this ship might be an education you'd regret,' he suggested with merriment. 'Two weeks under me and I reckon you'd be howling for mercy. I run a hard ship, Mr Darby.'

'I guess you probably do,' Ben said, smiling. 'Something tells me that if you said jump, I'd sure as hell jump.'

'But would you jump quick enough?' Taggart asked teasingly, his eyes narrowing to diamond-hard slits. Whether or not he was trying to be jocular was far from clear to Ben as Taggart added: 'There are lots of nasty bastards sailing the high seas, Mr Darby, but I bet there are damned few who can be as nasty as me when I really put my mind to it.'

Ben decided that Taggart *was* joking, that he enjoyed projecting a monster-image of himself as concealment for gentler instincts. He was on the point of accusing the Captain of a bark that was worse than his bite, when he realised that Taggart's attention was riveted elsewhere. He was staring beyond Ben, down into the waist of the ship; his face darkening with sudden anger. Pushing past the American and seizing the top of the guard-rail as if to steady himself against shock surging in his body, he let out a great roar.

'Hey, you! You down there!'

In the vicinity of the side-bunker hatch, a seaman paused in the act of lighting a cigarette. He was a tall young man with blond hair, his back and legs browned to mahogany in startling contrast. On a belt at the waist of his paint-stained working shorts, he carried a knife and marline-spike in a double sheath: proclamation of deck-sailor status. He looked up in idle curiosity at the sound of Taggart's voice and then glanced around him as if to determine at whom, other than himself, the shout had been aimed.

'Me?' he called out. 'Is it me you want?'

'Yes, you!' bawled Taggart. 'Are you bloody witless? Get yourself up here!'

With a puzzled shake of his head, the seaman made

his way to the ladder and mounted it to the lower bridge. His movements were unhurried, which seemed to make Taggart more agitated than ever. He faced Taggart, uncowed by the big man's size and angry demeanour. His tone, when he spoke, had a curl of irritation.

'What is it you want? Who are you?'

'I'm the master of this ship, laddie. That's who!' Taggart rasped. 'What's your name?'

'McCabe,' came the answer, a shade cautiously.

'McCabe, *sir*, when you speak to me!' Taggart snapped. 'And put out that cigarette when you're on my bridge! Have you got a shirt, McCabe?'

The man hastily nipped out his cigarette. He eyed Taggart uncertainly.

'A shirt, sir?' he asked.

'Yes, damn you! A shirt!'

'I've got plenty of shirts, sir,' the seaman said, perplexed.

'Well, go and put one on!'

The man called McCabe stared at Taggart as if, perhaps, he had not heard him correctly.

'Put a shirt on, sir? But I haven't had a shirt on my back since . . .'

'I don't want a discussion, McCabe. I've given you an order. Go and get a bloody shirt on! There'll be nobody running around the decks of this ship half-naked while I'm her master! Do you savvy plain English?'

'Yes, sir, but . . .'

'No buts, McCabe. It's an order. You can pass the word to your mates. Cover their backs or they are in trouble. If I catch one man on deck without a shirt, his name will be in the log-book and he'll be poorer a day's pay quicker than you can bat an eye!'

McCabe turned away as if to leave. He hesitated.

'The lads aren't going to like this, sir,' he mumbled.

Taggart fixed him with a glare that would have cut through armour-plating.

'McCabe,' he hissed, with menace, 'if I want a Gallup poll on the popularity of my orders, I'll let you know. In the meantime, just make sure that you and your mates carry them out. Now, get the hell off my bridge!'

McCabe hurried away, an unhappy frown clouding his young face. Taggart turned to Ben with a smile of satisfaction on his.

'That'll give them something to think about!' he said.

Ben looked at him uneasily. 'A little rough on him, Captain, weren't you? You can't really blame guys for stripping off to work in this heat.'

Taggart's smile died. 'That may be your opinion, Mr Darby,' he said icily, 'but on this ship, there's only one opinion that counts. And that's mine!' In the next instant, seeing the American's face fall and as if regretting the harshness of his rebuff, Taggart was conciliatory. He draped his arm round Ben's shoulder companionably and sought to explain himself.

'It's for their own good, Ben, my friend. If you had seen as many men go down with sunstroke as I have, you would have known that. Anyway, what's the harm with laying down the law right at the start? It'll save a lot of grief later on if everybody knows exactly who's boss.'

Still with an arm avuncularly round Ben's shoulder, he guided the American towards the ladder: 'Come on, my Yankee friend. Time I put you back on shore where you belong. I've got to collect my gear and have it ferried out, and a hell of a lot more to do besides, but you'll have lunch with me, won't you? My treat. I insist on it.'

They returned to the motor launch from which they had watched the *Kildare Glen* come to anchor. Ben, who had been more than a little bewildered by Taggart's disturbing fluctuations of mood, was relieved to find that the big man appeared to have left his bad temper aboard the ship. He was like a different person as the launch cut through the choppy waters of the Roads towards the shore: as congenial as, before he had been irascible. He drew the American's attention to the number of grey-painted merchantmen in the anchorage. There were more than twenty – not unlike the *Kildare Glen* – in the ten-thousand-ton bracket. All bristled with anti-aircraft armaments and most had squat houses built on their mid- and after-deck spaces. Taggart explained the significance of these solid but obviously temporary erections.

'Extra galleys, store-houses, ablution huts, that's what they are,' Taggart said. 'And these ships have all got converted spaces down below, too . . . In the tween-decks . . . with room to carry hundreds of troops. We're going to give the Japs a bloody nose, Mr Darby.'

Ben looked at him with interest.

'The new Burma offensive they keep talking about?'

Taggart did not answer immediately. He regarded the American almost coyly.

'We're not supposed to talk about it. Military secret.'

'Goddamnit, Captain, I've got about as high a security clearance as you can get. I don't print everything I hear. The least you can do is drop me a hint.'

Taggart laughed. 'If you haven't heard about it, you must be about the only bloke in Bombay who doesn't know what's in the wind. We're supposed to be invading the Andamans. We'll be off just as soon as they've scraped enough ships together.'

Taggart confided that most of the ships in the anchorage, including the *Kildare Glen*, had seen action in the Mediterranean during the summer: at beach-head landings in Sicily and mainland Italy. They had been diverted east in penny numbers as part of a build-up for similar landings against Japanese-held territory.

'If I know the Japs, we're not in for any picnic,'

Taggart said. With a teasing grin, he added: 'Still have a hankering to sail in the *Kildare Glen*?'

Ben laughed. 'That was the boy in me talking. The man has a job to do. When you're knocking off Japs, I'll be heading in the opposite direction.'

'Still set on Sierra Leone, eh? God help you!'

'Sierra Leone wasn't my idea. I just go where I'm told. The trouble is getting to the goddamned place.'

'How will you get there?' Taggart asked.

'God knows, Captain. I sure as hell don't. The word is that I have to hitch a ride on a plane to the Persian Gulf, and from there to Cairo. After that, it gets tricky...' He laughed. 'Maybe camel train across Africa. Nobody so far has come up with the answers. Maybe they won't – and I'll be sitting on my fanny in Bombay for the rest of the war!'

'Just steer clear of political meetings then,' Taggart advised cheerfully. 'You won't have me around to pick up the pieces.'

Taggart moved out of the Taj that day to join the *Kildare Glen* and Ben saw nothing of him in the days over Christmas. He had no reason to believe that he and the British sea-captain would ever meet again.

Later, reflecting on the strange vagaries of war, Ben was to conclude that in any situation where a variety of foreseeable eventualities exist, the one most likely to occur was the one that was totally unforeseen. So it proved, at any rate, in the projections of an itinerary that would take him from Bombay to West Africa. Air Transport Command could get him to Karachi or Abadan or Basra but could give him no guarantee that, having got him to any of these places, he would not thereafter be stuck in one of them for weeks, possibly months. A cable for help to Washington, however, elicited a response from the US Press Corps office attached to the Allied High Command in Delhi. The cryptic message advised Ben to contact Royal Navy HQ,

Bombay, without delay, and seek the assistance of HMSTO. This latter turned out not to be His Majesty's Ship *TO*, which was Ben's puzzled interpretation, but a person in the shape of His Majesty's Sea Transport Officer.

This gentleman – a grey-haired veteran – greeted Ben with news that he was in luck and that there would not be any difficulty in wangling him a sea-passage to Sierra Leone. Indeed, such was Ben's timing that a choice of several ships was likely to be available. He just hoped that the American wasn't in too tearing a hurry to get to West Africa because the journey would take anything from five to seven weeks. The bonus was a two-to-three-day stopover in South Africa, a land flowing with milk and honey. Ben reeled out of the STO's office in a daze, with the promise that all would be put in hand immediately and that he would be contacted at the Taj Hotel as soon as there was anything to report.

Thus it was that – only seven days after he had gone out to the Roads with Taggart to meet the *Kildare Glen* – Ben's travel problems were solved in a way that had never crossed his mind. A naval rating duly sought him out at the Taj and delivered to him a letter in a buff envelope: very official-looking and marked 'Confidential'. Ben had to sign a receipt for it.

The letter, from the STO, confirmed that a passage to Sierra Leone – with a provisional sailing date in early January – had been reserved in his name. But it was the ship's name, typed in capital letters, that leapt out at Ben from the document in his hand. It was the *Kildare Glen*.

CHAPTER 2

Sister Hewson

The prospect of a long sea-trip excited Ben Darby. But the mystery, of how the *Kildare Glen* should be designated as his ship, was still unresolved when he decided on a shorter journey in fulfilment of a promise he had made. For one reason or another, he had put off returning to the military hospital where he had spent three weary months. With his departure from Bombay imminent, however, he made up his mind to bid a final farewell to the people who had repaired his broken limbs and battered body.

To Ben's surprise, he experienced a strange sense of home-coming at the sight of the solid Victorian edifice. It stood grey and dignified in a pleasant acreage of green-lawned grounds, where a sprinkling of chalet-type wards had sprung up to accommodate a wartime increase in business. The main building could have been a replica of infirmaries in Leeds, Plymouth or Southampton. Like so many public and government buildings in Bombay, its design made no concessions to Indian style or climate but might have been transported lock, stock and barrel from damp grey England. But it was not the hospital's Englishneess that struck a coming-home chord in Ben's heart. It was the recognition of a familiar and secure environment which, for a time, had encapsulated his whole existence with its unchanging timetabled routines.

During his sojourn in Hastings Ward – one of the

prefabricated units in the grounds – Ben had looked on his confinement like a term of imprisonment that had to be endured. But returning of his own volition and secure in the knowledge that he could leave when he pleased he was able to indulge a nostalgic affection for the place.

He was welcomed, with the warmth that might have been shown for a long-lost son, by both the staff and the longer-term patients whose tribulations he had shared. Ben had come, laden like Santa Claus, with small belated Christmas gifts for all those whose kindness or friendship had made his stay in hospital more tolerable. He had forgotten no one, from the black-faced and perpetually smiling Madrasi cleaning orderly to the doctor who had reset his broken limbs.

Only one familiar face was missing as he made his rounds with the news that he would be leaving Bombay for good early in the New Year: there was no sign of Sister Hewson, for whom he had purchased a small bottle of perfume. Her absence was an intense disappointment, although Ben mentally chided himself for the acuteness of the feeling. If he were honest, he had to admit that Hewson wasn't really his type – in spite of any suppressed longings he might have entertained for her. While Ben had been under her jurisdiction, she had tantalised and frustrated him in equal measure. At the core of his disappointment now, however, was regret that he was being denied the opportunity of meeting Hewson, for once, on equal terms.

As one of her charges in Hastings Ward, Ben had been as beguiled as any red-blooded man by the flaunted sexuality of the doe-eyed nursing sister – but he had never tried to over-step the limits of the patient-nurse relationship that Sister Hewson dictated. There had been banter between them – often of a deliciously *risqué* nature – but its latitude and duration had been regulated by Hewson's whim to indulge in such games with patients. She was the boss and, in the sweetest possible way, she allowed no one to forget it.

Observing the way she controlled and manipulated his fellow men, Ben had been provoked to both amusement and admiration, especially as he knew that he was no more immune to her precocious charms than any other man. Anything in trousers was putty in her hands.

Nature had endowed Sister Hewson with dark and sultry good looks and parcelled them up in an enticingly voluptuous figure. She was aware of her sexuality and used it blatantly to instil starry-eyed subservience in her patients. She also employed it to keep her superiors – the doctors and administrative officers – in line. From them she extracted an uncritical deference that had her less pulchritudinous nursing colleagues gnashing their teeth in jealous rage.

Hewson's popularity with men did not extend to the nursing sorority, who referred to her snidely as 'Her Royal Highness'. The tart use of the honorific did not discomfit Harriet Rachel Hewson who, from her schooldays, had become used to teasing play being made of her initials. Indeed, she gloried in it: taking special delight in never signing her full name to the sundry order forms and report sheets that circulated daily in the hospital, as regulations demanded she should. Instead, she merely appended the initials 'HRH' – a habit that often triggered delicious uncertainty and misunderstandings. From time to time, the uninitiated drew from it the awing conclusion that a person of royal blood was labouring inconspicuously within the hospital walls. It pleased Sister Hewson never to be the one who enlightened them otherwise.

As a patient within her bailiwick, Ben Darby had yielded as meekly as any of the other inmates of Hastings Ward to the siren-like charm of Sister Hewson. But he had never come to terms with the inequality of the patient–nurse relationship. All the authority to command was weighted too heavily in favour of the allegedly weaker sex, making Ben feel constantly at a disadvantage.

Normally shy and reserved with women, Ben had been profoundly embarrassed by his first encounter with the captivatingly pretty Hewson. It had occurred soon after his installation in Hastings Ward and while he had been encased in plaster. He had been lying awake when Hewson had made her 6.30 a.m. circuit of the ward. Finding him awake, she had hoisted up his mosquito net to its statutory daytime drape and set about straightening his bed. She had discovered Ben's manliness manifesting itself like a signal-mast against the single sheet that covered him.

While Ben blushed with confusion, she had feigned admiration.

'Ah, what a splendid case of morning thickness,' she had teased, and reached under the sheet to locate the proud member with a hand that had lingered briefly as if in fondling admiration. Then had come the sharp painful rap that had reduced the muscular rigidity to limp repose. The blow had been delivered with a smiling apology from Hewson and with the murmured regret that it was a pity to waste such splendid ardour.

Thereafter, Ben had become almost used to the humiliation of an act which became something of a morning ritual. It preceded the presentation of a bedpan to relieve the full bladder – the cause of the involuntary arousal – and was followed by a longing for revenge. The revenge feelings invariably incorporated an aching desire to be accorded equal terms of intimacy with the luscious body of his tormentor.

But however longingly or lustfully the patients of Hastings Ward hungered after the tantalising person of Sister Hewson, she had remained the forbidden fruit that was forever out of reach. They could look but dared not touch. The grapevine had it that, in any case, she was the exclusive preserve of a high-ranking army officer of very jealous disposition – some said a colonel, others a brigadier – and that the common herd had no chance at all.

On his discharge from the hospital, Ben had resisted the temptation to test the availability of the alluring Sister Hewson by trying to date her. There was that inner suspicion that she was not his type and, in addition, he had no desire to compete with some frosty British brass-hat. If that was where Hewson's heart lay, good luck to her.

On his return to the hospital, however, it surprised Ben how deeply he was disappointed that Hewson was not there. Her absence gave his sentimental journey a piquancy of incompleteness. His farewells made, he was on his way across the gardened walk to the main gate when he came face to face with her. His heart leapt at recognition of her in an off-duty yellow frock and a short-brimmed black straw. For a moment Ben thought that she was going to walk straight past him. But she stopped suddenly and a beam of delight brightened her face.

'Why, it's Mr Darby!' she trebled, and laughed. 'I didn't recognise you with your clothes on!'

It was the kind of conversation-opener that was somehow typical of Hewson: a statement of indisputable fact but delivered with enough coquetry to invite the slightly salacious interpretation. The gambit led, in a natural progression, to Ben suggesting that they might spend the evening together. He was conscious of agreeable surprise when, instead of turning him down, Hewson expressed pleasure at the idea. Ben could not believe his good luck.

The evening was a disaster. Long before it was over, Ben was wondering why Harriet Rachel Hewson's enticing body and beguiling manner should have so captivated him that he had ignored all the other warning signs of other eminently less desirable traits in her personality. Of course, it was entirely his own fault. He had read all the signals but had chosen to turn a blind eye to them, so ready was he to obey the eager promptings of his own carnality. It had been naive of him to believe that Sister Hewson of Hastings Ward would, once he had her to himself, become the Hot-Lips Harriet of his fantasies. She was much too used to twisting helpless males around her little finger. In Hastings Ward, Ben had seen her play with the captive inmates' feelings until they were as docile and biddable as performing dogs.

Away from the ward, Ben was to make the discovery that the off-duty Harriet seemed to expect not only the same kind of docility from her men friends but that her right to was taken for granted. In exchange for the gracious favour of her company, it seemed, it was encumbent upon the favoured one to bend and bow to every shift and change of her mercurial will. The longer Ben spent in her company, the greater became his disenchantment.

Their evening out began inauspiciously with a visit to a cinema. Ben would have preferred some other way of escaping the torrid heat of the late afternoon but Harriet had brooked no discussion. The second feature – a western – had just started when they were shown to their seats. Ben settled down to watch the film and was enjoying the sensual pleasure of Harriet's hand clasped in his when the mood of togetherness was suddenly shattered.

Without warning, the slender hand encapsulated by his own was suddenly wrenched away. Mystified, Ben could sense rather than see the pout on his companion's pretty face.

'Anything wrong?' he enquired softly.

'I can't stand being pawed in public,' she hissed back at him, astonishing Ben, because the hand-holding had seemed the most innocent of familiarities. He sank back in his seat in disbelieving silence.

A few moments later, she was commenting none too softly that she hated western pictues and that the one on offer was the silliest and most puerile she had ever seen.

'Aw, relax, honey,' Ben murmured soothingly. 'The big picture's a weepie. They've got to put something on the programme for the little boys.'

Then this rubbish should be right up your street!' was her withering reply. The change in her mood from sweet to sour bewildered Ben. Once again, he found himself swallowing his annoyance.

'Look, honey, if you don't like it, there's nothing to stop us leaving. I'm easy, one way or the other.'

Already, their exchanges were attracting more attention than the wagon-train ambush up on the screen. Heads were turning and Ben grew uncomfortable as the stares increased. Harriet Hewson seemed oblivious to the attention. She stood up, but made no move to leave; ignoring a demand from behind to sit down as she adjusted the black straw more securely on the crown of her head. Then, with a disdainful glance at the person who had complained, she forced a determined passage along the row of seats. At the aisle, she looked back towards Ben.

'Are you coming or not?' she demanded imperiously, and turned on her heel.

Excusing himself embarrassedly as he disturbed the occupants of the seats for the second time, Ben made his way to the aisle. Harriet, walking quickly, had almost reached the exit. Ben caught up with her outside.

'What now?' he asked.

'We'll go somewhere more interesting,' she said.

In the gharry she remained stonily indifferent to Ben's attempts to humour her. No, she told him, she had not taken offence at anything he had said or done. She just did not like western films. They were made for juvenile minds. And no, she did not want to go to the Taj for a meal. It was far too early and, in any case, she was not the least bit hungry.

Eventually, after they had gone some distance out of the way, she redirected the gharry to an officers' club, where her nursing corps rank of captain entitled her to entry. Ben, his deep-dyed sense of courtesy strained but intact, agreed that a stiff drink would not go amiss.

Indeed, two *chota* pegs of whisky seemed to put Harriet in a much more affable frame of mind. Ben's misgivings slipped away as she treated him to the full beam of her come-to-bed eyes and became relaxed enough to tease him impishly about his shyness when he had been her patient in Hastings Ward. This was more the Harriet Hewson who had tantalised and attracted him: the creature who had the power to provoke and enchant with a mischievous candour of talk that acted like a honeyed aphrodisiac. Ben was succumbing, open-eyed, to the treatment – her earlier petulance forgiven and forgotten – when the radiance of her interest in him seemed suddenly to dim, as if she had become preoccupied with something else and she was only vaguely aware of his presence.

In hospital, this had always been the sign that she was drawing back to unreachability, but then the retreat was softened by murmured regret: duty called, another patient needed her. She would vanish from Ben's bedside as if she had been no more than a mirage in the desert of boredom that was hospital existence.

But now, sitting opposite Ben in the busy club, she ended the intimacy of their *tête à tête* with an abruptness that was little short of bad manners. One moment, she was rapturously hanging on his every word and treating him to the full brilliance of her seductive eyes and, in the next, not only had her attention wandered but so had she. Ben found himself talking to an empty chair.

Harriet Hewson had crossed to a table occupied by three army officers, who greeted her with obvious pleasure. She remained at the table – the object of much adulation – for fully ten minutes. No explanation nor apology for her sudden absence was offered to Ben when she returned.

'Friends?' Ben enquired.

'Yes. Are you jealous?'

'No. Should I be?'

'Not if you know what's good for you.'

'What is that supposed to mean?'

She shrugged, indifferent.

'It means anything you want it to mean. Can we change the subject?'

'Sure, if you want to. Let's talk about your job – about nursing.'

'Nursing?' She looked at him askance. 'Why, for heaven's sake?'

'Because I'm curious. A job like yours is full of situations and pressures. It needs a heck of a lot of discipline . . . Dealing with people who can be terribly ill . . . People who die on you in spite of all you can do . . . It must be awfully hard at times.'

'You get used to it,' she said.

'You mean you never get emotionally involved?'

'With patients? No. Never.'

'But you don't care for patients *impersonally*. By that, I mean you don't treat them as if they don't matter to you. You give something of yourself. Don't your patients sometimes get the wrong idea?'

'All the time. But it's the easiest thing in the world to put them firmly in their place. They get over it when they see that you treat everyone exactly the same. Did you ever see me show favouritism? Do you think I ever showed favouritism to you?'

The American smiled ruefully. 'No,' he admitted. 'But I sometimes felt that you sheltered behind that uniform of yours . . . behind your authority . . . that you took advantage of the fact that I was more or less at your mercy.'

'I don't ever remember you complaining.'

'I'm not the complaining kind.'

'But you're complaining now.'

Ben laughed softly. 'I'm not your patient now. Or is that how you still see me? The fractures case who needs a little jollying – but not too much in case he gets the wrong idea.'

'Now you're being bloody offensive,' she said angrily.

'I'm sorry. I apologise . . .' He searched for a way to explain himself. 'All I was trying to do was get your slant on things. I'm interested. I wanted to find out how you separate your working life from your personal life . . . if it's difficult to switch off, or what. Hell, what I'm saying is that I could never do your kind of job. In my job, I get involved. I identify with people . . . I suffer for them.'

'But I don't? You think that I am an unfeeling bitch?'

'I didn't say that,' Ben protested. 'I was trying to be objective. You are the only one who can tell me how much you feel or how much you don't feel. You are the only one who can tell me how keeping your emotions out of your work affects you personally. Does it make you . . . hardened? Or is it one hell of a strain? I'm genuinely curious to know . . . Because I'm the kind who faints at the sight of blood and would throw up if I had to change a baby's diaper!'

She regarded him with an expression that managed to convey both scepticism and amusement.

'Well, that's a line I haven't heard before,' she said. 'No man has ever asked me out before to strip away the veils over my psyche. They've tried to strip off just about everything else, but not that. I must admit that yours is a novel approach.'

Ben regarded her wearily. Why was it that she seemed

unable to talk about anything for any length of time without putting sexual connotation to it? Her sarcasm saddened Ben.

'Maybe you'd better keep that psyche of yours under wraps then, honey. Some things just don't stand up to strong light.' His tired smile took some of the sting out of his words.

'I intend to keep wraps on everything I've got,' she replied, and paused, letting Ben get the warning in her meaningful stare. 'Do we understand each other?'

'Perfectly,' he said. 'And it suits me fine.'

No more was said, but the tacit understanding was established. The evening was not going to produce a meeting of bodies. It was a fact that Ben was able to accept with considerably less dismay than the evening's failure to produce a meeting of minds. The sad truth facing Ben was that he and Harriet Hewson had little or nothing in common. All that remained to them now was to acknowledge that their relationship had no future and to end it in as civilised a manner as was possible.

They went to the Taj for supper, in token observation of the formalities, and even communicated companionship enough over the standard fare of steak, egg and chips. But it was arm's-length communication. The table between them was like a chasm that neither had the desire to bridge. It was when they moved into the lounge for a night-cap that Taggart found them. The sea-captain was in civilian clothes, looking debonair and younger than his forty-odd years in a light-grey suit, powder-blue shirt and with a blue-and-white tie at his neck.

'Ben!' he roared, when he was still a dozen paces from the corner table where the couple were seated. 'Ben, I've been looking for you all over. I've got news for you . . .' He stopped short when he realised Ben was not alone. He goggled down at Harriet Hewson. 'Why, Ben, you rascal . . . You've been holding out on me!'

Taggart continued to feast his eyes on Harriet Hewson. He seemed to like what he saw. She, on the other hand, seemed to be amused by the frankness of the inspection. As Ben performed the introductions, Taggart went on staring admiringly.

'You've got taste, my friend,' he said approvingly. He winked at Harriet. 'He's a real dark horse, isn't he? He didn't tell me he had a fancy bit.'

Ben almost choked at Taggart's choice of words but Harriet laughed softly.

'I'm not Ben's . . . fancy bit,' she corrected Taggart. 'Ben was a patient in my ward . . . We are . . . acquaintances. Nothing more.'

'Then he's bloody slow off the mark,' Taggart commented cheerfully. 'Just acquaintances, eh? By God, if I'd been three months in hospital, we'd have been more than acquaintances. I'd have had you in the bed beside me.'

Harriet Hewson made a mild pretence at being shocked.

'Really, Captain! We do have rather strict rules about that kind of thing. We try to keep our patients happy but our duties don't extend to hopping into bed with them.'

Taggart grinned. 'Are you saying you wouldn't enjoy it? You've got the shape and you'll not kid me that you never get the inclination. I always thought you nurses were a hot-blooded lot.'

Harriet Hewson coloured. 'We manage to restrain ourselves, Captain,' she said with icy sweetness. 'And if you'd been my patient, that wouldn't have been too difficult.'

'Ouch!' Taggart roared, and clutched his heart as if he had been wounded. But his delight was apparent. 'I like that!' he approved enthusiastically. 'I like it!' He beamed at Ben. 'She's not only a stunner, Ben, she can look after herself. I like her!'

Ben Darby had been quietly enjoying the role of neutrality to which he had been relegated. Taggart versus Hewson was an encounter to savour: the one, charging in with all the subtlety of approach of a jolly rhinoceros; and the other, full of feline grace and deceptively playful, but sharp-clawed and self-willed with it.

Round One Ben awarded to Harriet Hewson. She had parried Taggart's forceful vulgarity without turning a hair. Indeed, she had seemed even to relish the challenge and the pleasure of scratching back.

'Aren't you going to take the weight off your legs and have a drink with us?' Ben invited Taggart. He darted a quick look at Harriet Hewson. 'You don't mind, do you, Harriet?'

The flash of anger that glinted momentarily in Harriet's eyes vanished so quickly that he wondered if he had imagined it. The smile she offered him was guileless.

'Why should I mind?' she asked. 'The more the merrier. Your friend has a rather crude way of putting things, but I don't think he means any harm by it.' She smiled demurely up at Taggart. 'Do you, Captain?'

Taggart assumed an expression that bordered on cherubic.

'I am what I am, my dear young lady. You don't learn social graces in the fo'c'sle of a ship, which is the way I came up. I'm a rough sailor man with rough sailor ways.'

Ben grinned at the modest self-assessment.

'And he's slightly mad with it. You're looking, Harriet, at the man who saved my life . . . Rescued me single-handed from a howling mob.'

'Did you, Captain? Did you really?' Harriet Hewson regarded the big man with new interest. 'How exciting. Tell me about it.'

Taggart shrugged modestly. 'It was nothing.'

It befell Ben to recount the details, which Harriet Hewson insisted on hearing after a waiter had delivered fresh drinks to their table. Her wide-eyed admiration of the sea-captain seemed to grow as Ben graphically described the events on the *maidan*. So glowing was the testimonial that Taggart laughingly insisted that he should buy its narrator a double on the strength of it. And this he did, while modestly maintaining that the American's gift for embellishment was worthy of greater reward. Taggart did not seem to disapprove unduly of extravagance in Ben's story-telling, however, and positively basked in the esteem it provoked from Harriet Hewson.

She did not hide her admiration for what Taggart had done, confessing her own terror of the mob violence that erupted in Bombay from time to time. It made her go weak at the knees just to think of the courage it must have required for Taggart even to contemplate extricating Ben.

'You must be an exceptionally brave man,' she told Taggart to his face. 'You must have known the risk you were taking. I say you deserve a medal!'

'He's got quite a few already, Harriet,' Ben said. 'You don't seem to realise that Captain Taggart is quite a celebrity. You should see his war record. He's seen more action than any dozen of those fruity-voiced chums of yours up at that army club you took me to.'

'Ben's exaggerating,' Taggart said.

'He's had one whisky too many, if you ask me,' Harriet Hewson said severely. 'He should be upstairs, tucked in his little bed.'

'I've still got to see you home, sweetheart,' Ben reminded her cheerfully. 'And I haven't had one whisky too many. I've had just enough to make me feel happily benevolent to all mankind.'

'Well, don't feel that your benevolence has to stretch

to seeing me home. I'm a big girl and quite capable of looking after myself.' She had a sudden thought. 'If Captain Taggart's getting a taxi to go back to the docks, I'm sure he wouldn't mind a small detour via the hospital. He can drop me off.'

'I'd be delighted,' Taggart confirmed.

Ben looked at Harriet Hewson. 'I thought you were my date.'

She treated Ben to a smile of rare sympathy.

'Of course, Ben, and you've been perfectly sweet. But don't spoil things by getting all possessive. I'll be perfectly safe with Captain Taggart. So, be a good boy and we'll say no more about it. It's settled.'

She stood up, once more the no-nonsense Sister Hewson of Hastings Ward and not about to be diverted from her chosen course by a troublesome patient. Ben made no attempt to dissuade her from leaving with Taggart. If that was the way she wanted things, it suited him fine. He felt only relief as they disappeared outside.

Ben had come to the conclusion that Harriet Hewson did not really like men. She simply used them to serve her own consuming vanity. She used any male that was handy, like a mirror – to be picked up and laid aside as it suited her – with no aim but to fortify her narcissistic preening. It was sad. Being a mem-sahib in wartime Bombay – a city bulging with love-starved, home-sick sevicemen – had probably spoiled her. Here, with more admirers competing for her favour than she would normally have met in a lifetime, she could pick and choose and discard at will, without any fear of the queue shortening. Perhaps it was no surprise that her power to attract had gone to her head.

It was not until after Harriet Hewson had gone off with Taggart that Ben realised that the sea-captain had never got round to telling him the 'news' that had brought him to the Taj. Had he heard that he was getting Ben for a passenger? The opportunity had also come and gone for Ben to quiz Taggart on why the *Kildare Glen* should be going anywhere near West Africa when the ship had apparently been earmarked for operations against the Japanese. The lost opportunity to satisfy his curiosity annoyed Ben now.

He looked at his empty glass and wondered if, perhaps, Harriet Hewson had been right and that he had consumed one whisky too many. Maybe he had.

'Well, damn you, Harriet Hewson!' he thought. 'I'm going to have another one!'

With an air of determination, he made his way to the bar.

The great grey shape of the *Kildare Glen* loomed high above the wharf like a whale that had been stranded by the tide. From somewhere within the steel carcass came the echoing ring of hammers upon metal as unseen labourers toiled at some unknown task. Ben Darby – his boarding instructions document from the STO protruding from a breast pocket – stared up at the ship that was to take him to Sierra Leone. He felt again the rise of excitement that had filled him on his first acquaintance with the *Kildare Glen*, when she had been anchored out in the Roads. He could not quite believe that he really would be going to sea in the freighter. But the instructions, delivered before breakfast time, had been clear enough: naming the ship, the wharf, and the necessity to report to Captain W. F. Taggart before noon that day. Ben had wasted no time. It was now only six minutes after eleven.

Now that her cargo had been discharged, the ship looked bigger. A solitary railway wagon was parked below the ship's side, abreast the No. 4 hold, with a derrick swung out above it. Ben watched as a sling – loaded with twisted metal casing – came swaying out above the ship's side and was lowered into the railway wagon. Moments later, the empty sling was reeled back almost to the derrick head and then yanked inboard to an accompanying rattle of winches.

'What a bloody waste of money!' a voice said at Ben's shoulder. Ben turned at the sound of the voice to find that he had been joined by the man he recognised as the *Kildare Glen*'s Chief Officer, Mr Fowler. Fowler held in one hand the notebook in which he had been recording the ship's forward draught. His footsteps, as he approached Ben, had been drowned by the sound of the winches.

'What a bloody waste of money!' Fowler repeated, with a weary shake of his head. Seeing Ben's mystified expression, he pointed to the railway wagon into which the sling had been emptied. 'Scrap metal!' he said. 'Look at it – all good stuff! It's only a month since they fitted it into the ship at a cost of God knows how many thousands of pounds ... And now they're tearing it out!'

'What is it?' Ben asked.

'The last word in air-conditioning, that's what it is! Or rather was! They're ripping the whole lot out – panelled ducting, electric motors, the lot! It cost the bloody earth to install and they're not bothering to salvage any of it! Just pulling it apart any old how! It's bloody criminal.'

Ben was still a little mystified.

'Air-conditioning?' he queried.

'For the troop accommodation,' Fowler enlarged. 'The poor sods would have suffocated in the tweendecks without it. But we're not going to be carrying any troops now.' Fowler's face creased into a grin. 'We're only going to have one passenger now – you, Mr Darby. We've been expecting you. I'll give you a hand with your gear.'

The Chief Officer eyed Ben's single suitcase sitting on the quay.

'Is this all you've got?'

'Afraid so. I'll manage it myself.'

Fowler, however, insisted on carrying the case.

'I heard you were in a plane crash,' he said as he led the way up the companion ladder. 'Is this all the gear you salvaged?'

Ben laughed. 'I'm the only thing that was salvaged. What I have in the case are only bits and pieces I've picked up since I came out of hospital. But I'm having some more clothes delivered to the ship later today. I gave one of the local tailor johnnies quite an order.'

'The Indians are bloody marvellous at the old made-to-measure. They won't let you down.'

On board, Fowler led the way to a handsomely appointed cabin on the lower bridge-deck.

'This is where we lodge honoured guests,' he announced. 'You should be comfortable here. You've got your own private bathroom and shower – and your nearest neighbours are the Old Man and the Chief Sparks. I'll go and let the Old Man know you've arrived.'

Ben was happily surveying the spacious accommodation when Taggart appeared at the open door. He stood there, enjoying Ben's obvious approval of the cabin.

'Not a bad doss-me-down for a humble coal-heaver, eh, Ben?'

Ben stopped his admiring appraisal of a wall-fitted bureau bookcase in polished maple. He smiled uncertainly at Taggart.

'A humble coal-heaver?'

Taggart laughed. 'That's right, my friend. You!' His grin broadened. 'There was a hell of a lot I meant to tell you last night but I never got round to it. But we did get a wee bit side-tracked, didn't we? That nursery pal of yours is a real cracker, isn't she?'

'We did get kind of side-tracked,' Ben agreed. 'At least, I did!'

'Aw, come on, Ben. All's fair in love and war,' Taggart growled good-naturedly. 'You're not going to hold it against me because I took your fancy bit home. I didn't try to get my end away or anything like that, although I wouldn't say I wasn't tempted. I was a perfect gentleman. You can ask her when you see her.'

'I don't have any plans to see her. You did me a favour taking her off my hands.'

'Oh?' Taggart frowned. Then he chuckled, rubbing his hands together. 'Then it'll be every man for himself tonight. I'm throwing a farewell party on the ship . . . And she said she'd come . . . I'm sure she fancies me. And she's going to bring some of her nursey friends. I thought it would be a good way to welcome you to the *Kildare Glen* . . .' He cast an anxious look at the American. 'Have I done the wrong thing?'

'Don't worry on my account,' Ben assured him. He was surprised, nevertheless, that Harriet Hewson had promised to show up with a bevy of friends. Sharing the limelight with her own sex wasn't Harriet's style somehow. Ben changed the subject.

'What did you mean about me being a coal-heaver?'

His puzzlement delighted Taggart. 'Can't you guess?'

'I've never heaved coal in my life.'

'Of course you haven't,' Taggart agreed gleefully, 'but that's what you're down for on this ship. On paper, at least. It'll cut out a hell of a lot of red tape and it'll get you to Sierra Leone. So don't look so worried.'

'I'm not worried. I just don't understand.'

'It's simple,' Taggart explained. 'You'll travel on the *Kildare Glen* with all the comforts and privileges of a first-class passenger but, to save everybody concerned a lot of unnecessary work and inconvenience, you sign on as crew.'

'I sign on as crew?'

Taggart laughed. 'Maybe you'd rather walk the plank?'

When his merriment at his own joke had subsided, Taggart explained that ships without passenger-carrying certificates often resorted to the practice of accommodating fare-paying passengers by signing them on as supernumeraries. This circumvented a number of bothersome requirements on life-saving equipment and, at a stroke, eliminated the lengthy and often costly process of complying with a host of needless legal technicalities.

In Ben's case, he would not even be a supernumerary. The *Kildare Glen* was actually a man short of regulation strength and Ben would, ostensibly, fill the vacancy as no replacement was available in Bombay. The vacancy had arisen because one of the ship's three coal-trimmers had been paid off with an injured back. If Ben signed the ship's articles as a coal-trimmer, paperwork could be kept to a minimum.

'You'll just have to trust me not to put you to work in the bunkers, shovelling coal,' Taggart warned Ben jovially. He explained that the weakened stoke-hold watch would be brought up to strength by volunteers from the ship's complement of Navy gunners. The latter were queuing up to fill the twice-daily four-hour stint in the bunkers, which would enable them to share the money that would otherwise have been paid in trimmers' wages.

'You'll have to sign a disclaimer to this money,' Taggart told Ben. 'But just to keep things right, when you sign the articles, it'll be for a nominal wage entitlement of a shilling a month. Just think, you'll actually be paid for doing bugger-all but sitting on your backside and eating three square meals a day. A shilling a month ... That's nearly fort cents in your money!'

Ben smiled. 'Nearly half a dollar? Gee!'

'There's a catch, of course,' Taggart pointed out mischievously. 'Whatever you earn will be deducted for, say, personal laundry expenses ... So, don't be too ambitious planning what to do with your pay-off in Sierra Leone!'

'You're really going to take me there?' Ben squinted at Taggart from below arched eyebrows. 'What happened to the Andaman Islands and your date with the little yellow men?'

Taggart's face clouded. 'I don't know. They cancelled the show. All I know is that the *Kildare Glen* has been ordered back to the UK, via the Cape.'

'You don't look too all-fired happy about it,' Ben observed. 'Don't you want to go home?'

'No, damnit! I don't!' Taggart snapped testily. 'This ship's my bloody home now! And she was brought out here to do a job ... To have a go at the Japs ... So why the hell don't they just let us get on with it?'

Ben shrugged. 'Don't ask me.' The sea-captain's desire to be shot at by the Japanese in preference to seeing his homeland again seemed unnatural. He shook his head; a sad reflective action that betrayed puzzlement more than anything else.

'Why do you shake your head?' Taggart asked, in a shirty tone.

'Just thinking,' said Ben. 'It seems kinda crazy to want to go tangling with the Japs rather than see your folks. Don't you have anybody at home in England?'

Anger blazed in Taggart's eyes.

'That's none of your damned business! Is it?'

Ben winced at the unexpected rebuff. He bit down on his lip.

'I'm sorry ... I was curious, that's all.'

His hang-dog look and softly spoken apology drew instant contrition from Taggart. The big man's expression softened.

'There are some things I don't like to talk about, Ben. Family happens to be one of them ... I didn't mean to bite your head off.'

'I'm sorry,' Ben repeated.

Taggart regarded him sombrely.

'If you must know, I had a wife . . . once,' he said. 'I had a son, too. Now . . . Now, I have nothing to go home to.' He shrugged his massive shoulders. 'I was never a very good husband, Ben . . . And I didn't win any prizes as a father . . .' He lapsed into thoughtful silence.

Ben longed to ask questions, his curiosity made greater than ever by Taggart's surprised confession. But he remained silent, waiting for Taggart to enlarge on the little he had revealed. When Taggart did speak again, it was in a self-absorbed manner, as if he were thinking aloud.

'It's a funny thing, Ben . . . The way you remind me of him . . . Of Michael . . .'

'Michael?' the American prompted.

'He was his mother's son . . . Michael . . . Always much closer to her than he was to me . . .' Taggart's voice faded almost to a whisper. 'It's odd the way you remind me of him . . . He was never very sure what to make of me . . . Always asking questions – the way you have a habit of doing . . . And always apologising, saying he was sorry. Just like you do. I think he was frightened of me, Ben. Me, his own father!'

Ben could well understand a sensitive boy being in awe of this big, moody and unpredictable man, who could be jolly and laughing one minute and snarling the next. Ben said nothing, sensing that anything he did say might act like a goad on the deep raw wound that Taggart seemed to be exposing to him. The subject of his son was obviously a source of great pain to the big man. The hurt was there to see, shining like a light from his brooding eyes.

As if suddenly becoming aware that he was baring some private compartment of his soul, Taggart covered up, with the shock of a sleep-walker who wakes naked in a busy street. He blinked in confusion and turned away from Ben in such haste that he blundered into a chair and knocked it over. Then he stood for a moment, his back to the American: seeming to gather himself. He took three slow steps towards the door. There, he turned and faced Ben, his eyes bright, almost accusing. Then, without a word, he turned on his heel and went out.

Ben remained rooted to the spot, tense and more than a little unnerved by that silent stare. He let out his breath in a sigh: unaware that he had been holding it, as if the act of daring to breathe would have caused some cataclysm. He felt emotionally drained, torn between an anxious compassion for Taggart and a fear-filled foreboding.

For the briefest of moments, he had glimpsed once more into the troubled heart of the master of the *Kildare Glen* and sensed a loneliness that was dark with a confusion of feelings. But what they were he could only begin to guess. Because he had sensed, too, a rage of such torment bottled within the man that it chilled his own heart with fear. Taggart was denying an outlet to the fury of emotions that bubbled within him and, in so doing, was compounding the dangerously volatile nature of that seething mix.

Ben could not dispel the sudden fear that Taggart — as admirable and brave as he was — had the stability of a landmine with a trembler fuse.

CHAPTER 3

The Party

Two Indian ratings, with rifles and fixed bayonets, stood guard at the main door of the white-washed Navy building. A white ensign hung limply from the flagstaff above the door, which faced south across the Bombay Roads. A glimpse at the scrambled-egg braiding on Taggart's cap and the row of medal ribbons on his tunic front was enough to bring the two sentries to attention as he strode towards the door. At Taggart's heel, stepping briskly to keep up with the big man, was the *Kildare Glen's* young Second Officer.

Inside, a petty officer directed Taggart to the canteen, where the conference was being held. In this long room, the lino-topped tables had been stacked alone one wall and the chairs had been set out in rows facing a narrow platform. Close on fifty men – merchant-ship captains like Taggart, and their navigating officers – were crowded into the room. Few were seated, most preferred to jam the areas of floor space at the sides and rear of the rows of chairs, where they conversed in animated fashion. Nearly all were in uniform, with the majority favouring the wide-legged white shorts and knee-length stockings that were standard tropical wear.

Taggart ploughed through the throng, making his way to the front row of seats. His Second Officer stuck close behind him, pausing only briefly to exchange greetings with others of the navigating fraternity who spoke to him or waved a hand from a distance. Taggart selected a seat which seemed stout enough to take his bulk and reserved it by placing his brief-case on it. He looked round at the gossiping throng.

'It's like a meeting of the Mothers' Union,' he observed sourly. 'All girls together.'

'Sir?' The young Second Officer at his side snapped his heels together and bowed his head slightly towards Taggart, as if he had not heard. His stiff posture and the mannerism of the politely inclined head betrayed his origins as other than insular British. Taggart tried again.

'I happened to remark, Mr Prins, that this... this chattering assembly... was like a meeting of the Mothers' Union.' He glowered at the Second Officer. 'But maybe they don't have Mothers' Unions in Holland?'

The earnest young man's expression remained respectful but showed plainly that he had no idea what Taggart was talking about. Taggart snorted impatiently.

'It's like a bloody club – all friends together,' he persevered. 'Even you have chums here. I'm the stranger in the camp... The odd one out.'

Understanding glimmered in the young Dutchman's eyes.

'Ach, yes... Yes, sir. All friends! We meet many times before. Always the same ships... Sicily, Algiers, Salerno, Malta, Alexandria... It is, how would you say, sir? A reunion?'

'More like a bloody wake,' Taggart commented, surveying the gathering with an air of indifference. 'I've never seen so many knobbly knees under one roof.'

Not all that many knees were actually visible, although Taggart's remark was not entirely without foundation. Those that were on view were less than beautiful. Taggart preferred to keep his legs covered by long trousers, although his physique was such that he could have bared his knees without any loss of dignity.

He could never understand why elderly sea-captains – and he did not clas himself in this category – should be so careless of their appearance that they voluntarily displayed not only their ungainly knees but the blue ugliness of the varicose conditions from which so many suffered.

Willem Prins, the *Kildare Glen's* Dutch-born navigator, was still trying to work out a connection between knobbly knees and what Taggart described as a wake, when the company began to fill the empty seats. The young officer decided, not unwisely, that Taggart's brittle patience need not be tested by a request for an explanation. The question on the tip of his tongue remained unspoken.

The opportunity to ask it passed, in any case, with the arrival on the platform of the two naval officers. One, a man in his fifties, wore rear-admiral's braid on his epaulets. The other was a lieutenant. The junior of the pair immediately requested the gathering to be seated and there was a bustle as the seats filled up and the shipmasters and their navigators faced the platform with the hushed expectancy of a concert audience. The Rear-Admiral was introduced and made a short speech of welcome. He went on to declare:

'As you know, gentlemen, this sailing conference has been convened in place of the normal convoy conference, for reasons with which you are no doubt familiar. Only eight of the twenty-four ships represented here today will have the luxury of naval protection when they leave Bombay. Those of you with orders for Aden and the Red Sea will have the company of the two AS vessels that can be spared from this station by the Royal Indian Navy. There will be no convoy commodore. Command of this small Aden detail will devolve to the Senior Officer, Escort. More about that later . . .'

The Rear-Admiral allowed a frown to wreath his face before continuing:

'Alas, gentlemen, we simply do not have the ships to provide escorts for the majority of you. Those of you bound for South Africa must make the long and hazardous crossing on your own – what I call the Albatross Run. Because, although you'll be within range of friendly aircraft this side of the Line, once you're south of the Line you'll only have the wandering albatross to keep you company . . .'

'Is that the next best thing the Navy's got to a frigate bird?' a voice called from the rear of the gathering. There was laughter and, although the Rear-Admiral blinked in surprise at the interruption, he acknowledged it tolerantly.

'I'm not an ornithologist,' he admitted affably, 'but I believe the birds are cousins. The sad fact remains that we have not got round to equipping either species with Asdic and depth-charges . . . And, in the absence of any kind of frigate – the feathered variety or those that fly the white ensign – the only escort you're likely to have between here and Cape Natal is that far-flying denizen of the deep, the albatross. I trust, gentlemen, that he watches over you well.'

He paused gravely, as if to make sure that his words had had a suitably sobering effect, then continued briskly:

'You will sail independently from Bombay at intervals of twenty-four hours . . . following prescribed routes, which have been charted for you. These routes have daily rendezvous positions – their co-ordinates have been coded – that you must endeavour to maintain . . .'

He smiled grimly. 'We cannot go with you, we cannot guard you, we shall never know with *certainty* precisely where you are . . . But, gentlemen, if you make every effort to be within the rendezvous sector allotted to you for each day of your crossing, we *will* know exactly where you *ought to be*.'

'What's the purpose of this, sir?' a master in the

audience asked. 'Does it mean that, if we get the hammer, we can expect help?'

The Rear-Admiral eyed the questioner sadly.

'I regret that help cannot be promised if your ship is torpedoed. If you do have that bad fortune, you must assume that no assistance will be forthcoming.'

'That's a bloody great comfort!' commented one of the audience. 'Which way should we swim if we're halfway over?' There was enough jocularity in the remark for it to be greeted with a sally of laughter and a number of unhelpful answers to the question about swimming. The Rear-Admiral allowed himself only the faintest of smiles.

'I sincerely hope none of you even get your feet wet,' he said. 'But in the unlucky eventuality that any of you do catch a tinfish, I hope that you have time to get off an SOS and radio your position. It may be no comfort to you to know that a distress signal may be unavailing as far as your own fate is concerned, but knowledge of your position may provide the only means whereby we prevent other ships from sharing that fate. You all have experience enough to know that merchant ships that may be near enough to effect a rescue must be diverted away from the area in their own interests. I know it goes against all your instincts to abandon your wounded, gentlemen, but that is the dictum to which you must all reconcile yourselves when you make this ocean crossing. Any casualties must be left to their own salvation. If it is the unhappy lot of any one of you to become a casualty, embrace this terrible knowledge as best you can and know that your distress can only serve those who would rescue you by acting as a warning to stay away. Wish them God-speed and the luck to save themselves, not you.'

A foot, shuffled against a chair leg, sounded thunderous in the silence that greeted the Rear-Admiral's words. Then a sober-faced Second Officer in the rear seats spoke up.

'Just how great are the chances of submarine attack. Admiral? And are there areas where they are more likely than others?'

'The chances are not to be underestimated,' replied the Rear-Admiral. 'The Indian Ocean is, I know, a very big place – but not so vast that you will be able to relax your vigilance for a moment in any part of it. We know that the Japanese Navy has one surface raider and at least three submarines operating well to the west and south of Ceylon. And German U-boats are likely to be encountered anywhere between here and Cape Town. The Mozambique Channel and the waters off Lourenço Marques are their favourite hunting grounds but they have also been popping up well to the east of Madagascar. Since the Japanese have opened up base facilities in Malaya and Java for the Germans, their U-boats have been active in areas where we never encountered them before.'

The Rear-Admiral picked up what looked like a hard-covered ring-binder file and displayed it.

'Most of you already have a copy of this book. It is a comprehensive manual of zig-zag patterns, with all the more tiresome calculations worked out and illustrated. For instance, twenty-minute course alterations over the period of a normal four-hour watch come with the courses to steer and a table of distances, according to speed. Each four-hour pattern shows the mean distance, according to speed. Give this book pride of place on your chart-tables, gentlemen – because your best protection against surprise submarine attack will be to zig-zag continuously throughout the hours of daylight . . .'

There were some groans from the rear of the audience at the latter statement. The Rear-Admiral acknowledged them by raising a hand and shaking a forefinger in a cautionary manner.

'I know, I know...' he said. 'It's a bloody nuisance... Continuous zig-zagging means reworking all your fuel-consumption estimates. I know, too, that when you are homeward bound – as all you lucky chaps are – the shortest distance is in a straight line. But the important thing is that you get there. There's no point in making things too simple for any enemy submarine commander who sights your smoke and thinks he's on to an easy thing. Zig-zagging won't save you from submarine attack but it may confuse the enemy and make him advertise his presence. And anything you can do... *anything*... that can tip the unequal odds you face... must be done! That is why your sailing orders contain strict instructions for continuous zig-zagging between dawn and dusk.'

During the next half-hour, the Rear-Admiral went over every detail of the ships' sailing orders, pausing every so often to answer questions which the shipmasters raised. At the end of the discourse, he offered to clarify any points that were still unclear. There was a lengthy silence. And then Taggart rose. The Rear-Admiral looked down at him expectantly.

'Captain Taggart, isn't it?' He smiled. 'We haven't met, but you were pointed out to me as a renowned killer of U-boats. Is there something I can illuminate for you, Captain?'

'There is,' Taggart replied. 'And this seems as good a time as any. I would like some explanation for the way we've all been buggered about. I was given to understand that my ship, and all the others here, had been brought out east to do a particular job... And that was to land troops in the Andaman Islands. Now that you've got all the bloody ships you were screaming for, you're dispersing the lot and sending them back to the UK. I would like to know why, for God's sake!'

The Rear-Admiral was a little taken aback.

'Don't you want to go home, Captain?' he asked, in a disarming tone.

'If I had wanted to go home, I could have gone six weeks ago. Repatriated as a survivor.' Taggart was in no way mollified. 'I stayed because I thought we were being given a chance to kick the Japs where it hurts!'

The Rear-Admiral forced an uncertain smile.

'Your fighting spirit is commendable, Captain,' he said, and broke off to hold a whispered consultation with his lieutenant. Reassured, he faced the gathering again and beamed down at Taggart.

'There is no reason why any of you should not know the reasons why there was such a dramatic turnabout in your orders. The purpose will become plain to you soon enough, as it is. The truth is that London and Washington have decided between them that the needs of the European theatre of war are greater than those of South-East Asia Command. Much to the regret, even anger, of many of us in this theatre of operations, our plans to carry the war to the Japanese have been frustrated by those in charge of our global strategy. The decision has been made to concentrate our resources on the defeat of Germany and the opening of a second front in Europe at the earliest possible moment. That is why your ships have been recalled to the UK, gentlemen. They are needed for the blow which, hopefully, will bring about the end of the war in Europe during 1944 . . .'

The revelation triggered a hum of conversation in the audience. The Rear-Admiral smiled down at Taggart, who was still standing.

'Does that answer your question satisfactorily, Captain Taggart? If it's the chance of hurting the enemy you want, you'll get it all right. That's what you're going home for.'

'It's still a bloody long way to go,' said Taggart.

*

Looking around the *Kildare Glen's* saloon at midnight, Ben Darby thought that it resembled a battlefield from which most of the dead and wounded had been carried. The long dining-table was strewn with empty bottles, abandoned glasses, overflowing ashtrays and the scattered debris from what had been a sumptuous buffet supper. Four wall-mounted electric fans laboured wearily, circulating rather than dispersing the wraiths of tobacco smoke and the odours of alcohol and human bodies. The night was oppressively hot, even by Bombay standards.

Taggart's party had started sedately enough at 6.30 in the evening with more than forty guests from other ships and the port-based forces crowded into the saloon and adjoining smoke-room. As the bottles had been emptied and the platters of food had been picked clean, the atmosphere had thickened and the company had gradually thinned. Among the earliest departures had been four of the six khaki-uniformed nursing sisters who had arrived with Harriet Hewson. They had paired off with locally resident officers and slipped away, almost with stealth, from the predominantly male gathering.

By midnight, only a few hardy survivors of the hectic merry-making remained aboard the ship and reasonably upright. And they had divided into two distinct groups. At the untidy saloon table, Fowler and three seafaring disciples of Bacchus – dedicated, it seemed, to drinking the *Kildare Glen* dry – were, with nostalgia and much argument, refighting Tommy Farr's prewar battle with Joe Louis for the world heavyweight crown. In the smoke-room, Taggart presided with the august ease of a pharaoh over what was left of his company. This entourage included Ben Darby, Harriet Hewson, three captains from ships berthed nearby, and the two nursing sisters who had not been spirited ashore by smooth-talking suitors.

The latter pair were large jolly women who were not in the first flush of youth. Their generous use of cosmetics had softened but not hidden those cruel facial lines that reveal the relentless march of passing years. For all that, neither women had lacked attention from would-be Romeos. Both possessed a worldliness and robust humour that more than compensated for a shortage of more glamorous attributes. Both also possessed a formidable tolerance to gin, which had enabled them to see off a number of hot-breathed admirers who had tried to match them drink for drink. Now the circle of competitors with eyes only for them had shrunk. Only the three visiting sea-captains remained, continuing to vie with each other shamelessly in amorous intent and heedless of the mathematical deterrent that three into two does not go.

An unlikely phenomenon of the evening had been the absence of any jockeying by the males to single out Harriet Hewson from the outnumbered female herd. From the outset, there seemed to have been an unspoken understanding that she – by far the prettiest of the small nursing contingent – had a special position which exempted her from the rush for quick conquests. It was as if she bore Taggart's personal brand on her forehead, proclaiming that any dalliance with the host's property was strictly taboo. Much to Ben's surprise, Harriet had given no sign that any man in the company, other than Taggart, held the slightest interest for her. She had not moved far from his side throughout the evening and had played the consort's role as if it were her right.

Ben – no lover of noisy social gatherings nor the artificial gaiety and inconsequential chatter they generated – had been quite content to keep a low profile. In his polite, self-effacing way, he had remained in the background and indulged his hobby of people-watching: observing all the posturing and manoeuvring and guessing at the private doubts and inadequacies that lurked behind the public masks. In his detachment, he knew, he was seeking a kind of refuge of his own – but he preferred it to joining in and the pretence of pleasure that he did not feel. The conventions of the herd were not for the maverick. Indeed, it was perhaps his own maverick nature that had caused his interest to return again and again to the two people present, who, in their own ways, stood apart from the herd: Taggart and Harriet Hewson. They constituted a most unlikely twosome: natural enemies, in Ben's judgement. But, apart from some amiable spitting and sparking, there had been no jarring conflict between them. However, this had not been through any lack of effort on Harriet Hewson's part.

She had, by turns, flirted outrageously with the *Kildare Glen's* captain and then, with equal facility, provoked him into argument by choosing to contradict him over the most innocuous topics. It was as if, confident of her power to tantalise and command any man, she had deliberately set out to tame this fierce lion of a captain. From her obvious enjoyment it had seemed to Ben that she was playing some kind of game with Taggart for her own private amusement – and it made him uneasy. Taggart was not a toy to be cast aside when boredom set in. There were better ways to tame a lion than by alternately stroking its mane and pulling its tail.

Yet, with the company now reduced to a lingering few, Taggart's patience showed no sign of running out. He seemed prepared to accept Harriet Hewson's flights from melting sweetness to mischievous contrariness as the price he had to pay for her filling the role of first lady.

Then the argument rose about 'mind over matter'. The discussion started innocently enough, with one of the two jolly nursing sisters commenting on the childish fear that some men showed for a hypodermic needle.

Harriet Hewson, whose steady intake of gin was beginning to show in a flushness of face and a rather reckless loquacity, seized on the remark.

'All men are cowards,' she declared sweepingly, eyeing Taggart with unmistakeable challenge. 'I've seen them trembling with fright at just the mention of inoculation ... I've seen them pass out at the sight of the needle ... And, usually, the bigger the man, the bigger the baby!'

She stared at Taggart mockingly, inviting him to contradict her if he dared. Taggart dared.

'That's about the silliest thing I've ever heard. It shows, Harriet, how little experience you have of men.'

She cocked an eye at him, amused.

'I've seen enough. And they're all the same. They panic at the slightest hurt. They're not nearly as tough as women.'

'Me included?' Taggart asked quietly.

'You're a man, aren't you?'

'A real one, Harriet. The kind you don't know anything about.'

There was a sudden edge to his voice that made the others in the group look at him sharply. They had been talking across the exchanges between Taggart and Harriet Hewson, but now they were silent, like skirmishing brawlers conceding the ring to the principal antagonists.

'You're just a man like all the rest,' Harriet Hewson said. If she saw the angry glitter in Taggart's eye, she gave no sign that she did. 'What makes you think you're any different?'

'Needles don't frighten me. Pain doesn't frighten me.'

'That's easy enough to say.'

'I mean it. Fear is in the mind. And overcoming it has nothing to do with physical size or physical strength. It's strength of mind that matters.'

'Mind over matter?' Harriet Hewson's tone was more

mocking than before. 'Pull the other leg, it's got bells on it.'

'I can prove what I say.'

'You'll never convince me. I've seen too many people in real pain ... Screaming with it. That's why anaesthetic was invented, you know.'

'You don't believe me?'

'No.'

Taggart spread his left hand, palm-down, on the table in front of him.

'Say I was to take a knife and pin that hand of mine to the table, would that cause me pain?'

'You bet your sweet life it would!' Harriet Hewson affirmed. 'But you wouldn't be so daft as to try.'

'Wouldn't I? I bet I could do it and wouldn't turn a hair.'

'And I bet you wouldn't have the nerve! I'd stake anything I possess on that.'

'Anything?' Taggart queried meaningfully.

'Anything,' she replied, meeting his eye.

The others in the smoke-room were watching, goggle-eyed. One of the nurses gave a soft laugh.

'He's after your virtue, Harriet,' she warned.

'He's too late for that,' quipped the other.

'I know when a man's talking in drink,' Harriet Hewson assured the nursing twosome. 'Captain Taggart has more sense than to mutilate himself to prove anything. He's wrong and he just won't admit it if nobody calls his bluff. Well, I'm calling his bluff.'

Taggart smiled. 'We'll see,' he said. 'Excuse me for just one moment.' He got up and left the smoke-room.

'It's all right,' Harriet Hewson said into the uneasy silence that followed his departure. 'He'll not do it. It's some kind of trick.'

Ben Darby was unconvinced.

'You'd better damn well stop him, Harriet,' he warned. 'This could get out of hand.'

His warning drew a giggle of laughter from Harriet Hewson.

'Out of hand?' she chortled. 'Out of hand! That's the bit I'm looking forward to. How does he get it out of his hand?' She giggled helplessly at her own joke. And she was still giggling when Taggart returned. He dangled, from between his fingers, a brass filigreed sheath on a length of fine gilt chain. The sheath held a dagger with the narrowest of blades. The handle, only fractionally wider than the blade, was worked in the form of a coiled snake.

Taggart withdrew the dagger from its sheath and exhibited it to Harriet Hewson.

'You said something about calling my bluff. You said you'd bet anything?'

She smiled at him teasingly.

'Showing me a knife doesn't prove anything. I still say you're bluffing.'

The narrow blade glittered as light danced off the gleaming steel. He spread his hand firmly on the table in front of Harriet Hewson.

'You're not squeamish, are you?' he asked her.

She stared at him, eyes bright with excitement and challenge.

'You wouldn't dare.'

'Stop this! It's madness!' The heated interruption came from Ben Darby. He was on his feet, staring anxiously at Taggart.

'Keep out of this, Ben. It's between Harriet and me. Stay where you are!' Taggart snapped the warning and Ben, who was weighing up the chances of snatching the dagger, thought better of it. He stood, poised and watchful but stricken with uncertainty. The speed of Taggart's act, however, surprised all present with its suddenness.

In one swift, sharp movement of his right arm, he

brought the knife skewering down through the back of his outstretched left hand. There was a thud as the blade passed through his hand and bit into the table beneath. Taggart relinquished his hold on the coiled-snake handle, leaving the dagger quivering above his pinned hand.

'Oh, my God!' cried one of the nurses. 'Oh, you bloody fool!'

The second nurse had gone white-faced with shock. The three sea-captains could only stare at Taggart in stupefied disbelief. Ben turned his head away, his face contorted as if he had suffered the piercing pain of Taggart's self-inflicted injury. Harriet Hewson stared dumbly at the skewered hand in front of her, mesmerised by the small ring of blood that was seeping up at the blade's point of entry to Taggart's hand.

Taggart had not uttered a sound. He was smiling triumphantly at Harriet Hewson.

'Now, I'm pinned and at your mercy. What do you want me to do next? Sing you a song?' He grinned at her and began to sing: 'Sixteen annas, one rupee. Seventeen annas, one buckshee...' He broke off and turned to flash a grin at Ben Darby. 'You look sick, Ben. Are you going to leave me nailed to this damned table? I was hoping you would pull this toothpick out of my hand...'

Ben moved across to the table and pushed Harriet Hewson out of his way, so that he could get above the dagger's handle. He gripped firmly down on the handle with both hands and was astonished at the depth to which the blade had been driven into the table-top. He tried to pull the dagger free in one movement but it was too firmly anchored.

Taggart placed his free hand on the wrist of the imprisoned hand and pressed slowly down on it.

'Try again,' he said to Ben. 'And try not to cut off my nose when it comes out.'

Ben drew the weapon cleanly out of the trapped hand at the second attempt. Taggart calmly took a handkerchief from his pocket and wrapped it round the injured hand. Blood gushed from his palm before it was hidden by the fold of the handkerchief.

'I suppose I should go and bathe this bloody mess with antiseptic,' he said. 'I have some stuff in my room.'

'I'll come with you,' Ben said.

Taggart frowned at him. 'I really think it's a job for a professional.' He cast an enquiring look at Harriet Hewson. 'Harriet? What do you do in that hospital of yours besides making eyes at the patients? Can you tie on a bandage? I'd do it myself but I'm not too hot at tying knots one-handed.'

Harriet Hewson looked shaken and uncertain.

'I . . . I'll come,' she blurted out. 'You . . . I . . . You'd better let me have a look at that hand . . .'

Ben stood back and watched Taggart leave the smoke-room with a solicitous Harriet Hewson in tow. She had taken hold of Taggart's left arm and was already trying to peer below the blood-soaked handkerchief.

Ben became aware of Fowler, swaying at his side. The Chief Officer looked decidedly drunk.

'What the hell was that all about?' Fowler asked.

'Nothing that need worry you,' Ben replied. 'Everybody has had just a little too much to drink, that's all.'

'Hell, the night is young,' Fowler declared drunkenly, and staggered back to his cronies in the saloon.

In the smoke-room, the two nurses and the three captains had held a hurried conference and come to some kind of decision. One of the nurses was on her feet and came towards Ben.

'We're leaving,' she announced. 'At least, four of us are. Kate and I are going aboard the *Empire Seawind* for coffee and sandwiches. Captain Williams is going back to his own ship.' Captain Williams, it seemed, had drawn the lot of odd man out.

'Aren't you waiting for Harriet?' Ben asked.

The nurse treated Ben to what is known as an old-fashioned look.

'Her Royal Highness needs us like she needs a hole in the head,' she said. 'It was Harriet who started this nonsense and put a damper on the whole proceedings. She can sort things out for herself. She's pretty good at that. Doesn't give a damn for anyone.'

The group of five left together, asking Ben to thank Captain Taggart on their behalf for a party they would remember for a long time.

Ben went out on deck to escape the suffocating atmosphere of the saloon. The air was only marginally cooler. The humidity of the Indian night lay on Bombay like a heavy damp blanket. It brought no relief to the irritability and edginess that Ben felt. Why, he wondered, had he not just drunk himself to insensibility and that kind of escape, instead of hanging around the edge of the evening's merry-making like a disapproving puritan? He tried not to think of how Harriet Hewson was now coping with Taggart and his injured hand. The pair had not returned to the saloon and Ben felt no obligation to sit around indefinitely in expectation of an official announcement that the party was now over. As far as Ben was concerned, he was sorry that it had ever started.

He wearily climbed the ladder of the lower bridge – the simple effort being enough to start new floods of sweat running down his back. His brand-new made-to-measure white shirt – worn for the first time that evening – was sticking to him wherever it touched. Back in his cabin, he stripped it off and went into the bathroom. He turned on the shower and tested it with his hand. The lever was turned to 'cold' but the water running from the rose was tepid. Well, it would at least wash the sweat from his body. He let the water flow over him for fully five minutes.

He was towelling his hair when he heard voices as clearly as from a loud-speaker mounted in the bathroom wall. They came from a ventilator grille high up on the tiled wall. Taggart's bathroom and Ben's were back to back and Ben realised that the ventilator was common to both. The voices were coming from Taggart's bathroom and, apart from a slightly echoing quality, were as distinct as if no separating wall existed. There was no mistaking Harriet Hewson's voice.

'Let me go, damn you, you're hurting me!'

Nor was there any mistaking Taggart's tones.

'Only because you enjoy being hurt. You love it, don't you?'

'I'm not going into that shower!'

The protest from Harriet Hewson was followed by a series of squeals and gasps. Ben stood, transfixed, knowing that what was happening next door was none of his business and that he should not be listening, but he was unable to move: his scruples overcome by a shocked kind of curiosity. Taggart's voice was the next he heard.

'You look good without any clothes.'

'You bastard. You've torn my pants!'

'Get into the shower, sweetie. I want to have you when you're wet.'

'No! No! Keep your hands off me! I'm warning...'

The words died in squealing protest. There was a sound like that of an open-handed slap on bare flesh, followed by a cry of pain. Then all the sounds were drowned by the noise of running water. The shower had been turned on. It stopped just as suddenly as it had started and then the noises emanating from the grille on the wall were low and animal-like: the grunting moans and cries of creatures mating in the wild.

Ben fled from the bathroom, embarrassed by the lewd

morbidity of his eavesdropping. He felt tainted and ashamed by it. Whatever had happened through there had, he was sure, happened without the willing complicity of Harriet Hewson. Or had it? Was she just another woman who cried no when she meant yes? Ben asked himself a hundred times if, instead of listening, he should have intervened. But what good would intervention have done? It was really none of his business. He was not a keeper of the world's morals. And Harriet Hewson had told him that she was a big girl and could look after herself. If she had found out differently, she only had herself to blame.

When, almost guiltily, Ben returned to the bathroom to clean his teeth, a noise still came from the grille up on the tiled wall. It was the sound of a woman weeping.

CHAPTER 4

Outward Bound

Ben Darby woke up to heavy throb of sound from somewhere far below him and with the sensation that someone was gently rocking his bed. He sat up and stared about him, taking a moment to realise that he was not surrounded by the familiar trappings of his own room in the Taj Hotel. Nor was anyone rocking his bed. The entire room was lifting and falling in a gentle motion. The *Kildare Glen* was on the move and the dull sound was the slow beat of the ship's engines.

Casting aside the single sheet that had covered him – it was wringing wet with his body sweat – Ben stepped, naked, from the three-quarter-size bed. Peering through the mosquito-mesh of the port at the fore-end of the cabin, he could see Fowler and several seamen some distance away in the bows. The Chief Officer was engaged in conversation with a tall, gangly seaman, who had a 28 lb hammer resting on one shoulder. Ben was not yet familiar enough with the crew to have recognised the tall seaman as the ship's carpenter. Nor was the significance of the heavy hammer apparent to him. In fact, Fowler and his deck squad were standing by to drop the port anchor. The ship had left her quayside berth – now more than a mile distant – and was manoeuvring slowly in the Roads.

Ben padded across to the maplewood desk and groped along its top for his wrist-watch. It showed 7.45. He shook his head and ruffled both hands through his hair as if the act might clear his sleep-befuddled brain. But this merely intensified the dull ache behind his eyes and reminded him that, in spite of his careful drinking the night before, his total intake had still been immoderate. He showered and dressed quickly, in the belief that the *Kildare Glen* must have received sudden orders to put to sea. As he was pulling on his trousers the entire cabin began to shake and a deep rumbling of agitated machinery vibrated upwards from the bowels of the ship. The *Kildare Glen*'s massive engines were driving full astern. The noise and the shaking stopped simultaneously and from somewhere on the bridge above came the roar of Taggart's voice.

'Let go the port anchor!'

The order was followed by the thundering rattle of chain running out through the hawse-pipe. Then the deck below Ben's feet seemed to emit a grating metallic ratcheting as the bridge telegraph transmitted a final instruction to the engine-room and received an echoing reply. Ben went out on the lower bridge into eye-piercing sunlight. It stirred his incipient hangover, lancing through his skull, and he reeled towards the shady lee of the upper bridge ladder to escape the tormenting brightness.

He was standing there, blinking and unhappily reflecting on his general fragility, when Taggart came nimbly down the ladder from the navigating bridge. The *Kildare Glen*'s master, in pristine white uniform and looking fresh, seemed to glow with good health and well-being.

'Ben, you look like death warmed up.'

'I look better than I feel,' Ben said miserably. His eyes went to the neat bandage covering Taggart's left hand. Only his thumb and the tips of four fingers were visible. 'How's your hand?'

'It's fine.'

'And Harriet?'

'Taking some poor sod's temperature with a hangover, I should imagine. God, those nurses put away some booze between them.'

Ben studied Taggart. The *Kildare Glen*'s captain, if he had any morning-after regrets of rough-handling Harriet Hewson, showed none.

'I thought I heard Harriet crying last night,' Ben said, tentatively. 'I was in the bathroom ... And it's not exactly soundproof ...'

Taggart laughed. 'You're lucky if that's all you heard. Bloody women! They think they're so damned superior. But you only need to look at them sideways and they turn on the waterworks.'

'Then it *was* Harriet crying? I wasn't just hearing things.'

'Boozer's remorse,' said Taggart. 'She was crying buckets. That's the way gin goes for women, you know. Makes them all morose and weepy.'

'It was the gin, was it?' Ben managed to sound only vaguely interested. 'I didn't have her figured for the crying type. Not much fun for you.'

Taggart blinked at him, amused.

'Fun? It wasn't fun I was after. I just wanted to put that little tease in her place.'

'And did you?'

'Let's just say she won't forget me in a hurry. You don't take a soft line with play-acting bitches like her, Ben. They don't respect you if you don't show them who's boss. That other night at the Taj, you let her walk all over you – but she didn't damned well walk all over me! If a woman makes goo-goo eyes at me, she gets everything that's coming to her, whether she likes it or not.'

'And Harriet didn't like it? She put up a fight?'

Taggart's grin had a lewd quality as he leaned towards Ben.

'She put on an act,' he confided. 'Started playing the

virgin queen. Can you imagine it?' Ben could imagine it. Taggart went on: 'She must have thought I was one of those chinless wonders who ponce about the Taj. She can maybe kid them on that they're being given the kingdom of heaven if she deigns to let them touch her left tit – but I've met her kind before. When I buy a bike, it's not just because I want to ting-a-ling on the bell!'

Ben didn't want to hear any more. He had lain awake half the night tormented by the suspicion that something akin to rape had occurred in the neighbouring cabin, but how far Harriet Hewson had colluded in that unhappy fortuity he could only conjecture. She alone could point an accusing finger at Taggart. But would she? Ben thought it unlikely. Her pride would never allow her to expose her shame to public scrutiny and the chance, even, of ridicule. No, she would lick her wounds in private, extinguishing the memory. Perhaps she would even convince herself that nothing had happened.

Ben, however, would not forget. He felt like the bystander who had seen an accident coming and had done nothing to stop it. The terrible irony was that the two main participants would very likely dust themselves off and go on their way, relatively unscathed, while he carried permanent marks: the bystander, caught by flying glass. Taggart showed not a twinge of remorse for what had happened and, almost certainly, Harriet Hewson would attribute no blame to herself. It was left to Ben to feel guilt enough for both. From an acute awareness of his own weakness, it pained him that he was unable to save others from the consequences of theirs. He wanted so much to rejoice in the nobility of the human race – but the more he saw of it, the more he wanted to lament.

As they faced each other at the front of the bridge ladder, Taggart took Ben's self-absorbed silence to be no more than a hangover symptom. He was not unduly sympathetic.

'You'll feel better after a good plate of bacon and eggs,' he assured Ben jovially. 'Give me five minutes to powder my nose and we'll go down to breakfast together.'

'Sure,' said Ben, although he had no appetite. He watched Taggart stride off towards his cabin. He seemed a man without a care in the world, and Ben wondered what it was about the British captain that had roused in him feelings of profound sympathy and concern. Was it a mixed-up gratitude for saving his life? Was it the hero legend and some deep need to see Taggart live up to the heroic qualities the man undoubtedly possessed? He wanted to admire Taggart, to look up to him, to cast him as a man worthy of the greatest respect. But Taggart kept letting his image slip. There may have been an element of rough justice in his humiliation of Harriet Hewson, but after the event there had been an absence of magnanimity or compassion. No twinge of conscience. His cruelty had been calculated – it was an end in itself. *I just wanted to put that little tease in her place.* Then there had been that crazy exhibitionism of pinning his hand to the table. As if he were vaunting his power to destroy by saying: 'Look at me! I am strong enough to destroy all of you! And I can prove it, even if I have to destroy myself!'

It occurred to Ben that, perhaps, he had been wrong about Taggart needing a *friend*. What he thrived on was *enemies*. Enemies who could be beaten. And Taggart left no room for equivocation. Ben could be one or the other: a friend or an enemy. The choice was up to him – and sooner or later it would have to be made.

The saloon still retained a pungently stale odour from the night before. It had 'the pong of a Chinese whorehouse', according to Taggart, who wrinkled his nose in distaste as he took his place at the head of the long dining-table. The Chief Steward lurking at his elbow to take his breakfast order was immediately castigated for not fumigating the premises with pine-scented spray. The man accepted the public reprimand with a look of chagrin on his face. Since 6 a.m. his entire staff had worked like slaves cleaning up the appalling mess of the officers' party, and he considered it a small miracle that breakfast was going ahead on time at all.

The meal was Ben's first on the *Kildare Glen* with most of the deck and engineer officers present. They were grouped around the table in a pecking order that accorded to rank, with Taggart at the top. The junior engineer officers, the second and third radio officers, and the two apprentices ate separately from the hierarchy, at tables in the smoke-room. Taggart bade Ben sit on his right – the seat normally occupied by the Chief Officer and that directly opposite the Chief Engineer – and Fowler moved down a place to accommodate him. He did not seem over-pleased.

The Chief Engineer was a stocky grey-haired Scot called Ferguson. When the steward had taken the breakfast orders, he eyed Taggart with an air of innocent enquiry.

'Are you an authority on Chinese whore-houses, Captain?'

Taggart stared hard at him.

'That's hardly a subject for the breakfast table, Mr Ferguson.'

'It was you that brought the subject up. I wondered if you were speaking from expert knowledge.'

'Well, keep on wondering, Mr Ferguson,' Taggart snapped, and dismissed the matter by turning and facing Ben. 'Did no one tell you we were moving out to the anchorage this morning, Mr Darby?'

'No,' Ben replied, receiving a broad wink from Ferguson, who seemed in no way put out by Taggart's snub. 'I . . . When I woke up, I thought we were putting out to sea.'

'Mr Darby is a journalist, a war correspondent,' Taggart said to the table at large.

'He'll be doing a story on you then, Captain?' Ferguson said with a poker face. Taggart glanced at Ferguson, as if he had detected sarcasm in the Chief Engineer's voice.

'He could do worse,' he said, and looked at Ben with raised eyebrows. 'Will you be doing any writing while you're with us, Mr Darby?'

'The idea had crossed my mind,' Ben replied.

'Good,' said Taggart. 'I can promise you one hell of a story. You will get all the co-operation you want.'

Ben remained thoughtfully silent while the steward placed a glass of chilled tomato juice in front of him. When the steward had gone, he regarded Taggart with an air almost of apology.

'I hadn't thought about writing about you personally, Captain. I was thinking more of featuring some of the guys in the crew, whose jobs aren't quite so glamorous as yours.'

Taggart stared at him with astonishment.

'You're joking?'

'No, Captain, I'm not joking,' Ben said, and met Taggart's eyes with a level stare. He saw a glitter of anger there.

'Just what did you have in mind?' Taggart asked stiffly.

'I thought about doing something on the guys who shovel coal. On paper, I'm supposed to be one of them. That's how I got the idea. It must take guts to sweat away down there if there are submarines about. I guess it must take a special kind of guy . . .'

'That's an excellent idea,' said Ferguson, genuinely pleased.

Taggart did not think so.

'Who the hell wants to read about bloody firemen?' he asked petulantly. 'You'll be lucky if you can find one who can read and write!'

'Then maybe they're due a break from somebody who can,' Ben said. 'I'd like to work with them, get to know them, sweat with them, feel with them . . .'

Taggart laughed – a harsh grating sound.

'That man is out of his mind!' he exclaimed.

'You have to be to work in the stoke-hold,' Ferguson said. 'I say three cheers for Mr Darby.'

'I'd like to do it with your approval, Captain,' Ben said.

'You do what you bloody well like,' snorted Taggart.

A strained silence ensued and it continued while the officers ate their breakfast. When anyone did attempt to start a conversation, Taggart glowered at the offender and put him down with some biting comment of his own, discouraging further pursuit of the topic. Ben ate nothing, contenting himself with a cup of steaming black coffee. He was aware that he had earned a large black mark from Taggart, but he was unrepentant. The *Kildare Glen*'s captain might be good for yards of interesting copy but Ben Darby did not take kindly to direction in what he should or should not write about. He had his own highly personal way of developing his stories and he was not going to change his ways just to keep Taggart sweet. Indeed, the less Taggart had to do with it, the better!

The atmosphere at the breakfast table dismayed Ben. With the possible exception of Ferguson, the other officers seemed quite cowed by Taggart, which did not augur well for a happy ship. Ben got the distinct impression that, in the short time he had been in command, Taggart had succeeded in getting himself thoroughly detested. As the Captain smothered his extra-large helping of bacon and eggs with Worcestershire sauce and devoured it with the grace of a pig at a trough, Ben caught the revulsion in the surreptitious glances at the spectacle from the officers seated around the table. The loathing apparent in those stolen glances ran deeper, Ben thought, than mere disgust at the Captain's table manners.

When Taggart rose and left the table, with a grunt that indicated he had finished, his departure was greeted with evident relief. Smiles reappeared on faces and several conversations broke out at once. Everyone relaxed.

During the morning, several coal barges were towed out and moored against the *Kildare Glen*'s port side. With them came a regiment of Indian labourers, who immediately began to erect a complex of scaffoldings and timber walkways to allow the coal from the barges to be transferred to the *Kildare Glen*'s bunkers. Ben watched the operation, enthralled. Clad only in loincloths, the labourers swarmed like ants over barges and ship, hoisting or carrying baskets of coal in an endless stream to the bunker hatches. No mechanical aids were employed. The entire operation of transferring 750 tons of coal was done by hand, accompanied by a babble of voices. Ben had no doubt that, if coal-burning ships had existed in biblical times, this was the way they would have been bunkered.

When Ben returned to his cabin, it was to find the movable furniture stacked on the leather wall-settee and the floor rugs removed. On hands and knees a diminutive figure was propelling a scrubbing-brush across the dark-red compound surface of the cabin-deck. Alternately using scrubbing-brush and cloth, which he dipped into a bucket of muddy-looking water, the boy – for he seemed no more than fourteen years old – was intent on producing a sheen from the dark-red floor. He did not hear Ben's entry. When he suddenly sensed Ben's presence, he looked up with eyes that were wide with fright. He cowered away momentarily, like a startled fawn.

'It's OK, son. I live here,' Ben said. 'I didn't mean to scare you.'

The tension went out of the boy.

'It was your shadow ... Blocking out the light ... I thought you were the Old Man ...'

'Captain Taggart?' Ben grinned. 'Keeps you on the hop, does he?'

The boy smiled, making him look younger than ever. His face had a shining innocence about it, of the kind that makes women go all soft and motherly.

'The Captain's not easy to please,' he said.

'You're only a kid. How old are you?'

'I'm sixteen.'

'They let kids of sixteen go to sea?' Ben was shocked.

'Before the war, they let you go at fourteen. The apprentices and the galley-boy are only a month or two older than me.'

'And your folks let you go? At your age I was still in higher school.'

'I don't have any folks. I was a Barnardo boy. I came to sea straight from the home.'

'A Barnardo boy?'

'Haven't you heard of Dr Barnardo's? Maybe they just have orphanages where you come from.'

Ben considered this. 'Yeah ... I'm with you now. It was pretty tough for you there, was it?'

'Tough? No ... It was my home. I liked it there. But they can't keep you for ever, can they?'

'I don't suppose they can,' Ben agreed, with a wry smile. There was something engaging about the matter-of-fact acceptance by the boy of a lot that others would term disadvantaged. 'What's your name?'

'White, sir. Richard White. But everybody calls me Whitey.' He hesitated, an anxious little frown on his face. 'Is it true that you're a famous writer?'

Ben laughed. 'I'm a writer, yes. But famous? I wouldn't say so.'

'I want to be a writer some day,' the boy said, his eyes bright with enthusiasm. Self-consciousness overtook him at having had the temerity to admit the ambition.

'It's a bit of a joke really. People laugh when I tell them.'

'I'm not laughing,' Ben said.

The boy regarded him with wide-eyed hope.

'Maybe I can talk to you sometime? I know so little . . . And there's so much I want to find out about.'

'Sure,' Ben said. 'We can talk. Anytime.'

The boy chattered his gratitude, over the moon with delight at Ben's promise. Ben, warmed by the sheer pleasure he had awakened, experienced a rare glow of worthiness. Tyro writers could be a real pain in the neck, but he had recognised in young Richard White's enthusiasm a glimmer of the shy idealistic yearnings that had once burned in his own breast. If he could nurture them, he would.

Ben decided that waiting to sail from the Bombay Roads was an experience akin to that of early Christians awaiting their turn to walk down the tunnel into the broad arena of Rome's Colosseum. The analogy was perhaps extravagant, but on the ships ready to depart there was a fellowship of final farewell as each hour of sailing arrived and another friend weighed anchor and nosed out through the boom-gate, alone, to face the hostile wastes of sea beyond.

Already, ships and crews had come through much together. All had faced considerable ordeal by fire and tempest – but they had been sustained during their times of trial by the comforting presence of one with another. Across many miles of ocean, the dangers had been shared. Now, here in Bombay, was the parting of the ways.

As each dawn came, the number of mechantmen in the anchorage decreased by one. The departing ship would slip out from the Roads in the still of breaking day, her progress through the grey shapes of the anchored armada marked by winking Aldis lamps that blinked out brief messages of 'God-speed' and 'Safe journey'. Now and then voices called out greetings from ship to ship as friend recognised friend and waved farewell.

The days on the *Kildare Glen* started with the ritual of observing the dawn departure. No order had been given to summon the hands on deck well in advance of working hours. It just seemed to happen spontaneously. There was a solemnity to it, too, this largely silent demonstration of good-bye to old friends. It rose from a certain sadness that permeated the quiet groups lining the rails of the anchored ships like a chill morning mist – a sadness rooted in the unspoken acceptance that the ship heading so bravely seaward might never be seen again. For all the waiting men, now, the dice had been thrown. All the ships would sail one by one in their appointed order, but not all would reach the far side of the ocean. Thus those remaining viewed those leaving with a tense trepidation: knowing that possibly death awaited their comrades in the arena to which they departed, but knowing, too, that their own hour to face the waiting predators was not far off.

Ben, suddenly intensely alive to the unknown hazards of the ocean crossing he was about to make, marvelled at the calm of the men whose number he had joined. He sensed the awakening in them of gut-deep anxieties and fears that they did not parade openly but which were there, nevertheless. It was betrayed in nervous smiles and cheerful bravado that did not wholly conceal inner tensions. Indeed, Ben felt – in the quickening of his own blood – as if his nerve ends were tuned to the current of fear-edged anticipation which the men of the *Kildare Glen* were unable totally to conceal.

On four successive days, they made their dawn salutes. They watched the *Fort Buckingham* go, sedately, ignorant of the unmarked equatorial grave that awaited her within the week. All but one of her complement of seventy men would die in the trackless ocean beyond the boom-gate, but the morning of departure was serene. Next away was the *Ocean Pride*. She was followed by the *Fort Stager* on the third dawn and, on the fourth, by the *Empire Seawind*. On the fifth day, the *Kildare Glen* steamed out through the boom-gate.

By mid-morning, the land had faded from sight astern and the *Kildare Glen*'s bows were lifting in a long lazy swell. Some of the tension that had gripped Ben prior to departure remained with him as the cargoless ship, riding high in the water, ploughed south into the Arabian Sea. Course was altered frequently in compliance with the first series of zig-zag patterns, creating constant variations in the motion of the ship. One moment, she would be riding easily with the following north-easterly swell and, in the next, she would be rolling and sliding with the swell on the quarter. Ben parted company with his breakfast at eleven in the morning – but it was to be the only time he was troubled with sea-sickness.

The excitement of at last quitting Bombay and his general queasiness made him decide that his first day at sea would be one of inactivity: a day of acclimatisation. To the south lay twenty-eight and a half million square miles of Indian Ocean – and there would be plenty of time to commit story ideas to paper as the *Kildare Glen* tracked a zig-zag path across that watery wilderness. But the first day out was not to be free of incident.

Taggart – who had been cool towards Ben since he had mooted the idea of writing about the ship's 'black gang' instead of the ship's master – seemed to undergo a personality change from the moment the ship was in open sea. He kept himself more to himself and adopted a ferocity of manner that was unrelieved by occasional lapses into joviality. It was as if, before, he had merely been presenting a mild front to the world and biding his time until, at sea, he could let his incipient paranoia run riot.

Ben was in his cabin when he heard the sound of raised voices coming from the Captain's quarters. He went out to the lower bridge to find two deck-sailors and one of the firemen standing there in an anxious little group. The commotion in the Captain's cabin was still going on.

'What the hell's happening?' Ben asked.

'A complaint delegation,' one of the men said. 'The Old Man said he would allow one spokesman into his day-room to put our case. Sounds like they're having a right old barney.'

'A complaint delegation?' Ben frowned in puzzlement. 'About the food?'

'About the cigarette issue,' answered the seaman. 'We don't mind the Old Man and the Chief Steward making a modest bob on the fags, but charging double the going rate and doling out nothing but those Indian-made coffin nails is a bit bloody thick!'

The men were particularly incensed because they had got wind of the fact that the Chief Steward had a large stock in the bond of popular British cigarettes – such as Senior Service and State Express – in American packs, but he had been forbidden by Taggart to put them on sale. Taggart, meanwhile, had acquired a large quantity of Indian-manufactured Players – vastly inferior to the British-produced brand – and had insisted that these would have to be sold before the other stocks were touched. He had not endeared himself to the crew by putting an inflated price on the Indian cigarettes, thus ensuring that he made a considerable profit.

Ben was shocked, not only by Taggart's greedy profiteering, but to learn from the seamen that the ship's captain enjoyed a monopoly position with regard to the sale of tobacco and liquor at sea. He could virtually name his own price. One of the seamen was trying to explain the position to him when the mosquito door to Taggart's quarters burst open. A big red-haired man, who was almost Taggart's equal in size, was propelled through the door and forced on to his knees in front of the startled delegation. Taggart had the man in an armlock and had the redhead's arm twisted up his back.

Taggart let the man go and stood back, breathing heavily. His eyes burned with fury as he regarded the others.

'Take this upstart back where he belongs! And clear off my bridge, the lot of you!'

The red-headed man was still sprawled on hands and knees, his breath coming in great grunting heaves. He half-turned his head to direct a hate-filled stare at Taggart.

'I'll get you for this, you bastard!' he snarled.

'That remark will cost you another day's pay!' Taggart snarled back. 'That's another logging offence to go with the ones you've already totted up.'

One of the three seaman helped the redhead to his feet, mumbling something to him and clearly stifling a reply that would have antagonised Taggart further. Ben heard the red-headed man protest: 'It was him who started it! The bastard thumped me in the gut and started battering me. I didn't lift a finger to him!'

'You're a liar, McQueen!' Taggart growled. 'And lying won't help you. You don't get away with assaulting the master on this ship. Next time you won't be so lucky. Next time I won't restrain you with my bare hands – I'll take a pistol to you.' Taggart made a sweeping gesture to the redhead's three companions. 'Take that specimen away and see he behaves himself!'

Two of the three seamen got the redhead to his feet and began to support him towards the ladder. The third took up the rear but took only two hesitant steps before turning to face Taggart.

'What about the cigarette issue, sir?' he asked, tentatively.

'There isn't going to be one,' Taggart snapped. 'If you and your mates don't like my terms, you can damned well go without. We'll see how long it takes you to come to your senses.'

The man seemed about to make an angry reply, but thought better of it. He pursed his lips together, frowned angrily, and hurried after his mates. Taggart acknowledged Ben's presence for the first time.

'Well, Mr Darby, that concludes the entertainment for the time being. I hope you had your eyes opened. That's the kind of scum you want to write about.'

Ben met Taggart's mocking stare levelly.

' "Scum" isn't a word I would use about anyone. I write about people, and I write about them as I find them. "Scum" is not a word I would want to use. I try to be very selective about the words I use.'

'You have to be, Mr Darby. Because if someone doesn't like the words you use, they might knock your bloody head off. But you're not the master of this ship. I am. And I can say what I bloody well like. That trouble-maker McQueen is scum!'

'You called him a liar, too,' Ben reminded Taggart, continuing to meet the Captain's stare unyieldingly.

'He's a lying scum,' Taggart agreed.

'But who threw the first punch, Captain?'

'Are you suggesting it was me?' Taggart's eyes were glinting angrily.

'He might have provoked you,' Ben said, with a

deceptively reasonable tone. 'But, of course, there were no witnesses. It's his word against yours.'

'And on my ship, my word is law!' Taggart answered, with a snap of triumph. 'Never allow yourself to forget that, Mr Darby. Never forget it!'

With that, he turned on his heel and barged through the mosquito door, leaving it banging.

Ben did not see Taggart again until after the evening meal. The Captain had eaten alone in the seclusion of his cabin – to the unconcealed relief of the other officers who sat down to dinner in the saloon and, for once, enjoyed a range of conversations that were not dominated by the uncompromising opinions of their skipper. A few lingered on in the smoke-room afterwards, and it was the peace of this little group that was interrupted by the sudden appearance of Taggart, who was in a towering rage.

The target of his fury was Ferguson, the Chief Engineer, and the apparent reason for it was the miserable speed that the *Kildare Glen* was achieving. Oblivious to the others present, Taggart tore into the bemused Ferguson: his tirade laced with insult and obscenity. It was clear that he held the engineer directly responsible for the ship's failure to exceed a lamentably slow seven knots when she should have been spanking along at more than twelve and a half. The performance was entirely attributable to Ferguson's personal incompetence and that of his lazy and useless engine-room staff.

Ferguson did not take the onslaught lying down. Without resorting to insult himself, he angrily repudiated Taggart's accusations: arguing that the *Kildare Glen*'s dawdling speed was the result of two things beyond his control. The growth of barnacles and other marine growth on the ship's bottom was so great that a good four knots was being clipped off the speed and there would be little improvement until the ship was dry-docked and scraped: something he had urged in Bombay until he was blue in the face. The other factor was the poor quality of Indian coal, which was dirty and not a patch on good Welsh coal for raising and maintaining a good head of steam.

Taggart shouted him down. He didn't want excuses. He wanted the Chief Engineer to get off his backside bloody fast and do something about it! Ferguson was white-faced with suppressed anger. In clipped tones, he promised to do everything he could to improve the ship's speed but it was not his intention to listen to any more of the foul-mouthed abuse to which he had been subjected. He added the hope that, in the future, the Captain would consult him privately about any matters relating to his department because he, Ferguson, did not intend to discuss them in public.

'That's all I have to say on the matter,' he concluded with dignity and would have marched from the room if Taggart had not caught him by the shoulder.

'You, go, Mr Ferguson,' he snarled. 'You go and start lighting fires under those grease-monkeys you call engineers! And, by God, you had better produce results! Because, if you don't, I'll break you!'

He relaxed his hold on the engineer. Ferguson stared at him with contempt for a moment but said nothing. Then he turned and left. In the days that followed, the Chief Engineer was to register his disdain for the Captain's company by never returning to the saloon or smoke-room, and the engineer officers followed his lead. From then on, they ate all their meals in the small mess-room above the engine-room.

After the row between Taggart and Ferguson in the smoke-room, Ben selected a book from the shelves of the ship's library and escaped to the privacy of his cabin. The book he had chosen – a surprise discovery next to a trilogy of westerns by Zane Grey – was Oliver Goldsmith's *History of England*. He was deep into a hair-raising account of how the English got rid of one of their Plantagenet kings by thrusting a red-hot rod into his bowels, when there was a tentative knock at his door.

It was young Richard White, the cabin-boy. He clutched a dog-eared school exercise book in his hand and presented it to Ben.

'It's just some poems and things that I wrote . . . I've never shown them to anyone before . . . I thought maybe you'd read them . . . if it ain't no trouble . . .'

Ben took the book. 'I'd like that, Richard. I've been looking for something to read and all I could come up with was a stuffy old book on history. Come on in a minute.'

The boy hesitated, 'I don't know that I should . . . I've got supper mugs to get ready . . .'

Ben persuaded him that the supper mugs could wait five minutes. The boy came in and, at Ben's invitation, perched himself on the edge of the settee. Ben placed the exercise book on the open flap of his desk and parked himself in the armchair, where he had been reading.

'You must work long hours, Richard. It's getting on for eight.'

'I don't mind. You get used to it.'

'Tell me, what do you like to write about?'

The boy hung his head, still shy.

'Oh, you know . . . Things I see . . . Things that happen . . .' He got no further, looking up in sudden alarm at the roar of Taggart's voice from just outside the cabin door.

'You've got a light showing from a for'rd port, Mr Darby!'

The bawled warning preceded Taggart's bull-like entry into the cabin. With scarcely a glance at Ben, he strode towards the offending port at the fore-end of the cabin. The deadlight had been dropped but the heavy metal flap had not been clamped. Taggart flipped the locking nuts into place and screwed them tight. As he did so, he spoke over his shoulder to Ben.

'That's the kind of carelessness that costs lives at sea. A Jap sub could see that light five miles away . . .' He turned and, for the first time, saw the cabin-boy. He seemed to swell with anger.

'And what the bloody hell are you doing here, boy?'

Richard White had slipped from the settee and was standing nervously, as if poised for flight. He was trembling with fear.

'N-n-nothing sir,' he stammered.

'Nothing!' Taggart echoed. 'That's all you're good for – nothing! But it's not what you get paid for. You get paid for working! And working is something you're not very good at. Isn't that so?'

'I don't know, sir.'

'I don't know, sir,' Taggart mimicked in a high-pitched voice. 'But I know, sir. I wanted my bathroom spick and span this afternoon, didn't I? But you didn't make it spick and span, did you? You gave it the once-over-lightly – a miserable little spit and a promise. Well, you're going right back there and you're going to do it all over again, even if it takes you half the night. You understand?'

'Captain . . .' Ben had got out of his chair. 'It's my fault that the boy is . . .'

Taggart turned on him. 'Keep out of this, Mr Darby. I'll thank you not to interfere in matters that don't concern you. And this doesn't concern you!'

'For Christ's sake, go easy, will you? You don't listen to anybody!' Ben's voice had risen with anger, and he was determined to be heard. His vehemence surprised Taggart, who goggled at him in disbelief. His incredulity gave way to faint amusement.

'Well, well, well,' he mocked, 'I do believe you're trying to tell me something.'

'I'm trying to tell you to cool it!' Ben said, with an

urgent note of appeal in his voice. 'For your own sake as much as anybody's. Before you blow a fuse!'

'How very considerate of you, Mr Darby,' Taggart said in a calm voice, his manner icy. 'We'll resume this conversation in a moment. After I have attended to your young friend here. You will excuse me, won't you?' Sarcasm dripped from his tongue as he spoke. He turned and glowered at the cabin-boy. 'You! Hop it! Go get a bucket and a soogie cloth and get started on my bathroom. I'll look in later to see how good a job you're making of it.'

The boy fled. Taggart turned back to Ben.

'You seem to have reservations, Mr Darby, not only about my mental health but in the way I choose to run this ship. Perhaps you will tell me what qualifications you have to interfere on either count.'

Ben sighed. 'Look, Captain, I'm not trying to tell you how to do your job. But you act like you've got a grudge against the whole goddamned world. Why, for God's sake? You don't have to prove anything to anybody. I had a whole lot of respect for the guy who waded into a mob and saved my neck, but that respect wears pretty thin when the same guy treats his own men like dirt under his feet and gets his kicks by bullying a young kid who's barely old enough for high school.'

The muscles in Taggart's face quivered as Ben was speaking, but he let the American finish. He seemed to make a deliberate effort to hold himself in check.

'You're a brave man Mr Darby,' he said softly. 'Few men would say to my face what you've just said – and walk away in one piece. You've got more guts than I gave you credit for. But, having listened to you saying your piece, you can bend your ears back and listen to me saying mine. And you'd better listen good, because it might save you a lot of grief later on. Maybe you were right saying that I had a grudge . . . Maybe I do . . . because I don't give a tuppenny damn for what you or the whole damned human race think about . . . This stinking world gave me nothing on a plate. I've got nothing that I didn't have to fight for, and I mean *fight*! Since the day I was born, it's been me against the rest – and that's the way it'll be till the day I die. I don't need your respect, or any other man's – because your respect isn't going to be any goddamned use to me when the bastards who fawn on you and pin medals on you when it suits them try to push me back down where they think I belong . . .'

'You're wrong,' Ben said, in a voice so low that it was scarcely audible.

'Wrong, am I?' snorted Taggart. 'Wrong! There are only three kinds of people in this world, my American friend: those that are in the shit-heap; those that are trying to fight their way out of it; and those that are trying to push you back down. Well, I fought my way out of it . . . And out is where I mean to stay!'

'You're sick,' Ben said.

Taggart grabbed him by the shirt-front.

'Sick, am I?' His eyes smouldered. 'Not as sick as some I could mention.'

'What are you talking about?' Ben gasped.

'I'm talking about passengers who aren't ten minutes on the ship before they're entertaining lily-white cabin-boys in their cabin. I'm disappointed in you, Mr Darby. I didn't take you for one of them. But I should have known. Now I know why you were so keen to palm your girlfriend off on me.'

'You've got it all wrong!' Ben cried. 'For God's sake, let me go!'

Taggart released his hold.

'Just keep away from the younger members of my crew, Mr Darby.' Taggart turned to leave, but paused at the doorway. 'I'll be watching you,' he warned.

Ben was speechless, staggered at the vileness of Taggart's innuendo. He wanted to scream a denial, but no sound came from his dry throat. Denials were no real defence. He subsided into his chair, weak with shock.

He was still sitting there ten minutes later when he noticed Richard White's exercise book sitting on the open flap of his desk. He picked it up and leafed through it.

The pages were filled with the boy's spidery scrawl: short essays, diary-like observations, of events and places, poems. All were set down neatly and systematically, with headings in capital letters. Ben lingered over one page that had been devoted to a short poem. It was entitled 'Why?', with the line below the title, 'by Richard Stanley White'. Ben read:

> Last night, when the seas were mountain-high,
> I saw a ship go down.
> Last, night, I asked: Dear God, oh, why?
> Why must the sailors drown?'
> Last night, I saw the torpedo's flash
> And heard its angry roar.
> Last night, I cried to heav'n above:
> 'Dear God, what for? What for?'
> Last night, no answer came to me,
> As we our vigil kept –
> But was the rain upon my face
> A sign that angels wept?

For all that the lines lacked style and form, Ben felt moved by them in a way he had never been moved by the polished lines of Shelley or Wordsworth. The innocent trusting face of the boy who had penned them was too vivid in his mind, and he could share only too keenly the sensitive questing of a spirit that was awakening to the realities of a world less than perfect. Ben could feel a boy's wondering pain in his own heart and the slim comfort he snatched from rain upon his face.

A sign that angels wept?

Well might they weep, thought Ben. Well might the angels weep.

CHAPTER 5

Storms

The temperature in the stoke-hold was the wrong side of 120°F and sweat streamed from Ben's shoulders. A rag wound round his hand, McQueen opened the furnace door and nodded to the American.

'Let's have you then, Yank. Show us what you can do.'

Ben slid the broad shovel into the heap of coal that McQueen had barrowed for him and, with a step towards the furnace, heaved a full load far into the fiery orifice.

'Keep it going, Yank,' McQueen exhorted, but Ben was already stooping and a second shovelful was on its way. Ben was determined to prove himself to his tutor and he bent his back with a will, working with a feverish energy. The heat leaping out at him burned at the skin of his face and naked chest, but he ignored its searing torture to keep going without respite.

'OK, OK. Take a blow before you bust a gut.' The big red-haired fireman was smiling broadly at the determined fury of Ben's efforts as he called a halt. He took the shovel from Ben. 'Now watch me,' he instructed.

Ben retreated beyond scorching distance and watched as McQueen demolished the heap of coal with easy thrusts of the shovel and measured deliveries of its contents into the open furnace.

Finally satisfied, the redhead dropped the shovel and retrieved a flagon of water from where it hung on a hook in the open end of the ventilator shaft. He spilled some water over his head and face, drank deeply, and then handed it to Ben. The water was warm and coated with coal-dust but tasted like nectar.

McQueen grinned at the American.

'I'll give you your due, Yank. You're a real tryer. You'll come on once you get the hang of it.'

'I thought I did pretty well,' Ben said.

'Ten out of ten for effort,' smiled McQueen. 'But two out of ten for performance.'

Disappointment showed on Ben's glistening coal-streaked face.

'Surely I did better than that,' he protested.

'Don't get me wrong,' McQueen said. 'For a beginner you did hell of a well. But you were wasting all the energy you were using up. You were killing yourself for nothing.'

'I was getting the coal right to the back of the furnace,' Ben maintained, with a note of pride in his voice. 'You said I'd heap it all in the front.'

'Most beginners do scatter it all over the front. Some miss the bloody door altogether and put it all over the floor.' McQueen grinned more broadly then ever. 'You really did hell of a well. But throwing all the coal up the back of the furnace is as bad as blocking up the front. What happens when you throw the coal all up the back is that the whole bloody shooting-match gets clogged up and you don't get a nice even flow of heat to the boiler. When you let the coal leave your shovel, you try to let it go in an even spread. Not too much at the back and not too much at the front. There's a knack to it. You let the coal slide from the shovel, so that it falls in a nice fore-and-aft distribution. Not too much in one place.'

'What's the secret?' Ben asked.

'There's no secret,' McQueen said. 'It's just something that comes with practice. Like hitting a golf ball. You don't have to go at it like a hopped-up windmill. You've got to have rhythm and timing. You've got to keep your movements smooth and easy.'

'I'll try again tomorrow. That is, if you'll give me another lesson.'

'If it's OK with the Chief, it's OK with me,' McQueen said, and nodded in the direction of the far end of the stoke-hold. 'And talk of the devil, here he comes to check up on you. My bet is that he thought five minutes down here would crease you.'

Ferguson, in white boiler-suit and his Chief's cap pushed to the back of his head, had come through to the stoke-hold from the engine-room. His eyes took in Ben's begrimed appearance and McQueen's wide grin.

'How's our star apprentice coming along?' he asked.

'He's not afraid of hard work,' said McQueen. 'I'll have him in my watch anytime you like.'

Ferguson stared at Ben admiringly.

'I expected to find you'd been carried up the fiddley feet first, Mr Darby. That's a good hour you've been down here. Has Mac taught you everything he knows?'

'It seems I've still a lot to learn, Chief, but I'll get there. I don't intend to let it lick me.'

'Good for you, laddie,' Ferguson commended Ben. 'If you pass muster with Red Mac here, you've got what it takes. Faint praise from him is worth a testimonial on parchment from anyone else.' He arched an eyebrow at the fireman. 'Isn't that right, Mac?'

'Why, aye,' McQueen agreed, his eyes twinkling in his blackened face. 'You know what the Geordie Mafia say about me . . .? *Numero uno*. The best there bloody is!'

'The best there bloody is,' Ferguson confirmed, and winked at Ben. 'When he's sober.'

The smile left McQueen's face and he glowered reproachfully at the Chief.

'I never touch a drop when I'm at sea, Mr Ferguson. And you know it.'

Ferguson grinned. 'Of course I know it, laddie. Mind you, you make up for it in port. I daresay you'll have worked up quite a thirst by the time we reach Durban.'

McQueen nodded. 'Aye, and we'll never get there if I spend the watch gassing like an old fishwife.' He smiled at Ben. 'I'll get on wi' me work. It's only officers have time to stand around gossiping.'

Ben walked through to the engine-room with Ferguson, who was quietly chuckling at McQueen's parting remark.

'He's right, of course,' the engineer confided to Ben. 'Mac there is paid for what he does, whereas I get paid for what I know. It leaves time for the occasional natter and a cup of tea. D'ye fancy a cup of engine-room tea?' He glanced mischievously at Ben. 'Because the Fourth Engineer's going to be in a lot of trouble if he hasn't brewed up. I told him that you would be ready to trade your pension rights for a mug of his tarry swill.'

Ben laughed. 'I reckon I could drink a quart of engine-oil right now, Chief. I've got that kind of thirst.'

Ferguson pulled a face. 'You sound like you've tasted the Fourth's tea already. It'll take the back off your throat and put a lining in your stomach – but it's usually hot and wet!'

The most junior of the engineer officers was a man in his middle forties: a small wiry man who had been at sea for more than twenty years. He was uncertified, having made the jump from petty officer to engineer officer because of a wartime shortage of certificated engineers. Fourth Engineer was the highest rank he would attain.

He poured a mug of tea for Ben and laced it liberally with sugar and condensed milk. Ben sat in the fan of cool air issuing from the engine-room ventilator and drank it gratefully. As the Chief had promised, it was hot and wet.

Here, it was impossible to converse without shouting. Overhead, the great metal arms of the main engine kept up a continuous clangour.

'I don't think I could ever get used to this,' Ben bellowed at the Fourth.

'What?' the little man bawled back, holding a hand to his ear.

'This noise,' Ben tried again. 'I don't think I could ever get used to it.'

'I can't hear you for the bloody noise,' the engineer shouted, and Ben nodded.

'That's what I've been trying to tell you. It would drive me crazy. I could never get used to it.'

The Fourth suddenly began nodding and making signs that comprehension had dawned.

'The noise?' he shouted, and nodded his head even more vigorously. 'Can't hear yourself think?' More nodding. 'It's OK. You get used to it!'

The days began to take on a pattern for Ben after his first venture into the stoke-hold. For an hour during the forenoon watch he would go below for tuition by McQueen in the arts of firing a ship's boiler. In the afternoons he followed the shipboard custom of those not on watch and took a siesta between one-thirty and three-thirty. In the evenings he worked at his desk, writing: compiling his own personal log of the voyage: making copious notes; and putting on paper a range of ideas for future articles and the novel he intended one day to write.

Ben did not confine his curiosity about seafaring to the engine-room and stoke-hold. Mr Prins, the Dutch Second Officer, loved to talk to him about the mysteries of navigation and welcomed his company on the bridge. The other officers, Taggart among them, tended to make fun of the Dutchman's rather earnest manner and unfailing courtesy, but Ben found it engaging. In the small hours of the morning – when the heat of his blacked-out cabin made sleep difficult – Ben always found a welcome from the Second Officer on the bridge. His arrival there was always good for a quick brew of coffee and a discussion on astronomy or meteorology – subjects in which Mr Prins was a mine of information.

Ben came much less in contact with Mr Barraclough, the twenty-one-year-old Third Officer, who kept the eight-to-twelve watches. He had still to learn Mr Barraclough's Christian name, for no one had ever used it in his presence. The traditional use of 'Mister' among the officers was a custom which Ben found fascinating but quaint. He found himself resorting to the formality of 'Mister' long after Mr Prins had invited the use of Willem – and he even found himself taken aback when someone addressed him as Ben instead of Mr Darby. The rare familiarity came as a surprise.

Another reason why Ben saw little of the Third Officer was that Taggart had the habit of standing most of his watches with him, and Ben had no wish to cross the path of the *Kildare Glen*'s master after the unpleasant scene with him on the first day at sea. Indeed, six days passed in which Ben saw little of Taggart. It was towards the end of the sixth day, that Taggart offered his olive branch. Ben found a portable typewriter sitting on his desk with a hand-written note propped beside it.

The note said: *Ben. You were bemoaning the fact that you were unable to pick up a typewriter in Bombay. Want to try this trusty old machine of mine, with the compliments of the management? Let me know if you need some paper to go with it*. The note bore Taggart's initials at the foot and there was a postscript: *Drop in for a chat after scoff-time tonight*.

The evening meal was always served promptly at 5

p.m. Ben ate through the three substantial courses slowly, preoccupied by the unexpected invitation from Taggart and wondering if he should accept it. He decided that an invitation from the Captain was as good as a command and should not be ignored. Taggart had, as usual these days, eaten alone in his room and his steward – carrying a tray of dirty dishes – was descending the inside stair to the pantry as Ben took that short cut to the Captain's quarters and knocked at the door.

Taggart greeted him warmly and insisted on pouring him a post-prandial brandy. He was so solicitous of Ben's welfare that Ben felt faintly uneasy. Benignity did not sit easily on Taggart and he seemed to be overplaying it. The Captain seemed to know all about Ben's morning sessions in the stoke-hold and his nocturnal visits to the bridge but, far from disapproving of these activities, he was quick to express his admiration for the way Ben was acquiring practical knowledge of working conditions on board ship.

Abandoning his customary directness, Taggart arrived circuitously at the purpose of his surprise invitation.

'I look on you as a generous man, Ben,' he said. 'You're slow to condemn. You're the kind of man who will always make allowances. Am I right?'

Ben shrugged. 'I like to think I'm a tolerant sort of guy. Make allowances? I suppose I do. I'm a pretty easy-going sort of person.'

'Can you make allowances for a bloke who has a hell of a difficult job and sometimes blows his stack because of it?'

'Yeah. We all have pressures. The guy with a lot has more reason to blow off steam than the guy who isn't carrying a big load.'

Taggart seemed relieved to hear Ben say this.

'That's it exactly, Ben,' he agreed.

He splashed more brandy into Ben's glass and silenced Ben's half-hearted protest: 'You're my guest. I don't offer this stuff to everybody.' He frowned. 'Ben, I once said you apologised too much ... Because I never do ... It's a sign of weakness ...'

'Not in my book,' Ben said. 'It's a sign of strength ... Being able to say you're sorry when it needs to be said.'

'I want to say it to you, Ben. I was out of order the other night. I was in a foul mood and I'd had a bellyful of lip the whole blessed day. I'm sorry I spoke out of turn to you.'

'Then let's forget it ever happened,' Ben said.

'Good!' Taggart brightened visibly. He stuck out a hand. 'Friends?'

Ben took his hand. 'Friends,' he said.

The breach healed, Taggart seemed to thaw more than ever. Ben got the impression — as he had got the impression on the night when Taggart had come to his room in the Taj Hotel — that Taggart wanted to talk. *Needed to talk*. He talked about the isolation and loneliness of commanding a ship: about the friendless nature of the job. The decision-making process was impaired by too close a friendship with any other individuals affected by the consequences of a difficult judgement. The master of a ship had to remain aloof, free to exercise his judgement as he saw it. He, alone, carried the responsibility. Command could not be shared, nor diluted and weakened by the obligations of friendship.

'That's why it's good to have somebody like you aboard, Ben,' Taggart confessed. 'I can talk to you in a way I can never talk to Fowler or the Chief Engineer. They have their own little axes to grind. You don't. You're an outsider. Not involved. You're neutral. I can chat to you and know you won't try to capitalise on my mateyness by talking me into something that would be an error of professional judgement.'

Ben was quietly considering this when a sharp whistling sound startled him. Taggart smiled and, easing himself out of his armchair, reached for the cap of the speaking tube that ran down the forward bulkhead from the bridge. He listened at the open tube and then spoke back into it, firing off laconic questions. Answers came down and Taggart concluded the exchange with the promise to come up to the bridge in ten minutes.

'Something wrong?' Ben enquired when Taggart returned to the table but did not sit down.

'That's Fowler panicking like an old hen,' Taggart said. 'The Sparks has just picked up an all-ships call that has put the wind up our Chief Officer.'

'An all-ships call?'

'An SOS,' Taggart said. 'From the *Fort Buckingham*. She was one of the ships that left Bombay ahead of us.'

Ben sat bolt upright in his chair. Taggart's calm statement had sent a chill down his spine.

'She's in trouble?'

'Torpedoed and sinking.'

'Are we close enough to help?' Ben asked.

'She's more than five hundred miles away. And we have orders to steam like hell in any direction but the one that would give us a chance of picking up any survivors.'

'Jesus!' breathed Ben. 'What's going to happen to those poor guys?'

Taggart gave him a long and eloquent look but left the question unanswered.

'I'm going up to the bridge,' he said. 'I have decisions to make.'

Ben hurriedly got out of his chair, suddenly realising that he served no purpose on the ship. He was a passenger: as useful in the present situation as baggage to a marathon-runner.

'I'd better not keep you,' he apologised to Taggart.

Taggart told him to sit where he was.

'Finish your drink, Ben,' he said. 'We're more than

two days' run from the *Buckingham*'s spot of bother. There's no need for us to get our knickers in a twist. Fowler's only panicky because he's learnt that I don't treat Admiralty orders as holy writ. He's scared I'll go looking for survivors regardless.'

'And will you?'

Taggart smiled. 'At the speed this old tub's making, it's not going to make much difference what the hell I do. We're supposed to zig-zag during daylight, according to orders – but one day's steaming was enough to put an end to that particular nonsense. We'll be lucky to get to Durban by next Christmas as it is. Six and three-quarter knots is what we've been averaging! A hundred and sixty-four miles was our day's run to noon today – and that with a following current!' He smiled grimly to himself. 'I might just go and scare the shit out of Fowler by telling him to make for the *Fort Buckingham*'s position. No sub is going to sit around for the time it will take us to get there and, if the Japs left any survivors – which they're not notorious for doing – at least my conscience will be clear.'

Ben, who in the past few days had been well on the way to hating Taggart, felt a new stirring of admiration for him. There was no denying the fearsome burden of his job and the pressures it exerted. Whether or not those pressures were any excuse for the mean and tyrannical style of Taggart's command was a matter on which Ben was not yet ready to pass judgement. He was a bewildering paradox of a man: behaving like a vengeful Genghis Khan one minute and then – when it seemed that he was without redemption – betraying a streak of nobility that was wholly admirable. Taggart's quiet, almost reflective, assessment of what action he should take over the *Fort Buckingham* showed the strength of his finer instincts. His orders demanded that he ignore the plight of the stricken ship – and there was real danger in disobeying those orders – but Taggart had been ruled by the slim possibility that survivors might be found. There was no vainglory in the decision. A ship capable of less than seven knots could not dash to the rescue any more effectively than she could run and hide. Taggart had weighed the chances and made the decision that came closest in line with his instincts as a professional seaman.

When Taggart had gone up on the bridge to acquaint Fowler with his intentions, Ben did not return to his cabin, preferring instead to get some fresh air by promenading forward of the housing of the lower bridge. A wooden deck, which had been holystoned white, skirted the bridge accommodation and made a pleasant exercise area that was fanned by airs from the forward movement of the ship.

Ben found it fascinating to stare out over the foredeck as the bows of the *Kildare Glen* plunged and sent great surges of phosphorescent foam bubbling away from the ship's sides. The night was dark, with a thin scurrying overcast that gave occasional glimpses of the stars.

Even in the open air, with a moderate breeze blowing, there was no escape from the clammy heat. The wind was moisture-laden. Although rain was not falling, the wind's breath upon Ben's cheek and bare arms was warmly damp. It left tiny globules of water on the steel walls of the bridge-housing while, within the accommodation, condensation penetrated to every enclosed space, making the walls and surfaces run with dripping sweat.

Ben turned at the sound of Taggart's feet on the ladder from the navigating bridge.

'Is that you, Ben?'

'Over here. I'm taking the air.'

Taggart joined him, cap in hand and wiping his brow.

'Jesus, it's hot!' he complained. 'I'm steaming like an old kettle!' He replaced his cap on his head and slackened the neck buttons of his high tunic. 'It's ninety-four on the chart-room thermometer and the humidity's damned near dew-point. Not the weather for brass buttons – look, they're turning green!'

Ben stared at the buttons that Taggart was fingering, but it was too dark to verify the tarnishing effect of the clammy atmosphere. 'I'll take your word for it,' he said.

'We're in for a storm,' Taggart said. 'The glass is going down like the bottom's fallen out of it. We're going to get a real blow, Mr Darby.'

'Any more about that ship?' Ben asked.

'No. If they're lucky the poor buggers'll be in the boats by now. That is, if the Japs didn't blow 'em out of the water first. A storm'll be all they need. Say a prayer for them when you go to bed tonight, Mr Darby, because this ocean is a very unfriendly place. If you're not Jap-bait or shark-meat or don't get fried to a turn by the sun, this ocean won't give up on you. She'll toss you around like a matchbox in a mill-race and then swallow you whole when she's had her fun.'

Ben stared out at the ocean in question. It was becoming perceptibly angrier: the waves heaping to peaks of foam, from which spray leapt and danced.

'It's kind of scarey,' Ben said. 'All that emptiness and us in the middle of it. We've been going a week and never seen a sign of another living thing. I keep thinking how Columbus's sailors must have felt when they went for months without a sight of land... You know, feeling that the world really was flat and that every minute was taking them nearer the edge...'

Taggart gave a soft laugh.

'Those were hard days and hard ships. But life at sea has never been easy, Mr Darby. You ask anybody of my generation who did sea-time in the hungry twenties or thirties. That's what made me the hard-nosed bastard I am. The youngsters going to sea now – even with a war on – have it easy compared with us. That's why

I'm hard on them. I can't let them go soft – because the sea will never be a place for softies. If I don't sort out the men from the boys, the sea will do it eventually – and much more painfully. Because the sea never relents... Never gives in... Never stops being cruel and spiteful... Oh, it can put on a pretty face and look as beguiling as a Mayfair tart in midsummer – but don't you trust her, Mr Darby. Don't you trust her. Because her middle name is treachery and she eats regiments for breakfasts. There is nothing that she cannot or will not destroy.'

Ben smiled in the darkness.

'That's pretty impressive imagery, Captain. Can I quote you sometime?'

'In my obituary. Not before,' Taggart said, with a soft chuckle. 'And I don't want anybody writing that for a hell of a long time yet!'

For two days and two nights the wind seldom dropped below Force Six and the highest reading on the bridge barometer showed a mere 983 millibars. With the pressure low and the relative humidity continuing close to saturation point, conditions on the *Kildare Glen* became increasingly uncomfortable. The engine-room was like a steam-bath, and it required conscious physical effort to summon the energy for the simplest of tasks. The work of firing the boilers became a torture for the men involved: sapping the strength of the stokehold gangs so much that, at the end of each watch, they could scarcely haul themselves up the steep ladderways of the fiddley to the sweet air of deck-level.

The seventh day at sea produced a victory for Taggart. Those of the crew who had resisted the purchase of coarse Indian cigarettes at his price finally capitulated. Their craving overcame their principles. Ben learnt of the surrender from McQueen, who never hid his deep personal hatred of the Captain and seldom missed an opportunity to vilify him. During the sessions in the stoke-hold, McQueen delighted in gibes at Ben about him being the 'Old Man's spy' and an 'officer-lover', but Ben took them all good-naturedly. He tried neither to defend Taggart nor to indicate that he shared McQueen's opinion of him: adopting a stance of strict neutrality. It saddened Ben, however, that animosity existed. Taggart, he knew, was largely responsible for the poisonous hate he attracted to himself, but Ben could not free himself of a profound sympathy for the Captain. He sensed the elements of tragedy in the unyielding rigidity of the man. Taggart's life had taught him never to bend and now he was incapable of doing so. So that his strength was, at the same time, his weakness. The slightest crumbling in the edifice could lead to its complete disintegration.

On the second day after the SOS from the *Fork Buckingham*, Taggart stoked up more bitterness for himself by taking what seemed unduly harsh disciplinary action against three young members of the crew. Three of the catering staff – including the cabin-boy, Richard White – had been engaged in a major clean-up of the ship's galley. They had scrubbed and scraped and scoured for an afternoon in ninety-degree heat and, at the end of it, flopped down on the hatch-top of No. 3 hold to cool off. Clad only in shorts and sandals, they were prostrate and luxuriating in the feel of a stiff tropical breeze against their bodies, when Taggart had come out of his quarters and exploded in rage. He had interpreted the scene on the hatch below as a flagrant violation of his order about the wearing of shirts and accused the youngsters of sun-bathing. Their pleas of innocence were swept aside as he stormed mercilessly at them, not only for wanton disobedience but for inexcusable slacking. In spite of attempts by the Chief Steward and the Chief Cook to persuade Taggart that a reprimand would be sufficient punishment, the offences were officially registered in the log-book and fines imposed on all three boys.

Ben knew nothing of the incident until the following morning when he reported to the stoke-hold for his daily instruction in the art of handling a coal shovel. Taggart's latest injustice had been the talk of the firemen's quarters the night before and it was still the number-one topic of conversation in the morning. Rumour that the *Kildare Glen* was only a few hours' steaming from the spot where the *Fort Buckingham* had radioed a distress call had become a secondary concern. The sullen mutterings of the men were centred wholly on the short-comings of the dictator who ruled their lives from the bridge.

No one was more outspoken on the certainty of trouble to come than Ben's stoke-hold mentor. McQueen muttered darkly about the nasty things that happened to sea-captains who thought themselves bigger than God almighty and hinted that Taggart's day of reckoning would soon be upon him. It was a relief to Ben when he was finally able to make his escape from the sweltering heat and bitter resentments of the stoke-hold and go up on deck. He liked and respected McQueen, but he was growing weary of the way that he kept identifying him with Taggart: as if Ben's refusal to join in the general condemnation of the Captain signified approval of all that Taggart did.

Ben arrived on deck to find that the strong wind of the previous two days had died to nothing. The sun burned down through a thin wispy film of cloud and the sea was calm, with only an occasional ripple of white breaking gently at the heads of the wide valleys of swell. The *Kildare Glen*'s pitching and rolling had become less violent in the new conditions and there was a tranquillity to the way she now slid through the water with a constant gentle movement. The deep rhythmic labour of the ship's engines seemed to take on a muted note that was in harmony with the eerie still of the empty ocean.

The silent desolation encompassing the ship filled Ben with a strange uneasiness: a fluttering of the blood, no more. A tremor of expectancy made piquant by a total ignorance of what to expect. Was it a trick of the subconscious: his senses reacting to the knowledge that somewhere in these waters a ship had been sunk only three short days ago? Less than three days ago. Only sixty-five hours previously. Yes, there was that awareness but there was an indescribable something more. It was in the air, in the very nature of the calm. A sense of imminent catastrophe.

The tiny current of alarm would not leave him. It stayed with him as he showered and dressed and it remained as a nervous edginess when he took his seat in the saloon for the midday meal. Then he realised that he had not been singled out to experience this odd sensation. The others at the table were all affected and spoke of it. Willem Prins identified and explained the phenomenon.

'It is the calm before the storm, Mr Darby. It is not a myth but something you can actually *feel*. The barometer has been falling at about four points an hour. We have come through one area of low pressure but we're heading right into another that's twenty times worse. You wait and see.'

And wait was all Ben could do, with some trepidation. He had no intention of letting his edginess rob him of his usual siesta, but after ten minutes he gave up all attempts to sleep and went up to the bridge to keep Prins company. He was immediately drafted into service as an extra look-out. Prins pressed a pair of binoculars into his hand and allotted him the eyrie-like position of the binnacle-box on the monkey island to search the ocean for any sign of life.

On Taggart's orders, the look-outs had already been

reinforced from the thirty-odd army and naval personnel who made up the ship's gunnery force. A fo'c'sle-head watch was being maintained from the twelve-pounder gun platform in the bows by one gunner. Two more were stationed in the port and starboard Oerlikon nests on the foredeck and two in those abaft the engine-room. Two gunners also kept a stern watch from the Bofors position and four-inch gun platform on the poop. The watch look-out was in the crow's nest.

'Anything special I should be looking for?' Ben asked Prins, as he focused the heavy glasses on the horizon.

'A sail, a raft, floating debris, anything at all,' Prins told him. 'You see anything floating, sing out and tell me. We are almost right in the place where the *Fort* ship was torpedoed, so keep your eyes skinned. We are probably too late, but you never know.'

Ben found that his eyes quickly tired in the glare of sun and water but he systematically swept: from ahead to abeam, slowly, varying the distance on which he concentrated. As the afternoon wore on, the nature of the cloud formations changed. The high hazy film dropped lower and lower, turning into smoke-like wraiths that drifted rapidly over the ocean surface. The wind was no more than a damp breath and yet these misty wisps seemed to move at great speed. They grew thicker and thicker, and more numerous, obfuscating distances so that visibility varied from five miles to 500 yards, depending on the direction of the gaze. When the moisture formations passed over the ship it was impossible to see the fo'c'sle-head from the bridge. They flitted past, leaving everything they touched bathed in a fine dew and, in the next instant, the fore-deck would be bathed in sunlight and a visibility of two miles would be restored.

As swiftly and as silently as these fugitive swirls of mist had appeared, they suddenly lifted to a height of about two hundred feet, to dance above the mast-tops and gather in density. The ocean reappeared around the *Kildare Glen* in a two- to three-mile radius of visible water, with the ship at the centre of the shallow dome formed by the leaping clouds. The light became a dull, greyish yellow. It was a half-light, not dark enough for night nor bright enough to be termed day.

And into this half-light came a sound. At first Ben thought his ears were playing tricks with him. The sound came from somewhere in the yellow curtain of cloud; the drone of an aeroplane engine. Faint, approaching, then less distinct. Again it came. Ben heard the look-out shout from the crow's nest: 'Aircraft! Aircraft!'

From below came the sudden jarring clamour of the alarm bells as Willem Prins touched the button that summoned gunners and crew to their stations. Ben heard Taggart's voice shouting: 'I heard it! I heard the damned thing! But where has it come from? There isn't a bloody airfield within a thousand miles!'

As gunners appeared from below and manned the four gun-pits on the top bridge, Ben was almost toppled from the binnacle-box by a sudden gust of wind that seemed to hold the *Kildare Glen* at the full extent of an unexpectedly heavy roll to starboard. He found his feet and hung on the platform as that first gust proved to be but the harbinger of many. The wind shrieked and whipped at the bridge awnings. The canvas cover of the port bridge Oerlikon was lifted out from its pit to go tearing past Ben's head like a monster bat and wing far out to sea. Ben watched its soaring flight in amazement. The sight of the sea – a gentle heaving calm only moments before – was enough to unnerve the stoutest heart, so violent was its transformation. The swell pattern, so regular, was now almost indistinguishable as the waters leapt upwards to form thrusting peaks of angry foam. Spray filled the air above the convulsing ocean and the *Kildare Glen* reeled and lurched before the onslaught of confused seas. She rolled over on her side so far that it seemed to Ben, hanging on for dear life, that she would capsize. But after hanging for agonising moments at the extreme of the terrifying swing she began to jerk upright again, before corkscrewing into a similar roll in the other direction. Above the howl of the wind, Ben heard the stentorian roar of Taggart's voice from somewhere below, on the navigating bridge. It was directed at the helmsman. The ship slowly responded to the wheel and laboured round to ride into the sea. The pitching and rolling and corkscrewing were not arrested, but their violence became noticeably less severe.

With eight gunners on the top bridge, Ben decided that his role as a look-out had become unnecessary. Glasses slung round his neck, he judged his moment between rolls of the ship and clambered down the vertical ladder to the navigating bridge. A trifle white-faced, he peered into the wheel-house.

'Try and hold her on that,' Taggart was bawling at the helmsman, who was wrestling to hold two full turns on the wheel. Taggart caught sight of Ben.

'You'd better come in before that squall hits us, Mr Darby,' he said.

Squall? Ben didn't know what Taggart was talking about – but it became plain as a cloud of rain threw itself at the bridge and huge drops of water spattered against the wheel-house windows like bullets. Ben could hear water running in rivers on the wing of the bridge as the rain-cloud emptied and was gone as quickly as it had come.

'What's the glass reading now, Mr Prins?' Taggart shouted over his shoulder. The Second Officer came scurrying from the chart-room.

'Nine-five-three millibars and still falling, sir,' he reported.

'Bring the crow's-nest look-out down until further notice. And get the Bosun up here, will you? We shouldn't ship much water when we're light ship, but we'll have safety lines rigged anyway. I've been in an Indian Ocean cyclone before and I'm not taking any chances.'

As Prins moved towards the bridge telephone to carry out his orders, Taggart turned to Ben.

'Ever been in a cyclone?'

Ben clung to a radiator pipe as the *Kildare Glen* rolled drunkenly.

'I had a taste of a Florida hurricane once,' he replied, 'but that was on dry land. Is a cyclone as bad?'

'Much the same thing, Mr Darby. Different parts of the world, they give them different names. A hurricane in the Caribbean, a cyclone in these waters, a typhoon further east. A rose by any other name... In other circumstances we might have taken evasive action – but we can't get away from this one. It's moving too fast and there's nowhere to run. We'll just have to ride it out.'

'How long will that take?'

'Who can tell?' said Taggart with a shrug. 'We're still some way from the centre of it. This is just the fringe. It all depends on the course it takes. It could run west for a thousand miles before dipping up north of the Equator and then swinging north-east towards India. Or it could swing in a circle right around us and have us looking for a way out until this time next week. There's no telling. They are very unpredictable things.' He changed the subject. 'Did you hear the plane?'

'Yes. One of ours, you reckon? That got lost?'

'Wherever it came from, I reckon it was lost,' Taggart said. 'Unless it came from a carrier.'

'A British carrier?'

Taggart arched his eyebrows expressively.

'From Trinco? I think they would have mentioned it

to us before we left Bombay if we were going to have any big stuff floating around.'

'Then a Jap?'

Taggart's eyebrows went even further up.

'God help us if it is. But it can't be. The Japs wouldn't send a carrier as far west as this without a bloody great task force to back it up. You Yanks are keeping them far too busy for that. Jesus!' He broke off and suddenly cocked his head to one side. 'I can hear it again!'

He almost ran, with the roll of the ship, to the wheelhouse door and then, climbing uphill against the counter-roll, made his way to the wing of the bridge. Ben followed him, with Prins bringing up the rear.

'I heard it, too,' the Dutchman said, and pointed excitedly to the port quarter. 'There the swine is! Look!'

Taggart had seen the single-engined seaplane almost in the same instant as Prins and already had his binoculars to his eyes. Ben saw it emerge from low cloud at a height of no more than three hundred feet. The tiny aircraft with its huge floats was flying into the teeth of the wind and seemed to be suspended almost stationary. Then it banked and came towards the *Kildare Glen* in a long fast side-slip.

'It's a bloody Jap!' screamed Taggart. 'Where are our gunners? Why don't they fire?'

But even as Taggart spoke the Oerlikon directly over him on the port wing of the bridge was loosing off a burst of fire. The bark of the cannon came as a thunderous shock to the men on the bridge immediately below the nest, but they recovered their startled wits to stare in wonder at the stream of tracer shells from overhead. Needless to say, the violent rolling of the ship ensured that they sprayed everywhere except in a direction that would have endangered the fast-approaching seaplane. An advancing comber was raked with fire in one instant and, in the next, tracers were screaming high towards the heavens. The seaplane swooped low over the *Kildare Glen*'s foremast and raced away to starboard.

Taggart was swearing aloud at the gunner's incompetence, but Ben felt only sympathy for the unseen crewman. Trying to hit that plane must have been like trying to shoot clay pigeons from a roller-coaster.

The seaplane had disappeared into cloud away to starboard, but they could still hear droning. It reappeared a mile distant, crossing ahead of the ship from starboard to port and then it was in cloud again. But the engine note throbbed steadily nearer and there it was again, twenty degrees forward of the port beam: low and side-slipping directly towards the ship.

This time three Oerlikons on the port side opened up almost simultaneously. The aim of all three was as erratic as ever because of the rolling and plunging of the ship, but the three streams of tracer cut a criss-cross of arcs in the paths of the floatplane, as it dipped so low that it seemed certain to hit the wave-tops.

'He's coming straight for the bridge!' Taggart screamed. 'He's doing a *hara-kiri*! Move your backside, Ben, Mr Prins . . .'

Even as he spoke, Taggart was bundling Ben and the Second Mate towards the wheel-house door. But a massive sea lifted the *Kildare Glen* in the same moment and the three men tumbled in a heap. They were scrambling to their feet when the storm-tossed ship came back from a forty-five-degree roll to send her port rail dipping down to meet the sea. Ben, Taggart and Prins grabbed whatever they could to prevent themselves sliding towards the wing of the bridge and, in arresting themselves, were given a final glimpse of the floatplane. One moment they could see it, the next, it disappeared from view behind a mountain of a comber that dwarfed the ship. The wave, 600 feet across its frothing brow, seemed to blot the sky from view. It hung, poised and towering, a sixty-foot-high wall of water that seemed certain to swamp the ship, before crashing in a surge of foam. The *Kildare Glen* leaned into the breast of rushing water and, righting herself, began to climb up and over the advancing wall, her bow section leaping clear of the water. Then she was plunging down and rolling crazily to starboard and it was the stern that came clear of the heaving sea. There was the shuddering scream of the propeller as it raced wildly, with no water to brake its whirling blades. But already the bow was rising again to repeat the whole shuddering process.

Taggart had moved out to the wing of the bridge and was staring at the boiling sea with a wariness born of incomprehension. The aircraft roar had died as the giant wave had reared its crest above the *Kildare Glen*. Taggart strained his ears against the shrieking of the wind as if the aircraft sound must surely materialise again. But the only sound came from the wind and the sea and the thudding thunder of the ship's bottom as she hit the 'milestones'.

There was no sign of the floatplane.

'He must have gone straight under,' Ben shouted, as he edged closer to Taggart in the wing. Both men stared at the sea in disbelief.

'I was sure he was going to hit us,' Taggart said. 'That bugger was set on meeting his ancestors and he bloody well intended to take us with him!'

'We still don't know where he came from,' Ben said.

Taggart nodded. 'If we're lucky, we never will.'

When the watch changed at four in the afternoon, Ben did not go below with Prins. With the tacit approval of Taggart, he lingered on the bridge when Fowler arrived to relieve the Second Officer. By then the gun crews had been stood down from their stations, although the extra look-outs were to be maintained until half an hour after sunset. The strange light persisted. Somewhere above the rushing clouds, the equatorial sun was sending down its burning rays, but at ocean-level a gloom darkened the visible world: an eerie, tenebrous adumbration that constantly changed. This unnatural twilight and the cloying, oppressive heat seemed to Ben to touch at some deep and long-dormant instinct of primitive origin – an instinct rooted in the neolithic dark of man when the senses responded with superstitious awe to natural phenomena and, in terror, ascribed to them the properties of the supernatural. Ben did not quake with terror at finding himself encompassed by rolling mountains of water and a heaven that was a dark frenzy of shifting shapes and shadow, ballooning purple and black and every sombre hue of grey, and tinged a sulphurous yellow. It was not fear of the elements nor fear for his life that Ben felt; more an acute and dread-filled awareness of utter isolation from all that was benign upon the face of the planet. For the first time in his life, the much-used word 'godforsaken' burgeoned with new and terrible meaning. So impressing was the desolation that bore down on him in this hostile limbo, Ben felt a physical nausea.

Later, long after they had passed through the heart of the cyclone, Ben was to remember the darkness by day and his physical and mental reaction to the storm: searching for a rational explanation of the way he felt. He could not accept that the nausea – a debilitating feeling not unlike that associated with influenza – was a form of sea-sickness brought on by the sea conditions. He would have readily attributed his complete loss of appetite to that if he alone had been affected in this way. But even the oldest hands on the *Kildare Glen*, he discovered, all suffered similarly, and the general malaise lasted for the duration of the storm. This was to set Ben off on the track of investigating the effects of abnormally low atmospheric pressure on the human body, but his meagre findings were inconclusive.

Within an hour of the Japanese seaplane's dramatic disappearance, Ben was considering the prospect of the five o'clock meal in the *Kildare Glen*'s saloon with a decided lack of relish. Somehow, the violent rolling and plunging of the storm-racked ship was more tolerable on the bridge – and there was a fascination in watching from the shelter of the dodger the endless spectacle of the ocean in torment. Ben knew that, practised wordsmith though he was, he would never be able to describe adequately the ferocity of a storm at sea to anyone who had not actually experienced such conditions at first-hand. It was so much beyond what he himself had imagined that he knew there was no way he could convey to the uninitiated the awesome nature and power of those rolling mountains of water. There were no yardsticks that could be used, no similes, no adjectives, no extravagance of metaphors, that could convincingly impress on the most comprehending mind the scale and fearsome confusion of the ocean's unrestrained might.

Fowler flitted nervously about the bridge – doing his best, it seemed, to keep out of Taggart's way. Ben wondered if Taggart, like himself, had smelled the reek of whisky on the Chief Officer's breath and detected a slight unsteadiness on his feet that could not entirely be attributed to the unpredictable motions of the ship. If Taggart had noticed, he had given no sign. He treated Fowler with dissmissive contempt at the best of times and, on this occasion, he was content largely to ignore him.

The Chief Officer had just informed Taggart, in a voice like doom, that the barometric pressure had fallen below the 950-millibars mark, when there was a shout from one of the look-outs on the top bridge.

'Ship-ho! Ship! Dead abeam to port!'

Fowler scurried to the monkey-island ladder and scrambled half-way up.

'What kind of ship? Where? Where?' he screamed above the wind.

With a look in Fowler's direction that would have shrivelled the Chief Officer, Taggart strode into the wheel-house and pushed the alarm button, with its consequent shrilling of bells. He emerged clutching a telescope. Planting his feet firmly in the wing of the bridge, he focused it to port.

'I can see her!' he shouted. 'Stern funnel, straight stem, two tall masts, bridge amidships. Could be a tanker! And yet I don't know... Damn, she keeps disappearing!' He turned and bellowed at Fowler: 'Get the book of silhouettes, Mr Fowler. Let's see if we can identify her.'

Fowler disappeared towards the chart-room and returned moments later clutching a book. He got down on one knee, well below the dodger, and riffled through the pages.

'There are dozens of two-masted tankers with straight stems,' he moaned, as Taggart fumed with impatience. Finally, Taggart ducked down beside him and took the book from him.

'We're not worried about bloody tankers,' Taggart said, after a glance at the pages where Fowler had had the book open. 'And certainly not British ones!' He flipped pages rapidly. 'Where the hell is the Japanese Navy section?'

He found what he was looking for and ran his finger down a vessel-identification index. His finger stopped moving and he looked up at Fowler.

'Let's see what we've got under aircraft-carriers and seaplane-tenders.'

Fowler blanched. 'You didn't say anything about aircraft-carriers!'

'They're lumped together here, you ninny,' Taggart said, with a contemptuous upward glance. 'That bloody seaplane came from somewhere. She had to have a mother ship.' He returned his attention to the book on his knee, turning more pages. Ben edged closer to him and saw that the pages of the book were illustrated with the silhouettes of ships.

'Here we are!' Taggart exclaimed. 'If that's not her, it's a carbon copy. I want another look . . .' He stood up and handed the book to Ben, so that he could resight his telescope. 'Foot of the page,' he said to Ben. '*Notoro* class seaplane-tender.'

Ben found the silhouette and read the details printed underneath.

'*Notoro* . . . Fourteen thousand and fifty tons . . . Four hundred and fifty-five feet long . . . Maximum speed: twelve knots . . . Armaments: two four-point-seven-inch guns and two three-inch guns . . . Capacity: sixteen seaplanes . . .'

'She's Jap all right!' Taggart roared. 'Take a look, Mr Fowler. That crane abaft the bridge is the giveaway. And that stern like a duck's arse. Christ, she's an old-timer! I bet she's a good twenty years older than the *Kildare Glen*!'

Fowler peered at the distant ship through Taggart's telescope, while Taggart grabbed the book from Ben's hands and checked over every identifying feature of the silhouette listed as *Notoro*.

'Could be the *Kamoi*,' he muttered out loud. 'No, the *Kamoi*'s foremast's too far forward and the mainmast's too close to the smoke-stack. And she's got a stern crane . . .' He looked up as Fowler suddenly shrilled:

'She's turning towards us!'

Taggart reacted instantly, moving quickly to the wheel-house door.

'Starboard your helm,' he bawled. 'Easy now. Let her come easy.'

The other ship was now clearly visible to the naked eye. She was framed momentarily against a white streak of horizon, between dark waving sea and the lower lip of inky cloud. She was head-on and rolling crazily. Ben watched her disappear for long intervals, hidden by the intervening seas, then the cross-trees of her tall foremast would rise from the waves, followed by the stubby bows.

Taggart had disappeared into the wheel-house. Ben turned his back on the ship – which he did not doubt was an enemy vessel – and peered inside the wheel-house. Taggart was berating the helmsman for giving the ship too much wheel. Ben was thrown off his feet as the *Kildare Glen* was caught beam to the sea and began to roll almost on her ends. The rolling continued violently until the wallowing freighter came round to ride with the sea. Now she was roller-coasting. Sledging along on the powerful-running sea-crests, with the stern-rail almost awash in swirling foam and the bow section clear of water, before plunging down into a deep trough in what seemed an endless slide. But she would rise again, climbing through solid water and thrust upwards by the buoyancy of the great volume of air sealed in the fore-section.

Satisfied with the course, Taggart crossed to the telephone, set it at the appropriate number, and jangled the calling handle furiously.

'Four-inch platform?' he demanded into the mouthpiece. 'Is that you, Mr Prins? Oh, it's you, PO. No, never mind the Second Mate. You'll do. Is your crew at the ready?' There was a short silence while Finney, the Navy PO in charge of all DEMS personnel, reported the readiness of the crew manning the stern-mounted four-inch gun. He must have added some observations of his own because Taggart bawled at him: 'I don't want a bloody weather report. This is Captain Taggart here. Look, you seem to be unaware of it but there's a ship four thousand yards astern of us that happens to be a bloody Jap. I want you to open fire at will ... Yes, you blockhead – open fire at will ...'

Ben had no idea what it was the PO had to say to

Taggart but, whatever it was, it did not improve the Captain's patience. He again cut the other man short.

'I don't give a damn that you can't see anything, PO!' he shouted into the telephone. 'But you had better take my word for it that we have a Jap ship right on our tail and I want her to know we mean business. Tell Mr Prins to get up here fast! I want him on this phone directing your fire – so keep the phone manned. And if you use your eyes, you'll see a target soon enough!'

He crashed the phone down and strode past Ben.

'Calls himself a bloody gunner!' he muttered, as he went out to the bridge wing. Ben hovered near the door, feeling superfluous and wishing there was something he could do. Taggart must have divined the wish.

'Ben,' he called, 'Make yourself useful. Bring me my binoculars. They're in the chart-room.'

Ben fetched the glasses. Taggart took them and peered astern. He cursed as sooty smoke issued from the *Kildare Glen*'s stack and, as well as obscuring the view, showered the bridge with pellet-like particles of carbon.

'That's all we bloody need!' he growled, and bellowed to the helmsman: 'Come ten degrees to port and steady on that.'

The smoke, swirling in the gale-force stern wind, angled away to the other side of the bridge as the helm alteration took effect. Taggart raised his glasses again.

'She's gaining on us,' he said. 'And she's making more smoke than we are. Surely they can see it from the stern!'

As if in affirmation, the four-inch gun on the *Kildare Glen*'s poop spoke with a hollow boom, the explosion sounding strangely muted.

Taggart, scanning the sea astern, waited for evidence that the shell was near to target. He finally lowered his glasses.

'Not a thing,' he said. 'Never even saw the splash.'

He grimaced at Ben. 'The sea's too rough. You wouldn't see a salvo from fifteen-inchers in this bloody lot!'

Ben had certainly seen no sign of exploding shell. He had only caught occasional glimpses of the pursuing ship, but there was no mistaking her presence now. A tornado-like spiral of smoke was clearly visible against a light-grey wedge of sky at horizon-level.

Willem Prins arrived on the bridge as the *Kildare Glen*'s four-inch barked a second time. The result was no more discernible than the first. The shell could have landed anywhere in these leaping mountains of white water.

Taggart spoke earnestly to Prins, telling him that spotting for the gunners on the stern was probably a forlorn task, but that he wanted the gun to keep firing anyway. He explained his tactics in his own lurid way.

'That monkey back there can't fire at us without turning beam to the sea and he can try it any time he likes as far as I am concerned. Because he'll be rolling on his beam ends and has as much chance of a hit as a cow farting pancakes from a see-saw in a Force Ten wind. We show him our arse and keep popping away until it gets dark. After that we give him the slip.'

Two hours later, the following ship was still there: seemingly immune to the shells that the *Kildare Glen* had pumped steadily astern. She was now less than two miles distant.

CHAPTER 6

Ocean without End

The cabin-boy, Richard White, using his back against the wooden panelling of the inside stairway to steady himself against the pitching of the ship, made it to the top of the steps. He backed into the chart-room and deposited the laden tray he had been carrying on the settee. Fowler, who had been bent over the chart-table, turned.

'Oh, it's you, boy. What have you got there?'

'Two pots of fresh coffee, sir, and sandwiches. There's luncheon meat, chicken and pilchard. Will you tell the Captain, sir?'

'I'll let him know,' Fowler promised.

Fowler screwed up his eyes as he left the muted red glow of the chart-room's lights and went out to the Stygian gloom of the wheel-house. Taggart, Ben Darby and the Second Officer were out on the bridge-wing.

'Coffee up, Captain,' Fowler called. 'And assorted sandwiches. There's enough for an army.'

Taggart peered at him. 'Well, do the honours, Mr Fowler. Two sugars and plenty of condensed milk in mine. And the same, I think, for Mr Prins. How about you, Mr Darby?'

'The same for me,' Ben said. 'I . . . I'll give Mr Fowler a hand.'

'Mr Fowler can manage on his own,' Taggart said sharply. 'Can't you, Mr Fowler?'

'If you say so, Captain,' Fowler replied in a surly tone.

He retreated into the wheel-house, muttering under his breath.

'Bloody old woman,' Taggart growled. He turned to Willem Prins.

'Give Finney a buzz on the poop, Second Mate. Tell him he's wasted enough ammunition and confirm that order to cease firing.'

Five minutes earlier, with the flash of the four-inch gun doing no more than reveal the *Kildare Glen*'s position in the raging sea, Taggart had ordered the gun crew to hold their fire. Ten minutes had passed since they had last had a glimpse of the Japanese ship. Now blinding squalls were racing across the surface of the ocean and the gathering night had reduced visibility further.

'Shall I stand down the gun crew, sir?' Prins enquired politely.

'Not yet,' warned Taggart. 'We'll keep them standing by for emergencies. But they are not, repeat not, to fire a single round unless the order comes from the bridge. Make that clear. Oh, and tell the PO to organise some suitable beverage for his men. Soup and sandwiches, whatever the galley can muster. But I want a strict lookout – no let-up in that, tell him, or I'll have his bloody head on a plate.'

'Aye, aye, sir.' Prins departed to do the Captain's bidding.

'Port twenty the helm,' Taggart sang out at the top of his voice.

'Port twenty it is, sir,' came the reply from inside the wheel-house.

Taggart conned the ship slowly round until, again, she was heading close to the weather. The first of a succession of fierce rain squalls hit the *Kildare Glen*, coming in from forward of the beam, before he took shelter in the wheel-house and accepted the cup of coffee that Fowler brought him. The Chief Officer did not bring one for Ben, loftily informing him that he could get his own from the chart-room before it all spilled away.

Ben was glad to get his own. He emerged to find that Taggart had left the wheel-house and was sipping his coffee in the lee-wing. There was no sign of Fowler.

'Mind if I join you, Captain?' he asked. 'I've been feeling queasy all day and it gets worse if I'm inside. That's good coffee.'

'It hits the spot,' Taggart agreed. 'Mr Fowler has gone below. Call of nature, he said. He must think I'm bloody stupid.'

'Oh?' Ben was puzzled.

'Coffee's no good to Mr Fowler. Not unless it's been laced. The poor bugger can't go a whole watch now without his little stiffener.'

'I didn't know,' said Ben, although he was not altogether surprised.

'The man is a problem, Ben. His own worst enemy. He'll never get another command. A permanent one anyway. You know he blotted his copybook once?'

'No, I didn't know.'

'In peacetime he would have been out on his ear. Finished. He only got away with it because there was a war on. He hates my guts because I got the *Kildare Glen*, but I had nothing to do with it. It was that blot on his record that kept him from getting the ship, not me. Anyone else, they would have let him keep in command.'

'You sound almost sorry for him,' Ben said.

'Well, I'm not!' Taggart assured him sharply. 'I'm the poor bugger that's saddled with him. If he fell overboard tomorrow, I wouldn't miss him.'

'You've had your work cut out today,' Ben said, diplomatically refraining from making further comment on the Chief Officer and his short-comings.

'And it's going to be a long night,' Taggart said. 'We've got a long way to go to get out of the wood.'

'Because of that Jap ship? She's faster and, according to that ship-bible of yours, she outguns us.'

'She doesn't frighten me, Ben. We could take her on and maybe even beat her. We could certainly give a good account of ourselves if it comes to the crunch. It's what she was up to that makes things tricky.'

'I don't understand.'

'Don't you see the game she was playing, Ben? The Japs don't send clapped-out old-timers like that out into the middle of nowhere to play at surface-raiding. She hasn't got the speed or the guns to be any bloody good at it. Her job was to cruise around south of the Line and well out of harm's way.'

'But why?'

'She needs calm waters, Ben. Plenty of balmy ocean where she can send out her seaplanes – and get them back again. This weather must be driving her Old Man crazy. I bet he's gnawing his finger-nails right up to the elbow at this minute, because a blow like this makes his old tub useless. His is a spotting job, Ben. His job is to stay out of sight and send his winged chariots north, south, east and west looking for ships. When they spot one, they just whistle up a sub to close in and do the dirty work. That way, they can cover a hell of a lot of ocean between them.'

Ben stared gravely at Taggart. 'The big danger is submarines?'

'Before we left Bombay, we were told the Japs had three in these parts – but there are thin pickings for them in a wide, wide ocean like this. Looking for ships away from the coast is like looking for needles in haystacks. But a pack of spotter planes makes it what you would call a different ball game. We're on a hiding to nothing now. They've found us and they won't give up on us. The only thing on our side right now is the weather.'

'No flights from the mother ship until further notice, eh?'

'Not a hope. They must have launched that floatplane we saw before the sea got up. The pilot must have known he'd had his chips long before he chanced on us. He must have been cruising around watching the needle on his fuel gauge getting nearer to zero. No wonder he decided to cremate himself on my bridge. He was a dead man already.'

Ben let out a long breath.

'I sweat just thinking about how close he got.'

Taggart was peering into the darkness. The only light came from the leaping spume and the white-water fury of the crashing waves. The air was alive with spray. It leapt to mast-head height from the thundering break of water against the *Kildare Glen's* bows. Taggart murmured:

'Keep sweating, Ben . . . thinking how close that Jap ship could be to us at this minute. She could be four cables off and we wouldn't see her.'

'As close as that?'

Taggart laughed. 'Let's hope she's not. Let's hope she hasn't guessed we've turned around and that she's still bucketing along with the sea and the wind up her backside. The longer she keeps running before the sea, the tougher it's going to be for her if she decides to come about. Because this weather is going to get a hell of a lot worse before it gets better. Take my word for it!'

They were interrupted by the appearance of the Second Radio Officer at the door of the wheel-house. Coming from the light of the radio-cabin, his eyes were not attuned to the dark, but he recognised Taggart's voice.

'Captain Taggart? Is that you out there? I can't see a damned thing.'

'What is it, Sparks?' Taggart reached out a hand to touch the man, who nearly jumped out of his skin with fright when he realised how close the Captain was.

'Another SOS, sir. The *Empire Seawind*. Torpedoed and abandoning ship. I've got the position.'

Ben heard Taggart's sigh. It was weary with regret.

'That's John Sutherland's ship.'

Ben remembered a lean, elegant man who had taken a fancy to one of the older nurses at Taggart's party in Bombay.

'I'll put that position on the chart,' Taggart was saying to the Sparks. 'Ben, keep a look-out here, will you? Sing out if you see anything. I'm going inside for a minute.'

Taggart returned a few moments later. He resumed his stance at Ben's side in silence. Ben made no attempt to break into the other's thoughts. He reckoned Taggart was a man with a lot on his mind and that, if he wanted conversation, he would initiate it. In fact, five minutes passed before Taggart spoke.

'Well, we've got one thing to thank John Sutherland for now,' he said. 'We know where one of those Jap subs is.'

'Close?' Ben asked softly.

'Close enough, Ben. Close enough. Nearly four hundred miles south-west. And that tells us something else. The weather can't be quite so bad down there yet. I've seen submarines attack in bad weather, but not in a sea like this. The torpedoes could go anywhere.' He paused thoughtfully. 'I may be wrong, of course, but I'm going to assume anyway that south and west the weather is better . . . So we'll bear south and east. We're between the devil and the deep blue sea, Ben. Our choice is between the Japs and the cyclone – and we're going to take our chances with the cyclone.'

Staring out at the mountainous seas that dwarfed the ship and buffeted her about, Ben consoled himself with the thought that conditions could not get all that much worse. He was wrong.

The crash of noise from just outside his cabin sounded to Ben like the end of the world. He awoke from a fevered half-sleep in pitch darkness, with the *Kildare Glen* giving the impression that she was turning upside down. Ben — lying jack-knifed, with his shoulders against the bulkhead and his feet against the bedboard so that he was wedged against the bucketing movements of the ship — went tumbling out of the broad bunk as he tried to sit up. His ankle cracked against the leg of the well-anchored cabin table and he ended in a heap against the panelled settee. With every beam and steel plate in the ship's frame groaning and protesting, the *Kildare Glen* began the shuddering process of righting herself. Ben crawled towards the door and, pulling himself up, managed to locate the light-switch. The sudden flood of light eased the cloying claustrophobic dread that the darkness inspired but did not entirely eradicate it. He still felt a sense of entrapment between the box-like walls that rose and fell endlessly and between which he seemed doomed to be cast about like a dice in a cup.

Ben found trousers and shirt and pulled them on. His Bombay-purchased sandals were slithering from one side of the cabin to the other and had to be pursued and caught before he could buckle them on. The slight expense of energy required was enough to drench him in sweat. In spite of the bulkhead fan, with its leisurely side-to-side sweep, the heat in the blacked-out cabin was suffocating.

Taking care to switch out the light before hooking the door open, Ben found that a meagre grey light was filtering into the interior alleyway. The outside stormdoor, surprisingly, had been hooked to allow air to enter the accommodation through a six-inch gap. Water had come in, too, and Ben splashed through the saturated coir matting of the alleyway as he made his way along the inside stairway to the chart-room.

There was no one in the chart-room. Passing through, Ben noticed that the brass clock above the table registered a quarter to seven. A council of war was taking place in the wheel-house. It was milling with bodies. Taggart and all the deck officers were there. So, too, were the Bosun and Carpenter. Taggart, looking grey-faced with fatigue, was issuing orders.

'Cut the whole bloody thing adrift!' Taggart was telling the Bosun in a tone that invited no compromise. 'It's bloody useless as it is and not worth saving, so let it go! Mr Fowler, you get down there with the Bosun and take charge of things. I don't want anybody playing the idiot and going over the side!'

Ben, as unobtrusively as possible, tried to slip through the tense little gathering. He had reached the door to the outer bridge when Taggart called him.

'Don't go away, Mr Darby. I need every able-bodied man there is. So stick around.'

'I'll be just outside,' Ben acknowledged, surprised and flattered that there would be something for him to do in what seemed to be a major emergency. Nothing he had heard had given him any clue as to the nature of the emergency, but he did not judge it to be the right moment to seek enlightenment from Taggart. The Captain was already ignoring Ben and earnestly addressing himself to Mr Barraclough, the Third Mate. Ben eased himself thankfully into the open air and gulped in deep breaths. It seemed to relieve the faint nausea, which had hung on him for what was now the best part of the day.

He was aware that there was a pronounced difference, a noticeable irregularity, in the way that the *Kildare Glen* was battling into the sea. She seemed to be rolling less steeply to starboard and yawing desperately near to horizontal as she tilted to port. And when she lay over to port, she seemed reluctant to return the other way. The truth hit Ben as he emerged on to the wooden deck beside the chart-room: the *Kildare Glen* had developed a considerable list to port. The realisation triggered a fluttering of apprehension within him. There was no reassurance to be found in his simultaneous sight of the sea in the forbidding grey light of a new morning. The massive waves were still heaping into vast canyons of foaming water, and over everything swept blizzards of spray that rose and filled the air in a permanent curtain of white fury. The aspect was terrifying, exceeding by far all Ben's imagination of the unbridled ferocity of nature. This ship – which in Bombay had seemed so huge and solid – was tiny and insignificant in this maelstrom. She seemed as puny as a matchbox below the comberheads that hung as high as apartment-blocks above her before breaking in great half-mile-wide avalanches.

When he ventured to the port side of the bridge behind the radio-room and the full force of the wind threatened to claw him up with its surge, it became apparent to Ben what had caused the noise that had awakened him. The lifeboat, which had been slung outboard from the bridge-deck just outside his cabin, was no longer there. All that remained were the davits from which it had been suspended, and those stout metal posts were twisted and leaning at a strange angle. The stay linking the davit-head had parted, and from the after davit-head hung a tangle of wire and life-line and part of a five-purchase block that looked as if it had been cleft by an axe. The awning that had covered most of the port lower bridge had disappeared, leaving buckled stanchions and the splintered remains of the wooden support battens. The heavy boom that had supported the lifeboat in its outslung position had also gone and, with it, the big ring clamps that had secured it. They had sheered clean away. The remains of the slip wires had shredded and dangled uselessly on the deck, still attached to mangled ring-bolts which had taken so much pressure that their anchoring deck-plates were corrugated with undulations.

Looking aft towards the boat-deck above the engineers' accommodation, Ben saw that the larger No. 3 lifeboat had suffered a similar fate to No. 1. But it had not yet parted company with the *Kildare Glen*. The forward fall had carried away but the after fall had held and now the boat – its bow section almost smashed to pulp – was hanging crazily from the after davit. Every time the *Kildare Glen* dipped rail-deep to port, the sea smashed at the suspended boat and pulverised it a little more. The tarpaulin was shredded and crackling like a dozen whips as it flapped and sought to fly off in the wind. With every roll of the ship, the smashed lifeboat seemed to shed more equipment from within it: oars, a storm lantern, galvanised buckets.

Between the bridge and the boat-deck were ample signs of other sea-damage. The timber houses built on the deck as troop latrines and galleys looked as if they had been stood on by a heavy-footed giant. The roofs had been stoved in and they leaned inboard at a grotesque angle. The deck along the port side was a scene of devastation, with timber debris floating in trapped sea-water and mingling with lengths of twisted steam-pipe casing that had been torn from its welding.

Ben returned to the wheel-house as Fowler and the Bosun trooped off to complete the sea's job on the battered No. 3 lifeboat. It was plain to Ben now what Taggart wanted done. The boat was to be cut adrift.

Finney, the PO Gunner, was in sober conclave with Taggart when Ben re-entered the wheel-house.

'I'll get a dozen men down there right away, sir,' Finney was saying. He caught sight of Ben from the corner of his eye. 'And our American friend?' he queried Taggart diffidently. 'You say he'll help?'

Taggart nodded acknowledgement of Ben's presence.

'I'm sure Mr Darby will be only too pleased to render his assistance. He did sign on as a trimmer and this is an emergency. The safety of the ship is at risk.' He cocked an eyebrow at Ben. 'Am I right, Mr Darby?'

'What can I do?' Ben asked.

'The coal in the bunker has shifted, Ben. If we don't correct the list we've taken to port, we could be in a lot of trouble. We need to trim a hundred and fifty tons of coal over to the starboard side. It's a case of all hands to the shovels.'

'You're the boss,' Ben said.

'Good,' Taggart approved. 'Go along with the PO. He's organising the volunteers. The sooner you get down there the better.'

'Do I have time to put on my working rags?'

'Of course, but don't hang about, Ben?'

'Yes?'

'We need hands on deck, too. All we can muster. But it's dangerous work . . . with this sea. I thought you'd be better below. At least you've been learning to handle a shovel . . .'

'I'll be OK,' Ben said. He smiled at Finney. 'Let's go.'

He wasn't quite sure what it was Taggart had been trying to tell him: whether, in an oblique way, he had been trying to express concern for Ben or offer him some kind of warning. Or was it apology? Whatever it was, Ben quickly forgot about it in the sweaty discomfort of the next few hours. He was to remember his labours within the suffocating confines of the *Kildare Glen's* bunker hatches as the closest approximation of hell on earth as it was possible to contrive.

Directing the operation to move 150 tons of coal from the tween-deck area of the side-bunkers on the port side was the Second Engineer, a portly little West

Harpudlian whose nervous twitch and fluttering bird-like mannerisms were the legacy of privations suffered in an Arctic convoy. His name was Castle and he was a chronic worrier who had difficulty communicating with his fellow-men without stuttering away in sudden machine-gun bursts of excited chatter.

Ben and the gunners drafted in to assist the regular trimmers gleaned only a sketchy idea from Castle what had caused the dangerous shift of coal. It appeared that a chute blockage on the port side had led to the creation of an empty pocket immediately below it. When the blockage had suddenly cleared, it had triggered an avalanche of coal from the starboard side that had thundered down into the lower bunker and also piled high into the empty recesses of the side-bunker. There had been no equalising shift back, with the result that the coal would now have to be shovelled or barrowed across to the starboard side.

Castle was clearly afraid that the violent rolling of the *Kildare Glen* and the restless state of the coal would achieve in an instant what he hoped to accomplish with his gang of shovelling men – and that one and all would be buried alive. The fear was not lost on the men, and it added an urgency to their toil as they sweated away at the tasks allotted to them by the engineer. Ben found himself high near the roof of the side-bunker, working in tandem with Ryker, who was trimmer on McQueen's watch. Lying on their stomachs, with little head space and with little light reaching them from the portable cluster some distance below and behind, they raked away with their shovels, sending coal back downhill to their back-up pair who, with a little more working space, widened the distribution of displaced coal.

It was excruciating work, made infinitely more difficult by the sapping heat, the dust, the airlessness, and the agonisingly endless motion of the ship. Into this little side-cavern of hell, two deck seamen appeared –

having rigged a hose from a deck-line and let it down through the fiddley. They took one look at the mole-like scratching of Ben and his companions and made a quick escape to deck-level, thankful to face the flying spray and cyclonic wind awaiting them there. Ryker used the hose to dampen the coal and reduce the dust. Then he lay on his back and let the trickle of water fall on his head and chest. He passed the hose to Ben so that he, too, could cool his head and body. Ben did so gratefully, and passed the hose on. Then he and Ryker got on with the job of reducing the mountain of coal from the sides of the hatch.

With only the briefest respites, they worked throughout the morning. By midday, they had created a steel-walled cavern where, before, the coal had been heaped high. There was now plenty of room to walk and move about and wheel a barrow. The burden of activity was now concentrated on the starboard side of the ship, where corners had been filled and a gang of six were trimming coal down evenly into the outer reaches of the cross-bunker. The Second Engineer was flitting about nervously, cautioning here and encouraging there, but with plain signs that relief was tempering his fretful fluttering.

Just after one o'clock, Castle expressed his satisfaction and called a halt. Ben hauled himself up the fiddley ladder, scarcely able to lift one foot after the other. He was utterly drained. His back, arms and legs ached as if some torturer had stretched him on the Spanish Rack. His hands were blistered and bleeding. The raw flesh exposed by broken blisters was an ugly mess of blood, sweat and coal-dust: looking almost putrescent. Staring at his upturned palms when he reached the deck, the pain from them surprised Ben. Below, when they had been gripped round a shovel, he had been only dimly aware of their tenderness – perhaps because, in concentrating his mind on the effort of moving coal, he had managed to shut to the back of his mind isolated pockets of pain which were merely component parts of the more general bodily agony that had to be overcome. Hauling himself up the fiddley ladder by gripping the hand-rail, the fiery pain from Ben's hands had suddenly asserted itself as the most persistent and unpleasant torment of the many consuming his body.

Fifteen minutes in a tepid shower eased some of the aches and pains but merely intensified the mind-consuming irritation that tortured Ben's hands. He could touch nothing without setting off a riot of pain that brought tears to his eyes. Drying himself became a major battle because of the difficulty of holding a towel. He dabbed at himself tentatively, growing angry at himself because it was more than he could endure to continue with the ineffective dabbing for more than a few seconds at a time without wanting to scream out. When he tried to button a shirt, the act of trying to get his flesh-raw fingers around a button came near to defeating him.

For all the time he had spent under the shower, Ben had been unable to remove the coal-dust that had insinuated itself into his eyes and nostrils and, in particular, into the open sores of his hands. Looking at himself in the bathroom mirror, he was dismayed at his black-eyed appearance. The corners of his eyes seemed to be welling with black tears that left blotches on his towel when he tried to rub them away. His nose and throat were congested to a degree that made him constantly want to hawk and spit. Clearing his passages brought up gritty black fluid from his sinuses and lungs.

Determined to remove every gravel speck of coal from the blister sores on his hands, Ben resumed his painstaking toilet over the wash-basin in his bathroom; cursing bitterly as violent roll after violent roll of the ship emptied water from the basin almost as fast as he ran it in. The anger of the gods against him seemed complete when the water from the basin's taps trickled to nothing and gave out. The fresh water tank that fed the bridge accommodation was empty.

Ben was not alone in making the discovery. A cry of fury from through the wall in Taggart's bathroom suggested that the Captain, too, had been deprived of his water supply at a critical moment.

Indeed, both men emerged from their cabins simultaneously in the hope of finding someone to restore the supply. Taggart was in a towering rage, ready to commit murder. He quickly acquainted Ben with the reason. He had been on the bridge continuously for close on twenty-four hours and, snatching five minutes to run a razor over his face and freshen up, he had been denied that tiny luxury because some lazy bastard had forgotten to pump up water to the bridge tank.

It was a groggy-looking Richard White who appeared from the ship's pantry in response to Taggart's bellowing. He shrank on the stairs, near to tears, as Taggart berated him mercilessly and demanded an explanation for the empty tank.

The boy mumbled something that was inaudible against the external noises of storm and labouring ship which, without stop, provided an unrelenting accompaniment to all life on the *Kildare Glen*. Taggart's anger increased.

'Speak up, you snivelling little shit!' he screamed at the boy, his eyes bulging. 'I'm going to get an explanation out of you if I have to hang your head off the bulkhead to get it! Speak up, damn you!'

The boy cowered against the stair, quaking with terror. The look on his face was abject. After several attempts, he managed to stammer out a coherent reply.

'I . . . I . . . I wasn't feeling w-well, s-s-sir . . . I . . . I . . . I f-forgot t-t-to p-p-pump up the tank.'

'Captain . . .' Ben tried to intercede, but Taggart thrust him roughly aside and took two steps down the stairway, thus interposing himself between Ben and the boy. Ben was left with his view of the stair blocked off by the solid wall of Taggart's back and shoulders. He was powerless off by the solid wall of Taggart's back and shoulders. He was powerless to say or do anything while Taggart ranted on some more at the boy, warning him that if the water tank was not pumped full within the next half hour he would be made to regret the day he had ever been born.

When Taggart turned to ascend the stair, his fury-filled eyes still bulged from his face in an expression of simmering violence. He did not wait for Ben to step out of his path but jostled straight into him, forcing him back against the panelling of the alleyway with his chest. Ben was pinned by the other's weight against the unyielding wall. Taggart thrust his snarling face almost nose-to-nose with Ben's.

'I warned you once before about trying to interfere, Mr Darby. Now, I'm warning you for the last time. Keep your nose out of my business!'

He pushed Ben roughly aside and strode towards his cabin. Ben suddenly had an overpowering need to breathe fresh air. He went out through the storm-door on the lower bridge, where the need was more than satisfied the instant he stepped across the high threshold. The force of the wind almost swept him off his feet and the door was rattled back against its frame with a crash like a cannon's. Spray was blowing across the *Kildare Glen*'s waist to the height of the funnel. The rage of sea and heaven was awesome to behold. It occurred to Ben that, since he had been wakened early in the morning by the thunderous noise of the sea smashing the lifeboat from its davits, he had scarcely given a thought to the whereabouts of the Japanese ship. The enemy vessel, and the danger it represented, seemed to be the least of the *Kildare Glen*'s problems. All the indications were that Taggart's ruse, of turning tail and running from the seaplane-carrier and then doubling back on his tracks as soon as it was dark, had been completely successful. Some sort of alarm would have been raised if the other ship had been anywhere in sight – and Ben was certain that Taggart would never have left the bridge for a shave with the Jap in the vicinity.

No, the Jap was somewhere under the heaving horizon, and probably having just as much trouble as the *Kildare Glen* in surviving these violent but wholly neutral seas. Taggart had seen the weather as an ally, but it was showing little friendship that Ben could discern. The *Kildare Glen* seemed to be making no headway in the sea whatever, her screw labouring away with little evidence that it was more than holding the ship's head into the weather.

As he huddled against the bridge housing, Ben could see that the deck gang had been busy during his labours in the dark hell of the bunkers. The smashed No. 3 lifeboat was gone and her davits lashed inboard. Two of the troop deck-houses had been totally demolished and their debris removed. Only the most solid-looking of the temporary structures remained: a galley-cum-bakehouse, which enjoyed some protection from the bridge-house. The two starboard lifeboats had been swung inboard and secured in their chocks.

A door crashed shut somewhere below him and Ben saw the frail figure of Richard White edge his way along the coaming of the cargo-hold and head towards the ship's galley. The cabin-boy did not go in but unclipped a wrench, that was attached to a length of chain, from a clamp in the galley housing. This he used to turn a valve in the piping immediately below the clamp. Replacing the wrench, the boy then unhooked a T-shaped handle from its storm mounting and began to work the handle up and down. It dawned on Ben that what Richard White was operating was the hand pump that filled the fresh-water tank on the bridge from the storage tanks in the ship's double-bottom.

Ben watched the boy work the heavy metal handle a few times and then lean against it as if the effort was too much for him. The pump was located on the port side of the galley – the weather side – and flying spray was raining down on him in a constant deluge. There was something so pathetic about the boy's despair that anger seethed in Ben. It was stirred by a loathing for Taggart such as he had never felt for another living being, for there was no doubt in the American's mind who was directly responsible for Richard White's misery.

Ben slipped out from his relatively sheltered position and braved the fury of the wind and spray battering the port bridge-deck – now exposed where the No. 1 lifeboat had been – and clambered down the ladder to the main-deck. It was awash with water running like a river through the sheltered alleyway from the fore-deck. Ben splashed through it towards the galley. The boy was trying again to work the heavy pump-handle up and down when Ben reached him.

'I'll give you a hand,' Ben shouted above the scream of the wind, as he took over half of the T-shaped handle and added his efforts to those of the cabin-boy. He bit down on his lip, in pain, as his fingers closed over the hard metal shaft, but he set his mind resolutely against the torment to his torn hands and endured it. 'How long do we have to keep this up?' he shouted.

Richard White shook himself, water streaming down his face, as a particularly heavy deluge of water enveloped the pair. 'Until the tank overflows,' he shouted back, and stopped pumping. He pointed up at a cylindrical tank on the after end of the top bridge. 'That's it up there. You'll see it when it overflows. It takes about twenty minutes' to half an hour's pumping to fill it.'

Ben nodded grimly. 'Let's keep at it then.'

Ben forced his aching muscles to respond as he bent his back and arms into rhythmic manipulation of the heavy handle. Up and down, up and down, up and down . . . He soon became aware that the boy at his side was making only a token contribution, but he maintained a brisk action. He stopped when he realised that Richard White barely had the strength to hang on to the handle. More water broke over them as Ben slipped an arm round the boy's shoulder and helped him into a sitting position on the high step of the fiddley door.

'I'm sorry,' the boy moaned. 'I just can't . . .'

The child face was flushed and the boy seemed to have difficulty focusing his eyes.

'You're ill!' Ben shouted, arching his back as another curtain of sea-water descended in a flood.

'Me head's sore . . .' The boy's words were barely audible against the sea. 'I'm so tired.'

'Don't move,' Ben ordered and, lurching a few steps forward, tried to open the galley door. His rattling attempts brought the Cook to the door to unbolt it from the inside.

The Cook, a wiry little man with a crew-cut that accented his permanently pugnacious expression, scowled at Ben.

'Go round the other bloody side! What kind of sailor . . .?' The words died as he recognised the drenched and bedraggled figure as the *Kildare Glen*'s passenger. 'Good God, sir! Are you all right?'

'Give me a hand,' Ben shouted, without ceremony. 'I've got someone here who isn't.'

With the Cook's help, Ben carried the boy into the narrow galley. The blistering heat all but took his breath away. He sat Richard White on a narrow wooden bench away from the worst heat of the stoves while the Cook rebolted the port-side door.

'What's up with the lad?' the Cook enquired over Ben's shoulder.

'I don't know. A fever maybe, by the look of him.'

The Cook took one look at the boy's face and agreed.

'I'll get the lads to put him in his bunk. He don't look well at all.'

He went off, leaving Ben with the boy. Moments later, he was back and with him were the Second Steward and one of the assistant stewards. They insisted on taking over Richard White's welfare, promising to dry him off and tuck him up in his bunk.

'If you want to help, sir,' said the Second Steward to Ben, 'perhaps you'd report this to Mr Fowler. He has charge of the medicine cabinet. There might be something he can give the lad.'

Ben said he would see Fowler immediately.

He left the galley by the starboard door and was making his way forward across the lurching deck, when a shout made him look up. Taggart was standing at the rail that skirted the after end of the navigating bridge, glaring balefully down at him. The *Kildare Glen*'s master shouted again.

'Up here, Mr Darby! I want you up here!'

Anger welled in Ben, but he controlled it and made for the bridge ladder. It still bubbled away dangerously within him as he faced Taggart. There was no meekness in his stance nor his stare as he presented himself solidly in front of the ship's captain.

'What the hell has been going on down there, Mr Darby?' Taggart demanded belligerently. 'I saw somebody being carried aft.'

'It was that kid – the one you like to scare the life out of, Captain. Well, maybe you'll lay off him now. He's too weak to stand up . . .'

'You're talking rot!' Taggart blustered.

'And you've gone too goddamned far!' Ben hurled

back at him. 'That boy's sick with fever – and if you don't do something about it, I goddamn will!'

'You? You?' Taggart was almost speechless with outraged disbelief. 'What can *you* bloody do?'

Ben's temper had now slipped its leash. His anger had control of him.

'I'll make your name stink from Tokyo to Timbuktu!' he shouted at Taggart. 'I'll tell the world just what kind of shit you really are!'

For a moment, Ben thought Taggart was going to hit him. The big man's arm came up and the right fist was balled and ready like a brandished knobkerrie. But the blow that might have permanently flattened Ben's features was stayed and the fist was presented to within an inch of Ben's nose, where it remained in a threatening manner.

'You dare to threaten me on my own bridge! You, a newspaper hack!' Taggart's voice grated like metal in a stripping gear-box.

'You don't scare me,' Ben answered bravely. 'You don't own me life and soul like you seem to own everybody else on this ship!'

Ben, acutely aware of the menacing fist but beyond the point of caring, almost sagged with surprise when it was suddenly withdrawn. He was quite unprepared for the bewildering change in Taggart's manner, from one of towering threat to sudden astonishment and apparent delight.

'Ben, you rascal,' he roared, 'what the hell have we been feeding you on? Raw meat? You've really worked up a head of steam! By heaven, I never thought I'd see the day!'

Ben glowered at him, confusion. 'I meant every goddamned word I said!' The words were delivered defiantly, but Ben's uncertainty robbed them of total conviction.

'Of course you meant what you said!' There was

admiring approbation in Taggart's quick agreement. 'By God, you were ready to take me on tooth and nail! That takes guts, Ben. The kind of guts that I can respect.'

'What are you going to do about that kid?' Ben persisted. 'He's ill. And he needs looking after . . . Not the kind of treatment you've been dishing out to him!'

Taggart's eyes hardened and he stiffened perceptibly. But the reaction was momentary. He held back thoughtfully before replying with only the faintest air of aggrievement.

'You're a pretty hard customer, Ben . . .' He grined sheepishly. 'So I blow up now and then — and maybe I shouldn't . . . But I've been on edge. We all have . . . And that boy makes me see red! He's a lazy little sod, and a play-actor with it. He rolls his little-girl eyes at you and thinks you should feel sorry for him. The Chief Steward lets him get away with murder, but I bloody well don't. This is a ship — not a ballet school for pansies . . .'

'He's just a kid, for Christ's sake!' Ben interrupted vehemently. 'You expect everybody to be like Superman!'

'I expect everybody to do their job,' Taggart retorted. 'And it's that boy's job to keep that water-tank full. The little sod dodged it! And he has no excuse for falling down on the job any more than I have, Ben. God knows there's nothing I'd like better than to get down off this bridge for an hour with my feet up — but I bloody well can't. I've got to keep going even if I feel like hell. And God knows I expect a damned lot less from first-trip cabin-boys than I expect from myself! I get angry when what I get from them is bugger all . . .'

'He's ill, Captain. You're wrong if you think he was swinging the lead.'

Ben had no intention of giving an inch. Taggart had misjudged the boy and he had to be made to realise it.

'You seem pretty damn sure,' Taggart said, seeming pained by Ben's persistence.

Ben scented victory. 'I am pretty damned sure,' he confirmed emphatically. And from the look on Taggart's face he knew he had won. He should have felt triumph, but the untypical droop of Taggart's shoulders provoked a sudden pang of guilt. He suddenly realised how tired his adversary was. The foulness of Taggart's temper had been an obvious enough symptom of the big man's fatigue but it was only now that Ben saw the others: the rheumy bloodshot eyes, the grey pallor that tinged the weather-beaten face.

'What have they done with the boy?' Taggart asked wearily.

'They've put him to bed. He really is in a bad way.'

'OK,' Taggart conceded. 'We'll consider him on the sick-list. I'll get Mr Fowler to take a look at him.' He smiled. 'He fancies himself as a doctor, although he's the last person I'd send for if I had anything wrong with me.'

'Thanks,' Ben said. 'I appreciate it.'

Taggart studied him. 'You've cooled down now. Does that mean you'll maybe have second thoughts about telling the world what a shit I am?'

Ben bit his lip. 'I was all riled up. Forget I said it.'

Taggart laughed. 'Not a chance, Ben. You know I'm a shit. I know it. Fowler knows it. Ferguson knows it ... Everybody on this ship knows it! I don't give a monkey's fuck if the whole damned world knows it.' There was a warming gleam in his eye as he added: 'There's just one thing ... Me saying it is one thing. Other people saying it is something else again. Remember that, Ben.'

Ben met his stare levelly. 'I'll remember,' he said.

'There's another thing ...'

'Yeah?'

'You said I didn't own you like I owned everybody else on the ship . . . Don't take any bets on that.'

'What do you mean?'

'I mean, you signed the articles like everybody else on this ship. And that means that like everybody else thou shalt serve the Lord thy God with all thy might and with all thy strength or the Lord thy God will put the boot in.' He smiled. 'There is only one God, Ben, old fruit – and on the *Kildare Glen* that's me. So don't let your spirit of independence run away with you, eh? I like a man who has guts – but don't make a habit of calling me names on my own bridge. Some captains wouldn't take kindly to that at all.'

'You want an apology?'

Taggart considered this, as if savouring a private joke. For all his fatigue, there was a mocking brightness to the eyes that pierced at Ben from below half-closed lids. He shrugged his great shoulders.

'An apology is just words, Ben. You trade in words . . . I don't. Deeds count much more with me than words.' He smiled enigmatically.

His teasing obliquity was beginning to annoy Ben, dissipating the fragile accord that had emerged from the confrontation.

'Deeds?' Ben echoed, unable to keep a slight edge from his voice. 'Do I have to get down on my knees and beg forgiveness?'

'I wouldn't respect a man who did that, Ben. I have no respect for a man who grovels. It robs him of any dignity . . . It wouldn't impress me at all.'

'Just what would impress you, Captain?' Ben asked with exasperation.

Taggart's expression became almost sly.

'An act of pride maybe. A way of calling quits and thumbing your nose at me at the same time.' Ben stared at him without comprehension. 'Look,' Taggart went on, 'your touching concern for the health of one of my crew has robbed me of a pair of hands when they can least be spared. I'm sure you meant well but, thanks to you, I still haven't had the shave and wash to which I think I'm entitled after a day and a night on this bridge. A real man wouldn't hum and haw about saying sorry to me. A real man would say, "Bugger you, Captain" and go and do something about it.'

Ben stared at him in astonishment.

'You want me to go and pump up that goddamned tank?'

'Somebody's got to do it. I don't give a damn who. But it means taking a man away from other work that's just as important. Are you volunteering?'

There was a calculated challenge to the question and Ben's anger made him rise to it.

'Am I supposed to read that as an order, Captain? Is that an utterance from the mouth of God – to be obeyed?'

'I wouldn't dream of ordering you to do it, Ben. I only asked if you were volunteering. You know what they say . . .? One volunteer is better than ten pressed men.'

'OK, Captain. You've got your goddamned volunteer!' Ben ground the words out, blind to everything but the knowledge that to refuse would be a sign of weakness, an abject retreat. And he wasn't going to give Taggart that satisfaction.

'You're a man after my own heart, Ben,' Taggart said, and seemed to mean it. Heaven forbid, thought Ben, and tried to convince himself that the glint in Taggart's eyes was not one of triumph. The thought that it might be was enough to agitate him with anger as he left the bridge. Spray was still lashing across the ship's waist and he had to fight his way through it to reach the pump on the weather side of the galley. He threw a defiant look at the bridge. His pride was intact. He had faced Taggart head-on and he had not backed down. Taggart had. And that was a victory. But the alien thought was taking hold in Ben that his victory was a kind of defeat and that he had only been conned into thinking otherwise.

Although pain flared from the blood-raw flesh on his hands as soon as he laid hold of the pump-handle, he did not relax the fierceness of his grip. Face set in silent fury, he began to pump: his mind fully concentrated on the muscle-racking task as if the fate of the world hinged on any interruption to the rhythmic rise and fall of the heavy handle. Never once did he look up – although he knew that, from the bridge, Taggart was watching him.

There was no let-up to the storm. Normal watch-keeping patterns were restored in mid-afternoon, although Taggart did not end his vigil on the bridge.

'He'll probably stay there until we've run out of the cyclone,' Willem Prins told Ben as the pair lingered on in the saloon after the evening meal. Ben had eaten little. His meagre appetite had not been encouraged by having to eat off a table-cloth that had been soaked to stop the crockery from sliding and from a table that had wooden guards around it to keep his dinner-plate out of his lap. The meal over, Ben and the Second Officer now had the saloon to themselves.

'Did you hear about the signal from Colombo?' the young Dutchman asked Ben. Ben confessed that he had not, and was told that it had made Taggart very angry. It had emanated from Colombo as a result of the *Kildare Glen* breaking radio silence the previous day: giving her position and announcing that she was engaging an enemy surface ship, believed to be the *Notoro*.

'Colombo seem to think that our message was a phoney,' Prins told Ben. 'They were advising all ships to ignore our call until' – and he quoted – ' "authenticity of signal can be established". They said that the vessel of origin – that is us – was not in the area claimed and that the enemy ship *Notoro* could not possibly be in these waters because she had been sunk in Rabaul last year.'

'That ship looked pretty real to me,' Ben said. 'So did the seaplane.'

'They were real enough,' Prins agreed, 'although I'm not surprised that Colombo were suspicious about the position we gave. We haven't been where we were supposed to be from the first day out, and since the SOS from the *Fort Buckingham* we've been getting further and further away from the track we were supposed to follow. We're so far off course now that we're not even in the right *zone*.'

'Does that mean the Captain will get hauled over the coals when we hit port?' Ben asked.

Prins stared at him, digesting the idiom in his solemn way. When Ben's meaning dawned, a beam spread across his earnest face.

'Taken over the coals? Ah! I see! That does not trouble Captain Taggart, my friend. That is the least of his cares. He does not give damn for that. For him, the important thing is, as you say, to hit port!'

'And how long is it going to take us to get to Durban?' Ben asked.

The Second Officer contemplated the question solemnly.

'Two more weeks . . . But in this weather . . . Perhaps three. Who knows?'

Ben grinned. 'You're the navigator!'

Prins nodded grimly. 'But a navigator with his head in a sack, my friend. It is two days since we have seen the sun, and star-sights are out of the question when there is no horizon, even if we could get a glimpse of a star we knew. We are running blind, Mr Darby, and we could be running blind for another week yet. There is only one thing I can state with perfect certainty . . .'

'And what is that, Mr Prins?'

'We are not running anywhere very fast!'

The truth of the Second Officer's assertion was borne out in the days that followed. The weather all but stopped the *Kildare Glen* in her tracks for two days. The wind buffeted the ship with gusts that exceeded 130 mph and for forty-eight hours the sea remained a boiling white mass that was almost permanently hidden by driving spray. From noon to noon, the battling freighter logged a distance travelled of, first, twenty-four miles and then of forty-three. The third day brought a slight moderation of the conditions and the day's run leapt to seventy-three miles. On the fourth, eighty-eight miles were logged and, on the fifth, the century was topped with a run of 104 miles.

In five days, the *Kildare Glen* had covered a distance that was still some miles short of that which she had been built to put behind her in twenty-four hours of normal steaming. But the sixth day dawned bright and beautiful, with a burning sun. Only a long heaving swell persisted as a reminder of the days of storm.

The morning broke with the *Kildare Glen* alone on a blue ocean.

At 7.30 a.m. Taggart left the bridge for the first time since the afternoon when the seaplane had been heard above the clouds. Apart from short absences to attend to calls of nature, he had maintained a bridge vigil of nearly 140 consecutive hours. The only rest he had allowed himself had come in brief catnaps, hunched in a high-armed stool behind the wheel-house windows. As fatigue had taken its toll he had communicated less and less with those around him, keeping his own counsel and displaying choleric ill-humour on the rare occasions when he did have something to say.

On that morning, Ben and Willem Prins were first in for breakfast on the stroke of eight o'clock; with the Dutchman almost elated at the prospect of a good morning sight of the sun in advance of the run to noon.

Ben was in a happy mood, too: being hungry for the first time in a week and, for one, looking forward to a plate of fried eggs and bacon.

They had scarcely exchanged 'good-mornings' and seated themselves when the vast frame of Taggart filled the saloon doorway. He seemed not to notice them as he took his seat at the head of the table. He had shaved and donned a fresh white uniform but his eyes were sunken and he walked with the gait of a zombie.

'Good morning, sir,' Prins greeted him brightly. He might have spoken to the air. Taggart leaned his head in his hands and gently slumped forward against the table. Prins got quickly to his feet but hesitated at an eruption of sound from the hunched figure. The room was filled with a resonant snoring. Captain Taggart was sound asleep.

CHAPTER 7

After the Storm

The sores on Ben Darby's hands refused to heal. Bathing them several times a day in a weak solution of carbolic did not prevent the torn flesh from turning septic and suppurating in several places. Mr Fowler – with a grave and authoritative manner that would have done credit to a qualified medical practitioner – took a personal interest in Ben's hands that bordered on the proprietorial. Healing them seemed to become one of the major objectives in his life. He persuaded the American to report to his cabin at ten in the mornings and eight-thirty in the evenings, so that the hands could be bared for inspection, dressed with healing ointment and then carefully bandaged. As an antidote to the poison in his bloodstream from festing sores, Fowler prescribed a course of M and B tablets and, at the morning 'surgeries', issued Ben with his daily ration of four white pills.

In discourses designed to reassure his patient, the Chief Officer acquainted Ben with past challenges that had tested his knowledge of medicine. The cases ranged from particularly hideous instances of venereal disease to Fowler's first-aid treatment of a man whose leg had been all but severed by a runaway wire cable. Far from reassuring Ben, Fowler had him offering up prayers of thankfulness that his injuries were relatively simple. He steadfastly resisted Fowler's suggestion that the infected areas on his palms and fingers could be quickly cleaned up by lancing with a scalpel. Ben opted for continued application of ointment and allowing time for it to do its work. Fowler did not press the issue but was clearly disappointed.

It was through Fowler that Ben kept up to date with the progress of Richard White who, after a week in his bunk, was showing signs of much improvement. His illness had been diagnosed as heatstroke, which – from Fowler's point of view – was a rather boring kind of ailment. All he could do was prescribe quinine in the hope that it would bring the lad's temperature down.

Taggart made much of Fowler's diagnosis, waxing wrathful at mealtimes over an illness that he classified as a self-inflicted injury. He lectured the deck and radio officers on the human body's vulnerability to the harmful rays of the tropical sun. He reminded everyone that the cabin-boy was one of three crew members who had wantonly disobeyed his orders about exposing neck and spine to the sun by lying shirtless on the hatch. He made no differentiation between heatstroke and sunstroke and never used the former term when referring to Richard White's incapacity. The boy had suffered sunstroke – and the fact ought to serve as a lesson to everyone on the ship. No one dared contradict him.

Taggart would not let the topic go away, pursuing it to the point of eccentricity. Certainly, in the aftermath of the storm, his behaviour became markedly strange as he became increasingly obsessed with the dangers of sunstroke and insisted on the entire crew adopting precautions against it.

On the thirteenth day out from Bombay, he announced the first of these measures after appearing on the bridge in a garb that was a radical departure from his customary attire. Normally, he was fastidious in the wearing of the correct uniform – even at sea – and he was insistent on the officers following his lead.

On this day, however, he startled Willem Prins by striding into the wheel-house wearing a striped blue-and-white pyjama-jacket over his uniform white trousers. On his head was a khaki pith helmet, which had a white handkerchief draped from its rear rim to cover the neck.

The *Kildare Glen*'s captain looked for all the world like an actor in the guise of a mad explorer, who had strayed from the stage of a West End farce. Prins goggled at him, mouth open in wonder: a reaction that angered Taggart.

'What the bloody hell are you staring at?' he snarled. 'Are you keeping watch or having a wet dream?'

Prins stuttered an apology and galvanised himself into action. With only a moment of indecision, he made for the wheel-house door. He was stopped in his tracks by Taggart's bull-like roar.

'Where the hell are you running off to?'

'The . . . the compass error, sir . . . I was just going up top for an azimuth . . .'

'It can wait!' snapped Taggart. 'In any case, you're not going up topside dressed like that!'

Prins gaped at the Captain and then looked down at the spotless whites that he had pressed with an iron before coming on watch.

'Like what, sir?'

'I am enforcing new regulations for dress on the bridge, which will be observed while we're north of Capricorn,' Taggart informed him sharply. 'I came up to relieve you so that you could go below and change.'

The Dutchman stared at him blankly.

'I do not understand . . . sir.'

'Then that square head of yours is bloody thicker than I thought,' rasped Taggart. 'Can't you see what I'm wearing?'

'It . . . It looks like a pyjama-jacket, sir.'

'It is a bloody pyjama-jacket, you halfwit! Where's yours? You do have one, Mr Prins?'

'Y-yes, sir.'

'Well, get below and put it on in place of that stupid short-sleeved shirt you've got on!'

Prins could only stare at Taggart, bewildered.

'I do not understand, sir . . .'

'No, you do not understand,' said Taggart, mimicking the Dutchman. 'Because you're thick and you don't know anything about sunstroke. But I do know something. And one of the things I know is that when the *Poplar Leaf* went down, the captain – a friend of mine called Ronnie Laird – was the only one out of nineteen in a boat that didn't get sunstroke. And do you know why he didn't get sunstroke? Because he was the only one wearing a pyjama-jacket!'

It would never have crossed the Second Officer's mind to question an order from the master, and he did not do so now. If Taggart had ordered him to wear a sarong and a straw hat, he would have complied – because he had been brought up from childhood to regard as sacrosanct the commands of his elders or those in authority above him, no matter what his private feelings might be. He was absent from the bridges for less than five minutes. When he returned, his neat white shirt with the double-barred epaulets had been replaced by an exotically coloured pyjama-top with a floral pattern. He was blushing with embarrassment as Taggart inspected him.

'Button it up,' the master ordered the Dutchman. 'Right to the neck!'

Prins did so, having difficulty with the top button which had never been fastened since the garment's purchase. Taggart surveyed him.

'You look like a poof,' was his verdict, 'but appearances are secondary. What about a sun-hat? Don't you have one?' Taggart took off his pith helmet and waved it in front of Prins.

'I don't have one,' the Second Officer confessed.

Taggart snorted. 'I might have known you'd be schooner-rigged. You could have got one in Bombay for a few chips, you know. Still, can't be helped.'

He did not let the matter end there, but insisted that Prins attached a white handkerchief to the back of his uniform cap in the style of a Foreign Legionnaire's kepi. When Taggart left the bridge, the young Dutchman became aware that the helmsman at the wheel was having a fit of the giggles behind his back. Prins sharply reminded him to watch his course and stomped out to the wing.

The sniggering helmsman's turn was to come when Taggart issued orders for the deck sailors not to venture on deck without their heads and necks being covered to protect them from the rays of the sun. Most complied meekly. A variety of headgear promptly appeared: soft-brimmed sun-hats, a couple of panama hats with gaudy bands, even some Mexican sombreros.

One seaman decided to go bare-headed, as he had done throughout his years at sea. He was heard to voice the belief that the Captain was off his head. The lone rebel changed his tune after a brief but noisy encounter on deck with Taggart. Taggart had provided the noise: threatening to put the rebel in irons until he was of a more obedient frame of mind. Taggart did not accept as an excuse that the seaman did not possess a hat to wear, with the consequence that the man duly appeared on deck with a towel wound round his head like a turban, the ends hanging to provide a neck covering. The unfortunate was promptly greeted with much jeering and hailed by all and sundry as 'Gunga Din'. The label stuck and probably remained with the man for the rest of his days.

The compulsory headwear made the deck crowd the

immediate target of much ribald comment from the stoke-hold gang. This led to at least two vicious fist fights, which exacerbated the disharmony already prevalent on the ship. Before, Taggart had been the prime object of the acrimonious mutterings. Now the various departments vented their spleen on one another. Ill-feeling was rife and, like the painful sores on Ben Darby's hands, would not go away as the *Kildare Glen* ploughed ever south across an empty ocean.

The known presence of enemy submarines in that infinity of blue exerted its own pressure on worn nerves for twenty-four hours a day. The menace of the unseen enemy – the knowledge that the fatal strike might come at any minute of the night or day – was a constant companion to the man on watch and, equally, to the man below who tossed sleeplessly in his bunk. There is a destructive edge to the fear of unseen dangers that is often crueller and more corrosive to the spirit than that fear that rises in the presence of visible peril. If the latter is a stab to the heart, the other is a slow, devouring cancer. The strain of never knowing how close the enemy might be had an insidiously draining effect on the nerves of those cooped up within the steel walls of the *Kildare Glen*. It frayed the tempers of otherwise placid men. It made the quick-tempered ultra-sensitive: lowering flash-points dangerously. Each day was an agony of waiting for something to happen, an agony that grew no less when nothing did. The suspense merely intensified as the minutes and hours ticked away. They waited. They waited like a condemned man waits to hear his executioner's footsteps and only a silence prevails, until the silence itself becomes a torment.

In the fair weather that followed the storm, Ben Darby found himself almost longing for the crashing thunder of seas that the cyclone had provided. The battle then had been straightforward: one tiny ship against the elements, to the exclusion of all else. Clear skies and calmer seas brought a relief that was largely physical – normal living was less uncomfortable – but the bluer the sky and the smoother the sea the more agitated became the mind.

Ben, deprived of much physical activity because of his hands, found himself with too much time to think. He tried to read but found it difficult to sustain interest in the written word for more than half an hour at a time. He became restless and fidgety: claustrophobic when confined to his cabin and unable to concentrate when he tried to read in the fresh air. His eyes continually sought the skies, expecting to see a dot on the horizon and hear the drone of a scouting seaplane from the Japanese ship. *Where was that ship?*

It might have given him comfort to know that the same question was tasking the minds of three submarine commanders and Japanese Naval Headquarters in Batavia, because all contact with the ship had been lost. Her fate was to remain an unsolved mystery. Taggart's notification that the ship sighted by the *Kildare Glen* was the tender *Notoro*, and the lack of credence given to his radio signal, were to fog the truth for some time to come. Also, inquiry into the matter was overtaken by subsequent events. All hostilities with the Japanese were to be over before it was finally established that the seaplane-tender had not been a figment of the imaginations of Taggart and his crew. She was not, in fact, the *Notoro* but the equally aged and almost identical *Kaminari*. After radio contact with her had been lost by the submarines with which she had been acting in consort, the Japanese presumed that she had foundered with all hands in the Indian Ocean during late Janauary, 1944.

But omniscience of events, present and future, was not granted to Ben nor those who voyaged with him. Their entire world was bounded by that circle of blue water and dome of sky which could be seen by the eye, and it was governed by a loneliness that comes with the crushing awareness of trackless ocean waste stretching vast beyond the eye's compass. Ignorance of the presence or absence of hostile forces in the immediate vicinity brought no bliss to the men on the freighter as she ploughed her lonely path south. It sharpened their fears by day and darkened their nights.

Because Ben could feel some of this stress and recognise it for what it was, it depressed him that he was powerless to do more than watch the petty frustrations that turned friend against friend and touched every aspect of life in the ship. They stemmed, he knew, from the accumulated pressures of nearly five years of war. Without commitment to the running of the ship and disqualified even from minor involvement by his torn hands, Ben felt more keenly than ever his status as outsider. He felt like a remand prisoner who, by chance, had been closeted in an escape-proof penitentiary with stir-crazy lifers. From his brief taste of the conditions which it was their lot to endure, he could see all too clearly how continued stress eroded the stability of the most serene personalities. Real fears and real anxieties were kept bottled and never allowed an outlet – but the pressure had to escape sometimes and, when it did, the explosion usually came in the shape of uncharacteristic aggression or untypical over-reaction to the most trivial of slights.

Because of the taut state of his own nerves, Ben found it easy to understand and sympathise with the shortcomings of almost everyone around him. To him, it was nothing short of a miracle that, having endured for so long, they were able to endure still. They should have been coming apart at the seams: gibbering and demented. But no, they were not yet reduced to that. They flared up at little things, they snapped and snarled and came to blows – but they did their work and the watches changed on time. The trailing log kept clocking up another nautical mile for every 576 revolutions of the propeller. There was not much laughter in the *Kildare Glen* and the reason – Ben realised – was that she was a ship of tired men. Most of the faces were young but the eyes were old with the weariness of too much war.

Even the joke of Taggart having his bridge officers stand their watches in pyjama-tops – for a joke it seemed to Ben at first – provoked little hilarity after the amused disbelief of the first day. Once the spectacle had ceased to be a novelty, the bizarre uniform was so speedily accepted as normal that it might have been the approved standard of attire throughout the Merchant Marine.

Tempted as Ben was to laugh at Taggart's absurd obsession with the prevention of sunstroke, he was quickly sobered by the recognition of all the elements of tragedy in a situation that had the trappings of farce. Of all the men on the *Kildare Glen* wearied and worn down by war, none showed the signs of disintegration more visibly than Taggart. It was as if all those weary days and nights he had spent on the bridge during the storm had finally unhinged him. In his days as a junior feature-writer, Ben had once interviewed an eminent psychiatrist who had conducted tests associating sleeplessness with madness. He remembered now the doctor's claim that the easiest way to drive a man insane was to deprive him of sleep. He remembered, too, how Taggart had in a rare moment of confidentiality confessed to sleeplessness.

Was the accumulation of all those sleepless nights and the way that, at sea, Taggart drove himself beyond human limits, finally exacting a terrible price? Was this the final crack-up?

The belief that Taggart was on the brink of madness was not the exclusive preserve of Ben Darby. Ferguson had been saying as much to his engineers from the first day out from Bombay. The deck sailors and the firemen openly lamented in their messes the foul luck that cursed them with a crazy man as their skipper. Only Ben seemed to see Taggart as a figure of tragedy – perhaps because the American's detached position allowed him to do so. He felt a sorrow for Taggart, like that evoked by the sight of a great oak smitten by the rotting disease which will bring it low.

However, from the Chief Officer down, the crew of the *Kildare Glen* took a narrator view of Taggart. He spared little of the milk of human kindness for them and they despised him for it. They saw him as a man who abused his position and authority and, as a consequence, had forfeited any right he had to their respect. In the line of duty they respected the uniform but loathed the man. They obeyed his orders, but from habit and grudgingly. They lived for the day when they would be paid off from the *Kildare Glen* and walk away from his hated face for ever. What might have made Taggart the man he was or what would happen to him in the future did not matter to his men. They saw him only in the context of the present, the day that had to be lived. The possibility that Taggart was suffering from mental breakdown was not seen as Taggart's misfortune but their own bad luck. Skippers came in all shapes and forms: the good; the bad; the fussy who played it by the book; the kind who had religion and the kind who drank too much; the worriers; the womanisers; the tight-fisted; the tyrants. What you got was the luck of the draw. Like good cooks and bad cooks, captains came and captains went. If you got one who was clean off his trolley, well, hard luck, shipmate. You can't expect to win 'em all.

There was no doubt in Ben's mind that the day when Taggart ordered Willem Prins to put on a pyjama-jacket was a kind of milestone. If at that particular moment morale on the *Kildare Glen* was low, from then on it took a dizzy downward spiral from which it never recovered. Taggart's edict about headgear and pyjama-tops – silly and trivial as it seemed – may have been only unfortunate in its timing, but it supplied the spark which ignited many subsequent outbursts of feeling. They spread with rippling effect, one leading to the next, until the whole fabric of discipline on board was threatened.

Feuds broke out all over the ship, and were not confined to the fo'c'sle hands. Ben never expected to see the mild and earnest Second Officer lose his temper, but he did. The Dutchman remonstrated with Barraclough, his friend, because the Third Officer seemed always to occupy the bathroom to wash out his shirts and underwear when Prins was wanting a shower. The shouting went on for ten minutes and the pair might have come to blows but for the intervention of the Chief Steward, who had heard the noise from his cabin on the other side of the ship.

The row was typical of many. Only Ben seemed immune from involvement, thanks perhaps to the fact that his cabin was relatively isolated. And he did not have to rub shoulders with any of the others unless he chose to do so. When he saw a row brewing, he had the good sense to walk away from it. One evening, with a handful of officers in the saloon listening to the BBC news on the temperamental short-wave radio, the storm signs were easy to read. Tuning the radio was a delicate operation and several of the officers believed that they were the only ones who could do it. Fowler, the Chief Steward and the Second Radio Officer all vied for the honour this evening, when reception proved very difficult. Ben took this as his cue to go out on deck for some fresh air. A few minutes later, he heard raised voices emanating from the saloon and the air was filled with angry recriminations.

The food on the *Kildare Glen* had, at best, been

indifferently cooked since Ben had joined the ship. In the third week out from Bombay, the quality of the meals coming from the galley deteriorated spectacularly. The fact did not escape the notice of the crew, who had long ago nicknamed the Cook 'Borgia', in the belief that it was his life's mission to poison them. The deck-seamen, in particular, were constantly at war with the Cook. They had complained in vain about his bread – made from weevil-infested flour – which was spotted so badly that they called it fruit load. With equal lack of success, they had complained about his 'cockroach soup'. On the sixteenth day at sea, however, they rebelled over the Cook's mutton stew. Led by an AB called Clinton and carrying mess-tins containing the offending culinary concoction, they marched forward in a body to complain to Captain Taggart.

Taggart, in pyjama-jacket, was eating in the saloon when a steward informed him that the deck-sailors were outside and demanding to see him. He did not take kindly to the interruption, but he pushed aside the corned-beef salad that figured on the officers' menu and had mercifully been spared from the Cook's attentions.

Ben, who had finished eating, waited until Taggart had left the saloon before he, too, slipped out. He climbed the inside stair and stepped out on to the lower bridge, which gave him a grandstand view of the meeting on the deck below of Taggart and the angry seamen.

Clinton, a big man with a barrel chest, was in no mood to be cowed by Taggart. He thrust a slopping mess-pan in front of the Captain.

'We'd like you to taste that, Captain,' he demanded. 'I wouldn't feed it to my dog at home! It's uneatable!'

Taggart peered at the dish.

'What is it?'

'It's supposed to be mutton stew – but it never came off no bloody sheep. Indian goat is what it is! And an

Indian goat what died of malnutrition and bloody old age by the taste of it! You taste it, sir!'

Taggart dipped a paw into the dish and fished out a morsel, dripping with partly congealed gravy. He put it in his mouth.

'Nothing wrong with that!' he snapped. 'What's your complaint?'

'It's bloody uneatable!' Clinton protested angrily, and he was joined by men behind him, who made their own comments on the edibility of the stew. Taggart glowered at them.

'You can eat it or go hungry. Now get back aft where you belong or there'll be a few names going in the log-book. Starting with yours,' he said, with a stare at Clinton. The AB stood his ground.

'I bet the officers aren't eating bloody goat-meat,' said a man at the back.

Taggart rounded on him. 'The officers are making do with bully out of a tin, so that you lot can get what fresh meat is going. It's more than you deserve.'

'We'll settle for bully beef any time instead of that muck,' another man said. There was a chorus of agreement.

Taggart pushed through the throng until he was face to face with the man who had spoken.

'Do you suffer from deafness, sonny?' he asked in a growl. 'I've told you once to clear off aft. I'm not going to do it again.'

He pushed the man away and then shouldered his way towards the alleyway door. He paused on the step.

'I'm going in to finish the food that was set in front of me,' he announced. 'You lot had better not be here by the time I'm finished.'

He turned his back on the seamen, climbed the weather-step, and disappeared towards the saloon. The men did not disperse: standing angrily about and arguing with each other about what they should do next.

With lamentable timing, the *Kildare Glen*'s cook chose that moment to poke his head round the galley-door and add his voice to the proceedings. Enraged by the deck-sailors' unflattering reference to his stew and delighted that the Captain had sent them packing, he sought to hurry the proceedings.

'You heard what the Old Man said,' he shouted. 'You don't deserve good food. Why don't you get back where you belong?'

Clinton took one look at the Cook and glared murder at him.

'This is what I think of your stinking pig-swill!' he roared, and hurled his mess-tin of stew high over the gunwale into the sea. The Cook let out a cry of anguish at the sacrilegious treatment of food he had prepared. He came charging at Clinton, brandishing a large soup-ladle in his raised right arm.

Clinton stood his ground, laughing at the wiry little man's furious charge. It was clear that the able seaman believed that the Cook would not force home his attack against a man almost twice his bodyweight. He under-estimated the fury of the little man. The Cook brought the ladle down on the top of Clinton's skull with all his strength. There was a loud metallic sound, as sharp as a pistol shot, and Clinton staggered back, dazed and reeling. He was still gathering himself in groggy incredulity when he saw a second blow coming. This time he caught the wrist of the Cook as the ladle descended. A shake of that thin wrist was enough to send the ladle clattering on the deck. Now pain added to Clinton's anger. He seized the Cook, lifting his feet clear off the deck and, for a moment, Ben – watching from the lower bridge – thought the big seaman intended to throw the unfortunate Cook into the sea after his stew.

Clinton staggered some ten paces, still holding the

Cook above the deck. The little man was lashing out with his feet and it was no surprise when his captor suddenly let him go and hopped around, clutching a knee-cap. The Cook did not wait to see what damage he had inflicted with the toe of his heavy working boot, but dodged into the galley and attempted to bolt the door.

Hobbling, Clinton went after him and succeeded in getting through the door. By now, some of the catering staff from the pantry had abandoned their saloon serving duties and were coming to the rescue of the beleaguered cook. The sailors from the fo'c'sle decided to stop them and scuffles broke out on and around the No. 3 hatch.

Suddenly, from the galley came a piercing scream. Clinton had again seized the fighting Cook and, having again lifted the little man of his feet and been kicked, had deposited him backside-first on the top of his own stove. The coal-fired iron stove was almost red-hot and scorched the seat of the Cook's trousers black before the cloth flickered into flame. There was a smell of burning flesh.

Watching bemused from his gallery, Ben jumped as the door behind him was suddenly thrown open and a wild-eyed Taggart appeared. In his right hand, he clutched a .45 revolver and, in his left, a pair of handcuffs. He ignored Ben and went running for the ladder, laying into the men scrapping near the hatch and scattering them in all directions. Then he fired a shot in the air and the hostilities ceased as if by magic.

'Aft!' he screamed at the top of his voice. 'Get aft, the lot of you!'

The brawlers took one look at Taggart's contorted face and another at the gun in his hand and scurried like rabbits for the safety of the after-deck. Taggart plunged into the galley from which ringing sounds emerged, as if someone was playing ten-pin bowls with empty milk churns and a cannon ball.

Hearing the noise, Ben could only assume that every pot and pan in the galley had been sent flying. A hint of what had taken place was given when Clinton was bodily ejected from the port-side door and Taggart came bounding after him. He fell on top of the seaman like a lion on its prey and, in a trice, had turned him on his stomach and handcuffed his hands behind his back. Then he yanked him to his feet and, although Clinton could scarcely stand unsupported, frog-marched him towards the bridge. The Captain's face was twisted with fury. As he neared the bridge ladder, he caught sight of Ben standing on the lower bridge. A roar issued from him.

'Don't just stand there like a stalk of bloody rhubarb! Get someone to see to the Cook. This bugger has burnt the skin off his arse!'

A strange paralysis gripped Ben as he decided which way to turn. He could not take his eyes off the seaman, who was swaying and tottering in Taggart's grasp. Clinton's face was bloodied from a split eyebrow and he seemed ready to collapse in a heap. As if reading his thoughts, Taggart roared:

'I'll see to this hooligan. A spell in irons will take some of the sauce out of him! You get hold of Mr Fowler and see to the Cook.'

'Right,' Ben said, dazedly, and moved towards the door to the inside stairway. From the deck below came Taggart's voice as he offered encouragement to his charge:

'Come on, you dung-head! Walk! You're going down the forepeak!'

The galley looked as if it had been hit by a hurricane. Among the debris, Ben and Fowler found the Cook groaning over the sink. He was hanging on to it for support, intent only on making certain that his scorched posterior was free from contact with anything that would aggravate the pain. He did not make a pretty sight. Most of the seat of his pants and the jockey-shorts beneath had been burned away. The skin was blackened and blistered, and adhering to it were flakes of cloth that crumbled at Fowler's gentle touch.

'Better get the pants right off,' Fowler concluded. 'By God, Cookie, you've been done to a turn. I think you'll live, but you won't be sitting down for a month!'

The Cook's reply was a drawn-out wail and a string of obscene references to an able seaman named Clinton and the horrible revenge that he would suffer. The Chief Steward arrived to offer such help as he could provide. Between them he, Ben and Fowler managed to carry the Cook in a face-down position to his cabin above the engine-room. It was Ben's first glimpse inside the quarters there. When, finally, he left Fowler and the Chief Steward to attend to the Cook's discomforts, Ben heard his name called from the adjoining cabin. The door to the room had been fastened back and a curtain fluttered in the entrance. The voice came again.

'Is that you, Mr Darby?'

Ben entered a large cabin with three sets of upper and lower wooden bunks. One of the six bunks was occupied by Richard White.

'How's the invalid?' Ben greeted the boy.

'I'm not too bad. I feel a bit sick and dizzy most of the time, and the heat gets me down. But better than I was.'

'It *is* pretty sticky in here,' Ben said.

'The engine-room ... The heat and the fumes rise – and we get the lot here.'

Ben looked down at the flushed perspiring face.

'Maybe I could speak to the Captain about having you moved? There's a sick bay up forward. They could put you in there.'

'No!' The boy was emphatic, almost shouting the word. He stared at Ben, his eyes pleading. 'Please don't say anything to the Captain.'

Ben shrugged. 'If that's the way you want it. He really scares you, doesn't he?'

'He scares everybody . . . But he hates me.'

'It's his manner. Maybe it's himself he really hates.'

'No, it's not that. He just hates to look at me and I can feel his hate. I don't know what it is — some devil in him. He can't help himself . . . It takes control of him. He just can't bear the sight of me . . . I don't know why . . . There's no reason for it.'

'Forget him. Think about getting better.'

The boy stared up at Ben, his eyes grave and questioning.

'Why is he afraid of *me*? What harm can *I* do him?'

The expression on the boy's face and his questions disconcerted Ben.

'I don't really think you scare the Captain too much, kid,' he said.

'I dream about him all the time,' the boy said, as if he hadn't heard Ben. 'At first, the dreams were bad . . . nightmares. But it's different now. I'm not the one who's frightened. It's him. All I want to do is ask him why it is he hates me but all he does is run away, telling me not to come near him. I run after him but I can never catch up with him . . .'

The boy was so intense that Ben did not know what to say.

'We all get dreams,' he said, acutely aware of how trite he sounded. 'Think about all those stories you're going to write, eh?'

The boy's face brightened.

'Did you read any of my poems?'

'Yeah . . . They're good. And the other stuff, too. I've been meaning to have a talk with you about them but... Well, I've never got round to it. Maybe when you're better, eh?'

'Yes, yes... I'd like that.' The boy sank back on his pillow, a look of contentment on his face. 'I'd like that very much.'

Ben took his leave and walked along the alleyway, emerging from shadow into the bright sunlight of the after-deck. As he blinked against the glare of the sun, he suddenly shivered as if ice had been dangled against his spine. There was no accounting for the unexpected shudder that convulsed through him and chilled his blood. Later, he was to remember it and wonder if it was a presentiment of events to come.

The more the day wore on, the more it seemed to Ben that he was a lone inmate in a floating mad-house where the entire staff were hopelessly crazy and he, alone, was sane. It was no consolation to him that, in displaying their varying degrees of imbecility, his custodians did not pick on him but seemed blissfully unaware of his existence. If they were aware of him at all, it was on the periphery of their excesses of temperament – a distant spectator, who did not count because he had no stake in their battles.

The lower bridge had been the scene of constant comings and goings throughout the afternoon. With Fowler in attendance to act as witness and clerk of the court, Taggart had dealt summarily with all who had been involved in the scuffling that had taken place in the vicinity of the galley, logging the offenders and imposing hefty fines. Any protests of innocence earned the protesters even harsher fines for insolence. The Chief Steward became involved when he tried to plead on behalf of his catering staff who, he maintained, had done no more than try to rescue the Cook from a homicidal attack. Taggart gave him short shrift and ordered him to remain confined to his quarters until further notice.

Not even the Cook escaped Taggart's wrath. On the Captain's orders, he was brought – face-down on a stretcher – to the lower bridge, where he, too, had his name entered in the log-book and his misconduct recorded. Then he was carried back to his bunk to lament the loss of a week's wages in addition to the loss of dignity he had already suffered.

At the behest of his watch, Willem Prins agreed to act as spokesman for the deck-sailors on behalf of the AB, Clinton, who had been incarcerated in the forward paint locker and handcuffed to a stanchion. When he came off watch, at four in the afternoon, Prins sought an audience with Taggart and made the point that, if the ship were torpedoed, a man who was chained below decks in a compartment that was kept battened down would have little chance of escape. He pleaded that, if Clinton had to be restrained, a more humane kind of confinement might be found.

Ben never learned precisely what transpired between the Captain and the Second Officer, although Taggart's shouting was clearly audible in his own cabin. The word 'mutiny', erupting from Taggart, was heard distinctly several times – although it was not quite clear if Prins was being accused or if Taggart was referring to Clinton's crime. Certainly, the *Kildare Glen*'s master was not disposed to relax the nature of the able seaman's confinement, which he considered to be mild to the point of sentimental folly on his part. He listed a number of barbarous alternatives, which he believed would have been much more appropriate but which, in his enlightened way, he had shrunk from employing.

Perhaps if the matter had been left at that – with Taggart simply rejecting the Second Officer's intercession – the courteous young Dutchman would have taken it less to heart. But Taggart did not let it rest at that. He abused the young officer verbally in the most wounding manner, decrying his countrymen as half-German and weaklings who had lain down before the Nazis rather than fight them. He accused Prins of gross disloyalty to his captain and the flag that had given him sanctuary and he threatened the young man with an end-of-voyage report that would finish him as a deck officer and make it hard for him to get work as a deckhand on a Mersey ferry.

At the time, Ben got only an inkling of the cruelty and injustice of Taggart's verbal assault on a young man whose personal record and achievements gave the lie directly to all the vile abuse heaped upon him and his compatriots. What Ben did witness was the effect the incident had on a self-effacing and sensitive officer. Prins went about his duties thereafter like a man in deep shock, withdrawing into himself and indulging in long broody silences that made him unreachable even to those who sought only to be friendly. He did not protest or retaliate or seek to redress the wrong that Taggart had done him. It was just as if some fine and vital spark within had been brutally extinguished.

Before the day was out, the ship's gunners made their own contribution to the unrest that now seethed through the *Kildare Glen*. Half were Royal Navy personnel and half were soldiers of the maritime section of the Royal Artillery and, normally, a friendly rivalry existed between them. A simple game of cards ended all that. An accusation of cheating was the signal for war to break out.

In the free fight that ensued below decks, most of the crockery in the gunners' mess was broken, several noses flattened and a number of lips cut and eyes blackened. A near-fatality also occurred. The gunners messed and slept in converted quarters located in the tween-deck of No. 5 hold. During the free-for-all, one gunner slipped near the hatchway and fell into the empty lower hold.

He was lucky. He could have been killed outright and, at first sight, it looked as if he had been. But when he had been hauled out and cleaned up, it was discovered that his injuries were comparatively light. He had a broken leg, a broken wrist and a face that looked as if it had been battered by a shovel, but he could talk through his broken teeth and the fractured limbs would mend.

The realisation that one of their number had gone down the hold and was possibly dead brought the brawling to an end. It also resulted in Taggart's arrival on the scene, like an avenging angel. Breathing fire and threatening the wrath of God on the now subdued gunners, he supervised the injured man's removal to the sick bay and conducted an investigation, which he pursued with the zeal of a Holy Inquisitor. Although Petty Officer Finney had known nothing about the rumpus until after it was over, Taggart carpeted the senior navyman and let him know that he was being held responsible for the breakdown in discipline of all the DEMS personnel. Taggart's report on the matter would go to the appropriate Navy Authority in Durban, with a recommendation that court-martial proceedings be instituted and the culprits charged with causing an affray, 'to the endangerment of the ship'. Finney did not need to be told that, in time of war, the kind of charges that Taggart intended to press carried penal sentences, and he was a shaken man.

When he tried to persuade Taggart that less drastic action could ensure that the fracas in the gunners' quarters never happened again, the unrelenting ship's captain rounded on him venomously. It was all the PO's fault. He was lazy and inefficient and a bad example to his men. How the PO had ever qualified for three good-conduct stripes was beyond Taggart's understanding. He could only assume it was by subverting his superior officers in the way that he was now trying to subvert

Taggart from what was his plain duty. Well, no amount of pleading and wheedling was going to change Taggart's mind. Indeed, he intended to make Finney the subject of a separate report, listing his failings and laying the blame for the indiscipline of the DEMS personnel where it belonged.

Finney made his way aft to his quarters on the boat-deck, a demoralised and broken man. In all his long service he had never encountered a more vindictive and inflexible will than that shown by Taggart. He had no doubt that Taggart was capable of stirring up the kind of trouble for him that would end his long unblemished career in dishonour and ignominy. With Finney's despair came anger. At heart, he was a tolerant and even-tempered man but – in that moment – if he could have called down a bolt to strike Taggart dead, he would have done so and rejoiced.

They were moving into the benign southern latitudes around Capricorn, where the sun rises and sets with a splendour that is the preserve of the Indian Ocean. The morning serenity of sea and sky was like Nature's apology for the cyclone's rage, but it was lost on the joyless men who surveyed it from the *Kildare Glen*. Taggart had decreed that all hands, with the exception of men on watch, were to muster amidships. Even Ben Darby had been included in the summons and he joined the mill of bodies around the No. 3 hatch, as curious as the next man to learn why Taggart had called the assembly. Unlike several – such as those from watches below who were having to forgo precious sleep to be in attendance – Ben was not eaten by bitter resentment at the unexpected departure from routine. He did, however, wonder what particular bee the master of the *Kildare Glen* had in his bonnet that had kept Taggart awake and pacing the lower bridge for most of the night.

At the best of times Ben slept only fitfully, and he had wakened several times during the previous night to become aware of Taggart's pacing. Up and down, up and down, the heavy footsteps had continued throughout the night, as Taggart had paraded the wooden deck on the fore-side of the bridge cabins. Ben was no less disturbed by the pacing than by the question in his mind as to what new furies Taggart was stoking in the confusion of his.

At precisely ten, Taggart emerged through the screen door of his cabin and took up a Mussolini-like stance at the rail of the deck above. He wore the now customary pyjama-top and pith helmet, but there were two additions to his get-up that did nothing to lesson his slightly ridiculous appearance. Round his waist was fastened a webbing belt and holstered .45. In his hand was a black rolled umbrella. While his astonished crew looked on, Taggart unfurled the umbrella and raised it above his head, so that he stood in shade.

His action was greeted by an audible aside from someone in the throng on the deck:

'He thinks he's the bloody Emperor of Ethiopia.'

The remark brought a titter of laughter and a roar for silence from Taggart. He pointed an accusing finger into the crowd.

'I've got your number, McCabe! Which watch are you on?'

The sailor was startled to have been identified. He hesitated at first, as if thinking of denying responsibility for the remark. But then he smiled weakly and answered Taggart's question.

'Twelve-to-four . . . sir.'

'You'll do day-work, too, until I say otherwise. Seven to eleven every morning.' Taggart's gaze searched the crowd and alighted on the Chief Officer. 'Mr Fowler, take a note of that, will you. See that that man gets a little unpaid overtime. The bridge brightwork needs soogieing. Get him started first thing in the morning.'

Taggart surveyed the faces below him, his bright eyes watchful.

'Is there anyone else who has something clever to say?' he invited. No one spoke. 'Good.' Taggart nodded in a satisfied way. 'Because what I have to say won't take long. All you have to do is listen. And you'd better listen good.'

Taggart allowed his admonition to sink in. Then he began:

'It may not surprise you to know that you are the scummiest lot of work-shy layabouts that I've ever put to sea with. You are *the dregs*. Not fit to call yourself sailors. But that is going to change. Here and now I am reading you the riot act. I am warning you ... I am warning all of you that things are going to be very different. Until now, I've been soft with you ... But that's all over ... From now on, you're going to learn that this is not your Daddy's yacht you're on but *my* ship! *My ship*, d'you hear? And I run a ship the way it ought to be run! If I say work, you work till your back breaks. And if one man steps out of line, *I'll break him*! D'you hear that? I, personally, will break him in small pieces!'

Such was Taggart's vehemence as he delivered the homily, that spittle slavered from his mouth as he bellowed his words. His sullen audience heard him out impassively.

Taggart ended by drawing attention to the number of men who — because of fights, negligence, or their own stupidity — had that morning sought to be excused their duties on the grounds of illness or injury. He glowered down at the Chief Officer.

'Mr Fowler ... I want the name of every man who has not appeared at this muster. My order was for all hands, with the exception of those who could not legitimately leave their posts – but I can see for myself that there's at least half a dozen faces missing. I want a list of the absentees at once. I'll be in my cabin.'

He turned and went through the screen door. His departure triggered a hum of talk as the gathering sheepishly dispersed. Fowler, running around the deck and screeching to be heard, halted the dispersal so that he could check off names against the crew-list he clutched in his hand.

A short time later, Fowler presented himself at the Captain's cabin. Taggart took from him the piece of paper on which had been pencilled seven names and read the list aloud. He paused as he came to the seventh name on the sheet, his face suffused with colour.

'Richard White? The cabin-boy?' Taggart's fierce stare bored at Fowler, flustering him.

'Yes, sir. He's still pretty wobbly on his legs.'

Taggart sucked in his breath.

'He'll be a damned sight wobblier by the time I've finished with him!' he snapped. He waved the sheet of paper in Fowler's face. 'There are some people who seem to think they've signed on for a pleasure cruise, Mr Mate. Well, I'm not having any malingering on this ship! These lead-swingers are going back to work if I have to go and tip them out of their bunks myself!'

Ben's first intimation that young Richard White was on his feet again, and working, came that evening. In expectation of another spectacular Indian Ocean sunset, he went out on the lower bridge to take the air in the last of the daylight. The sight that greeted him, looking aft, was the unexpected one of the cabin-boy labouring to manipulate the fresh-water pump near the galley. His immediate reaction was one of pleasant surprise that the boy had recovered sufficiently to resume his duties.

'Hi there,' he called out. 'How's it going?'

With the intention of speaking to the boy, Ben

descended the ladder to the deck and picked his way along the hatch coaming towards him. The boy seemed to panic when he realised Ben was making for him.

'Hey, don't run away,' Ben called, but with one frightened look over his shoulder, Richard White scrambled through the door to the fiddley and vanished. Ben reached the fiddley door in time to see the boy reach the far side of the grating cat-walk and pause briefly at the starboard-side door.

'No, please . . .!' the boy shouted. 'Stay away from me!'

With that, he clambered over the high step of the far door and disappeared.

Ben made no attempt to follow him, but stood, dismayed and puzzled by the boy's behaviour. Then he shrugged, made his way back to the bridge and promenaded on his favourite piece of deck alone. The boy's flight disturbed him, taking the edge off his pleasure at a sunset more breathtaking than any he had ever seen. The western sky was shot with a magnificent combination of colours, from mother-of pearl white, through duck-egg green, to turquoise, and descending to ribbons of flaming gold at the rim of sea.

'You wouldn't think there was a war on, Mr Darby, would you? Not with a sky like that?'

The voice came from somewhere above Ben and, looking up, he saw Fowler. He was leaning against the safety rail on the bridge above, gloomily surveying the rapidly darkening sky. 'Come on up,' Fowler invited. 'You get a better view from here and there's not long to go. Soon it will be gone for ever.'

Ben joined the Chief Officer on the higher level.

'We've got company tonight,' Fowler said, pointing aft through the haze of smoke billowing from the funnel. Ben followed the pointing hand with his eyes and gave a gasp of delight when he saw the albatross that was following the *Kildare Glen*. It was a magnificent bird, with a wing-span of fully twelve feet. The American watched as it wheeled gracefully across the ship's wake and circled back towards the mainmast before soaring skywards again.

'It's the most majestic thing I've ever seen,' Ben breathed.

'She found us at about five this afternoon,' Fowler said. 'She'll stay with us now . . . Until her fancy takes her somewhere else. She's a long, long way from home.'

'Where do they come from?' Ben asked.

'That one probably came from Kerguelen, way down at the south end of the Roaring Forties. At least, that's where some of 'em breed. But they're not land birds. They spend more time at sea than most sailors . . . as much as nine months at a stretch. God knows how they navigate. They travel thousands of miles.'

'How far is Kerguelen?'

'Well, it's damned near fifty south. Best part of two thousand miles.'

Ben watched the albatross until it was too dark to see it. Next morning, he was out on the lower bridge soon after sun-up. His heart lifted when the first thing he saw was the great long bird. It came gliding in over the waist of the ship, as if to greet him good-morning. Ben was fascinated, and spent much of the day watching the silent albatross wheel in flight.

Several times throughout the day, he became aware of Taggart watching him, watching the albatross. For some reason, Ben's fascination seemed to annoy the Captain, although Taggart said nothing.

The following morning, the albatross was still keeping the ship company. After breakfast, Ben borrowed a set of bridge binoculars and went aft to the four-inch gun-deck to study the bird at close quarters. As he left the bridge, he passed Taggart on the ladder. Taggart ignored Ben's polite greeting, his eyes fixed on the binoculars hanging round the American's neck. The look he flung at Ben as their eyes met was one of naked fury.

At the stern, Ben found that the best viewpoint for watching the bird in flight was from the Bofors nest, which afforded the highest platform. The albatross favoured a circling track astern and liked to loop in low over the poop. As if aware of its admirer, the great bird treated Ben to a series of gliding swoops close to his watch-tower. It was only by chance that, as the bird winged out high to port, Ben happened to glance forward towards the bridge. Taggart was standing on the area of deck outside the radio-room and a movement he made caught Ben's eye. It was enough to make the American's blood run cold.

Ben focused the glasses on the bridge, and the close-up view of the *Kildare Glen*'s captain brought instant confirmation of the fear that had shocked through him seconds before. Taggart was holding a rifle in his hands and the movement Ben had detected was the Captain's act of raising it and aiming it out over the port quarter in the direction of the soaring albatross.

CHAPTER 8

Durban

Anger gave speed to Ben's feet as he ran along the afterdeck. Heart racing, he pounded through the alleyway that skirted the engineers' quarters. With every step he took, he expected to hear the sharp report of a rifleshot from the bridge. But none came. He took the two bridge ladders three steps at a time. His breath was coming in long panting gasps when he hauled himself on to the navigating bridge. In his haste to cut the corner as he mounted the top step, he fell and went sprawling. He looked up to find Taggart grinning down at him evilly.

'Going somewhere in a hurry, Mr Darby?' There was a taunting tone to Taggart's voice. He stood, feet apart, the rifle crooked over one arm. Ben scrambled to his feet and stared at the Captain, still breathless.

'I . . . I thought . . .'

'You thought I was going to shoot that overgrown Antarctic chicken,' Taggart provided. 'And you were going to stop me?'

'Yes.' Ben gulped the word out.

Taggart laughed. 'You disappoint me, Ben. I didn't think you were the superstitious sort.'

'What has superstition got to do with it? You've got no cause to kill that bird.'

'Oh? You're just a bird-lover, is that it? You don't go for that stuff about them being the souls of departed sailors and it being twenty years' bad luck if you put a pellet up their backsides?'

Ben stared at him sullenly.

'I just don't hold with killing defenceless creatures. So why don't you put that rifle away and put my mind at rest?'

Taggart's face darkened. 'Don't tell me what I should or shouldn't do on my own bridge, Mr Darby!'

'I was asking you, politely . . . Please.'

'You go and get stuffed, Yankee! If I fancy a bit of albatross pie, you're not going to stop me.'

Ben persisted. 'Please, Captain. Please put that gun away.'

Taggart affected not to hear. He turned away and made a show of scanning the sky towards the starboard quarter. 'Now where the hell is the airborne turkey?' he murmured. He glanced slyly at Ben and, satisfied that he was watching, began to call in a loud voice: 'Here, goosey-goosey. Here goosey-goosey. The Captain wants a pie for his supper . . .'

At that moment, the albatross came winging in from starboard, less than twenty feet above the mainmast, and glided out over the port quarter. Taggart already had the rifle to his shoulder and was aiming it carefully. Ben could see his finger whitening on the trigger as he moved. He flung himself forward and his upraised hand struck the pointing barrel of the rifle in the instant that the crack of a single shot rang out.

With a cry of anger, Taggart jerked the rifle down in a short jabbing action. The butt struck Ben in the chest and sent him crashing against the housing of the radio-cabin. He leaned back against it, winded and hurt by the blow. But the hurt and the paralysing shortage of breath did not stem the sudden upsurge of hope he felt as he saw the albatross, still in regal flight. The bullet must have passed close, because the bird seemed to change direction sharply. It dived down almost to the surface of the ocean and then, with a single thrust of the great wings, it soared high.

'Looks like you missed it, Captain,' Ben ground out.

'It'll be back,' Taggart said. 'I won't miss a second time.'

But the albatross showed no sign of returning. Ben's heart soared with it as it climbed in the distance. He willed it to keep going and not turn back. An absurd joy filled Ben as the bird continued to distance itself from the ship until it was a speck in the sky, growing even smaller.

'Keep going, old girl,' Ben murmured. 'All the way to Kerguelen or wherever it is you come from.'

Taggart turned on him sharply.

'What did you say?'

'Nothing that would make sense to you, Captain. She's gone – and she won't be back. Looks like you won't be getting any albatross pie.'

Taggart seemed to bite back an angry reply. His face cracked into a forced smile.

'I could have hit it if I'd wanted to. You don't honestly think I would have killed the damn thing, do you?'

Ben met his eyes unwavering.

'You're mean enough.'

The weak smile left Taggart's face.

'Yes, Ben. I'm as mean as you're soft. That bird'll be back. If not today, tomorrow. I've had enough sport for today, though. I'll bag it tomorrow.'

But the next day came and the albatross did not return. And before the day was over, the fate of the albatross had become a matter of secondary importance to Ben. By then, the life or death of a seabird had ceased to matter. What was at stake was a human life.

As Fowler bent over to peer at Ben's hands, the American got the full blast of the other's whisky-laden breath.

This evening, the Chief Officer seemed to have other things on his mind than the slowly healing blisters that Ben displayed. His examination of the sores was cursory.

'They're getting better,' was his quick verdict. 'Give 'em a dab of ointment but leave them open to the air. That'll give them a chance to dry up a bit. I've done as much as I can for them.'

Fowler threw the soiled bandages from Ben's hands into his waste-paper basket.

'Won't be needing them again,' he said. He looked at Ben with an air of uncertain enquiry. 'Can I offer you a snifter, Mr Darby? I've been dying for a snort since eight bells. Keep me company.'

Was it guilt about his drinking that made Fowler lie? As on previous evenings, Ben had waited half an hour after the end of Fowler's watch at eight o'clock before presenting himself at the Chief Officer's cabin. He knew Fowler's first act on escaping from the bridge was to pour himself a stiff tot, and he was sure the Chief Officer had made no departure from the custom this evening. His fiery breath was a giveaway. Ben sensed a purpose in Fowler's invitation, however, and he was curious.

'I'll join you in a small one,' he said.

Fowler fished a whisky bottle from the recesses of his wardrobe, took two glasses from the water-bottle rack on the bulkhead and half-filled both tumblers. He seemed surprised when Ben opted to have his topped up with water. He took his own neat. Fowler bolted back most of the drink in a single gulp and stared at Ben unhappily.

'I'm worried about the Old Man,' he blurted out.

'Captain Taggart?' Ben was taken off guard.

'I . . . I think he's unbalanced. Something will have to be done.'

Ben sipped his drink in order to delay replying and

hide his surprise. Did Fowler want an ally for mutiny? He side-stepped the issue with a question.

'Do you have something in mind?'

'I don't know what the hell to do,' Fowler burst out. It was the confession of a greatly troubled man. Ben was perplexed.

'Look, maybe this is something you shouldn't be discussing with me. I'm a passenger . . . An outsider.'

'Who else can I turn to? You know what he's like. And you've nothing to lose. An independent witness could make all the difference if things come to a head. You must see that! Things can't go on as they are.'

'I . . .' Ben hesitated. 'I . . . I wouldn't do anything desperate if I were you, Mr Fowler. You . . . you could make things worse.' He saw Fowler's quick look of despair and quickly added: 'Look, saying somebody's unbalanced and then having to prove it opens up a whole new can of beans . . .' Ben floundered. He felt impelled to counsel caution. He did not want to be placed in a position of conspirator in any plot to overthrow Taggart – not necessarily because he was unsympathetic to those whom Taggart had pushed to the point of rebellion, but because of a deep uncertainty that open revolt was the right course or that it would achieve anything. If Fowler or anybody else believed that the Captain would meekly accept his own overthrow, then they were crazier than Taggart. There was no saying how he would react, but he would not give up his beloved command without a fight that could have the *Kildare Glen's* decks awash with blood.

'You're on his side, aren't you?' Fowler accused Ben.

'I'm on nobody's side,' Ben declared firmly.

'Then why won't you back me up?'

'Because I don't know just what you have in mind, Mr Fowler – and I don't think I want to know. It's none of my business. If you're not happy with the way the Captain run things and you want to do something about it, why not wait a couple of days or so until we get to Durban and go about it in the right way? Out here in the ocean, you'd just be asking for more trouble than we've already got.'

Fowler poured some more whisky into his glass and seemed to brood over what Ben had said. He did not offer more drink to the American, who, in any case had scarcely made an impression on the level in his glass. Fowler threw some more raw spirit down his throat and glowered at Ben, tormentedly.

'I'll wait,' he decided. 'But I intend to get the bastard. He cooked his goose when he doused that boy with water. That was criminal assault. He could go to gaol for it and, by God, I intend to see that he does!'

'Doused who with water?' Ben had no idea what Fowler was talking about.

Fowler seemed not to hear him. His eyes glinted with malicious triumph at some private prospect of how he would bring Taggart low. 'Yes, I'll wait till Durban,' he said, more to himself than Ben. 'I'll leave him without a leg to stand on. This time, I have the bastard by the short hairs. I'll make him pay for that stupid temper of his. He refused to listen to me . . .'

'What the hell are you talking about, Mr Fowler?' Bewilderment sharpened Ben's tone.

Fowler looked up, as if he had forgotten Ben.

'Didn't you hear about it? That day he read the riot act and called us all scum? He slipped up badly, Mr Darby . . . I tried to tell him that boy would be better left in his bunk, but Captain Bloody Taggart wouldn't listen to me. 'I'll waken the rotten little lead-swinger up!' he said . . . And he half-drowned the little beggar with a bucket of water. . . Nearly washed him out of his bunk . . .'

Ben was staring at Fowler in horror.

'He did that to the kid? The one they call Whitey . . . ?'

'I was right there when he did it,' Fowler confirmed.

'The poor little beggar could hardly stand up, but that didn't stop our great hero of a captain. 'Back to work, you little sod!' he was shouting. And back to work the little sod had to go! Oh, and your name came up, Mr Darby, but you must know about that.'

'I don't know about any of this,' Ben cried. He had risen, agitated, from his seat on Fowler's couch. In his anxiety, he seemed ready to tear the rest of the story from the Chief Officer. 'For God's sake, tell me what you're talking about!'

'Don't tell me Captain Taggart used your name in vain?' Fowler's voice had a mocking ring. 'He accused the boy of having pestered you about something or other – and he said it was to stop . . . that you were getting fed up with it. He threatened to have the boy's hide if he as much as spoke to you. But there's not much chance of that now, is there?'

'What do you mean?'

Fowler frowned. 'You haven't heard then?'

'Heard *what*?' Ben almost shouted.

'The boy collapsed this afternoon. He's back in his bunk and there's not a damn thing I can do for him. He should be in hospital, with proper doctors . . . He's in a coma . . . He'll be lucky if he sees Durban . . .'

The five catering staff, whose quarters Richard White shared, were gathered round the boy's bunk. One of the five had shouted 'Come in' in response to Ben's knock. The youngest of the assistant stewards – a freckle-faced lad of eighteen – was sponging Richard White's face with a cloth. He looked up with anxious eyes from his task to see who had come in.

'How is he?' Ben asksd, whispering without being aware of it. The faces staring at him were grave.

'He just lies there,' one of the five said. 'He hasn't moved an eyelid.'

'He needs a doctor,' said another. 'Old Fowler's out of his depth. He doesn't have a clue, so he does nothing.'

'Does the Captain know how bad he is?' Ben asked.

'He knows, all right! But he says there's nothing he can do for poor Whitey.' It was the young Second Steward who spoke. His tone was bitter.

'Do you think there's something he can do and isn't doing?' Ben stared at the corpse-like form in the bunk, fearing that the boy was already beyond aid of any kind. He seemed scarcely to be breathing. Only the barely perceptible tremble of the half-open mouth gave an indication of flickering life.

'There's plenty the Old Man could be doing,' said the Second Steward. 'We're not that far from the African coast now. We could put into Fort Dauphin or make for Lourenço Marques... Or we could put out a call for other ships with a doctor aboard... We know it means giving our position away for anything that's listening – but there isn't a man on the ship who's not ready to risk that if it means giving Whitey a chance.'

'Maybe if I spoke to Captain?' Ben murmured.

'You'd be wasting your breath,' said the Second Steward. Again his tone was bitter, but as he looked at Ben the angry face softened. 'And yet... Would you talk to him, Mr Darby? Maybe he would listen to you.'

'I'll talk to him,' Ben promised. 'And right now.'

'Thanks... We're all grateful,' the Second Steward said softly. He half-smiled. 'Whitey said you were all right, Mr Darby.'

'I... I can't promise anything. But I'll do my best.' Ben turned to go but paused in the doorway. 'There's just one thing. My geography isn't as good as it should be. Where the hell is Fort Dauphin?'

The Second Steward smiled. 'It's in Madagascar.'

Taggart was in his day-room. Ben's rap on the door was answered with a firm command to enter. He found the *Kildare Glen's* master seated at his desk with his back to the door, writing. Taggart glowered over his shoulder and his eyes seemed to light with pleasure when he saw that Ben was his caller. He sat, listening gravely, as Ben launched without preamble into the reason for his visit. A sixteen-year-old boy was dying because no one on the ship seemed to have appreciated just how ill he was. Ben wasn't blaming anyone, yet, but he guaranteed that there would be hell to pay if something wasn't done pretty damn quick to get the boy medical assistance that would save his life.

Ben spoke with a vehement urgency, rattling on like a runaway train and fully expecting Taggart to flare up and interrupt him before he was finished. But Taggart did not flare up. There was no trace of anger in him as he invited Ben to sit down so that they could talk the matter over calmly.

'Look, Ben,' he said, 'I want you to know that I'm every bit as concerned for the life of that boy as you are. I know I've been hard on him, too hard perhaps, and I'll probably regret it for the rest of my days – but I just can't fly in the face of reality and break all the rules on the outside chance that it'll save that boy. I've been a bastard to him, I know, and making for Fort Dauphin might ease my conscience and make you happier, but it isn't as easy as you seem to think. This ship and the rest of the men in her are far too valuable to the war effort for me to gamble with for the sake of a gesture. And that's all it would be, no matter how humane or well-intentioned – a gesture. Not only is what you are suggesting impractical, there's no guarantee that it would do the least bit of good.'

Ben had never encountered Taggart in this mood. He was calm, he was reasonable, he did not fly off the handle. He took pains to explain that Richard White's best chance of survival would be achieved by the *Kildare Glen* making a quick run into Durban. He had already ordered the Chief Engineer to sit on the safety-valve and drive the ship along as fast as she could go. Ferguson was to double-bank the watches, if necessary, to gain more speed.

Taggart had carefully considered the other options open to him. Fort Dauphin was the nearest port, but the ship was already well to the south of Madagascar and there were a number of reasons why diversion to this French colonial backwater could be ruled out. As for Lourenço Marques ... Well, it was a toss-up whether the Portuguese port was any nearer than Durban. Considering only distances, it was a case of six of one and half a dozen of the other – with Durban getting the vote, not only because it was the ship's destination anyway but because there were rather more compelling reasons for giving Lourenço Marques a wide berth. Taggart showed Ben the transcripts of two radio signals that had been received only that day and which the Captain had not even shown to Fowler. Both were SOS messages from torpedoed ships. The positions given in the distress calls were both close to Lourenço Marques: one, 100 miles off the coast; the other, only twenty-five miles from the port.

'If you or I were dying ... If half the damned crew were dying ... I wouldn't risk the ship by going anywhere near LM,' Taggart told Ben. 'And, for the same reason, I'm not putting out an all-ships call for medical assistance. The risk is too great. It would be an open invitation to any U-boat in these waters to move in – and, if one did, she'd get more than the *Kildare Glen*. She'd get any other damned ship that was stupid enough to answer our call.' He turned an anguish-filled face to Ben. 'You've got to understand, Ben, I can't risk this ship, and other ships ... And maybe hundreds of lives ... for the sake of one boy.'

Ben did not know how to take this new and strangely contrite Taggart. His arguments made sense, cruel sense perhaps, but Ben had no answer to them. If the big man had blustered and bullied and shown no cares or regrets for the plight of Richard White, Ben had been ready to stand his ground and return measure for measure. But he was disarmed and defeated by Taggart's authoritative reasoning and by the visible agony of the decision he had elected to make. This strange man had a genius for destroying all Ben's conceptions of him almost in the very instant that they threatened to become solid certainties. No sooner was Ben convinced that Taggart was mad and evil with it than the man revealed unexpected humanity and the startling clear-sighted sanity of a leader of men who was striving valiantly to overcome the immense stresses placed on him.

When he left Taggart's cabin, Ben sought the dark and silence of the deckway that fronted the bridge accommodation. There, in the draught of cool breeze that whispered from the fore-deck, he tried to sort out the jangling mess of doubts and uncertainties that turned in his mind and undermined his ability to think straight. A moment before, he had heard himself agreeing with Taggart that no more could be done for Richard White than what was already being done. But now Ben shirked the task of relating the outcome of his talk with the Captain to the young men who were gathered anxiously round the cabin-boy's bunk. He felt he had failed them and Richard White. But what more could he do? Ben asked himself the question a thousand times and the same answer came back at him a thousand times. *There was nothing he could do.*

The Jekyll-and-Hyde captain of the *Kildare Glen* had been totally convincing on that point, as he had been in his arguments against diverting the ship from her appointed course.

Ben finally summoned the calm he needed to go aft and face the Second Steward and his young shipmates. He told them about the ships being torpedoed not far from Lourenço Marques and that Taggart had been genuinely concerned for Richard White, in spite of all that had gone before. He found himself arguing Taggart's case for him.

'He's done a con job on you,' the Second Steward told Ben flatly. 'He's got the wind up that poor Whitey's going to snuff it – and he's done a con job to get you on his side.'

'It wasn't like that,' Ben protested. Taggart could be devious, but he wasn't *that* devious. He hadn't been putting on an act for Ben's benefit. He would have over-egged, given it away.

'Why are you sticking up for him then?' asked the Second Steward. 'He's crazy. Everybody knows he's crazy.'

There were plenty of times since they had left Bombay when Ben would have agreed with the young steward – the paranoid behaviour he had witnessed, the mad obsession with sunstroke and the absurd belief that pyjama-jackets had some mystical property of absorbing the sun's rays, the unaccountable desire to shoot a harmless albatross. Oh, there were plenty of reasons why Ben should agree with the common consensus that Taggart was mad. But now, as before, he stepped back from making that judgement.

Ben stood silent before the Second Steward, aware that his silence set him apart: allotted to him the status of alien within the camp. He was not one of them. The young steward spoke into the silence, his voice bitter.

'If Whitey snuffs it, it'll be murder – and it'll be that nut-case on the bridge who done it. Will you stick up for the Old Man then, Mr Darby?'

'Whitey'll make it,' Ben said, but it was fervent hope and a measure of defiance that gave weight to his words. *The boy must not die.* The awfulness of that eventuality was more than he wanted to contemplate.

Ben escaped from the hurtful hostility of the stewards'

quarters but he could not escape from the haunting dread that the comatose boy's life *was* ebbing away. *Will you stick up for the Old Man then, Mr Darby?* The Second Steward's words echoed in Ben's brain, accusing him. They seemed to think that he was some kind of apologist for Taggart, when that wasn't the case at all. Taggart had a lot to answer for, but all that was secondary. All that mattered and all that concerned Ben was that Richard White should hang on to the thread of life that held him.

Taggart was on the bridge with Barraclough when Ben returned to his cabin. It was about ten when he heard the heavy footsteps descending the ladder. He was quickly out of his chair and intercepted the *Kildare Glen's* master as he stepped through the door into the bridge accommodation. The big man stared, startled, at Ben's troubled face.

'Ben . . . anything wrong?'

'It's about Richard White . . . I need your permission . . .'

Taggart listened gravely while Ben outlined the idea that had come to him. He felt that a cabin with five others in it wasn't the best place for anyone as ill as the cabin-boy. And, since the sick bay was already occupied by the injured gunner, why not move Richard White up to the lower bridge, to his own cabin? Ben could sleep on the settee if he had to, but that wouldn't matter. He'd be able to keep an eye on the lad twenty-four hours a day. It was something he wanted to do and he was the only person on the ship who didn't have watches or other duties getting in the way.

Taggart was delighted. Great minds, he said, must think alike. He had come to the conclusion that his own bedroom could be put into use as a temporary hospital room. He had not used his bed since Bombay, preferring to sleep sitting up in the big winged chair in his day-room. Not that he slept very much in any case. But

Ben's idea was the better one. It solved a problem which had been much on Taggart's mind. He was grateful.

The transfer of Richard White to Ben's cabin was effected immediately. The Second Steward and the others in the catering-staff cabin were surprised when informed of the move, but all were agreed that it was a wise one, if somewhat overdue. They willingly helped to stretcher the sick boy to the bridge and see him safely installed in Ben's roomy three-quarter-size bed. But their co-operation was given without indication that Ben had risen any in their estimation. They were polite but coldly distant with him, leaving him aware that the new arrangement was best for Richard White, but that they still considered Ben the Captain's ally.

Taggart remained aloof from the transfer, staying in his cabin until all the activity was over. The stewards had no sooner left Ben with his charge, however, when Taggart's head appeared round the entrance curtain.

'Everything all right, Ben?' he asked, and advanced into the room to stare at the figure on the bed with unhappy eyes. 'I could have done without this trial,' he murmured.

Ben bathed beads of perspiration from White's forehead. The sweating skin was the only sign that the boy lived.

'I'll do everything I can for him,' Ben promised Taggart. 'God, I wish there was more that I could do than this!' He impatiently returned the cloth in his hand to the bowl he had wedged in the chair at the side of the bunk. Then he dried the boy's forehead with a towel. Standing back, he heard Taggart's whisper from behind him:

'There is *something* we can do . . . We can pray . . .'

It was an unlikely assertion, coming from Taggart, and Ben made no reply. He was totally unprepared when Taggart suddenly seized him by the wrist and dropped on his knees at his feet. Ben was pushed awkwardly against the bunk and could only stare in astonishment at the Captain's upturned face. The leathery features were misery-ravaged and the eyes were wild with beseechment as Taggart cried: 'Join with me, Ben. Join with me in asking help!'

Without waiting for Ben's assent, he bowled his head against the American's knee and launched forth words in a flood. Ben, imprisoned against the bunk, was forced to remain uncomfortably upright, a captive witness to Taggart's fervour and disconcerting petition for divine help.

'Dear God in Heaven,' he cried, 'if you exist and if you really give a damn for us poor sailors, listen now to the blackest-hearted sinner that ever walked on two legs and cursed your name... If you really are there, you don't need me to tell you what a rotten bastard I've always been... You'll know, won't you? If you created me, you'll know that I'm not some mealy-mouthed saint but just a sinning sailor that's kicked up hell all his life... Whether, since you made me, you want to take some of the blame for that, I have no way of telling... but I'm not asking any favours for myself... We've got a young lad here who needs you a damned sight more than I do... He never did no harm that I know of... so, if you've got any decency, the least you can do is give him a fighting chance...'

Taggart calmed for a moment, but the pause was short-lived. In a quieter voice, he went on:

'He deserves a fighting chance, God. The little sod is sick because he wouldn't listen to me and got too much sun... It was maybe a stupid thing to do, but when you're a lad of sixteen, you don't always do what you're supposed to do – so please don't hold it against him. If you want to take it out on anybody, take it out on me. I'm the one that deserves it. That's about all I have to say. Except amen.'

He got to his feet and looked sheepishly at Ben. His

face had lost the strained look, and the fervour that had gripped him was dissipated.

'I should have left the speaking to you, Ben,' he mumbled. 'I'm not religious . . . Never was any bloody good at that sort of thing.'

Ben was still a little stunned from the performance. He had never before heard the Almighty addressed with such impassioned irreverence, as if Taggart had been brow-beating an arbiter whose credentials were highly suspect. And yet, for all Taggart's profanity, there had been a simple sincerity in his invitation to be selected as the target of any divine retribution that was coming. It may not have moved God, but it had touched and disturbed Ben Darby. Taggart had never exhibited penitence as one of his strong points.

'I . . . I'm not a very religious kind of guy myself,' Ben murmured. 'I . . . I reckon you took care of things . . .'

Taggart straightened and moved about the cabin, eyes alight, like someone emerging from a trance who is familiarising himself with his surroundings anew and is pleased by what he sees. He seemed almost light-headed. He gave a start of surprise when, having completed a prowling circuit of the cabin, he came face-to-face with Ben – as if, until that moment, it had slipped his mind that he was not alone in the cabin. He stared at Ben, confused, and then beyond the American to the boy in the bunk.

'I . . . I . . . Something came over me.' He stammered the words out in a final rush. He shook his head in bewildered fashion. 'I must be getting old. I feel washed out . . . I . . . I never used to feel this tired.'

'Maybe you should try to get some rest,' Ben said, not unkindly.

'You're right,' Taggart murmured. 'But after eight bells . . . I'll try to grab forty winks after Mr Barraclough has been relieved.'

He left then, with a request to Ben to call him if there

was any change in Richard White's condition or if Ben needed anything. Ben promised to do so, but the moment the Captain had gone he resolutely tried to shut all thought of him from his mind. He resumed his gentle bathing of the unconscious cabin-boy's face and head and settled down for what he knew would be a long vigil.

During the next fifty hours, Ben spent only brief spells away from Richard White's side although there was no shortage of volunteers to take over from him. He was absent only for meals and occasional naps on Taggart's settee.

A third midnight of waiting and watching had passed when Richard White suddenly opened his eyes. He saw Ben and the tremble of a smile passed across his face.

'I'll be all right,' he murmured, and then the eyes closed again.

Ben, in a fever of anxiety, felt for and found the boy's pulse. He heaved a sigh of thankfulness as he detected a flickering beat. Hope rose in him that the boy's brief awakening and moment of recognition meant that a crisis had been reached and passed. But by two in the morning he was less certain. Instead of perspiration moistening the boy's forehead, the skin had become cool to the touch. The pulse beat was scarcely discernible. It was still there, but depressingly faint.

Another beat also changed. The steady rhythm of the *Kildare Glen*'s engines took on a decidedly slower tempo. Ben had to know why. It meant, surely, that Durban harbour was in sight and that the help that Richard White needed was within reach. Not wanting to leave the still figure but in an agony to know what was happening, Ben ran from the cabin and along the alleyway to the stair that led to the chart-room.

'Are we there? Have we reached Durban?' he hollered up the stair. 'Will somebody answer me?' No one did. He dashed back to his cabin. There had been no change in the boy. He continued to lie there, almost corpse-like in the stillness of his repose.

Ben was feeling again for the feeble pulse when he heard footsteps. There was a short knock on the door and Willem Prins was at Ben's side. The Dutchman's face was drawn and unhappy, as it seemed permanently to be these days.

'The Captain heard shouting. Was it you?'

'The ship's slowing down,' Ben said. 'Are we there? Have we arrived? The boy's sinking, I think.'

Prins frowned. 'We'll be in the Natal Roads at first light – we're not allowed to approach the port in darkness. The Captain ordered the engine-room to reduce speed to forty revs . . .'

Ben straightened, his face white with anger.

'We're marking time until it's light?' His voice was shrill with disbelief. 'But every goddamned second is precious. It could mean life or death to this kid!'

Prins shrugged unhappily.

'The Captain gives the orders. Not me.'

'Well go and tell him to change his goddamned orders!' Ben shouted. 'You tell him that we've got to go in, whether it's light or not!'

Prins stood, tight-lipped. He nodded.

'I will tell him the situation.'

Five minutes later, Taggart himself came down. Ben immediately stormed at him, asking him what kind of sailor he was that he refused to risk a port entry at night? Were there rocks? Were there shoals? What was to stop them getting close enough to the shore for a doctor to be sent out? Taggart waited until the American had run short of breath and angry words. He was very calm, ominously so.

'Now shut up and listen to me, Ben Darby,' he snapped. 'I look on you as a friend and that's the only reason you're not getting a fistful of knuckles down the back of your throat. You're the only living person that

I'd let speak to me like that and get away with it. But you're upset and I know why you're upset. These last couple of days must have been hell for you ... But you'd better keep a curb on your tongue because this time you don't know what you're talking about. Taking this ship into Durban is my business! And I *know* my business! You keep your goddamned American nose out of it!'

With that, Taggart turned and walked out. Ben sagged back against the bunk, limp and defeated. He felt utterly drained of strength and hope.

Richard White's skin was now icy to the touch. Ben draped a second blanket over him. The boy's lips seemed dry and were almost white in colour. Ben dribbled water from a teaspoon over the pale mouth: a task at which he had become practised during the previous two days. The boy had had no other nourishment.

The minutes dragged by. Hope began to burgeon again in Ben at sounds of movement on deck: footsteps and voices from the fore-deck; the crack of steam reaching the pipes that skirted the forward hatches; the jarring ring of the bridge telegraph to the engine-room.

The Chief Steward stuck his head round the cabin-door.

'How's the patient, Mr Darby?'

Ben looked up. 'There's still a heart-beat, but he's gone awfully cold. I don't like it.'

The Chief Steward came into the room.

'You look bushed,' he said. 'We're nearly there. Why don't you let me replace you?'

Ben blinked his eyes. They felt like they had weights attached to the lids. He was faint from fatigue, his mind and body functioning in slow motion. Over all crept a pervading dizziness.

'I could use some fresh air,' he admitted.

First he went to the bathroom and splashed water over his face and neck. It revived him a little. Then he walked like a drunk from the cabin and along the alleyway to the outer door. He had to concentrate on lifting a leg over the storm-step. On the lower bridge the cool air of the morning greeted him and he leaned against the guard-rail, looking aft. The ocean rim on the quarter was edged with golden light. Dawn was only minutes away.

Ben abandoned the support of the rail and lurched towards the starboard side. His fatigue fell away at the sight of waves breaking on golden beaches and, beyond, a sentinel array of apartment blocks and majestic hotels. He hurried to the fore-end of the bridge-house, gripped by a heady excitement.

Almost a mile ahead but looking astonishingly close was a breakwater gap of, perhaps, five hundred feet in width. Beyond the breakwater to starboard, the masts of ships in the harbours stood tall. Grey funnels and silo towers and high heron-like cranes rose stark against the sky. To port, the view was dominated by a high, densely treed hill – Durban's famous Bluff, the wooded peninsula that is Cape Natal.

A sleek white launch, flying a red-and-white flag, was gliding over the swell towards the *Kildare Glen* and, as Ben watched, came expertly alongside below the bridge. Two seamen standing by the ladder that had been streamed from the deck helped the pilot aboard. He was followed by three more uniformed officers.

An hour later, the *Kildare Glen* was berthed at a wharf on the Point. But even before the ropes were secured Richard White was being lowered by line on a stretcher to an ambulance that waited on the quayside. Ben watched as the ambulance nosed away from the wharf and headed for the traffic of Point Road. The doctor, who had come out with the pilot, had not been very communicative: refusing to speculate on the boy's chances and saying only that he had to be got into hospital as quickly as possible. Ben got the impression that the doctor simply did not know what was wrong with Richard White and was keeping his options open.

Quarantine regulations had been relaxed because of U-boat activity off Port Elizabeth and a decision made not to keep ships at anchor in the unprotected Natal Roads, but the doctor ruled that no one would be allowed to leave or board the ship until the cabin-boy's illness had been identified.

Ben was in no hurry to rush ashore. His first priority was sleep. He collapsed onto his bunk and, within seconds, he was unconscious.

He was wakened from deep sleep to find Taggart standing over him.

'I've got bad news, Ben,' he said. 'They got the boy to hospital, but he was dead on arrival.'

CHAPTER 9

Ship of Hate

Ben stared up at Taggart, open-mouthed, trying to take in the awful purport of his words. He closed his eyes tight-shut and then opened them again, as if by doing so he might convince himself that he was having a bad dream and that Taggart's sudden manifestation had been imagined.

But Taggart was still there, as solid as ever before him.

'The boy's dead?'

'Yes, Ben. I'm sorry . . . I truly am.'

Grief rose in Ben like a flooding tide. Grief, and a terrible rage. He sat up, swung his legs over the side of the bunk and drew a deep breath, not daring himself to speak. He wanted to flail out with his fists at Taggart. It was *his* fault! The boy was dead because of *him*! And he stood there saying he was *sorry*!

'You're blaming me,' Taggart said. It was a statement, not a question.

Ben made no sign of having heard him, his emotions still churning dangerously. When, finally, he did speak, it was in a voice charged with almost defensive vehemence.

'I'm trying to get it through my head that the boy is dead, for God's sake! He was just a kid . . .' The rising pitch of his voice gave his words an agony of protest. He wanted to scream out against the injustice of Richard White's dying, against the awful finality of death, against its utter and terrible irreversibility. Richard White had been so young, so full of dreams and trusting hope. Now his life was over before it had scarcely begun.

'You're blaming me,' Taggart said again, in the same flat tone as before and, looking at him, Ben saw tears in the big man's eyes. 'They'll all blame me,' he went on. 'And they'll all be right. I didn't want it to happen ... I never wanted him dead ... But it was me who lost him ... Me, who'll have to answer to God for his dying ...'

'You'll have to answer to man first,' Ben said bitterly, reading only self-pity in Taggart's wet-eyed sorrow. Taggart winced, as if Ben had struck him. He stared at the American with the sad air of a man who has been betrayed by a friend, of whom he had expected better.

'Do you include yourself in that, Ben? Do I have to answer to you? Will you sit in judgement over me? Am I already judged?'

'I'm not your goddamned judge!' Ben snapped angrily, disconcerted and confused by the other man's demeanour.

'But you blame me for the boy's death?' Taggart said quietly.

'I din't say so, damn you!'

'You don't need to, Ben. And it doesn't matter anyway. I'm saying it. I blame myself.'

Taggart suddenly looked a hundred years old. His shoulders dropped. His weather-beaten face which, until that moment, had always shown the strength of hewn granite, now seemed crumpled and sagging. He not only looked old, he looked defeated.

'It doesn't matter what happens now,' he said, with weary resignation. 'There's nothing that anybody can say about me or do to me that'll hurt me any more than my own knowledge that maybe I could have saved that boy. I'll bear that hurt with me to the grave. God help me, but his face will haunt me for the rest of my days.'

Taggart's face was bleak with remorse as he spoke and, in spite of himself, Ben could feel only a burdening pity for the big man. It stifled all the anger that, moments before, had seethed for an outlet. Ben had wanted to vent that anger on the man who – if he had not shortened the life of young Richard White – had certainly added to its misery. But rage in the face of Taggart's own misery was meaningless: like striking a man who stands defenceless and invites harder blows as the punishment he seeks.

When Taggart had gone, Ben lay on his bunk, trying to come to terms with the reality of Richard White's death. A few weeks before, he had not even known of the boy's existence; nor Taggart's, for that matter. Now it was as if he himself had scarcely existed before Bombay and he was inextricably entrapped amid the shuttling life-forces of an alien, 10,000-ton floating planet that was a bewildering microcosm of the world he had left. He felt a longing for release to a happier sphere. For here was only tragedy, and more tragedy loomed.

When sleep eventually came to him, Ben's dreaming world was filled with the majestic soaring flight of an albatross that seemed to fill the sky. He woke suddenly with the nightmare vision of the great sea-bird plunging to the deck of the *Kildare Glen* with blood spilling from its breast. It lay there lifeless until Taggart, smoking rifle in hand, came to claim his prize and bear the feathered corpse away. Even as he did so, the hooked bill seemed to dissolve and the bird's head melted into human shape with the waxen face of Richard White.

Ben woke in a lather of sweat. He was trembling, as if seized by fever. He stumbled into the bathroom and let the tepid water from the shower stream over him for more than fifteen minutes, until the terrible images faded from his mind.

The waking nightmare of life on the *Kildare Glen* was only slightly more tolerable. When Ben awoke, it was to find that the *Kildare Glen* had been moved from her berth at the Point to a special quarantine wharf at Salisbury Island. The Port Health Authority officers were taking no chances on a rampant disease being introduced to Durban while the cause of Richard White's death was still unknown. All movement to and from the ship was restricted and Ben, like all the officers and crew, was forbidden to set foot ashore until every man had been subjected to a rigorous medical examination. Three days — they seemed like months to Ben — were to pass before the quarantine was lifted and the *Kildare Glen* was reberthed at a dock on the Point.

While the quarantine lasted, with more than seventy men cooped up on the ship — so near and yet so far from the waiting pleasures of the South African port — the tensions grew. If hatred for Taggart had been rife before, it now permeated the ship like a poisonous cloud. Outrage at the death of the cabin-boy triggered a simmering unrest in all the seamen's messes and reached, on a slightly muted level, into the officers' saloon. While the object of their hatred remained alone and remorse-stricken in his quarters, his name came up in every conversation and, with it, the tag of 'murderer'.

It was impossible to escape from the talk — but Ben tried, by simply walking away when the subject of Taggart came up. Much of the speculation was wild but what appalled Ben, much more than Taggart's degree of culpability for Richard White's death, was the lynch-mob emotion that stoked the dark mutterings. There was more than a desire to strike at Taggart for any wrongs he might have committed against the boy. There was an added, uglier dimension that none tried to conceal: a savage will to exact vengeance for real or imagined personal wrongs, with Richard White's death the excuse.

In trying to remain aloof from the whispering hate directed at Taggart, Ben found himself distanced from those who had hitherto been friendly. He became more and more excluded from their confidences and no longer asked to join the poker and cribbage games in the saloon of an evening. He was pushed into an isolation that he had not deliberately sought. So unpleasant was the atmosphere on the unhappy ship and so much did he feel himself to be the outsider that Ben decided he had had enough of the *Kildare Glen*. He decided that, when the quarantine was lifted, his first priority in Durban would be to investigate other ways and means of completing the journey to Sierra Leone.

Ben was ready to go ashore an hour before the *Kildare Glen's* gangway was lowered when she reberthed on the Point. In his pocket was the cable he had composed for dispatch to Washington. At the US consular office, Ben and his particular problems were taken over by a young officer called Cy Markham, who was prepared to go out of his way to be helpful.

'Leave everything to me,' he advised Ben. 'It may take a little time but, with a little help from my friends, you can kiss that freighter good-bye.'

Ben did not announce his intentions to anyone on the *Kildare Glen*, preferring to wait until Markham had done his work. Nor did he book into an hotel ashore, as Markham suggested. Now that he had put his plans into motion, he had strange flutterings of guilt about quitting the *Kildare Glen*. He assuaged these feelings by continuing to use the ship as his base while he took the opportunity to see as much of Durban as possible.

When he was on the ship, notably in the mornings he found that although the tensions of the days in quarantine had not gone, they had markedly subsided. It was as if the high emotions of that period were being held in abeyance. Two events had produced a sobering effect. The first was the arrival on the *Kildare Glen* of a police officer, apparently at the behest of one of the crew, to interview members of the ship's company about the circumstances of Richard White's illness and death. The second was the display of a notice announcing a coroner's inquest. From the ship's agent Ben received an official summons requesting his attendance, with the advice that he should hold himself in readiness to testify.

Ben saw little of Taggart, who had a constant stream of visitors in the mornings and spent the afternoons and evenings ashore. He looked more bowed and careworn than ever and Ben wondered how he managed to face up to the considerable demands of normal port business, with the added worry of what would come out at the looming inquest. The *Kildare Glen* was to be drydocked and gangs of workmen had already boarded the ship to repair the damage wrought by the cyclone.

The prospect of having to give evidence at the inquest dismayed Ben. He foresaw only one outcome: the public disgrace and downfall of Captain William Taggart. Fowler, for one, had predicted nothing less when he had button-holed Ben one evening at the Salisbury Island quarantine berth. Ben had walked away, uninterested in the Chief Officer's boast that he held Taggart's future in his hand and that he intended to make the Captain regret tipping water over Richard White.

'That was criminal assault,' Fowler had crowed. 'It's the one thing he can be nailed for — and it'll finish him. He could go to gaol for it!'

Ben had excused himself, without being too polite about it. He said he didn't really give a goddamn, one way or the other. For all that, he found Fowler's malice a little more than he could stomach.

On the morning after he had first met Markham, Ben

set off ashore at ten-thirty and was dismayed to find himself overtaken by Fowler as he neared the dock gate. The Chief Officer was also heading for the city and suggested that they share a taxi. Abhorring the idea, Ben got out of the situation by resorting to a lie. He said he didn't want transport and intended to walk into town. He liked to explore. Fowler accepted the explanation but plainly thought Ben was mad: a conclusion with which Ben was willing to concur an hour later as he trudged along Point Road in ninety-degree heat. The road between the docks and central Durban led through the least salubrious part of the city. Here, black skins predominated, and beyond the frontage of mean shops and shabby stucco dwellings Ben glimpsed the conglomeration of shanty homes that housed tens of thousands of Durban's Bantu population.

White pedestrians were a rare sight in Point Road. Nor was there any welcome for them, Ben decided, as he found himself on the receiving end of sullen and resentful stares. The silent hostility he encountered was unnerving. Loungers at street corners spat in the dust at his feet as he passed. The resentment saddened Ben and made him uneasy. For a man whose faults did not include the usual prejudices of race and nationality, it was an uncomfortable experience to feel despised because his skin was white.

His long sweaty walk along Point Road was to sour all his later impressions of Durban, because no matter where he went in the city he was unable to escape from the undercurrent of tension created by the sharp divisions between white society and black. Although he was assured that Durban was one of the most liberal of communities in the Union of South Africa, the feeling never left him that, below the surface calm and orderliness, a time-bomb was quietly ticking away. One day it would explode.

Although, in India, he had been vilified by a street-corner politician and set upon by a mob, Ben had never felt threatened by the Indian people as a whole. The Indians were generally friendly and welcoming. South Africa was uncomfortably different. No one threatened violence, there was no visible sign of political unrest or rebellion – and yet the air shimmered with menace, like a tinder-dry prairie in a hot spell. One spark could set the firmament alight from horizon to horizon.

Ben spoke to Markham about it when, after his walk into town, he lunched with the consular officer in a smart city restaurant. Markham, who hailed from Memphis and came from an old Confederate family, had a rather cavalier attitude to racial questions and seemed to find Ben's sensitivity amusing. The Union of South Africa, he reckoned, was the most stable place in the whole continent of Africa, and Durban, climatically and socially, was one of the most pleasant places to live on the face of the earth.

To impress on Ben what a delightful place Durban could be, Markham insisted on showing him around. They toured in his lively little two-seater sports car, circling as far as the Umgeni River in the north and meandering through the fine residential homes that dotted the low-lying hills of Berea. Coming back to the central sprawl of Durban city – which was unremarkable architecturally and lacked a focal point with the confluent character of Times Square or Piccadilly Circus – Markham parked in a broad avenue where a line of rickshaws waited for hire. They were tended by tall Zulus wearing the full tribal regalia of leopard skins, ostrich-feather head-dresses and a colourful assortment of body adornments, strung from neck and limbs.

Ben could not be persuaded by Markham to engage one of the rickshaws for a short run. There was something repellent to Ben in the sight of these descendants of a proud warrior race reduced to tourist gimmickry in order to earn a living. He was reminded of the circus Indian braves he had seen as a boy and their re-enactment of wagon-train attacks. The redskins always lost the battles, and to a boy brought up on the wilderness stories of Fenimore Cooper, with his concept of the noble savage, there was something grotesquely pathetic about the sideshow debasement of the native Americans.

'You're a funny cuss,' Markham told him good-naturedly. 'You're the first newspaper guy I've met who's a starry-eyed romantic. You can take my word for it that these rickshaw Zulus are sharper than New York cabbies when it comes to making a buck. They don't need spears any more. They'd take you for your last dime and make you feel they were doing you a favour.'

From the sea, Durban had reminded Ben of Miami. A trip to the city's sea-front revealed other similarities and heightened yet again his uneasy awareness of the divisions between black and white. A golden shore — where bathers and sun-worshippers thronged from dawn to dusk — fronted a mile or more of hotels and luxurious apartment blocks and was reserved for the golden-skinned. This was the playground for those fair-skinned tribes of Africa, whose origins were Britannic and Germanic, rather than Bamangwato or Basuto.

The two men sat at an umbrella-shaded table, sipping ice-cream sodas and watching the passing parade of nubile blondes in scanty swim-suits. They descended to the beach by means of a white gate, which proclaimed 'Europeans Only'.

'This must be paradise after Bombay,' Markham said to Ben.

'The scenery's good,' Ben replied, refraining from voicing his deeply felt unease that, perhaps, it was a fool's paradise. If the sun-worshippers on the beach were unaware of the silent resentment he had encountered on his walk from the docks, then their golden skins must be a great deal thicker than they looked.

Later, Ben apologised to Markham for being such rotten company. The consular officer waved away his apologies.

'It's that goddamned ship,' he said. 'You've had a rough time, what with one thing and another. Which reminds me ... I've fixed up for you to have a medical check the day after tomorrow. Your people in Washington have been worried about you.'

'You've heard from Washington?' Ben was surprised.

Markham smiled. 'I wasn't supposed to tell you but you might as well know. I've got orders to look after you and treat you like you were precious china. They got the idea in Washington that you skipped hospital in Bombay sooner than was good for you and they're frightened you'll crack up. You must be well-connected in DC. I've been told to pull out the stops because you're a very valuable property.'

Ben declined, nevertheless, a fresh invitation by Markham to install himself in a Durban hotel.

'I'll quit the ship when you've found me another way to get to Freetown,' Ben told him. 'Until then I'll stick with it.'

'Freetown isn't an easy place to get to,' Markham said. 'I don't want to make any promises. The only alternative might be another ship heading round the coast from here. But is that what you've got in mind?'

'I've got only one thing in mind right now,' Ben said. 'And that's the inquest that's coming up about that kid's death. I don't sleep easy at nights thinking about it.'

'I'll make a point of being there,' Markham promises, 'if only to give you moral support.'

It was a promise that Markham was unable to keep. On the day of the inquest, he was refused admittance to the court. The proceedings were to be conducted *in camera*.

The long narrow chamber looked more like a schoolroom than a court-room. Along one side ran a gallery for the public and press. It was stepped only about two feet above the floor of the court and was empty. The bench, from which the Coroner would preside, was a plain oak table, slightly elevated above almost identical oak tables in the well of the court. A blackboard to one side of the Coroner's bench augmented the school-room impression, as did the desk-like wooden benches in neat rows in the body of the chamber.

After inspecting Ben's papers at the door, an official directed the American to the cross-benches where a number of men from the *Kildare Glen* were already seated. Ben could see Taggart deep in conversation with a plump, neat-suited civilian at the very front. In that area of the court there was a small enclave of naval officers and civilians, whom Ben took to be lawyers. All seemed to be flourishing sheaves of paper.

The Coroner entered the court from a door somewhere beyond the blackboard. He was a tall man, with a slight stoop and with horn-rimmed glasses perched on the bridge of his aquiline nose. He invited the court to be seated – they had been summoned to their feet in anticipation of his entry – and he surveyed the gathering over the top of his spectacles.

His first remarks were addressed to a court officer.

'Have the identities of all present been verified and the names recorded?' he asked. The official confirmed that they had and that Lieutenant-Commander Brook was in possession of the list. The Coroner asked if Lieutenant-Commander Brook would kindly make himself known to the court.

A naval officer with smoothed-down blond hair stood up.

'Commander,' said the Coroner, 'the military authorities have seen fit to place certain restrictions on the normal function of this court . . . for reasons that I fully understand . . . But am I correct in taking it that those now present include all who may be required to testify?'

'With the exception of expert witnesses, your Honour. That is, civilians who were not directly involved in the events preceding the tragedy in question but who may be able now to throw light on it because of their special qualifications in medicine and so on.'

'I understand. And these gentlemen are in attendance? They are in the building?'

'Yes, your Honour. They may be called when required.'

'And those officers and men who served in the same ship as the deceased and whose testimony may be required – they are all in court at this time?'

'Yes, your Honour.'

'It is not your wish to exclude them from the proceedings until their testimony is required? Their interests may conflict.'

'It was hoped, your Honour, that in the interests of naval security, these proceedings would be short and decisive and that any conflicts of interest – if there are any – would be speedily resolved. It may not be necessary to hear any or all of the witnesses whose presence has been requested if a formal verdict is inevitable.'

The Coroner sucked in his breath audibly.

'You may not presume on the inevitability of any verdict,' he said sternly. 'That will be decided by the court and the facts put before it. However, I see no reason to exclude from the proceedings those officers and men who served with the deceased and whom he no doubt counted as his friends and shipmates. Those who wish to testify will be given an opportunity to do so.'

After what seemed an age, the inquest into the death of Richard White finally got under way, with press and public excluded under the terms of the War Emergency Act. The first witness called was the doctor who boarded the *Kildare Glen* and accompanied Richard White to the Point Hospital. His evidence was formal and brief, amounting to little more than stating that the boy had died between 7.05 and 7.25 a.m. on the journey from ship to hospital.

'Did you certify that the young seaman was dead?' the Coroner asked.

'I did, your Honour.'

'And you certified the cause of death as cardiac arrest, which could apply to any fatality from death by gunshot wounds to straightforward heart-failure?'

'That is true, your Honour.'

'You did not know what had caused the cardiac arrest, only that it had occurred?'

'Yes, your Honour. The deceased was in a coma when I found him. The captain of the ship informed me that he had suffered sunstroke.'

'But you had your doubts, Doctor?'

'I was almost certain that the deceased's comatose condition was not the result of sunstroke.'

'But you had no certainty what had caused the condition?'

'None at all, your Honour. I was quite baffled by it. I suspected all sorts of things . . . The admission to the blood-stream of a drug . . . or a poison such as curare, which would have affected the neuromuscular system. For that reason, I hesitated to administer stimulative or reviving drugs. I decided that the only course was to get the patient to hospital as speedily as possible.'

'I see,' said the Coroner. 'Did you suspect any kind of foul play?'

'No, your Honour. An accident, perhaps, but not foul play.'

'And you are still of that view?'

'Having seen the post-mortem report, your Honour, I now have no doubt that the boy's tragic death was from natural causes.'

'Ah, yes, the post-mortem report. Let us not anticipate that. We shall come to it in due course. In the meantime, Doctor, you may stand down ... unless anyone has any questions ...?'

No one had any questions for the doctor. The Coroner consulted a piece of paper in front of him and then looked around the court-room over the top of his glasses.

'I propose to leave the pathologist's report until later,' he said. 'It may be expeditious, first, to deal with a contentious issue of which I have been given warning. Will Walter Brownsmith McQueen please take the stand?'

Heads turned to watch McQueen's progress from the cross-bench in front of Ben to the witness-stand. The red-headed fireman was clad in denim trousers and a bright checkered shirt. While he was sworn in, he kept his eyes firmly fixed on Taggart with unwavering hostility. The *Kildare Glen's* captain, who was sitting only a few feet away from the witness-stand – facing it – affected not to notice the unrelenting stare.

'Mr McQueen,' said the Coroner, 'I should warn you that it is tantamount to public mischief to waste the time of a court of law and that it will be doing neither the court nor yourself a service if it is your intention to waste its time. You volunteered certain allegations to the police of this city, on which they have not so far acted. As a result of your persistence, however, I have agreed to let you air those allegations in this court, so that they may be answered. If your allegations are found to have substance – and they are serious charges you make – then this court has the authority to recommend any action that is deemed appropriate. Do you understand?'

'Yes, sir.'

'Well, will you tell the court in your own words why, in the first instance, you saw fit to complain to the police?'

'I did it for the dead boy, sir. I say he was murdered.' McQueen's eyes levelled on Taggart and the fireman raised an accusing finger. 'And it was that bastard there that did it!'

The Coroner rapped sharply with his gavel.

'Mr McQueen! Mr McQueen! We will have no more outbursts like that! And you will moderate your language. Do you hear?'

'I'm sorry, sir,' McQueen mumbled. 'It's just that me blood boils when I think of what he done to that lad.'

'That may be so,' said the Coroner, 'but it is not enough to make accusations. You must be able to substantiate them. What facts do you have to back up your grave allegation that the deceased, Richard White, was murdered?'

'The facts speak for themselves, your Honour. I know it was murder . . . Everybody on the ship knows it was murder. I'm just the only one with the guts to say it!'

The Coroner frowned impatiently.

'Facts, Mr McQueen. Facts. Whom do you accuse of committing this murder?'

'Taggard did it! Captain William Bloody Taggart!'

Again the Coroner rapped with his gavel.

'I shall not warn you again, Mr McQueen. If you do not control your language and your emotions, I shall have you removed from this court.'

Chastened by the warning, McQueen allowed himself to be led by the Coroner to relate the events of the voyage from Bombay. Taggart sat with head bowed as McQueen told of the Captain's bullying of the cabin-boy: how he was overworked to the point of collapse and how, despite his obvious illness, the Captain forced the boy back to work by tipping a bucket of water over him. Everything came out. McQueen alleged that Taggart was insane. He told how Taggart had assembled the officers and crew and called them all scum, how he had been obsessed by the idea that the entire crew would come down with sunstroke and had instituted all kinds of crazy regulations. At the end of it, the Coroner asked if anyone wished to question the witness and it was then that the plump civilian in the well-tailored suit came forward. His name was De Gruyt and he had been retained as counsel to act for Captain William Taggart and the owners of the *Kildare Glen*.

He stared at McQueen with contempt.

'You have a sorry record, Mr McQueen – is that not so?'

'My record is as good as the next man's.'

De Gruyt raised his eyebrows and turned to the Coroner.

'With your permission, your Honour, I should like to read out to the court the copies of several entries in the official log of the *Kildare Glen*.'

'Are they relevant, Mr De Gruyt?'

'They say something about the character of this witness, your Honour. It is a list of misdemeanours, involving violence and other misconduct, for which the witness was punished but which left him with an abiding grudge against a master seaman, whose own record is not only without blemish but quite illustrious.'

'Proceed, Mr De Gruyt.'

McQueen's crime sheet was considerable. When De Gruyt reached that part of it that reported the logging that followed the protest about the cigarette issue, McQueen interrupted angrily:

'It's all lies. It was him that punched me! I never lifted a hand against him!'

De Gruyt waited with a pained expression on his face while the Coroner sharply reprimanded the fireman, warning him yet again that such outbursts would not be tolerated. Turning to De Gruyt, the Coroner suggested that the court had heard sufficient about McQueen's disciplinary record. Perhaps he could now get on with questioning the witness? De Gruyt accepted the direction gracefully.

'Mr McQueen,' he said, 'does the official record lie? Is it not true that because of your drunken behaviour in the *Kildare Glen*'s last port of call, Captain Taggart had to take disciplinary action against you?'

'Yes, but...'

'No buts, Mr McQueen,' interrupted De Gruyt. 'A straightforward yes or no will suffice! Is it not also true that on the two occasions when you attempted to assault the master of your ship and he was forced to defend himself, you failed because he is much the stronger man?'

'It was him that went for me!'

De Gruyt shook his head wearily.

'Mr McQueen, please answer the question. Was it not the case that you came off second best?'

'I was the one that was hurt, if that's what you mean.'

'Hurt, Mr McQueen? You had bones broken? You were cut about the face? You were badly marked?'

'No, but...'

'A straightforward no is sufficient, Mr McQueen. You were not seriously hurt. That's strange, Mr McQueen. Because Captain Taggart is a very big man. I would suggest that if he seriously chose to mix it with anyone, he could put that person in hospital for a month. Wouldn't you agree?'

'Maybe he could.'

'I *know* he could, Mr McQueen. But the fact is that on those occasions when you sought to attack him, Captain Taggart chose not to assert his superior strength. He used only sufficient force to make you desist from your folly.' McQueen tried to interrupt but De Gruyt ignored the attempt and talked across him, raising his voice. 'You did not like being overpowered, Mr McQueen. You fancy yourself as a tough guy and it was humiliating to be brought to account by a better man. You hate Captain Taggart for it, don't you?'

'I hate him all right!' McQueen agreed passionately.

'And you'd do anything, say anything, to get your own back on him, wouldn't you?'

'That's not how it is!'

'You deny harbouring a grudge against Captain Taggart?'

'No, I don't deny it. I bear a grudge against him all right, but . . .'

'There's no need to qualify it,' De Gruyt broke in. 'Is it not true that, not once but many times, in the presence of witnesses, you swore that you would get your own back on Captain Taggart? That you would get your revenge?'

'Yes, but . . .'

'Yes, Mr McQueen. Yes!' De Gruyt echoed the admission. 'And this is your way of getting that revenge! By making this vile accusation that Captain Taggart was somehow responsible for the death of the cabin-boy, Richard White.'

'It's justice I'm interested in!' McQueen cried out defensively. 'Taggart murdered that boy!'

De Gruyt stared at the fireman with icy contempt.

'You dare make the accusation again? Let us have some facts then, Mr McQueen. First, let us examine your allegation that the Captain criminally assaulted the boy by dousing him with water while he lay ill and defenceless. You saw the incident?'

'No, but everybody knows it is true.'

'Do they? Do they, indeed! If you did not witness the incident, how did you come to learn of it?'

'Somebody told me.'

'Ah, hearsay! Who told you?'

'I don't know. Everybody was talking about it.'

'But you cannot name anyone who actually witnessed the incident?'

'No.'

'No, Mr McQueen. You cannot name any witnesses because there are no witnesses. The whole thing is no more than a malicious rumour that gained circulation because it suited people like yourself to blacken the Captain's name.'

'The Mate was there. He's supposed to have seen what happened.'

'You're referring to Mr Fowler, the Chief Officer? Are you saying that Mr Fowler started this wicked rumour?'

'You'd better ask him.'

'Oh, I will, Mr McQueen. I will! But it is your testimony that interests the court at this moment. It seems to be somewhat lacking in substance, wouldn't you agree?'

'I'm telling the truth.'

'Are you?' De Gruyt grimaced in a way that left the court in no doubt of the value he placed on McQueen's assertion. 'How well did you know the deceased?'

'Not very well.'

'He was not a friend? And you seldom came in contact with him as a result of your work or his?'

'We were in different departments. There's not much mixing.'

'You lived in different parts of the ship, you did not mix socially, you hardly had any communication whatever with the deceased?'

'I don't know what you mean.'

'Did you ever hold a conversation with Richard White?'

'Not that I can remember.'

De Gruyt allowed the court to savour his look of incredulity.

'You had no contact with this boy and yet, earlier, you furnished this court with a catalogue of injustices which, you say, the boy suffered at the hands of Captain Taggart. Did you actually see any of this bullying that you spoke about?'

'I heard about it.'

De Gruyt threw a look to the heavens.

'Hearsay is not evidence, Mr McQueen. Do you not think it strange that you alone from the crew of the *Kildare Glen* have seen fit to make the preposterous allegations you have? Why has no one else come forward?'

'Because they don't have the guts. They're frightened.'

'Frightened of what, Mr McQueen? Frightened of being shown to be malicious trouble-makers like yourself?' De Gruyt gave McQueen no time to voice the angry reply that was on his lips. 'No!' he commanded. 'Do not trouble to answer the last question. I think that this court has heard quite enough from you.'

'All you've done is twisted my words,' McQueen protested, before De Gruyt leapt in to silence him.

'No, Mr McQueen! You are the one who has done the twisting. Because your whole outlook is twisted . . . Twisted with hate for a good and conscientious officer.' He turned abruptly to address the Coroner. 'Your Honour, I have no further questions for this wretched man. I submit that his testimony is worthless.'

The sentiment was one with which the Coroner seemed to be in accord. He scowled over his glasses at a bewildered and unhappy McQueen.

'You may stand down,' he commanded. 'But before you do, let me give you this advice. On your own admission, you are a man who has been activated by malice. I caution you against further acts that needlessly consume the time and patience of those who serve the law in Natal Province. I would remind you that the law is equipped to deal with those who seek to bring it into contempt and that the full weight of that law will be brought down upon you if you seek to use it as a vehicle for the pursuit of your own misguided ends. It is only by the indulgence of this court that you are being allowed to step down without being made to answer elsewhere for conduct that could be construed as public mischief, at the very least. You may consider yourself fortunate under the circumstances.'

McQueen stepped down, but seemed reluctant to leave the centre of the court. He turned, wild-eyed, to face the Coroner.

'Is this justice?' he cried. 'Is this what you call justice?'

It was more than the Coroner could take.

'Remove that man!' he ordered, and two burly officers hurried to obey his command. McQueen was bundled, protesting, from the chamber.

Stunned by the drama, Ben was scarcely aware that the name being called from the bench was his own. He made his way forward, almost in a daze, and took the oath, repeating the words haltingly from the card that was pushed into his hand. He longed to be anywhere in the world but where he was at that moment. There was nothing he could say that would bring Richard White back from the dead, so what was the point of all this? Ben was still shaken by the ordeal to which McQueen had been subjected. He liked McQueen, although he himself was unable to view the world in the same uncompromising black-and-white terms that McQueen saw it.

All through McQueen's time in the witness-stand, Ben had been tortured by the dread that here, in this court-room, was where he was finally going to have to take sides. The issue would be forced on him. He would not be allowed any room for equivocation. He would not be given any latitude to say yes, McQueen is right but it's not nearly so straightforward as McQueen seems to think. No more would he be allowed to say yes, Taggart did treat the boy atrociously but not by the standards by which he drives himself. Taggart's standards were not Ben's standards and, although he shrank from condemning them, he would have had equal difficulty in bringing himself to defend them. His picture of the man was still incomplete and, until it was complete – until he comprehended – he could not say that what he saw was the *truth*. Until he was face to face with the *truth*, he could not come down from the fence on which he sat. His need to *understand* was greater than his need to right a wrong. McQueen had screamed for justice, but justice would not be served by crucifying Taggart – and certainly not if it was encumbent on Ben Darby to supply the first nail. No, that kind of devotion to justice had to come from those who cherished revenge with an equal fervour – like McQueen, perhaps, or Fowler, who had vowed vengeance on Taggart in Ben's presence.

In the witness-stand, it took Ben conscious effort to pay attention to the Coroner while the thoughts flashing in his mind were so clamorous a distraction. He looked up, startled, when he realised that the Coroner had addressed the same question to him twice.

'You are a war correspondent, Mr Darby?'

'Yes, your Honour.'

'And you fully realise that you are forbidden to write or report on these proceedings because of the secrecy that, by necessity, must surround the movement and identification of merchant shipping in time of war?'

'I have signed a document to that effect, sir.'

'We shall not take up much of your time, Mr Darby. I did, however, wish it to be placed on the record that your appearance here was not in a professional capacity but by virtue of the fact that you knew the deceased and demonstrated some concern for his welfare during the last days of his life.'

'I did what I could . . . It was not enough.'

'Nevertheless, Mr Darby, from depositions before me, it is plain that you sacrificed your own comforts to provide a degree of privacy and quiet for the deceased when it was apparent how ill he was, and that you tended him quite selflessly when there was certainly no obligation on your part to do so. You have heard allegations that Richard White's death was, at the best, the outcome of criminal negligence on the part of the *Kildare Glen*'s master. As someone who was closely involved with the deceased, do you have evidence to offer that would support those allegations.'

Ben stared unhappily at the Coroner. He could feel beads of sweat moistening his brow.

'No, your Honour.'

'You hesitated, Mr Darby. Is there doubt in your mind? As someone who showed himself to be concerned for the deceased, you are in a unique position to acquaint the court with the circumstances that prevailed aboard the *Kildare Glen*. Did you witness any acts of brutality or other irregularity that contributed directly or indirectly to the death of Richard White?'

'Acts of brutality . . . in a physical sense? No.'

'The deceased was ill-treated in other ways?'

'He was made to work very hard . . . He was not strong.'

'Isn't hard work part and parcel of life at sea? Are you suggesting, Mr Darby, that the deceased was worked excessively? To the detriment of his health?'

'That's a judgement I should not like to make, sir. He seemed too frail for the work he had to do.'

'In the Captain's preliminary deposition, he states that the deceased first took unwell on deck and that it was you who drew his attention to the fact. He says you were angry and upset because you thought the boy was being driven too hard. Is that correct?'

'Yes,' Ben said, surprised that Taggart had made such an admission and wondering what else he might have said in his deposition. The Coroner frowned across at Ben.

'And what action did the Captain subsequently take?'

'Mr Fowler, the Chief Officer, treated the boy for fever.'

'The illness was diagnosed as sunstroke, I believe. The deceased was running a high temperature and complained of blinding headache. He was kept in his bunk for seven days?'

'Yes,' Ben said.

'You were quite satisfied then with the outcome of your – hem – talk with the Captain? He took seriously your – hem – representation that the boy needed rest?'

'Yes, your Honour.'

'And what do you know of the circumstances of the boy's return to normal work . . . and the alleged water-throwing?'

'Nothing, sir. The first indication that I had of his return to work was when I saw him on deck.' Ben had no intention of repeating what Fowler had said about the water-throwing. Quite apart from the fact that it would have been volunteering hearsay, Ben had no wish to be associated with that particular bombshell. He was already dreading the moment when Fowler would unleash it and the malicious pleasure with which he would do so. Ben had no doubt that Fowler's testimony was what would finally damn Taggart – and he was surprised that the knowledge pained him. He wondered if Taggart suspected how intent Fowler was on revenge and how the Chief Officer intended to exact it.

The Coroner had few more questions for Ben but De Gruyt rose and indicated that he would like to question the witness. He smiled at Ben, encouragingly.

'Mr Darby, you were present on the bridge, were you not, when Captain Taggart ejected the fireman, McQueen, from his quarters on the occasion of some complaint about a cigarette issue? Is that not so?'

'Yes.'

'McQueen threatened the Captain, did he not?'

'Yes,' Ben said softly.

'Do you remember his words?' asked the lawyer.

'Not the exact words . . .'

'But they were threatening words, you do remember that?'

'He said something about getting his own back.'

'Mr Darby, I put it to you that his exact words were: "I'll get you for this, you bastard!" Would you agree that these were the words McQueen used?'

'Yes,' Ben said, his voice a whisper.

'Speak up, Mr Darby.'

'Yes,' Ben repeated, more loudly.

'Thank you, Mr Darby,' De Gruyt said. 'There is just one more thing I should like to establish. Captain Taggart himself will testify that he is a hard man, a stern disciplinarian. There were times, were there not, when you thought he was unduly hard on the cabin-boy, Richard White?'

'Yes,' Ben said, again his voice faint.

'Yes,' repeated De Gruyt, 'and you had a couple of altercations with the Captain as a result of this?' Ben stared at the lawyer, his lips dry. 'You may speak freely, Mr Darby,' De Gruyt encouraged. 'Captain Taggart has been very frank on this matter. He expects you to be equally so. The Captain thought the boy was lazy and a shirker but you didn't agree and you told the Captain so.'

'Yes,' Ben said.

De Gruyt smiled. 'Mr Darby, as a rule, ships' captains do not take kindly to passengers advising them on how their ship should be run . . . But Captain Taggart is not an unreasonable man. He accepted that, in his preoccupation with the preservation of his ship from destruction by enemy forces and from the ravages of exceptionally severe weather conditions, he may have been unduly harsh in dealing with the deceased. He heeded what you said and took action accordingly. Is this not so?'

'Yes . . . Yes, he did.'

'He accepted that the boy might not be well and he got Mr Fowler, the Chief Officer, to attend to him medically? As a result of which, the deceased was excused all duties and confined to his bunk for a week?'

'Yes,' Ben agreed.

'Where the boy's condition steadily improved?'

'So I was told. I don't know . . .'

'No matter. Let us move on to the time when it was appreciated that Richard White was seriously ill and needed expert medical attention. You sought out the Captain and pressed on him a number of ideas about how that expert attention might be obtained?'

'Yes.'

'How did the Captain react to these suggestions — some of which, you may admit yourself, were less than practical?'

'He was . . . upset.'

'Upset, Mr Darby? Was he angry because you were once more suggesting to him how he should run his ship, or because the suggestions were unrealistic, or what?'

'He wasn't angry,' Ben said.

'He was upset, would you say, because he was powerless to produce the miracle that would save the life of one of his crew? Would you say that, more than anything in the world, Captain Taggart wanted that boy to live?'

'Yes,' Ben said hoarsely.

'Thank you, Mr Darby,' De Gruyt said. 'I have no further questions.'

When Ben returned to his seat in the rear of the chamber, it was to sit in a daze of reaction to the ordeal of occupying the centre-stage. The Coroner's thanks to him had echoed hollowly in his ears.

Ben was followed into the witness-box by an officer from the Special Investigation Branch of the Durban police. The burly Afrikaner told how he had taken depositions from the Captain and Chief Officer and also investigated the complaint made by the fireman, McQueen. He had discovered that Captain Taggart was heartily disliked by most of the crew but McQueen was the only one prepared to make an official complaint against the Captain.

As a result of the SIB officer's inquiries, his department had concluded that there were no grounds for the institution of criminal proceedings. A full report of the officer's investigation had, however, been forwarded to the Coroner's Office, together with copies of various depositions. De Gruyt had few questions for the police officer, establishing only that, since Richard White had died on South African soil, the prosecution of a criminal offence in connection with that death was the responsibility of the Province of Natal. Had White died at sea, the responsibility for any proceedings would have devolved to a British naval court or awaited the *Kildare Glen*'s return to the United Kingdom and the finding of a court of inquiry set up by the Ministry of Shipping and Transport.

De Gruyt then begged leave to address the Coroner. He submitted that, whereas this was a civil inquiry into the death of a civilian seaman, the impression might have been given so far to his client, Captain William Taggart, that he was on trial before the court.

'Your Honour,' said De Gruyt, 'I know it is not your intention that this impression be given and I would not wish to protract these proceedings unduly but, in the interest of clarifying matters – which are distressful to

my client – may I ask you now to hear his testimony
... so that the court can judge the manner of man
against whom baseless allegations have been made. He
has committed no crime ... He has not been negligent
of his onerous responsibilities ...'

'We do not need a speech at this stage, Mr De Gruyt,'
the Coroner interrupted. 'As it happens, the court shares
your anxiety that these proceedings are not protracted
unduly. I propose to accede to your request that Captain
Taggart take the stand at this time.'

De Gruyt smiled and bowed. Taggart, his face set
grimly, took the stand. He took the oath in a loud clear
voice and regarded the Coroner with an unwavering
stare.

CHAPTER 10

The Finding

Ben's full attention was on the big man in the witness-box. As Taggart enunciated the words of the oath in his ringing voice, Ben waited, dry-mouthed and filled with a weary resignation, for what he believed would be the final act of the tragedy. Taggart's law did not prevail in this court. Here he would not be able to assert his authority and will with sheer physical presence and weight of voice. Here, even with a Coroner who seemed to be not unsympathetic to authority in the established order and a lawyer who would try to lead him, Taggart was in an element that was alien to him. The most innocent of questions could raise that devil in him that would cause him to reveal the violent streak of paranoia that shimmered just below the surface of the man. No matter what De Gruyt or the Coroner said to the contrary, it was Taggart who was on trial. And this was one trial that Ben could not see Taggart winning. He could turn the tables on enemy submarines and bring his ship through an Indian Ocean cyclone but here – in this closed court – he could only injure his own cause. His capacity for self-destruction would assert itself.

That was the scenario of the tragedy that Ben felt was inevitable. If Taggart did not crack under the strain of trying to vindicate himself before the court, then his Judas was waiting in the wings. When Fowler took the stand and revealed the truth about the water-throwing incident, the final act of betrayal would be done.

In the event, Taggart's performance in the witness-box came as a total surprise to Ben. Whereas McQueen had been truthful but wholly unconvincing, the *Kildare Glen*'s captain was less than scrupulous with the truth but presented his version of it with utter conviction.

Taggart told the Coroner that Richard White's death had distressed him deeply. He felt a degree of culpability for which he would never be able to forgive himself. Unfortunately, White had a verifiable record of laziness and malingering which had perhaps influenced Taggart into believing that the boy was less seriously ill than he actually was. Seafaring was, however, a hard school. The youngsters who came through it did not come through it because they were molly-coddled.

Questioned about Richard White's illness, Taggart repeated his view that the symptoms were consistent with mild sunstroke.

'Sunstroke can be serious enough, even fatal,' cautioned the Coroner. 'What did you do?'

'I ordered the boy to rest in his bunk. And I took a personal interest in his condition because, in the absence of any doctor, the master of a ship must bear conscientiously his responsibilities towards the health of his crew.'

'You considered the possibilities of diverting to a port where medical aid might have been available or of seeking the assistance of ships in the vicinity?'

'I did, your Honour. But the overriding factor was the safety of my ship and the lives of all aboard. In wartime, ships cannot radio for assistance as they do in peacetime. Nor can they disregard their sailing orders. If I had opted for either of these alternatives, I would have been wilfully endangering my ship. I think that Lieutenant-Commander Brook and his naval colleagues will confirm that to have broadcast the ship's position or to have departed from my sailing instructions would have been the height of irresponsibility.'

'Quite so, quite so,' murmured the Coroner. 'Although I am a layman in these matters, I should have thought that these propositions were not viable in the circumstances facing you. To return to the state of the deceased boy's health, Captain . . . Do you feel everything that could reasonably have been done to alleviate his illness was done?'

Taggart faced the Coroner with troubled eyes. He seemed to make an effort to surmount deep distress before replying.

'I have to answer no, your Honour. With the advantage of hindsight, I have to say that there must have been more I could have done . . . and should have done. That knowledge haunts me deeply today.'

The statement seemed to move the Coroner.

'Your candour does you credit, Captain Taggart. I am sure that a lesser man would have chosen to answer that question differently. Painful as this must be for you, there is still one question I must ask you. The witness, McQueen, alleged that when you decided that the boy had spent long enough in his bunk, you entered his quarters and threw water over him as he lay asleep. Such an act would have constituted a common assault, an offence punishable by law – and one which, if answerable by a man in your position, would have most serious consequences. What do you have to say to that allegation, Captain?'

Taggart spread his hands in a gesture of injured innocence.

'I sincerely hope, sir, that the court will treat that wicked allegation as a total misrepresentation of the facts. It is the raving of a vengeful and bitter man who is determined to injure my reputation at the expense of the truth. I have had occasion to discipline McQueen, as the court has heard, and he seems set on getting back at me in any way he can.'

'Then the incident was pure fabrication?' prompted the Coroner.

'It was not what it seemed,' Taggart replied sorrowfully. 'The Chief Officer and I went to the boy's quarters to see how he was. He had been feverish and Mr Fowler took with him a bowl of fresh water – with the thought of bathing the boy's face, if it was necessary...' Taggart shrugged in a helpless kind of way. 'We found White sitting up in bed reading a book. He didn't seem to be in the least bit ill...'

'And what happened, Captain?'

'I asked Mr Fowler to take the boy's temperature and I held the bowl of water as he did so. But the boy didn't want his temperature taken. He pushed Mr Fowler away and what happened was an accident. Mr Fowler bumped into me and the bowl of water was knocked out of my hand. It was the fault of neither of us that most of the water went over White. He was wet and so was his bunk.' Taggart sighed. 'I'm afraid I found the boy's behaviour unreasonable. I was angered by it. Any sympathy I had for him vanished. I was driven to the belief, rightly or wrongly, that his illness was more sham than genuine and that the situation had lasted long enough. I ordered him to return to work. I shall never forgive myself if, as a result of that decision, I contributed in any way to the boy's death.'

It would have been possible to hear a pin dropping in the silence that followed Taggart's statement. He stood there forlornly, seeming weighed down by a profound sorrow: a tough disciplinarian blaming himself for an eventuality which no one in his shoes could possibly have foreseen. He seemed clearly to be judging himself much more harshly than any court would dare to do.

Ben Darby stared open-mouthed at the figure in the witness-stand, scarcely able to contain the cry of disbelief that had threatened to erupt from him. Until that moment, he had been as convinced as everyone in the court-room that Taggart's projection of himself as the hard but penitent man was utterly genuine. Now, in an instant, he knew it to be false. Whatever had happened in Richard White's quarters with the bowl of water had certainly not happened in the way that Taggart had told it. Taggart's version was a monumental lie. From all that Ben knew of Richard White, it was a lie. And from what Fowler had confided, it was a lie. Ben sank back in his seat. He could not understand why Taggart had taken the trouble to make it so elaborate. Surely he knew that the one person who could corroborate his story hated his guts. In trying to make the water-throwing incident look like an unfortunate accident, Taggart had dug a pit for himself in which Fowler would surely bury him.

The scenario was not unfolding in the way that Ben had anticipated, but the end he had foreseen now seemed more inevitable than ever. It did not matter anymore how convincing a case Taggart managed to present for himself: the more he made of his rectitude and deeply felt regret, the greater would seem his lack of these qualities when his pose was revealed as bogus.

Ben settled back to await the inevitable. He listened to De Gruyt extract from Taggart a reluctant catalogue of the deeds that had won him decorations and a brief period of world fame, then suddenly sat up and took notice when the lawyer moved on to unfamiliar territory. De Gruyt questioned Taggart about his strange obsession with the dangers of sunstroke.

'Captain Taggart,' the lawyer said solemnly, 'you have more reason than most, do you not, to be acutely aware of the perils of exposure to the tropical sun?'

'I suppose you could say so,' Taggart admitted reluctantly.

'You had a brother who idolised you, Captain Taggart,' De Gruyt persisted. 'He idolised you so much that he followed you to sea, did he not? He even contrived to get a job as a deck boy on the same ship as you. Is that not so?'

Taggart looked helplessly at the Coroner.

'Must I talk about my brother?' he appealed.

The Coroner regarded Taggart sympathetically over the top of his glasses.

'I believe Counsel is trying to establish reasons why you have a particular horror of sunstroke, Captain. If the question about your brother is relevant, I must advise you to answer it.'

'I tried to talk my brother out of going to sea,' Taggart said. 'But he wouldn't listen to me.'

'You were shipmates together on the *African Flower*, Captain,' De Gruyt encouraged. 'You were an able seaman at the time and, as I said, he was a deck boy. And, like all boys, he was anxious to acquire a splendid golden tan like most sailors have. Isn't that so?'

'Yes,' Taggart said, scarcely able to utter the word.

'Yes,' repeated De Gruyt. 'But he ignored your warnings about the need to go about things easily. Your ship passed through the Mediterranean in winter when it wasn't sun-bathing weather. From experiencing snow in Greece, you passed through the Suez Canal and, within a few days, you were experiencing the considerable heat of the Red Sea, where your brother exposed himself to more sun than was wise for him. Is this not so?'

'Yes,' Taggart whispered. 'He was terribly burned. He went crazy with it.'

De Gruyt turned appealingly to the Coroner.

'Your Honour, although all this happened many years ago, my client still finds it difficult to talk about. He was extremely fond of his brother. The tragic fact is that the boy died after days of derangement and physical agony and was buried at sea. Ever since then, Captain Taggart has held very strong views about the dangers of sunstroke and has enforced measures of a preventative nature on every crew that has been his responsibility. His zeal in doing so may seem strange to some but, to me, is wholly understandable. It is ironic that he should find himself suspected of having done too little to save a boy who – it is recorded – wilfully ignored his warnings about exposure to the sun. I put it to the court that Captain Taggart could do no more to save Richard White than he could for his own brother.'

'Thank you, Mr De Gruyt,' said the Coroner. 'The court accepts that Captain Taggart went to rather extraordinary lengths to ensure that his crew took adequate precautions against sunstroke and no one will dispute the validity of his reasons for doing so, but I suggest you move on from this particular line of questioning. As you said earlier, it is not Captain Taggart who is on trial.'

'I was endeavouring, your Honour, to answer allegations that have been made in this court about my client. The absurd charge that Captain Taggart was a murderer was backed by claims that his behaviour was not that of a sane man. The court can see from his conduct on the stand that Captain Taggart is in full possession of his faculties. I wish to underline the fact by showing that while, at times, my client's attitude towards the dangers of sunstroke may have appeared strange, it was at the worst, idiosyncratic – not insane – and it was motivated by the deepest fear that any man under his command might suffer the same terrible fate as someone who was very dear to him.'

'You have made the point, Mr De Gruyt,' the Coroner said, with an air of impatience. 'Do you have any further questions for the witness?'

De Gruyt had several. He was anxious to establish the punishing nature of the many responsibilities borne by a ship's captain on an ocean voyage such as that made by the *Kildare Glen*. He left no one in doubt that it was something of a miracle, in the midst of all that had happened, that Taggart had had any time at all to concern himself with the health of one of his crew. He concluded by reminding the court that Taggart had suffered much and for long on behalf of his country.

'Is it not the case, Captain Taggart,' De Gruyt asked, framing his final question, 'that, in addition to your valorous service throughout four-and-a-half years of bloody war, you have not spared yourself even in the face of great personal tragedy? A loss that has accented for you and made more harrowing the untimely death of your young crewman, Richard White?'

Taggart seemed completely startled by De Gruyt's question. He stared at the lawyer, face clouded and stricken.

'No ... please ...' The words came out in a scarcely audible croak. Taggart bowed his head, unable to say more. De Gruyt turned to the Coroner.

'Your Honour, I apologise for springing that question on my client. However, I made it my business to find out all I could about the man I was representing here today and I said at the outset that I wanted the court to learn the manner of man I represent. Because he is a man who does not publicly parade his wounds. The court should have a full picture of him – and that picture is incomplete without knowing that he carries the burden of a faith's sorrow. His only son, Gunner Michael Taggart of the Royal Artillery, was killed in action in North Africa almost a year ago. I have no further questions for the witness, your Honour.'

'Thank you, Mr De Gruyt,' the Coroner murmured. His expression was kindly and concerned as he directed his gaze to Taggart. The captain of the *Kildare Glen* was standing, shoulders hunched and head staring down, clearly in the grip of private emotion. 'You may stand down, Captain Taggart,' the Coroner said softly.

'The court acknowledges the forthright nature of you co-operation. Thank you for your help.'

Ben watched as Taggart half-stumbled towards his seat at the front of the court. He sat down and continued to sit with head bowed. He did not look up when Fowler took the stand and was sworn in. There was no doubt in Ben's mind that De Gruyt's mention of his son had come as a shattering surprise to the *Kildare Glen*'s captain. It had shaken Ben, reminding him of the one brief occasion that Taggart had ever spoken about family. Why was he so reluctant to talk about a son who had died in the service of his country and of whom he could justifiably have been proud? Ben sensed that in the answer lay the key to the *whole* Taggart. Somewhere in those hidden shadows was the solution to the black nature that erupted in the man. Ben cursed that he knew so little about the sea-captain. After the lie about the water-throwing, Taggart's testimony had continued to depart from Ben's anticipated scenario. It had come as a shock to learn of his younger brother dying from sunstroke. As De Gruyt had said, it *did* make some kind of sense of Taggart's bizarre obsession with sunstroke. But it had shaken Ben to learn that Taggart had even had a brother. He had never imagined Taggart with a brother – or sisters or parents for that matter. In Ben's mind, he seemed a man eternally *alone*.

But now Fowler occupied the witness-stand, with the fidgety manner of one who was embarrassed to be there. He answered several questions from the Coroner with guarded caution, as if suspecting verbal tripwires laid to bring him crashing down. The Coroner's expression revealed that he was less than impressed with the demeanour of the *Kildare Glen*'s Chief Officer. It was almost with disdain that he passed him over to the waiting De Gruyt.

'I wish only one thing from this witness, your

Honour,' De Gruyt acknowledged. 'I should like Chief Officer Fowler to tell in his own words what transpired when he accompanied Captain Taggart to the deceased's cabin on the day that the cabin-boy was deemed fit enough to resume his work.' He stared at Fowler. 'You remember that day, Mr Fowler? You were carrying a bowl of water, I believe, and the Captain instructed you to take the deceased boy's temperature. Will you tell the court what happened subsequently?'

At the rear of the court, Ben Darby learned forward, his eyes on Fowler. Without being aware of it, he was bracing himself for the revelation that Taggart had lied on oath. He caught his breath sharply and sagged back in his seat at Fowler's reply to the lawyer, which confounded Ben's anticipated scenario yet again.

'There's not much to tell,' Fowler said, with a surreptitious glance in Taggart's direction. Taggart was still sitting with his head bowed and betraying not the slightest interest in the proceedings. 'The Captain asked me to take White's temperature but the boy seemed more interested in the book he had been reading. I had handed the bowl of water to the Captain to hold and the boy tried to push me away. I bumped into the Captain and the bowl of water was knocked out of his hands. It tipped over White.'

'It was an accident?' asked De Gruyt.

'Yes,' said Fowler, managing to sound defensive. De Gruyt turned away.

'I have no further questions, your Honour.'

Fowler looked up at the Coroner, startled.

'Is that all?'

'That's all, Mr Fowler,' the Coroner replied wearily. 'You may stand down.'

The Chief Officer hurried from the stand as if unable to believe his good fortune. Ben watched his scurried progress to his seat, at a loss to comprehend the turn of events. He could not believe that Fowler had lied to him when he had first told him of the water-throwing incident. Taggart had gone too far — the Chief Officer had gloated at the time — and Fowler had intended to use his knowledge of what had happened 'to cook Taggart's goose'. So what had happened in the interim? Had Taggart done a deal with him? Had the Chief Officer chickened out?

The Coroner and De Gruyt had no further questions for Fowler, but Ben had plenty.

From the bench, the Coroner informed the court in general that he saw no particular purpose in seeking further testimony from the officers and crew of the *Kildare Glen* but proposed to call the pathologist who had performed an autopsy on the deceased. That gentleman's report had contained one surprising conclusion and, for that reason, the Coroner had delayed calling him. It was proper that the contentious matters relating to the conditions on the *Kildare Glen* be thoroughly aired and evaluated before the court heard expert testimony which would, perhaps, put these matters into clearer perspective.

The pathologist was called and had to listen whilst the Coroner made apology to him for having kept him waiting so long. He promised that his detention in the witness-box would be of as short duration as was possible.

'Did you conduct a post-mortem operation on the deceased seaman, Richard White?' the Coroner asked without further preamble.

'I did, your Honour.'

'And did you establish the cause of death?'

'I did, your Honour.'

'Will you now tell the court — without too much extravagance of medical terminology, if that is possible — what your findings were?'

The pathologist, a small portly man with wispy hair and a goatee beard, beamed.

'The deceased succumbed, your Honour, to the effects of the infectious disease known as poliomyelitis, or as it is known more commonly to the layman, infantile paralysis.'

'You are in no doubt about that?'

'None whatsoever, your Honour. The disease gets its name from the Greek word *polios*, meaning grey. It affects the grey matter of the spinal cord. This grey matter in the deceased young person bore evidence of intense inflammation, consistent with an advanced stage of the disease. The signs of muscular atrophy and motor paralysis associated with the disease were less marked than is often the case when the condition proves fatal. There were, nevertheless, quite sufficient indications – as I have detailed in my report – to satisfy me that the viral infection was of a strain powerful enough to cause degeneration of that vital machinery of heart and brain that sustains human life.'

'Does it surprise you, Doctor, to learn that the ship's officers, who were concerned for the boy's health, believed him to be suffering from sunstroke?'

The pathologist smiled. 'That evinces no surprise at all, your Honour. The symptoms of sunstroke and the symptoms of the onset of poliomyelitis are very similar. It is not uncommon for experienced medical practitioners, with many years of diagnostic success behind them, to make the mistake of identifying one condition when it is the other that prevails.'

'Then it is not to the discredit of the officers concerned that what they took to be a mild case of sunstroke turned out subsequently to be poliomyelitis? Remembering, of course, that these officers were not qualified doctors.'

'It is perhaps to their credit,' said the pathologist, 'that they came so close in their diagnosis. I have said that for a case proving fatal, the signs of muscular atrophy were much less marked than might have been expected. I must assume from that that the deceased retained some muscular function after the virus had taken hold and that the principal outward sign was feverishness and a general weakness in limb and body function. The absence of even partial paralysis could quite easily mislead an experienced doctor and cause him to make an incorrect diagnosis.'

'Thank you, Doctor. It may not surprise you to learn that in the case of the young seaman, the true nature of his illness was not discovered and that he recovered partially as a result of a period of rest. The recovery was short-lived, however, and he collapsed and sank into a coma from which he never emerged. He died within three days of the second collapse. I must ask you: if the boy's final collapse had occurred on dry land instead of upon the high seas, what are the chances that the boy might have responded to hospital treatment and been alive today? Would he have had a better chance of survival?'

The pathologist frowned. 'You ask me to make an hypothesis, your Honour. I can only offer you an opinion.'

'I understand that,' smiled the Coroner. 'Your opinion would be valued.'

The pathologist smiled. 'I have already been acquainted, your Honour, with a time-table of the deceased seaman's illness. Having ascertained the cause of death, I wished to add to my knowledge by familiarising myself with the history, as it were. I have come to the conclusion that hospitalisation at the first sign of illness would have afforded the seaman a chance of survival. But only a chance. Not a certainty. We cannot arrest the effects of the virus as yet. We can only alleviate them with good nursing and tender care. The seaman might have responded to both these commodities had they been available to him. From the moment he entered the coma, however, I have to express doubt that the best care in the world would have saved him. It is my opinion that he was already beyond aid. The rapidity of the advance of the disease in the final stages was such that death was the inevitable outcome.'

When the pathologist stood down from the witness-box, the Coroner began the process of summing-up. After comments on the inevitable sadness aroused by the death of one so young as Richard Stanley White and his personal regret that the circumstances of his death should provoke some bitterness and acrimony, he had special words of consolation for Captain William Taggart.

'Captain Taggart should,' he declared, 'rid himself of any guilt that he might attach to himself over the death of this young seaman. A ship's captain is not a qualified doctor and cannot be expected to make medical judgements with the facility and expertise of a trained practitioner. All he can do is act humanely within the limits of his knowledge and experience. This, I am satisfied, is what Captain Taggart did. It is easy to be wise in hindsight and argue, after tragedy of this nature has taken place, that this or that might have been done. It is quite a different matter, however, to act with equal wisdom when confronted at the time with the facts of a situation such as this. We have heard a medical expert give his opinion on the likely chances of survival of Richard Stanley White if, at the very outset of his illness, its gravity had been appreciated and the young man had been given the full facilities of a modern hospital. The likelihood is that the young man would have died in spite of the best care in the world. It would, therefore, be mischievous in the extreme if I or anyone else were to suggest that Richard Stanley White died by the default or neglect or lack of concern of his employers and their servants. Where and when the young seaman contracted the deadly virus that ended his life is not known to this court, but what is known is that the contraction of that virus was the instrument of his death. His dying was a natural process begun when the grey matter of his spinal cord was invaded by a paralysing infection to which medical science has still to find a counter-agent. I therefore find that the said Richard Stanley White died from natural causes.'

CHAPTER 11

Confessions

Ben emerged from the court-house buildings to be dazzled by piercing white African sunlight. He stopped to shield his eyes and take his bearings. Markham had told him that he would leave word where he could be found at the consular offices in Smith Street. He had been rather put out to be refused admission to the inquest and had opted not to hang around waiting for it to finish. He had said he would meet Ben later, hopefully, with news of new travel arrangements to Sierra Leone.

Ben was pondering the quickest route to Smith Street when he felt a hand on his sleeve. He turned to find himself looking into the faintly mocking gaze of the *Kildare Glen's* Second Steward.

'Satisfied then, Mr Darby? A nice little whitewash job, wasn't it?'

Ben shook off the arm and moved to go without replying.

'Don't want to talk about it, eh?' the Second Steward persisted. 'Your chum Taggart gets a clean bill of health, so you don't want to be seen talking to the lower orders? That it?'

'That isn't it,' Ben said. 'But I've got to push off. Excuse me.'

Again the hand detained him as he made to move.

'You funked in there, didn't you?' The accusation was delivered with a sneer. 'You could have stitched it up good and proper for Taggart but you went easy on the lying sod. Did he say he'd see you all right?'

Ben's anger flared. He shook himself free of the younger man's hold.

'You've got a big mouth, sonny. Now would be a good time to keep it shut. The place to say anything you had on your mind was inside that court.'

The steward backed away a pace.

'And get the bum's rush like McQueen? You got to be joking, matey. The whole thing was a fix. Nobody listens to the likes of us.'

'I'm sure as hell not going to listen to you!' Ben snapped. 'Go run off at the mouth at somebody else. And next time you want to call a guy 'funk', take a long look in the goddamned mirror!'

Ben turned and strode off, followed by the hostile stares of the young steward's coterie of friends from the *Kildare Glen*'s catering staff who had spilled from the court in time to catch the end of the exchange between Ben and their shipmate. Their hostility, on top of the steward's accusation, made Ben's blood boil. If they had any quarrel with the Coroner's absolution of Taggart, then it was their own goddamned fault! They could have asked to be heard in the witness-box, but not a single one of them had. Instead, they had left McQueen to be pilloried on his own and take all the flak that was going.

What had stunned Ben – even more than the surprise revelation that Richard White had died from poliomyelitis – had been the performance of Taggart in court. Was he mad, a consummate actor, or what? He had been so utterly convincing as the hard but just man who blamed himself for the cabin-boy's death – but he had robbed the display of all sincerity with the lie that Fowler had supported. The Captain's calm mendacity had astounded Ben, but it was not his lying that made him more of an enigma than ever. Ben could not erase from his mind the image of Taggart during the final part of De Gruyt's questioning. He had lost all composure. And that had not been an act put on for the benefit of the Coroner. Taggart had been devastated by the lawyer's reminder of a dead younger brother and by the revelation to the court of a lost son. Taggart's desolation had not been feigned. De Gruyt's intention had been to win the sympathy of the court for his client, and the ploy had been successful — but the cost to his client had been visible for all to see. None was left in doubt that a wound had been exposed that was the source of considerable agony for Taggart. It ran deeper and was more distressful than the loss of a son, which was agony enough for any man. *Was it guilt?* Guilt perhaps at being unable ever to express the affection he felt for his son? It was more than grief, *but what?* Ben did not know the answer, but the need to discover the true source of the dark pain that Taggart kept hidden worried him now with a persistence that threatened to become obsessive. It helped him come to a decision.

Markham was not at the office in Smith Street when Ben got there shortly before one — but he had left a message: he had adjourned for a prelunch drink and would linger over it in the hope that Ben would catch up with him. He would be at the Playhouse — (a) because it was central and Ben would have no difficulty finding it and (b) because they mixed the best whiskey sour in Durban.

Ben found the Playhouse without difficulty. His compatriot was at a table near the central concourse of the huge lounge. He was lolling back in a cane armchair with a long, frosted glass in his hand, idly contemplating the constellations represented in the high starry-heaven ceiling. Markham looked up, beaming, at the sight of Ben.

'Ben! I didn't think you'd make it.' He was on his

feet in an instant. 'How did the inquest go? Are you allowed to tell?'

'It's no secret that it was one hell of an experience. One I could have done without.'

'You were called?'

'Yes, although God knows why. My ten cents' worth of testimony didn't matter a bean.'

'You look as though you could use a drink,' Markham said, and signalled to a waiter. To Ben, he said: 'It was pretty upsetting, eh?'

'The verdict was death from natural causes. The kid had infantile paralysis, although the pathologist had another name for it. Polio-something or other. It seems his chances were never very good. The best he could have looked forward to was a lingering death in a wheelchair.'

Cy Markham shook his head sadly.

'Gee . . . rough. Sometimes it's better they go.'

'Don't tell Franklyn Delano Roosevelt,' Ben said with an edge of bitterness. He immediately became contrite. 'Sorry, Cy. I've no right to sound off at you. I've put you to a hell of a lot of trouble.'

Markham grinned. 'You are official business, Ben – and business always comes before pleasure in the Service. Well, most of the time. And I get paid for it. So don't look unhappy.'

'The trouble is, Cy . . . I've changed my mind about everything. I've put you to a whole lot of trouble for nothing.'

'You mean you don't want to go to Freetown?'

'Oh, I want to get there all right. But I'll stick with the ship.'

'I thought you wanted to get off that goddamned boat.'

'I did – but not now.'

'After what you've been through?'

'*Because* of what I've been through. I can't quit now.

And don't ask me to explain, because I'm not sure I can.'

'You'd better try, Ben. Goddamnit, two more days and I could have had your problem licked. I even had two options lined up. One, was to get you over to Walvis Bay and on to a fast Navy ship heading north. Two would have been trickier, but interesting – a train ride all the way to Northern Rhodesia and then across the border into Portuguese territory by mail plane...'

'Cy, I've made up my mind,' Ben interrupted. 'I'm staying with the ship. Another three weeks and I'll be in Freetown.'

The consular officer shrugged.

'You're going to miss seeing an awful lot of Africa. What's suddenly so goddamned important about the freighter?'

'That's the crazy bit... The bit you wouldn't understand. A kind of riddle I have to solve for myself or I'll be haunted by it for the rest of my life. Have you ever gone into a picture-show when the big movie has already started and then had to come out before the end?'

'I can't say I make a habit of it.'

'Well, that's what it's been like for me on this ship. I missed the start of the story and I don't know how it's going to end. All I've got is the bit in the middle.'

'There was trouble on the ship coming over from India. Are you expecting more?'

'I hope to God not,' Ben said with feeling.

'So maybe there isn't an ending. Things go on and nothing happens. Maybe your run up to Freetown will be one great big anti-climax and this riddle of yours – whatever it is – will stay that way. Something without an answer. I know that three weeks at sea would bore the pants off me – especially if I had a chance to see Africa by train, plane and boat. Which is what you're passing up. Instead of looking at nothing but ocean, you could be seeing half a dozen different countries. The dark continent is a mighty interesting place, Ben. Full of mysteries and fascination.'

Ben smiled. 'Sure, Cy. Like they got here in Durban. Zulu warriors all decked out in ostrich feathers so that they can pull tourists around in rickshaws. That I can live without. The dark continent that interests me, Cy, is the dark continent of the human mind. It's the last great unexplored continent.'

'They should have told Stanley and Livingstone.'

'Maybe they should have,' Ben said. 'Guys like Stanley and Livingstone were maybe legends in their own lifetimes – they opened up darkest Africa – but what I would have opened up would have been their skulls. Because what would have fascinated me was what went on in their minds. In the dark corners. What made them live with danger and disease and just about every goddamned discomfort known to man, when the likes of you or me might have thought twice and three times about it and chickened out? What drove them, Cy? The need for fame and glory, or what? Were they just plain cussed or maybe wanting to get away from their womenfolk for a time?'

'You tell me, Ben,' Cy Markham said with a grin.

'Take Livingstone,' said Ben, warming to his theme. 'They say he was a saint. But did you know that all his life he suffered from bleeding piles? Piles, for God's sake! Can you relate the two conditions – piles with saintliness? To me, that opens up a thousand questions about the guy that I'd like answers to... About his state of mind. About the pain that was always with him. Did he think that his only way to heaven was through his own private hell? Did he never curse the God he took to the heathen?'

Cy Markham held up two hands in a token of surrender.

'Ben, I'm just a guy that works for the State Department. And the name's Markham, not Freud.'

The *Kildare Glen* had moved from the dry dock on the day before the inquest to one of the five coaling berths on the Bluff. It was one of the least accessible places in Durban harbour, being reached only by the ferry that trundled back and forth across the spit of water between the Point and the Bluff. It was getting on for ten at night when Ben's taxi deposited him at the Point and he made his way to the ferry. His timing was good. The launch was just about to cast off as he stepped aboard.

It was a warm evening and Ben made his way to the bows to catch the cool whisper of air stirred by the boat's movement. A lone figure was already there. It was Fowler. He swayed away from the rail to peer at Ben.

'Well, if it isn't our American friend,' he announced, slurring the words. 'How went the day with you, Mr Darby?'

'It's been a long one,' said Ben. He eyed the unsteady Chief Officer. 'You been celebrating something?'

'Not shelebrating, old boy. Drowning my shorrows.'

'Well, we've all got those. Who's looking after the ship tonight?'

'Mr Prinsh volunteered. Been aboard all day. Funny chap, Mr Prinsh. Never wants to go ashore . . . Didn't want to go to the inquest . . . He's one who likes to be alone with his shorrows.'

'The inquest was full of surprises,' Ben said, his tone casual.

'Could have knocked me over with a feather,' Fowler agreed, lurching suddenly but succeeding in retaining his balance by clutching the rail. 'Of coursh, I knew young White didn't have sunstroke. Old Man wouldn't have any of it.'

'It was what you said in the box that surprised me,

Mr Fowler. I seem to recollect you telling me a different story. There was something else you said. Something about cooking the Captain's goose . . .'

Fowler staggered back against the rail as if Ben had hit him. His stare was fear-filled.

'We'll shay no more about that,' he ground out.

'Something on your conscience, Mr Fowler? Like perjury?'

Fowler was trembling. Ben thought he was about to burst into tears.

'Please,' he said, beseechingly. 'You mustn't talk about thish . . . Please.'

'But I want to talk about it, Mr Fowler. I want to know why you lied on oath.'

'He made me do it. Taggart made me do it, damn you!'

'Made you, Mr Fowler?'

The Chief Officer became more agitated than ever. Then the words came out in a rush.

'I had to do what he told me . . . Two nights before we docked, he caught me drinking on watch . . . Said I was drunk . . . The bastard knew I had a bottle hidden in the chart-room . . . He's been spying on me . . . He was going to make a big thing of it . . . Have me in the log-book . . . I would have been finished . . . Finished!'

'Unless the pair of you got your stories straight on what happened over that business with the water?'

Ben could feel no anger for the drunken Chief Officer, only a pitying disgust. The man was a jelly. He fastened on to Ben's shirt-front with his bony hands.

'Please,' he begged, 'please . . . you won't tell anybody? For my sake . . . If it ever comes out, I'd be washed up . . . It would be the finish of everything . . .'

Ben removed the hands from his shirt-front.

'I won't blow the whistle on you, Mr Fowler, but I would like to give you a piece of advice. Do yourself a favour and give the booze a miss. It might finish you quicker than Captain Taggart.'

He turned and walked aft as the boat came alongside the wharf at the Bluff. Ben stepped ashore without another glance at Fowler. As he made his way along the coaling quay to where the *Kildare Glen* was berthed, he could hear Fowler's stumbling progress behind him. The Chief Officer was following the railway lines that ran the length of the quay and he seemed to be tripping over every other sleeper. Ben did not look round once.

There was still an hour to breakfast. To escape the stuffy heat of his cabin, Ben went down to the quay for a walk in the cool of the early morning. The coaling gantries had not yet started their noisy loading of the *Kildare Glen's* bunkers and the air had an invigorating crispness that would vanish when the sun got up and the coaling operation generated clouds of black dust in all directions to coat the ship's paintwork and darken the seared leaves of the Bluff's tangled vegetation.

Beyond the landing stage a tall-masted catcher with a harpoon-gun at the bow had moored at the whaling station. Two great whales – which she had been towing against her flanks – were being hauled up the slipway, where a gang with long-handled fleshing knives waited to do their work. Here the air was not so pleasant and Ben wrinkled his nose at the stench from the bloodied quay. He noticed that the sides of the whales had been mutilated. Ugly gouges had been made in the belly flesh to expose grey rubbery blubber.

Ben was wondering what had caused the mutilations when, as if the unspoken thought had been divined, a voice at his elbow supplied the answer.

'Sharks, Ben. One of the problems of whale-catching in these waters when the big fellows you're after are as big as your ship. You've got to get them back to port before the sharks eat your catch.'

Ben turned to look into Taggart's unsmiling face. In the course of a few days, the *Kildare Glen's* captain seemed to have aged twenty years. The eyes were sunken and the tanned face had a greyish pallor.

'I saw you slip ashore,' Taggart said, when Ben did not answer. 'You're up and about early.'

'I wanted some fresh air,' Ben replied.

'You'll not get it here.' Taggart sniffed the air. 'These places have a stink all of their own. And it'll get worse when the butcher boys get to work and the sun gets higher.'

'I wasn't intending to stick around.'

'Mind if I walk back with you?'

Ben looked at Taggart closely.

'You make it sound as though I should.'

'You hold me responsible for the death of your young friend.'

'I've never said so.'

'But it's what you think.'

'Maybe it's what you want me to think.'

'I don't want you to think badly of me, Ben. What the rest of them think doesn't matter a damn – but you're different. You're like the conscience I never had, or couldn't afford to have. You bother me. Even now . . . the way you're looking at me with that hurt-spaniel expression . . . not saying anything but thinking plenty. I think I can take silent condemnation from anyone, but not you.'

'I'm not condemning you for anything, Captain. Would it make you feel any better if I did?'

'Yes,' Taggart cried. 'Yes, it would! Young White was your friend. Even when I told you he was dead, you showed no real anger. I expected an explosion from you . . . fury, accusations, threats, something . . . But there was nothing . . . Just a kind of cold, sad disappointment . . . pity almost.'

'I'm not your conscience, Captain. I have a hard

enough time living with my own. If it's absolution you're after, you've come to the wrong guy...'

'Damn you, Ben,' Taggart cried with vexation. 'It's not absolution I want from you, it's a sign that in spite of everything that's happened you won't despise me the way every other bastard on that ship despises me. At the inquest yesterday you could have put the knife in. You could have come right out and said, yes, that bastard Taggart killed the boy. You could have said I was as guilty as sin – but you didn't. You took my side.'

Ben shook his head. 'I didn't take sides, Captain. I was on oath. I was trying to tell the truth. Maybe that seems strange to you.'

'Strange? Why?' Taggart seemed perplexed. 'Why should it be strange?'

'Because you and Mr Fowler weren't quite so particular, were you? Goddamnit, I was really taken in by you. I was lapping up every word... How sorry you were... How you blamed yourself... How you could never forgive yourself... And then you spoilt it by telling that lie about the water! It fooled the Coroner, Captain, but it didn't fool me. It just knocked one hell of a dent in the admiration I was building up for you. Now I've got to admit there's damned little of it left.'

Ben's vehemence bemused Taggart. He made no attempt to deny his perjury, seeming only surprised that Ben should make so much of it. His main reaction was one of relief.

'Oh, Ben, what the hell am I going to do with you? You're too damned honest for words. Don't you realise that I couldn't tell the truth about that? It was an inexcusable thing that I did and if I had admitted it in court, I would have been hung, drawn and quartered.'

'Do you expect me to applaud?'

Taggart looked hurt. 'I expected you to understand. Damnit, man, it was a question of self-preservation! I wasn't to know that McQueen was the only one who was going to stand up in court and shout murder. I thought they were all going to gang up on me, like the sharks went for that whale down there. What good would the truth have done me then? It would have been a bloody marvellous consolation when I found myself in the dock for manslaughter, or worse.'

'It would never have stuck.'

'Maybe not. But I would have been finished either way.'

'Like Fowler will be finished if you make a song about his drinking?' Taggart looked at Ben sharply.

'Has that fool been talking to you?'

'He didn't need to. I worked it out all on my own. He's another who would sell his grandmother to keep his precious job. What is it about you guys that makes you so goddamned jealous of your jobs that you don't turn a hair at using blackmail and perjury to keep them? Is it just so you can play God on a ship? Is that what it's all about?'

Anger glinted in Taggart's eyes but he kept his voice even.

'That's exactly what it's about, Ben. When you work hard all your life for something, and get it, you fight like a tiger to keep it. Look anywhere in this stinking world and that's what you'll see – men fighting any way they know how to keep what they think they've earned, whether it's a piece of gold that they dug up half a desert to find or four walls and a roof that they've slaved with their hands to possess. It's easy to make moral judgements, Ben... Easier when you've got nothing to lose.'

'I'm not making moral judgements,' Ben said wearily. 'I just wish to God things were different.'

Taggart smiled and draped an arm round Ben's shoulder.

'Let's go and get some breakfast, Ben. Your trouble

is that you're not just my conscience. You're the conscience of the whole damned world. That's much too big a load to carry without a bowl of cornflakes inside you.'

They walked together along the quay.

'I had a visit from the police at three o'clock this morning,' Taggart said suddenly, and seemed amused by Ben's start of surprise.

'The police?'

'Yes. It seems that a friend of yours has got himself into more trouble.'

'A friend of mine? Who?'

Taggart grinned. 'Your chum, McQueen. He keeps picking on the wrong people. This time, it was the Durban police force.' Taggart shook his head sadly. 'Some people just never learn.'

'Has he been hurt?'

'I gather he may have a sore head – and not just from what he had drunk. He did not, as they say, go quietly. The two constables who arrested him had to send for reinforcements.'

The information pained Ben.

'What'll happen to him?' he asked.

'He's due to appear before the break at ten this morning. I said I would be there. Maybe you'd like to come along. He's going to need all the friends in court he can get.' Taggart saw Ben's look of uncertainty and said: 'It's OK, Ben, you won't have to go into the box as a character witness. I'll take care of that . . .'

'You'll speak up for him?' Ben could not hide his incredulity.

'I'll do my best for him,' Taggart said. 'The fact that he hates my guts is incidental. As long as he's a member of my crew, he is my responsibility. I can't be held accountable for his actions, but I do have a duty to him to make sure that he doesn't make things worse for himself than they already are.'

Ben and Taggart were seated in the magistrate's court long before McQueen was led up from the cells. First they had to sit through the cases of a dozen or more miscreants. 'All the boozers and the losers', was how Taggart described them in a whispered aside to the American as the overnight prisoners were summarily fined or had their cases referred to a higher court.

McQueen looked rather the worst for wear as he was pushed into the dock, but he stared around him defiantly. His lip curled angrily as a clerk read out the charge. After what Taggart had told him about McQueen fighting policemen, Ben was surprised at the relative mildness of the charge: no more than being drunk and disorderly.

'How do you plead?' the magistrate asked McQueen.

'Not guilty,' the fireman answered, in a voice that was anything but subdued.

The magistrate blinked at him.

'Have you been advised on this plea or are you seeking to waste the time of this court?'

'I was not drunk and I was not disorderly,' McQueen replied defiantly. 'I'm not guilty of anything. I was beaten up for no reason at all.'

The magistrate pursed his lips.

'You insist on pleading not guilty?'

'I *am* not guilty!' McQueen asserted.

The magistrate held a hurried conference with the clerk of the court. When it was over, the magistrate asked if the arresting officer was in court. He was. He was summoned forward and asked to give his account of the accused's arrest.

Reading from his notebook, the policeman related in a heavy Afrikaans accent the circumstances of McQueen's arrest. He had been observed pestering members of the public and it had been noted that he was unsteady on his feet. When apprehended, he had become violent and had to be forcibly restrained. The efforts of two officers had been insufficient to subdue the seaman, with the result that help had to be summoned from a mobile patrol. In the van taking him to the station, the accused had made further resistance and he had created more disturbance at the station, where he was charged and removed to the cells.

The magistrate heard the policeman out and then turned to McQueen to ask him if he should now like to change his plea to one of guilty. McQueen's adamant refusal was accompanied by the angry claim that the policeman was a liar and the denial that he had been pestering anyone in the street. His attempts to explain that he had simply been seeking directions to the Point Ferry were cut short by the magistrate. Silencing McQueen, he announced that he did not intend to waste his or the court's time any further. He found the accused guilty and fined him £10 or seven days in prison.

He goggled in disbelief when, from the dock, McQueen proclaimed that it would have to be seven days in prison because he certainly was not going to pay £10 for something he hadn't done.

'You will pay the fine and consider yourself lucky that you are getting off so easily!' ordered the magistrate. 'If you think that you're going to live off the tax-payers of this province for a week in order to avoid the financial penalty. I have imposed, you are quite mistaken!'

'Well, you'd better ask the police for your money,' McQueen roared from the dock. 'Because they took every penny I had! And they took my wrist-watch!'

The magistrate looked across the court at the policeman, perplexed. McQueen's defiance was clearly something that was quite new to his experience, and he was looking for help from any quarter.

'The accused had no money when we got him to the station, sir,' the policeman said. 'And if he had a watch, I never saw it. Maybe it came off in the scuffle.'

It was at this point that Taggart decided to take a

hand in the proceedings. He stood up and identified himself as the captain of the ship to which the accused belonged.

'Perhaps you will allow me to settle the matter of the fine?' he offered.

There was a groan from McQueen in the dock. 'This is all I bloody need!' he muttered audibly. He was told sharply by the magistrate to keep quiet. Taggart was invited to approach the bench.

The magistrate latched on to Taggart's intervention like a life-line. It was his instinct, he said, not to be harsh on men who had dangerous jobs in wartime and there had to be some tolerance of sailors who wanted to have a good time in a port like Durban. Their behaviour, however, had to be kept within certain confines. It could not be allowed to run out of control. In the circumstances, he was prepared to accept payment of the accused's fine by his captain, on the condition that the captain stood guarantor for the accused's good behaviour for the remainder of their stay in Durban. Any breach would result in the guarantor and his charge being brought again before the court and punitive fines being levied on both.

Taggart paid McQueen's fine in cash and was given an official receipt. McQueen was then released into his safe-keeping at the door of the court-room, where Ben joined them. The fireman was fuming with anger at the turn of events and might have made a scene if Taggart had not warned him that he would personally break both his arms if he said a word out of place. Gripping McQueen by an upper arm and wrist, he marched the fireman out of the building to the street, with Ben in close attendance.

'You're going back to the ship, sunshine,' he growled in McQueen's ear. 'And you're damned well going to stay there until we sail!' He turned to Ben. 'See if you can find a taxi, Ben. I'm not going to let this head-case out of my grip until he's safely aboard.'

It took Ben ten minutes to find a taxi and bring it back to where Taggart was standing at the kerb with McQueen still pinioned in his hold. In the taxi, McQueen was made to sit between Ben and Taggart.

'That's a tenner you owe me, boyo,' the Captain informed the fireman.

'You'll have to take it out of my hide,' the fireman snapped back. 'I'm sure as hell not paying for something I never done.'

'Of course not, you were just minding your own business and the nasty cops came along and started laying into you with their truncheons,' Taggart mocked.

'That's just about the size of it, *sir*,' McQueen said, with controlled fury. 'But then, you're not interested in the truth. You wouldn't know it if it walked up to you in the street.'

'Just watch your tongue, boyo,' Taggart warned icily.

McQueen turned contemptuous eyes on Ben.

'Your Yankee chum wouldn't know much about the truth neither, would he? Talks very grand, he does, but what does he bloody care about the likes of me? Shovelling coal is all I'm good for. To hell with my rights!'

'You poke a South African policeman and you say good-bye to your rights,' Taggart chimed in. 'So don't you start insulting Mr Darby. He came along to bail you out of the goodness of his heart . . . Which is more than I did. The sensible thing would have been to let you rot in gaol . . .'

'That's what you should have done!' McQueen interrupted angrily. 'By paying that fine, you just let those Afrikaans bastards win. They've got my money and they've got my watch and they had their bit of fun kicking hell out of me. I bet they're laughing their heads off right this minute. And all because I asked a couple of darkies how to get to the ferry!'

'Just what did happen, Mac?' Ben asked softly. He was disturbed by the fireman's tenacity in sticking to the story he had tried to tell in court. McQueen rewarded him with a sudden look of gratitude.

'Don't tell me I've suddenly got through to you, Mr Darby. What I've been saying is the truth.'

'Well, tell us, won't you?' Taggart prompted mockingly. 'Mr Darby and I could use a good laugh. Tell us what happened.'

McQueen flung Taggart a look of hatred, then concentrated his attention on Ben.

'It was like I said. I asked a couple of darkies how to get to the ferry. But not even the darkies in this town have much time for sailors. I never did them no harm and I wouldn't lord it over nobody, but that's not how they see it. They don't trust anybody with a white skin and they didn't want me speaking to them. I tried to tell them I just wanted to find the way back to the ship but they just jabbered at me in some lingo I couldn't understand. That's when the two cops came along...'

'This is beginning to sound like *Uncle Tom's Cabin*,' Taggart commented disdainfully. 'For God's sake, get on with it.' McQueen ignored him.

'The two darkies took off the minute they saw the cops, so the cops button-holed me. They wanted to know what I was doing talking to a couple of Kaffirs. They seemed to think that I was trying to fix up a short time with a black woman and wouldn't believe me when I said that all I was interested in was getting back to my ship...'

'The cop in court said you were drunk. Were you?' Ben asked.

'I'd had a couple of beers, that's all. I wasn't drunk. It was the two cops who were looking for trouble, not me. When they said they were going to run me in, I cheeked them, I suppose, but they weren't exactly polite and I hadn't done nothing.'

'So you poked one on the nose?' Taggart suggested.

'I didn't!' McQueen denied vehemently. 'I never raised a fist to either of them. I just wouldn't let them put the cuffs on me. They both went for me then. I thought they were going to murder me.'

'That's why they sent for reinforcements?' Taggart's scoffing tone gave no indication that he believed a word.

'They didn't need no reinforcements,' McQueen said, with disgust. 'The two of them got me down and cuffed me with my hands behind my back. Then one of them sat on me while the other one went and whistled up a van. It was when they had me in the van that they took my watch and my money. And they gave me a going-over. In the van that is. They gave me another going-over when they got me in the cells.'

'Did you have much money on you?' Ben asked. He had sat, quietly listening to McQueen's account, as the taxi travelled half the length of Point Road.

'Not enough to pay that ten-quid fine,' McQueen answered. 'I had maybe six or seven quid. But the watch was a good one. Swiss make and real gold. I got it in Aden. Do you believe what I'm telling you, Mr Darby?'

'I believe you,' Ben said. 'And I think the Captain does, too.' He looked across at Taggart. 'Isn't there something can be done about it, Captain?'

Taggart seemed highly amused by the situation.

'I'll give you this, McQueen . . . You made it sound convincing. The only snag is that, without witnesses, there isn't a damn thing that you, me, or anybody else can do about it. Even if you were the Archbishop of Canterbury, nobody is going to buy a story that you were robbed and beaten up by the police just for the hell of it.'

'It wasn't just for the hell of it. It was because I was speaking to these darkies. They went on about how it was against the law to go with black women and it didn't matter that I hadn't been caught in bed with one. I was a dirty Kaffir-lover, they said, and they had ways of dealing with Kaffir-lovers. They just wouldn't listen to me...'

'Mr Darby will listen to you, McQueen,' Taggart said, with a wink at Ben. 'It's all good material for that piece he's writing about the unsung heroes who fire Britain's merchant ships. How about it, Ben?'

Ben met the taunting challenge in Taggart's eyes with a sad little smile.

'Somebody should listen,' he said. 'Why shouldn't it be me?'

'And who's going to listen to you?' Taggart came back, still mocking. 'Who's going to listen to you, Ben? Do you honestly think anyone gives a damn if a couple of South African cops pick up a drunken bum like McQueen here and give him a quiet little going-over?'

'I give a damn,' Ben said. 'Next time they pick on somebody, it could be me... Or you.'

Taggart laughed. 'They're welcome to try – but they've got more sense, Ben. It's the nobodies they pick on.'

'You should know,' McQueen snarled bitterly, 'it's your style!'

Taggart grabbed a handful of McQueen's shirt-front and thrust his face to within inches of the fireman's.

'The only complaint I've got against those Afrikaners, laddie, is that they didn't do a proper job on you and put you in hospital. That way, we would have been rid of you! Now pipe down! Between yesterday and today, I've heard enough of your tongue to last me for the rest of my life!'

There was murder in Taggart's eyes and, for a dread moment, Ben thought the *Kildare Glen's* captain was about to smash a fist into McQueen's face. But the fist unclenched and Taggart pushed the fireman away, so that he slumped against Ben. Taggart sat forward in the taxi, gulping breath in what seemed an intense effort to control the fury raging within him.

When they reached the dock, he paid off the taxi and strode towards the ferry, leaving Ben and McQueen to follow some distance behind.

'He's like a boiler with a full head of steam and nowhere to put it,' McQueen muttered softly to the American. The comment put in a nutshell exactly what Ben had been thinking. 'I thought the bastard was going to kill me! Did you see his eyes?' McQueen whispered agitatedly. 'Calling me a drunken bum! He's the one that ought to be locked up!'

Taggart turned and glared at McQueen.

'You got something to say?'

The fireman had a sudden attack of discretion.

'Not a word, Captain,' he said, holding up his hands. 'Not a word.'

'You keep it that way,' Taggart said, his tone threatening. 'You keep that evil tongue of yours between your teeth. That way, nobody'll be tempted to haul it out and wring your neck with it.'

Taggart turned on his heel and marched towards the ferry. When they had crossed to the Bluff, the Captain's big strides again took him ahead of Ben and McQueen as they walked along the coaling quay. He was first to reach a knot of workers clustered around an empty railwagon. Their attention was directed under the wagon.

'What you got under there?' Taggart demanded of a shunter with a pole in his hand.

'A dog's trying to get itself killed under the wheels,' the man replied. 'Won't come out and won't let anybody near it.'

Ben and McQueen arrived in time to see Taggart crawling underneath.

'She'll have your hand off!' the shunter warned

Taggart. 'They're sending somebody down to shoot it. It's been living wild and it's half-starved.'

Taggart disappeared under the wagon. Ben could hear the low, angry growl of the frightened animal, then he heard Taggart's voice.

'Come on, old girl. I'm not going to hurt you. Come on then . . . There's a good lass . . . What's this you've got here?' The dog's snarling stopped.

Taggart emerged, crouching, and cradling a brown furry bundle in his arms.

'Jesus!' exclaimed the shunter. 'Will you look at that? There's two of them. She's got a pup.'

'She thought you were after her pup,' Taggart scolded the man. 'Look at her, how meek she is.' The bedraggled fox-like dog was licking the chocolate-coloured pup nestling against her belly and the hand with which Taggart was protecting his find.

'She knows I wouldn't hurt her,' Taggart said proudly.

'What the hell you going to do with them?' the shunter asked.

'They're homeless,' Taggart said. 'I'll give them a home.'

The shunter looked at him as if he were crazy.

'You're welcome,' he said.

Taggart caught sight of Ben and his face lit up.

'Don't just stand there, Ben. Get yourself aboard and tell the Steward I've got a couple of unexpected guests for lunch. I'll need milk and any scraps of meat he can find. Go on . . . I'll follow you.'

'Sure,' Ben said, dazedly. He went off along the quay towards the *Kildare Glen*, still unable to equate the man lavishing affection on the cradled strays with the fury-consumed individual of a few moments before.

CHAPTER 12

Detour

A single tug assisted the *Kildare Glen* out from the coaling wharf in the first light of morning. Her work was quickly done. With the freighter's bows pointing towards the gap between the Point and the Bluff, the tug cast off the hawser and stood clear as the *Kildare Glen* gathered way and steamed out through the narrow harbour entrance. A dumpy corvette of the South African Navy was waiting in Roads and she wheeled in a slow circle as the *Kildare Glen* dropped her pilot and was followed out to sea by two more merchantmen.

Taggart manoeuvred the freighter at dead-slow speed to allow the following ships to pass and take up station ahead of her. A wispy land haze screened the still sleeping city and the lower slopes of the Bluff as the trio of ships headed out to sea with their escort.

From the fore-end of the lower bridge, Ben observed the small convey form its steaming line. He had been wakened while it was still dark by movement to and from the bridge, and had dressed in order to watch the *Kildare Glen*'s unceremonious, almost stealthy, departure in the dawn. A flutter of excitement had teased the pit of his stomach at once more being on the move. It must always be like this for the sailor, he had thought, as the ship had met the long heavy swell of the open sea and he had felt the adrenalin rise at the thrill of going out to meet her unknown.

The sprawling city behind was soon lost from sight

in the whitish land haze. It would soon become no more than a memory. He would remember the golden beaches and the great green Bluff but, more than anything, he would remember the stark grassy plot and the hard yellow earth where Richard White had been buried. There had been no gravestones in that corner of the cemetery and none would mark the boy's grave, only a wooden peg with a name. The discovery, after the funeral, that the plot was paupers' ground had shocked and dismayed Ben. Once the extravagance of wreaths from the *Kildare Glen* had withered, the small wooden peg would be Richard White's only memorial.

With fifteen minutes to go until the breakfast-gong sounded, Ben decided there was no more to be seen from his promenade-deck. He rounded the bridge-housing to be met by a furious onslaught of affection from a four-legged friend. Her bushy rudder wagging fiercely, the fox-like bitch that Taggart had claimed as his own leapt joyfully against Ben's legs and contorted herself around them in a display of recognition.

Taggart had named her Bluff and, once bathed and fed, she had turned out to be the most handsome of creatures. In a matter of hours, she had made herself so much at home on the *Kildare Glen* that it would have been easy to assume that she had been resident for years. She and her pup had settled down immediately in Taggart's day-room. Both were allowed the freedom, not only of Taggart's quarters but the whole of the interior on the deck-level, including Ben's cabin. The stairs to the chart-room and the saloon-deck had proved sufficient deterrent to the younger dog to prevent it venturing further afield, but not to Bluff. She had quickly explored both escape routes and had even learned to mount the weather-step and push open the mosquito-door to the open bridge-deck, taking advantage of these egress points to familiarise herself with the ship in general. But she seldom left her offspring for long, returning regularly from her explorations to check on the stilt-legged little pup.

The pup – chocolate-brown, with white flashes on the chest and fore-paws – bore little physical resemblance to her mother, whose coat was reddish brown. Bluff also had a sharp snout that gave her a fox-like appearance, whilst the pup was snub-nosed and floppy-eared. Inspired by the pup's chocolate colour, Taggart had promptly christened it Bourneville.

As swiftly as Bluff had taken to the ship, she had taken to the ship's master as her own: obeying his commands in a way that suggested that, in her unknown past, she had been trained by an expert.

'Here, Bluff.'

The single command was sufficient for the bitch to disentangle herself from Ben's legs and go scurrying to Taggart as he descended from the navigation bridge. He patted the head raised to greet him.

'That's a good girl,' he praised, and smiled at Ben. 'Good morning, Ben. It's good to be loved, isn't it?'

'We all need love,' Ben said wryly.

'And me more than most?' Taggart laughed. He stretched his great bulk. 'By God, it feels good to be at sea again! Everything's simpler out here. The air's cleaner!'

Ben smiled at his exuberance. Taggart showing happiness was a rare sight.

'It's good to have company, too ... that corvette and the other ships. Do we have them all the way to Freetown?'

Taggart frowned suddenly. 'We're not going to Freetown, Ben.'

Ben went cold. 'We ... We're not going to Freetown? But ...'

'I'm sorry ... I meant to tell you last night. We'll get you to Freetown all right ... Eventually ... It's just going to take two or three weeks more than we bargained for ...'

Ben could only stare at Taggart, completely nonplussed.

'Oh, great! That's goddamned marvellous!' he wailed. 'Just where the hell are you taking me now?'

'You'll like the Argentine,' Taggart said, brightening. 'Buenos Aires is one of the most beautiful cities there is . . .'

'Buenos Aires!' Ben's voice was shrill with disbelief.

Taggart began to enjoy the American's dismay.

'Just treat it as a kind of extended holiday, Ben. I thought you'd be delighted. There was no sense in sending us home empty when there's all that bully beef going spare in Argentina. We'll be loading for the UK at BA and Montevideo . . . It's only a short trip across the South Atlantic and won't be taking us much out of our way . . .

'Oh no – not more than three or four thousand miles,' Ben agreed, with heavy sarcasm.

'Nearer five thousand,' Taggart corrected him, with a smile. 'More than five and half if you include the steaming distance between here and Cape Town.'

Ben groaned. 'Don't tell me . . . that's still ten thousand goddamned miles to go to Freetown! I was nearer the goddamned place before I ever stepped on this ship!'

'You were just waiting at the wrong bus-stop.' Taggart grinned. 'In lots of ways, you were lucky we came along and gave you a lift. You could have been stuck in Bombay for ever.'

In rolling blue ocean south of Cape Town, the *Kildare Glen* parted company with the corvette and the other merchantmen. There was a flurry of flags from the corvette to indicate a new course to her remaining charges. Then, with a single siren blast from the leading freighter, the small column turned to starboard and headed north towards the distant platform top of Table Mountain. The corvette wheeled briefly towards the

Kildare Glen to flash a farewell message: 'You're on your own now. Good luck and a safe journey.'

By evening, the distinctive top of Table Mountain was well below the horizon and the *Kildare Glen* was once more alone on the ocean. The next sight of land would be four-and-a-half thousand miles to westward, in the broad estuary of the River Plate. The three-day run along the South African coast had given Ben time to get used to the idea that, in the immediate future, he would be getting further and further away from his West African destination rather than nearer to it.

In Durban he had exchanged cables with his Washington office and detected, if not an impatience with his lack of productivity, a distinct off-handedness about his usefulness to the Bureau. It was as if, after the air crash, they had been prepared to write him off as a spent force. They were the ones who had wanted him in West Africa – on the strength of his dispatches from China – but they now seemed luke-warm about the whole thing. Maybe they were regetting the way they had billed him as 'the reporter who will trek to hell and back for stories from the world's least-known and least-accessible war zones.'

Ben realised, however, that he was perhaps being unfair to the Washington Bureau chiefs by reading too much into their missives. It was just possible that what he took to be disinterest on their part was, in fact, tolerance. They did not want to put undue pressure on a man who had been badly smashed up. Ben wondered what the Washington reaction would be when he failed to show up in Sierra Leone in mid-March, as he had confidently forecast. He only wished that a camera could record for him the consternation on the faces at head office when it was discovered that their intrepid globe-trotting reporter was in the wrong continent. The first intimation they would get that Ben was in South

America instead of West Africa would be his cable from Buenos Aires announcing the fact.

If the stop-over in Durban had done nothing to improve the morale on the *Kildare Glen*, it had at least worked wonders for the ship's performance. With the marine growths scaled from her bottom and the bunkers filled with good-quality steaming coal, the *Kildare Glen* had been given a new lease of life. This was evident almost as soon as the ship parted company with the Cape Town-bound convoy. Freed from the ten-knot pace of the convoy, Taggart had rung for full speed and the ship had vibrated as she had bowled along at nearly thirteen knots: almost twice the speed of her crawling progress across the Indian Ocean.

A startling change had also taken place in Taggart since Durban. It was as if he had resolved to win back the trust of his crew by affecting a less severe style of command. To Ben, whose company he sought more and more, he confided the hopes he had of making the *Kildare Glen* 'a happy ship' – an ambition that, hitherto, had not been in evidence. To Ben, his efforts appeared to be genuine. He promised an improvement in the quality of the catering and, with the Chief Steward's stores restocked with South African produce, the menus for both saloon and fo'c'sle underwent a spectacular change. The feeding became almost lavish in choiceness and variety.

Taggart lost no opportunity in revealing that his was the will behind this and other changes designed to make life on the *Kildare Glen* more agreeable. He cut tobacco-issue prices to a miniumum – a reversal of his previous policy – and relaxed the beer ration to the crew from a maximum of two bottles per man per week to two per day. The Steward was ordered to issue clean bed-sheets and towels to the crew once a week instead of the previous once-a-month. And Taggart himself made an effort to present a more human face to those under him: attempting to be hearty and tolerant where, before, he had been brutally demanding.

Ben observed all this with growing disquiet. What made him uneasy was not the fact that Taggart was trying to make amends for his previously uncompromising style, but that the Captain seemed certain that this new attitude would win him lasting gratitude and respect. Because it soon became clear that the more Taggart tried to court the favour of his men, the more they despised him. They saw every improvement in their conditions as no more than their rightful due and they viewed the instigator as a man doing too little and too late to assuage a guilt-ridden conscience.

Ferguson, the Chief Engineer, rejected Taggart's clumsy peace overtures with unwavering contempt. The engineer had endured his self-imposed exile from the saloon for more than a month without any attempt at reconciliation by Taggart and he now distrusted the Captain's sudden change of heart. He suspected an ulterior motive. Nor could Taggart penetrate the wall of unreachability that Willem Prins, the Second Officer, had built around himself – although he tried. The young Dutchman went about his duties like an automaton, communicating with others only when these duties demanded it and then retiring immediately behind his shell of silence.

As the days passed and the more Taggart tried and failed to elicit anything other than sullen contempt for his pains, the greater became Ben's unease. The Captain was mystified by the seeming ingratitude that he encountered. The more benevolent he made his regime, the less appreciative became its beneficiaries. His mystification turned slowly to deep-seated anger. His visits to Ben's cabin to unburden his frustration became more frequent.

'If it weren't for you and the dogs, I'd go mad,' he confessed to Ben, one evening. 'I've had my fill of the scum on this ship. I feed them like fighting cocks and do you know what one of them said to me on rounds today? He wanted to know why they couldn't have custard with their tinned pears more often, instead of ice-cream! Can you believe that? Jesus, when I was his age, if we'd seen ice-cream or a tin of pears, we'd have thought it was Christmas!'

'You've got to make allowances for the modern generation,' Ben said, knowing that he sounded banal.

'Make allowances?' Taggart echoed angrily. 'The more I go out of my way to make things better for them, the more they hate my guts. It was a mistake to go soft on them – the biggest mistake of my life. They see it as a sign of weakness.'

Strong south-westerlies slowed the *Kildare Glen*'s progress as she made her lonely westward passage, but she still averaged daily runs in excess of 260 miles. Compared with the daily rates towards Durban, this was positively flying along. Every mile seemed to feed the anger that was growing in Taggart at his total failure to overcome the bitter enmity of his men. Watching him, Ben wondered anxiously when the flash-point of that anger would be reached and the gathering fury would be released in volcanic eruption.

When Taggart had confessed that but for Ben and the dogs he would go mad, Ben had been uncomfortably aware of a closeness to the truth in the remark that was disturbing. Ben and the dogs were Taggart's safety-valves. From the dogs Taggart received an affection that was notably absent from any other source, and in Ben he had a patient listener on whom he had come to depend.

It was ironical, therefore, that when Taggart's anger did finally flare out of control, Ben should find himself the target.

It stemmed from a triviality. The occasion was a post-lunch discussion at the saloon table over the possibility that the war could be over by Christmas. Fowler was of the opinion that it could drag on for several years. Taggart, however, advanced the theory that a second front in Europe and a declaration of war on Japan by Russia could bring an end to the war in weeks.

'It's perfectly feastible,' he declared.

'You mean feasible?' Ben enquired, without rancour.

'I mean feastible,' Taggart snapped.

'I'm sorry,' Ben murmured, 'I've never heard the word. I thought you meant feasible.'

'I know what I bloody meant!' Taggart flared. 'The word is "feastible." '

'It's a new one on me,' Ben said. 'Let's forget it.'

'I won't bloody forget it!' Taggart persisted. 'You're trying to make out I'm bloody ignorant. I don't need a bloody American to teach me English!'

'I'm not trying to teach anybody anything,' Ben said, keeping his voice several decibels lower than Taggart's. 'I just happened to say I hadn't heard the word before. I'm interested in words . . . They're my business.'

'If they're your business, you should know that the word is "feastible". '

'I think you'll find that there's no letter "t" in it.'

'And I think you'll find there is!' Taggart shouted.

Ben was conscious of Fowler's smirking stare and the stares of the others. He got up from the table and crossed to the book-case in the smoke-room. He picked out the *Concise Oxford Dictionary*.

'There's an easy way of settling this,' he said, returning to the table. He thumbed through the dictionary. 'There it is in black and white, Captain. "Feasible" . . . meaning practicable, manageable, convenient, serviceable, plausible . . . I'm afraid I can't find the word "feastible" . . .'

Taggart seized the dictionary from Ben's hands and studied the page, his face thunderous. When he looked up, he stared murder at Ben.

'This doesn't prove anything!' he snarled. 'Not a damned thing! It's time we had a decent dictionary!' He hurled the book across the saloon. It crashed against the bulkhead and fell on the desk, with the covers hanging off and exposing the spine. 'It's trash!' he thundered. 'Trash!'

Then, with a final venom-filled stare at Ben, he marched out of the saloon.

Fowler sat grinning wickedly at Ben.

'Tut, tut, Mr Darby,' he admonished. 'You seem to have blotted your copy-book. He won't forgive you for this. You really took him down a peg.'

Ben looked round the faces at the table. They were all grinning. Taggart had been shamed in front of them and they had enjoyed his humiliation. Ben was already hating himself for what he had done. The grinning faces sickened him.

'Have your goddamned fun!' he burst out. He saw the surprise register on the faces before he turned his back on them and hurried out of the saloon.

Accounts of the incident spread throughout the ship like wildfire. Whether Fowler or the stewards were responsible, Ben did not know. His first indication that the 'galley wireless' had broadcast details of Taggart's humiliation came the following morning from encounters outside the pantry with a deck sailor and a gunner.

'Lovely feastible morning, Mr Darby,' the sailor greeted him, with a broad grin.

Two minutes later, it was the gunner's turn. As he went forward, he gave Ben a friendly wave and winked at him.

'A change in the weather looks feastible, Mr Darby,' he called.

It was quickly apparent that 'feastible' was on everyone's lips. Overnight, it had become the vogue word. From the bridge to the stoke-hold, it was used in every conversation and in any context. It replaced a well-known Anglo-Saxon adjective in every uttered epithet. Everything was suddenly 'feastible'. And, overnight, Ben had become a hero in the eyes of the crew. The consensus in the messes was that 'the Yank' was OK.

Ben's new popularity pained him. Taggart was a man who had overcome the handicap of little formal education and Ben had shamed him by airing a superior vocabulary. He had not intended to wound but, unwittingly, he had done so grievously. Taggart's pride had been hurt by being publicly corrected and Ben should have known that the man's pride would not have allowed him to have admitted graciously to a misconception he had probably held for most of his life. Ben had won the argument but, in his own eyes, with a low blow. He had hit below the belt.

The triviality of it all nagged at Ben in the aftermath of the incident. He recalled Taggart's revelation to him of his struggle to make the jump from deck seaman to officer in his early twenties. Having left school at fourteen, Taggart had required all his will and tenacity to achieve the necessary educational standards to sit his 'tickets'. It had meant hours of study while still working as an able seaman, and much sacrifice: learning mathematics far beyond the rudimentary knowledge that his schooling had given him and coming years late to such mysteries as spherical trigonometry. Like many men who had come up the hard way, Taggart was always quick to remind others that he had done so – but he was also ultra-sensitive to that gaffe or slip which made him look foolish to those with more privileged starts in life. Ben, in his innocence, had done the unforgivable: he had made Taggart feel inferior.

When, after two days, Taggart had not shown his face in the saloon and the tongues had wagged incessantly in ridicule of the Captain, Ben felt obliged to take some step to end his sulking. His knock on Taggart's door was greeted with the call to enter.

He found Taggart sitting on his settee, with a blanket thrown to one side. His hair was dishevelled and his face unshaven. He looked hollow-eyed and ill.

'You were resting... I'm sorry,' Ben stammered. 'I didn't mean to disturb you.'

'It's all right, Ben. I'm glad to see you. Sit down.'

Ben did not take a seat immediately.

'I want to say I'm sorry... About the other day.'

Taggart waved away the apology with a weary sweep of the hand.

'You showed me up as an ignorant bastard. So what? I am an ignorant bastard.' He gave a weak smile. 'Sometimes I like to kid myself I'm not. That's why I get shirty when a really smart johnnie like yourself proves I'm not half as clever as I'd like to be.'

'I wasn't trying to prove anything, Captain,' Ben said. 'I should have kept my big mouth shut.'

'Forget it,' Taggart said, and brightened as there was a movement from within the blanket draped over a box in the corner of the day-room. Bournville's chocolate-coloured head appeared. 'Go back to sleep,' Taggart ordered. The pup gazed up at Ben, yawned, and then sank back again into the makeshift bed.

'Where's Bluff?' Ben asked.

'Roaming somewhere,' Taggart replied. 'She'll be back before long.'

'She's a born sailor, that one,' Ben said, glad to pursue a topic other than the one that had brought him to Taggart's cabin. 'I think she was born with sea-legs.'

'You could be right,' Taggart agreed. 'She's no stranger to ships. Probably came from one. I think...' Taggart broke off before he could say more. He drew his breath in quickly and made an involuntary gasp. Ben took a step towards him but the Captain shrugged away from him, so that his face was hidden. 'It's OK, Ben. Just a touch of wind.'

'Are you sure?' Ben regarded him anxiously.

'It's nothing,' Taggart assured him irritably. He turned and managed a rueful smile. 'I've been lying here, trying to make another of my theories work. I never thought that a touch of indigestion would knock it into a cocked hat!'

'What do you mean?'

'Mind over matter, Ben. Mind over matter. Remember me shooting a line in Bombay, so that I could show off to the ladies what a tough guy I was? I said that a man could control pain . . .' He laughed. 'I didn't think that a touch of indigestion would make me eat my words.'

'You've been in pain?'

'It comes and it goes. I've really gone soft. At times I feel that my gut's on fire.'

'Something you've eaten?'

'Sure,' Taggart laughed. 'It's time I stopped breakfasting on barbed wire and rusty bolts. My digestive system can't cope with them any more.

'You're really ill, Captain, aren't you?'

Taggart looked at Ben wearily.

'I'm getting old, Ben – that's all. I'm tired . . . of fighting with everybody and everything. I'm tired of this bloody war. . . . I'm tired of this bloody ship and the people in her . . . I'm tired of having to be strong and prove I'm strong by carrying the heaviest load, when all I want to do is sleep and let some other poor bastard do my share. Sometimes I just want to sit down and cry. . . . But I can't sleep . . . and I can't cry, can I? Big Taggart. . . .'

Ben felt his compassion stir. He was sorry for Taggart and felt he always had been – an instinctive feeling that had been wakened the day that the big man had saved his life in Bombay. It had persisted in the face of all that had happened since Bombay and had been the enduring factor throughout their brief and stormy relationship. It had prevented Ben hating Taggart with the same sustained strength of animosity that the Captain provoked in just about every other human being. Always Ben drew back — stirred by some indefinable instinct to respond with forbearance to the worst that Taggart could do to offend his sensibilities. It was not just indebtedness to the man who had saved his life, but something far more profound: that instinct deep within Ben to answer not to what he saw with his eyes or heard with his ears but to what he sensed these surface things concealed. The stronger call came from what was unspoken and unseen and he could no more ignore it than he could the cries of a drowning man.

'Is there anything I can do to help?' he asked Taggart. 'Maybe there's something in the medicine cabinet that'll fix your stomach?'

'No, Ben, I'll soldier on, if you don't mind.'

'It's not an ulcer?'

Taggart laughed. 'An ulcer wouldn't stand a chance in my zinc-lined gut. No, it's just a touch of wind.' He stood up with an air of resolution. 'I'm going to have a shave and a shower and take a turn on the bridge. Show the flag. And do me a favour, will you? Don't say a word about my having a sore gut, or Fowler will be creeping around here with a bottle of black draught in one hand and his thermometer in the other and hoping that, whatever it is I've got, it's nothing trivial.'

'I won't say a word,' Ben promised. 'You take care.'

'Not feastible likely!' Taggart declared with a grin.

It was close to midnight and Ben was lying on his bunk, reading, when Taggart burst into the room, more agitated than Ben had ever seen him.

'Have you seen Bluff?' he demanded in a tragic voice. 'Have you seen her, Ben?'

Ben sat upright. 'No . . . Not for a couple of hours, anyway. She was in here running around with one of my sandals in her mouth — but I haven't seen her since.'

'She's gone!' Taggart cried brokenly. 'She's gone!'

Ben slid from the bunk.

'Gone? But how?'

'I don't know how,' Taggart snarled. 'I just know she's gone! I can't find her anywhere. She was on the bridge with me until about six bells and then she vanished. I thought she was with Bourneville . . .'

'Have you looked in the galley? They leave scraps out for her . . .'

'I've tried the galley!' Taggart was almost beside himself with angry grief. 'The bastards have done her in! I know it!'

Ben stared at him with shock.

'Nobody'd touch Bluff, Captain. I'd state my life on it. Everybody loves that dog.'

'Not half as much as they hate me! Somebody's done for her, I tell you! And, by God, when I find him, I'm going to take that man apart with my bare hands. I'll murder the bastard!'

There was no pacifying the angry captain. Not that he stayed around to be pacified. He went reeling off, in a state bordering dementia, with the intention of rousing the entire crew. While Ben dressed he could hear, above the howl of the wind and the *Kildare Glen*'s groaning progress into the rising seas, the sound of Taggart's raised voice from somewhere on the deck below. The southern summer night had a chill to it and Ben shivered in his short-sleeved shirt when he ventured on deck and felt the force of the wind sweeping up from the Antarctic. Already men were gathering in the waist of the ship in answer to Taggart's summons to assemble amidships. They huddled about, bewildered, as the Captain moved amongst them, ranting at each new arrival and demanding to know if any had seen the missing dog. None had.

A kind of bedlam reigned on the *Kildare Glen* for the next three hours. Taggart was in its centre, screaming and exhorting as every inch of the ship was searched. From bow to stern, from top bridge to every corner of living space, no part was missed. The holds, the engine-room, the bunkers, the gun-nests, all were searched, with scarcely an individual escaping during the process from the questions, accusations and threats that Taggart unleashed.

On one occasion, Taggart seemed to lose all reason. The victim was the PO Gunner, Finney, whom Taggart had promised to have court-martialled by the Navy in Durban because of the fracas that had taken place in the gunners' quarters. Nothing had ever come of the threat, but no one knew if that was because Taggart had failed to report the matter or if he had and his report had been ignored. At the height of the search for Bluff, however, Finney was imprudent enough to remark to the Carpenter that he had never seen such a ridiculous fuss over a stray dog. He was unaware that Taggart was immediately above him, on the boat-deck, and heard every word.

Finney and the Carpenter were sheltering in the lee of the engineers' accommodation and their first indication that the PO's remark had been overhead was when Taggart materialised from the deck above with a roar of rage. He almost fell down the ladder in his haste to get at Finney, literally landing at the gunner's feet and then seizing him like an enraged bear.

'You're the bastard who did for her?' he screamed at the shaken gunner, as his fingers closed round Finney's throat. 'You dumped her over the side, didn't you?'

At Finney's strangled denial, Taggart began to shake the terrified gunner. It was Ben, arriving hurriedly from the boat-deck in Taggart's wake, whose intervention saved Finney. He threw himself bodily between the two men and, yelling at the top of his voice, managed to distract Taggart sufficiently to make him relax his grip. Taggart vented his anger on Ben.

'This bastard killed my dog!' he shouted in Ben's face.

'He didn't!' Ben screamed back at him, with equal passion. 'Let him go!'

Taggart let go. Finney dropped to the deck and cowered there, shaking and gasping for breath. The Captain stared wildly at Ben, as if struggling to identify him. It took an agonising moment for recognition to dawn.

'Ben . . . Why did you stop me?'

'Because you would have killed him!' Ben shouted the words. Fear gave them vehemence. Not fear for himself, but fear that he could not get through to Taggart in his deranged state. The American turned on Finney. 'Tell him you didn't hurt his dog! Tell him, you son of a bitch! Tell him!'

'I swear I didn't harm it! I ain't seen it! That's the God's honest truth,' the frightened gunner bleated.

Taggart stared down at him, not wholly convinced.

'He'd say anything to save himself. Look at the lying rat!'

'I never touched no dog,' Finney whimpered. 'For God's sake, leave me alone!'

'Come on, Captain,' Ben coaxed. 'We're wasting valuable time here when we could be looking for Bluff. Let's keep searching. We'll find her.'

But they did not find Bluff. At just after three in the morning, Ben persuaded Taggart to let the searchers return to their bunks. The ship could be combed again in daylight. Ben led the Captain to his quarters. Much of the anger had gone from him now, leaving only a wordless grief. He seemed a broken man, withdrawing inside himself, saying nothing, and allowing Ben to lead him like a drunk who has lost his bearings.

In his cabin, Taggart slumped into a chair. Ben stared at the shell of the man who had fought U-boats.

'Can I fix you a drink, Captain?' he offered.

'No,' Taggart murmured, the first word he had spoken in fifteen minutes.

'She must have fallen overboard.' Ben forced himself to say. 'It's the only explanation.'

Taggart looked up at him with disbelieving eyes.

'A sea-dog like her?' He shook his head.

'You're sure you don't want a drink?'

Again, Taggart shook his head.

'Just leave me alone.'

At that moment there was a whimper, and Bourneville's sad little face appeared above the rim of the box that served in his bed. The little animal heaved itself over the edge and came on floppy legs towards Taggart. The big man scooped up the chocolate-coloured bundle and let the pup nestle in his lap. He stroked the flaps of its ears.

Ben had not moved and Taggart raised his eyes to meet his. Tears rolled down the weather-beaten face.

'Why, Ben?' Taggart whispered throatily. 'Why. . . ? Why do I destroy everything I touch?'

On the crossing from India. Ben had watched the stress of the encounter with the Japanese ship and the cyclone take its toll on Taggart. His behaviour had become more and more eccentric but it had not, as Ben had feared, degenerated into complete mental breakdown. Somehow, the Captain had come teetering back from the brink and shown remarkable resilience in the face of pressures which would have caused other men to buckle. Now Taggart was slipping over the brink again. As the days passed, it seemed that the mysterious disappearance of his beloved Bluff had loosened his hold on the precipice, and every day saw him slip further and further into the abyss.

Witnessing the disintegration of the man was an agony to Ben, made worse by the fact that he was unable to do anything to arrest the process. His impotence to help was made all the more unbearable by the knowledge that he alone was the only human being who cared. Taggart had so alienated himself from his mess that they were utterly indifferent to his decline. Some even gloried in it.

It amazed Ben how the loss of the foundling bitch could have such a profound effect on the hard-bitten skipper, until he realised that Bluff's disappearance was not the only factor. It had acted like the proverbial straw on the camel's back, providing the fatal overload.

In an effort to help Taggart, Ben tried to spend as much time in his company as possible. The more he talked to him, he believed, the more he would be able to alleviate the anxieties preying on the Captain's mind. But Taggart would only tolerate Ben's company on those occasions of lucidity when he was something like his old self – and such moments rapidly became rarer. More and more, the Captain retired into a private world of his own, into which no one was admitted.

One morning, Ben was wakened at about five by the sound of a voice coming from the fore-deck. Pulling on shirt and trousers he went outside but could neither see nor hear anything. He climbed the ladder to the navigating bridge. Fowler was leaning against the dodger.

'I heard a noise up forward,' Ben told the Chief Officer. 'It woke me up.'

'It's the Old Man,' Fowler said. 'He's still looking for his bloody dog.'

At that moment from somewhere in front of the forward mast-house, Taggart's voice rose.

'Here, Bluff. Here, Bluff . . . Where are you, girl?'

Taggart himself came into view on the fore-deck immediately below the bridge. He was bare-footed and clad only in his underpants. Now he was whistling for the dog.

Ben stared at Fowler, feeling both distress and anger.

'Aren't you going to do something?' he demanded.

'What do you suggest? Put him in a straitjacket and lock him up? You can, if you like.'

'It's your job to do something. You can't let this go on,' Ben protested.

'Don't tell me what my job is, Mister,' Fowler retorted. 'What that madman down there needs is a keeper, and I'm not volunteering. As far as I'm concerned, it would save a lot of grief if he just went over the side like his bloody dog.'

'Yes,' Ben agreed angrily, 'that would suit you fine, wouldn't it?'

Fowler grinned. 'Careful how you speak to me, Mr Darby. I could be running this ship after BA — after we get your chum in the booby-hatch where he belongs.'

'Will you manage to stay sober that long?' Ben asked acidly. He turned on his heel and hurried down the ladder, ignoring the heated rejoinder that Fowler hurled after him — something about him not having touched a drop since Durban and that Ben had better watch his step.

On deck, he approached Taggart and tried to persuade the Captain to return to his cabin. Taggart looked at him without recognition and without paying any attention to his words.

'Are you the standby man?' Taggart demanded in his bridge voice.

'It's me, Ben Darby,' Ben tried patiently. 'Look, Captain...'

'I *am* looking, you fool,' Taggart interrupted. 'I've been looking everywhere. She must be around somewhere. Why aren't you looking?'

'She's maybe gone back to your cabin,' Ben said, deciding to humour him. 'Let's look there.' He could feel Fowler's eyes on him from the bridge above. The Chief Officer was probably loving this. To Ben's relief, Taggart fell for his suggestion.

'Of course, my cabin!' he agreed, as if the thought had been a stroke of genius. 'She'll be worried about Bourneville.'

Ben accompanied him all the way to the door of the day-room. As Taggart was about to enter, he suddenly blundered against the door-post and doubled up, clutching at his side. He allowed Ben to help him inside and on to the settee, where he rolled over and brought his knees up still clutching at his midriff.

'Oh, God,' he groaned, 'this gut of mine is killing me.'

Ben tried to make him comfortable, without much success. Taggart shed the blanket that the American laid over him as he rolled in agony. Ben was perplexed. He tried to question the writhing Captain.

'It's the same pain, isn't it, Captain? And it's not indigestion – not way down there.'

'It's getting worse all the time,' Taggart gasped out. 'But there's bugger-all you or anybody else can do about it. So you might as well clear off and leave me to it.'

'I'm not going anywhere,' Ben said stubbornly. 'I'm not leaving you like this.'

He bullied Taggart into allowing him to probe the seat of the pain. He drew a finger across the naked abdomen, suspecting what the trouble was, and was rewarded by Taggart's wince of pain under the featherweight touch.

Taggart looked up at him grimly.

'Well, Doctor, now you know.'

'Yes, Captain. Now I know. The problem is what's to be done about it.'

'Nothing can be done about it. I keep it until we get to port.'

'And if we don't get to port in time?' Ben asked.

'Then, most likely, I'll kick the bucket.'

The pain seemed to have eased momentarily and Taggart's brain now seemed to be as clear as, previously, it had been confused. Possibly the reality of the pain had induced lucidity. Ben said.

'I'll have a word with Mr Fowler. You need surgery . . .'

'Sure, Chippy can have a go at me on the saloon table. No, Ben, no amateur's going to open me up.'

'That wasn't what I meant, Captain. There could be a ship nearby with a doctor . . .'

'Forget it. I keep my appendix until we hit the River Plate or the damned thing bursts before we get there.' He smiled. 'It's ironic, isn't it? History repeating itself so soon.'

'What do you mean?'

'I mean I'm in the same fix as that cabin-boy friend of yours. The same options are open.'

'It hadn't crossed my mind.'

'Well, it has crossed mine. I'm still in command. I've got to make the decisions.'

'And you've made your decision?'

'The ship comes first. I don't matter. We don't break radio silence and we don't back-track to Tristan da Cunha on the off-chance they've got a surgeon there. We keep going and, with a little bit of luck, we'll make the Plate before I snuff it.'

'You can't keep this secret, Captain. I still think you should tell Fowler.'

'You can tell him, Ben – over my dead body.'

'That's what I'm afraid of.'

'I'm not asking you, Ben. I'm telling you. Now bugger off and leave me to get some sleep. The pain's better now. I'll maybe get half an hour while I've got the chance.'

Ben left him then but did not return to his own bunk. Sleep would have been an impossibility. He sat in his chair, staring at the hands that could type out more than sixty words a minute and cursing their uselessness. Why couldn't they have been trained to hold a scalpel and used in a positive service to humanity? Ben had always been proud of his calling and how, in his own humble way, he had been dedicated to the promulgation of ideas and ideals that influenced the minds and lives of men. But, for the moment, he despised his role of useless onlooker and felt only disillusion. He could spend his life recording man in all his nobility and all his frailty and man would take no notice. He would still be as blind and cruel and avaricious as he had been in the dawn of time, and no amount of chronicling his errors and transgressions would prevent him repeating them for all eternity.

The same evening when Ben looked in to see Taggart, he found the Captain sitting in his armchair with a glass in his hand and a half-empty whisky bottle before him.

'Good to see you, Ben,' he greeted the American. 'Sit down, help yourself to a glass of the soothing spirit.'

'How's the pain?' Ben asked, as he poured some whisky for himself.

'So-so,' Taggart replied. 'It comes and it goes. At the moment, it's gone. Whisky is the perfect balm.' Ben was relieved to find that apart from being a little drunk, Taggart was enjoying one of his more rational periods. Twice during the day he had confused the American with someone from the dim and distance past and had insisted on calling him 'Nobby'. He had also caused some confusion on the bridge during the afternoon. At noon, he had given orders for boat-drill to be carried out at 3 pm. Then, when the alarm bells had been sounded, he had raised hell with both Prins and Fowler for holding boat practices without his say-so.

'I have been exercising my mind,' he announced to Ben.

'That sounds interesting,' Ben said, and waited to be enlightened.

'I've been contemplating the difficulty of dying with

dignity.' Taggart went on, not noticing that Ben almost coughed up his whisky in surprise at the calmly delivered statement.

'I can think of more cheerful topics,' Ben said, hoping he could turn the conversation in another direction. But Taggart was not to be diverted.

'I have a revolver in my desk over there,' he said. 'I thought that if the worst comes to the worst ... if it comes to a point when I know it's too late ... that it might be a good idea to blow my brains out rather than thrash around on the deck with a ruptured appendix spewing poison all over my insides....'

Ben would have interrupted but Taggart silenced him with a wave of his hand.

'Suicide doesn't appeal to me, Ben, so don't get agitated. There's nothing very dignified about suicide ... unless, of course, you go about it the way the Japanese do, with a bit of ceremony. But it's messy and not exactly painless. It would be just as easy to try to dig out the appendix and be done with it.'

He laughed. Ben did not join in.

'I also thought,' Taggart went on, 'that I could give my forty-five to somebody else and ask them to put me out of my misery. Would you do it, Ben?'

The American shook his head.

'No, Captain. Sorry. I'm much too squeamish and I'm a rotten shot. I'd probably miss.'

'I could always ask for volunteers,' Taggart said, thoughtfully, and then laughed again. 'No, I wouldn't need the bloody gun if I did that. I'd be killed in the rush!'

'You've still got your sense of humour. Captain. So can we talk about this some other time ... Say, in twenty years?'

Taggart took no notice of him.

'Is there ever any dignity in dying?' he asked the air, as if scarcely aware of Ben's presence. 'Or is it just the final indignity? Not the final glory, but the final humiliation.' He let his head slump forward. 'In some ways I'm looking forward to being dead,' he mumbled. 'It'll be the first decent sleep I've had in years.'

'Let's change the subject, eh, Captain?' Ben tried.

'No, Ben! Taggart's sudden stare reflected his fierce adamance. 'I've thought about death for a long time. I've thought about it and thought about it and thought about it. I've dreamed about it and had nightmares about it and it won't go away. Now I want to talk about it.'

'You could go crazy,' Ben began, before instantly regretting his thoughtless choice of words. Taggart immediately pounced on them.

'Crazy ... You said it, Ben ... Crazy! That's what thinking too much does for you. It drives you crazy. It's been driving me crazy ... Thinking things ... Getting angrier and angrier inside until you want to smash everything within reach ... You want to hurt ... Cause pain ... Even to those that means everything to you ... And they don't understand ... They hate you for it ... And you hate yourself for being able to show what you really feel and why you did this or why you did that ... And everything becomes confused and twisted and not the way it shoud be at all ...'

Taggart closed his eyes, as if he was trying to block out the things that his mind's eye could see.

'Go easy on yourself, Captain,' Ben said softly.

'No, Ben, I've got to talk. I've got to talk to *somebody*! Because I can't live with it any longer. I can't bear the obscenity of it any longer!' His voice rose almost to a screech. 'I don't know who I am any more, or who I was, or why I was ever born!'

Ben stared at the ravaged face.

'What is it you can't live with any longer, Captain?'

Taggart stared back at him, his eyes searching Ben's face.

'It's too horrible Ben. It will make you sick to your soul. I want to talk about it but it will scar your mind as it has scarred mine. It may not be personal to you – as it's personal to me ... I want to tell you ... but I want to spare you, too.'

Ben shivered at the intensity of Taggart's scrutiny.

'Forget me, Captain. Just tell me what it is.'

CHAPTER 13

Revelation

Taggart talked for almost an hour. A strange calmness gripped him as he spoke. He was like a man in a trance, recounting under hypnosis the particulars of a traumatising experience that had left him devoid of all emotion. Ben listened with growing awe and horror. At times he wanted to close his ears, but he heard Taggart out: absorbing the Captain's agony of mind, understanding it at last and knowing that, for ever more, some of that agony would be his.

Much of Taggart's story was like a confession. He talked about his son, whom he loved dearly but to whom he was never able to convey the depth of that feeling.

'I was a God to him, Ben, and he went in awe of me – always afraid to get too close in case he incurred my wrath. I was pretty good at laying down the law, mind. I expected to be obeyed in all things. But I wanted his life to be better than mine. I wanted him to have the chances that I'd never had. He was more like his mother than me – not exactly soft, but not a fighter like me who could look after himself. He needed protecting – and I wanted to protect him. The trouble was that, from about the time he was able to walk, he wanted to go to sea like his dad. His mother was dead against the idea – and so was I, although she never quite believed me. She thought I encouraged the notion...'

Young Michael Taggart had tried to run away to sea when he was sixteen.

'Norah, my wife, blamed me for it,' Taggart said. 'She never forgave me, even when I managed to get Michael brought home and put the kibosh on his seafaring ambitions. He, of course, never quite forgave me for stopping him doing what he wanted to do. And I never forgave Norah for not believing that it wasn't me who had stuffed the boy's head with the notion of sailoring.'

Norah Taggart had walked out on her husband. His long absences at sea had not made her heart grow fonder of the man she had married. They had embittered her. Taggart had been powerless to stop his son going with the mother. The boy had known no other home but with his mother and had been left with little choice but to follow her. The boy, however, had resisted his mother's attempts to make him sever all connections with his father. He had kept in touch and, occasionally, they had met at stiff, awkward reunions, at which Taggart had been unable to unbend and let his emotions speak and the boy had been unable to shed his awe of his father.

Then in the early months of the war, Taggart had become a celebrated hero. He talked bitterly to Ben about his hour in the limelight.

'At first I couldn't understand what the fuss was all about,' he said. 'I had done nothing exceptional. What they didn't tell the newspapers about the *Kildare Cape*'s fight with the U-boat was that the sub was crippled and couldn't submerge. She was at the end of her patrol and had no torpedoes left. All I was interested in was getting the hell out of it. And that's what we were doing when we got off a lucky shot and blew half her conning tower away. All that about me turning and fighting was a lot of crap.'

A Royal Navy patrol boat had picked up a dozen

survivors from the sunken U-boat, including the commander who had been blown into the sea with the *Kildare Cape*'s shell-burst. Later, Taggart had been photographed with the man whom he had vanquished.

'The propaganda boys really rubbed that poor Jerry's nose in it,' Taggart recalled. 'They made him out to be some kind of Nazi monster, but what I remember about him most was his dignity. Dignity mattered to him. He said no more than a dozen words to me, but I can remember them as clear as if it had happened yesterday. 'Captain,' he said, 'my one regret is that your gunner didn't get me and give me the dignity of dying with my ship.'

At this stage of his account, Taggart had broken from the flat monotone of his delivery to show a glimmer of emotion. He had briefly seized Ben's shirt-front and spoken with some vehemence.

'Beware of live heroes, Ben. Beware of supermen touched with glory, who live to get a ticker-tape parade. They could be like me – frauds who have had glory thrust on them. I didn't want the adulation I got. I never wanted any of the fuss or the damned medals. The damnable thing was that it made me believe I was somebody that I wasn't. I began to believe the bloody lies they told about me! I began to think I was some kind of superman. And when the fussing stopped, I missed it. I craved for it! I wanted the glory they made me believe was mine by right . . . But there is no glory, Ben . . . It doesn't exist . . . It's a myth . . .'

One person had been more affected by Taggart's sudden fame than any other. Michael Taggart had been caught up in the wake of all the ballyhoo. Then a medical student, he had been found by the newspapers and interviewed about his father's exploits.

The reports had highlighted the contrast between the buccaneering sea-dog father and the rather frail-looking and mild-mannered son. Michael had publicly expressed unbounding admiration for his father and admitted that it was far from easy living in the shadow of such a legendary figure. Everyone expected him to be a chip off the old block. Michael made no mention to the press that his father had thwarted his own ambitions of a sea career.

A few months later, Taggart had been staggered to receive a letter from Michael revealing just how unsettled his son had become. 'Your exploits,' Michael had written, 'have made me realise that medicine can wait. It's high time that I was making some kind of contribution to this war and I intend to get in on the action while there's still some action available. I can't let my old man grab all the glory, can I? With luck, there should still be some left for me.'

Michael had gone in search of glory by quitting university and enlisting in the Army. The letter to his father had been written on the eve of his departure for North Africa with the field battery to which he had been assigned. He had been killed three months before the final defeat of the Germans in North Africa.

Taggart had recited the bare details of this dreadful blow to him with great tears rolling down his cheeks. Some time after the official notification, he had received a letter from Michael's commanding officer. It had contained the usual condolences and extolled Michael as a young man of outstanding qualities that had made him a fine soldier and a much-loved comrade.

'You must have been very proud of him,' Ben had prompted Taggart, almost whispering.

'Proud? Oh, I was proud all right – if it's possible to be proud and broken-hearted at the same time. Oh, I was proud all right. But I couldn't leave things at that, could I? I had to know more. I had been told so little ... I wanted to know the place where it happened and how it had happened ... I wanted to know where the grave was ... I wanted to speak to the lads who had known Michael and been his friends . . . I wanted more than just the few memories I had of a boy I'd hardly got to know . . .'

During his stay in Bombay, prior to joining the *Kildare Glen*, Taggart had gone out of his way to find out more about his son's death. He had pestered the Army authorities there for information. As a consequence of one of those coincidences, that occur in war – and defy all mathematical laws of probability – the answers he sought were close at hand. Three twelve-inch gun-batteries from the Middle East had recently arrived in Bombay and were occupying a transit camp in not-too-distant Poona. One of them was Michael's former unit. The division of which it had been a part had been pulled back to the Suez Canal and disbanded soon after Michael's death. His old battery had been posted east to become part of a new division for Burma. The battery had a new commanding officer and there had been many replacements amongst the personnel, but the Battery Sergeant-Major was the same as the one under whom Michael had served.

Taggart had gone to Poona and sought out the veteran soldier. From the moment of their meeting, Taggart had found him very reluctant to say anything at all. He seemed most unhappy at the Captain's sudden appearance.

'We went for a walk on the edge of the sports field that was part of the camp,' Taggart told Ben, 'and it was like drawing teeth, trying to get a word out of the man. Apart from telling me that Michael had been killed in an artillery attack near a place called Medenine in Tunisia, he just clammed up. He didn't want to talk about it. I finished up losing my rag with him. I accused him of deliberately holding back and I threatened to knock his bloody head off if he didn't tell me what he was trying to hide.'

Taggart had eventually bullied the truth out of the

reticent warrant officer, who had not wanted to say too much out of respect for Taggart's feelings. There had been an unspeakable horror in the circumstances of Michael's death that made the veteran plead, even in the face of the Captain's threats, not to press him further. But the more he had pleaded, the more Taggart had insisted on being given every appalling detail.

At seven in the morning of that fateful February day in 1943, Michael Taggart and his closest friend in the unit had stood down from their gun after a dawn barrage on enemy positions. The front had been static for several weeks and the British battery had been dug into positions on nameless terrain well to the west of Medenine and not far from the Wadi Akarit. The two men had been the only occupants of the battery's field latrine when the British artillery emplacements had come under bombardment from German guns. The latrine was of the most primitive variety: a wooden pole stretched across a deep open trench, and surrounded by a burlap screen. Michael and his friend had been squatting on the pole, defecating into the trench, when a shell had landed nearby. A metal shard from the shell had ripped through the sacking screen and taken the top off Michael's head. His body had fallen into the pit of excrement.

The task of retrieving the body had proved too loathsome to Michael Taggart's fellow gunners. They had tried but had been overcome with vomiting revulsion whenever they had entered the stinking trench where he lay. It had been left to a team of medics, summoned from close at hand, to complete the grisly undertaking. The incident had had a profoundly demoralising effect on the entire unit, not least on Michael's friend. He had been untouched by the shell-burst that had killed Michael but had become so psychologically disturbed by the trauma that he had been hospitalised.

In his day-room on the *Kildare Glen*, Taggart forced

himself to repeat to Ben every ghastly detail of his son's grotesque end. With his voice breaking and tears streaming from his anguished eyes, he brought into the open the unendurable horror with which he had lived in torment for so long. Now the agony of it seemed to exude from him like the sweat dripping from his forehead and mingling with his unchecked tears. He released a great wailing cry and covered his face with his hands.

'Oh, Michael, Michael,' he sobbed through the fingers clasped about his mouth, 'is this your glory? Is this what I brought you into the world for? To die face-down in a pit of stinking shit?' He screeched, half-shouted the words; his eyes staring at Ben, not seeing him but fixed only on the tortured images of his mind. Then he dropped his head suddenly into his hands and began to cry like a child.

Ben got up and went over to him. He could think of no words that would comfort nor any action that would console. He laid a gentle hand on the massive shoulders of the whimpering man, stricken with a trembling compassion for him that was beyond the art of expression.

'Oh, Captain,' he murmured hopelessly. 'Oh, Captain . . .'

Ben hoped that, having brought himself to talk about the nightmare that haunted his mind, Taggart might have exorcised some of the horror that was destroying him. But sharing his terrible secret and private agony with the American brought about no slowing in the Captain's lapses into a confused world of his own. If anything, his behaviour became more muddled and irrational and his periods of complete disorientation became longer. At these times, it was impossible to converse with him sensibly and he had to be humoured like a child. His more lucid moments usually came in the wake of the bouts of severe abdominal pain, which also increased in frequency and duration.

Somehow, Taggart managed to conceal his pain from all but Ben, but there was no concealing the instability of his mind. His failure to remember where he was and who the people around him were led to incidents which the crew greeted as high comedy but which to Ben were depressingly tragic. He did not find it funny when the ship's captain suddenly took it into his head to chip rust from the fore-deck. Taggart had noticed the heavy flaking beside the coaming of the No. 2 hold and, obtaining a chipping hammer from the Bosun, he had sat on the deck for more than an hour quite happily chipping away at the offending rust. On another occasion, he had insisted on personally shining up all the brass on the wheel-house – much to the amusement of the helmsman, to whom he gave a running commentary in the mistaken belief that he was a Swede with whom he had sailed some twenty years before.

With just over a thousand miles to run to the River Plate, Taggart's concealment of the physical pain that had been racking him ceased to be a secret. He collapsed in agony on the bridge during the Second Officer's watch. Willem Prins summoned help and three men were needed to carry the Captain down to his day-room, where he insisted on being laid on the settee, rather than in the broad double-bed in the adjacent room. He also insisted that he wanted no one in attendance except Ben.

When Ben arrived, it soon became obvious to him that the latest attack was not of the spasmodic nature of its predecessors. The pain was continuous and showed no sign of relaxing in intensity.

'I'm done for this time,' Taggart informed him, between gasping breaths. He was rolling from side to side, knees up and hugging at his abdomen. He was flushed and bathed in perspiration.

'You'll make it,' Ben promised him. 'But you're going to have to let me get you something for the pain.'

'No medicines!' Taggart waved him away, and groaned convulsively.

'I'm not taking no for an answer,' Ben said, then left him and sought out Fowler. The Chief Officer was amused by Ben's anxiety.

'It's probably colic,' he said. 'Why get yourself in a tizzy?'

'It's appendicitis,' Ben replied, in a tone that brooked no argument. 'And the condition's acute. You're going to open that medicine chest of yours, Mr Fowler, and you're going to give me something to help the Captain cope with the pain!'

'So you're the doctor now?' Fowler taunted. 'What makes you think you can give me orders.'

Ben stared grimly at the sneering face.

'I'll tell you what,' he threatened. 'Everything I know about you, Mr Fowler . . . How incompetent a son of a bitch you are . . . How fond you are of the bottle . . . How you get drunk on watch . . . You don't do just what I tell you and I promise you that I'll make your name stink so far and so wide that you won't even want to know yourself!'

Fowler paled. 'You wouldn't dare.'

'Try me.' He paused to let Fowler savour the seriousness of his intent. 'Now, get the key to that goddamned medicine locker!'

Fowler got the key and accompanied Ben to the big double-doored recess next to the saloon where the medical supplies were stored. The interior was surprisingly roomy. The shelves were well-stocked with a wide variety of medicines and there was a dispensing table with scales, a mortar-bowl and pestle, and a case of surgical instruments. In a drawer of the dispensing table were several books and pamphlets, including the *Ship*

Captain's Medical Guide and a copy of the *British Pharmaceutical Code, 1923*.

Ben consulted the *Medical Guide* while Fowler looked on with a disdainful expression.

'Where are the morphine tablets?' Ben asked, when he had read enough.

Fowler unlocked a cabinet within the recess and lifted out a large brown bottle. He handed it to Ben.

'Sure you know what you're doing?' he enquired.

Ben glared at him. 'I'm doing your job for you, Mr Fowler. And the only reason I'm doing it is because the Captain wouldn't trust you to give him a glass of water for fear you'd put cyanide in it.'

Fowler laughed. 'Then he can't be as insane as I thought he was. Is there anything further I can do for you, Mr Darby?' He smirked.

'You can tell me why the ship seems to have slowed down.'

'My orders, Mr Darby – in the absence of a master who is *compas mentis*. The Chief Engineer consulted me about the bunker situation. We've been burning coal too fast. So we've reduced revs to keep going at a comfortable ten knots. I trust you have no objection.'

'Well you trust wrong, Mr Fowler! The captain of this ship has acute appendicitis and unless we make double-quick time to the River Plate and get him into hospital, he's going to die. I'm not going to let that happen and, more important, I'm not going to let you let it happen. So you just run straight along to the Chief Engineer and tell him to squeeze every last ounce of speed out of this rust-bucket that he can goddamned get! Do you understand me, Mr Fowler?'

Fowler eyed him uncertainly.

'Very well, Mr Darby. I'll see what he can do.'

'You do that,' Ben said, warningly. 'Because yours is the head I'm going to have if the Captain doesn't make it. Do I make myself clear?'

'Very clear,' said Fowler.

Ben returned to Taggart, who was in so much pain that he offered little resistance when coaxed to take two of the morphine tablets. The drug had some effect almost immediately. The Captain's writhing subsided and he settled back on the settee to stare, open-eyed, at the deckhead. He gagged once or twice as if he were about to be sick, but then his breathing became more even and a drowsiness overtook him. He slept fitfully.

Ben sat in one of the armchairs, watching him. With Taggart reasonably peaceful, he turned his attention to the books and pamphlets on drugs which he had found in the medicine locker.

He was alarmed to find a tract on morphine, which listed warnings on when the drug should not be used. He scanned it, praying that Taggart had no chest disorder or asthmatic or bronchial troubles, but found no mention of the drug's prohibition in connection with suspected appendicitis. The effects of the drug were also itemised and Ben was relieved to find that it was shown to be doing its work when the patient showed signs of relaxation and sleep. The opposite effect could also occur: the patient showing mild anxiety and fear, particularly if doses were continued. Mental clouding was likely and, also, constriction of the pupils and sweating.

Ben put the literature aside. The more he read, the more easily he would convince himself that he had made a dreadful mistake in trying to alleviate the big man's suffering. But it was a responsibility which no one else had seemed willing to shoulder.

As the minutes passed, the awesome nature of that responsibility bore down with increasing weight on Ben's mind. Taggart was now sleeping, not peacefully, but emitting short panting breaths. Ben tucked a blanket over him and sponged his beads of sweat away from his fevered brow. He drew a little comfort from the fact that, for the moment, Taggart seemed to be suffering no pain.

During the next twenty-four hours Ben was only vaguely aware of a truculent resentment building up against him in the *Kildare Glen*. It stemmed from the illusion created that in taking over personal control of the Captain's welfare he had somehow taken over command of the ship. It seemed that a landlubber, without any qualifications or experience, was giving all the orders – and there was a decided reluctance to obey these orders. It escaped no one's attention, however, that the Chief Officer – the man with every entitlement to put the American in his place – grudgingly obeyed whatever he was directed to do. This gave the impression that Mr Fowler still acknowledge Taggart's authority in the ship and recognised Ben as the Captain's sole agent in the exercise of that authority. So there was no rebellion against Ben's dictates – merely resentment.

In fact Taggart was in no position to give orders of any kind. Within twenty-four hours, he had become dependent on the four-hourly morphine doses as his only relief from pain and was begging Ben for the tablets long before it was time to get them. And as he became dependent on the drug, so he became more and more psychologically dependent on the person who supplied it. Ben became his personal angel of mercy. He looked to Ben for everything, in the way that a helpless baby clamours for its mother.

The big man's utter dependence on him did nothing for Ben's peace of mind. He was horrified by the speed with which the drug had exerted its power of addiction and his instinct was to withhold it because of the lasting damage it might be inflicting. But he was in a cleft stick. Taggart's pitiful pleading and the sight of his suffering were the factors that made him overcome his misgivings.

Ben felt no misgivings about using the unique position in which he found himself in order to speed the *Kildare Glen*'s progress towards the River Plate. He buttonholed Willem Prins in the chart-room and elicited from him the mileage still to run and an estimated time of arrival, impressing upon the young Dutchman that minutes saved could mean the difference between life and death for Taggart.

'Why do you come to me?' Prins asked. 'I cannot make the ship go faster.'

'You're the navigator,' Ben replied. 'I know there aren't any short-cuts to South America, but you have the ship's performance at your fingertips. You know what the ship can do and you can make it your business to see that she performs better than she's ever done before.'

'That is up to the engineers.'

'I'll take care of the engineers,' Ben said, 'if you give me the facts and figures that tell me how fast we're eating up the miles.'

'The Captain has ordered this?'

'The Captain's life depends on it.'

'Then God help him,' said Prins.

'Meaning you won't?'

'I shall do my duty, Mr Darby. No more than that. But I shall not mourn if the Captain dies. He is a monster.'

'Because he had a spat with you? Because he called you a few names when he was half out of his mind with other worries?'

'He said things that I can never forget, or forgive . . . Insults, lies, all of it . . . Not just against me, but my people . . . His words made me ill . . .'

'He was ill, Willem – even then. He didn't mean any of the things he said to you. He was letting off steam . . . And you happened to get the full blast . . . Maybe if you'd blasted back at him, he would have respected you more. He's like that.'

Willem Prins looked shocked.

'But he is the Captain.'

'Yes, Willem. He is the Captain. And right now he needs you on his side. You've got to do everything you can to see he makes it to the Plate.'

Prins drew himself erect.

'I told you I know my duty, Mr Darby. If . . . if the Captain does not make it, it will not be because I failed him.'

Ben came down from the bridge, feeling not dissatisfied with the brief conversation he had had with the Second Officer. It was probably the longest conversation the Dutchman had had with anyone in a month, ever since his row with Taggart and his Trappist-like withdrawal into brooding silence. Ben was sure that he could rely on Prins to treat Taggart's illness as the emergency it was, in spite of any ill-will he bore the Captain. His deeply imbued sense of duty would see to that. He would do his job dispassionately and to the very best of his ability, and it was important that he should. Ben did not have the same trust in Fowler.

Armed with the information that Prins had given him, Ben's next call was on the Chief Engineer. He found Ferguson in his port-side cabin above the engine-room. The Scot looked up with a wry smile when he saw who his visitor was.

'Well, well, well, this is an unusual honour, Mr Darby. You're not looking for more lessons in the stokehold, are you?'

'No, Chief.'

'What can I do for you then?'

'I want you to make up your silly feud with the Captain,' Ben said.

Ferguson got up from his desk and faced Ben.

'You want me to shake hands with the Devil, do you?

Kiss and make up? No, you're wasting your time, Mr Darby. He's had his chances to make his peace with me. If he wants to call a truce, he knows where I live.'

'He didn't send me here,' Ben said. 'I came on my own accord. This is my idea.'

Ferguson studied Ben's face.

'I've always thought a lot of you, Mr Darby. I've never been able to understand what you and Taggart have in common. And I've never been able to make up my mind whether you're bosom pals or deadly enemies. Me, I'm pretty particular in my choice of friends.'

'The Captain's a very sick man, Chief.'

'I'm well aware of that. He's off his bloody head!'

Ben nodded grimly. 'You could say so. He's sick in the mind. He has been for a very long time. And there are reasons for it. He's had things preying on his mind that are so terrible that I'd rather not even talk about them. I want you to take my word on it that it's a wonder he hasn't cracked before now. He needs your pity, Chief . . . Not your scorn.'

'Scorn is about all I've ever had from him. What about this belly-ache of his? The Mate says it's colic and says you say it's his appendix. Who do I believe?'

'There's not a lot that Mr Fowler says that I would believe. But you'd better believe me, Chief. The Captain's going to die unless he gets to hospital soon. Maybe he's got a few days. More likely, it's just hours . . .'

'You're no doctor. What makes you so sure?'

'Because I've seen it all before, Chief. And I know what I'm seeing now. Last time it was my mother . . . We were on vacation – the family . . . At a cabin in the woods . . . Miles from anywhere . . . At first, my old man thought it was just something she'd eaten – some fish we'd caught. . . . Then we knew it was more than that and we tried to get her to a doc . . . We drove through half the night . . . But we were too late . . .'

'I'm sorry,' Ferguson murmured.

'I don't want us to be too late this time, Chief?' Ben said fiercely. 'Fowler said he was going to get you to pull the stops out.'

'He didn't put it quite the way that you're putting it,' said the Chief. 'He said could we squeeze another knot out of the old sewing-machine without putting too much strain on the bunker position? I told him that he was the one who was worried about the coal lasting out, not me. We've got plenty...'

'The son of a bitch!' Ben burst out. 'You mean we could be going faster?'

'We're just dawdling along. If I double-banked the watches and got the deucer to sit on the safety-valve, we could get another two-and-a-half to three knots out of the old girl.'

'Well, you'll do it, won't you?' Ben stared at him anxiously.

Ferguson glared at the American.

'Of course I'll bloody do it! What do you take me for? I hate the guts of that overgrown gorilla up there, but I don't want his death on my conscience/'

Ben grinned, liking the man.

'I knew I could count on you, Chief.'

'Don't count too hard,' cautioned the engineer. 'We did our best to save that poor laddie of a cabin-boy remember? And the Almighty still took him. He's got no reason to be doing Taggart any favours. Have you any idea how far from the Rio Plata we are?'

'It was just under eight hundred miles at noon. According to Mr Prins, that's about sixty hours' steaming.'

'Aye,' Ferguson said, calculating mentally, 'assuming we get thirteen knots out of the old girl. Well, let's not waste time talking, Mr Darby. Let's see what she can do!'

*

Ferguson was as good as his word. Within minutes of his descent into the steamy cavern of the engine-room, the shuddering increase in engine revolutions could be felt throughout the ship. The *Kildare Glen* seemed to Ben to be thundering through the water, an impression that was reinforced by the fact that the wind had dropped to the lightest of airs and by the way that the ship was surging across the tops of the long lazy swell.

Ben found Fowler preparing to go on watch – and caught him in the familiar act of fortifying himself for the occasion. He tried to conceal the bottle at the sound of Ben's knock but was not quite quick enough. Ben entered the cabin without waiting for a summons.

'Well, well,' he said. 'Every picture tells a story.'

'What the hell do you want now?' Fowler snapped at him, flustered. 'Can't a man get any bloody privacy?'

'I've just been talking to Mr Ferguson.' Ben said, ignoring the gibe. 'He tells me he's not the least worried about the bunker coal. We've got plenty. There's no reason why we shouldn't have been flat out all day. I don't think you've been playing it quite straight, Mr Fowler. I could get the impression that maybe you don't want us to get to the Plate too fast.'

Fowler's glare was filled with fury.

'Don't interfere with things you don't know anything about, Mr Darby. You've got no standing on this ship!'

'And you haven't got ten cents' worth of integrity! All your goddamned authority comes out of a bottle!'

'I'm in nominal command of this ship,' Fowler blustered. 'That's the law, Mr Darby! That madman up there isn't fit to tie his shoe-laces and, as second-in-command, I'm obliged to take over – whether you happen to like it or not.'

'I don't like it, Mr Fowler,' Ben said, grinding the words out evenly. 'I don't like it one little bit. And I'll tell you why I don't like it. Because when it comes to tying shoe-laces you're the one who's not fit to tie anyone's. Not your own, not mine, and least of all the laces of the man up there that you call mad. You want him dead, don't you? Well, I want him *living*!'.

'I could have you locked up,' Fowler threatened.

'You could have me locked up,' Ben agreed, 'but you're never going to shut me up! You can lock me up any time you like, but you sure as hell are not going to gag me!'

Fowler stared at Ben uncertainly, his confidence wavering.

'You don't frighten me,' he said, but less than convincingly. 'And you can't blackmail me.'

'Oh, but I can,' Ben said with a grim smile. 'We both know you can be blackmailed.'

'What the hell do you want of me?' Fowler cried, his voice an unhappy screech.

'Just a little awareness of the urgency of the situation,' Ben said, in an almost calming tone. 'That's all I want. Just a sense of urgency and some good sense. Thanks to you and your goddamned lies about the coal, we've lost more than seventy miles since yesterday. That's nearly six hours' steaming, Mr Fowler – when every goddamned minute could mean the difference between life and death for Captain Taggart. Your account is in deficit, Mr Fowler, and from here on in I'm going to keep a very careful note. You'd better not get any further into the red. You'd better start paying back what you owe or, so help me, there's going to be a day of reckoning that you'll regret.'

With the help of the Chief Steward, Ben managed to transfer Taggart from the narrow settee in the day-room to the bedroom. Ben, then commandeered the Captain's settee for his own use, napping there when the opportunities arose to relax his vigil over the ailing giant in the next room. It was like travelling a familiar road, a road he had been down before – and a road of unhappy memory. The memory of those days and nights when he had stood by Richard White was still fresh, although they already seemed a lifetime away. Then, as now, time had been the enemy. Taggart then – to some extent – had seemed its ally: a frustrating obstacle in a race that had no winners, only losers. This time, it was Taggart's life at stake and one of the obstacles was much more vicious in character. Fowler's indifference to Taggart's fate was inspired by malevolence and Ben had felt no need for scruples in smashing through it. The unconcern of men like Ferguson and Prins had been more readily understandable and more easily broken down. To the credit of both men, neither had been prepared to allow their considerable dislike of Taggart to stand in the way of their efforts to save him.

Ben's hopes rose when just before midnight – when Taggart was due another dose of pain-relieving morphine – the Captain showed no signs of his growing dependency on the drug nor of the pain that had racked him. He was drowsy but lucid. He wanted a whisky and he wanted to talk. He seemed totally reconciled to the fact that he was ill and would have to stay confined to his bed. He apparently had a clear grasp of his situation: that all now depended on the *Kildare Glen* reaching Montevideo quickly for his immediate transfer to hospital. Ben, deciding that he would give the big man no more morphine unless the pain returned with its former intensity, told Taggart that the *Kildare Glen* had been breaking all her previous speed records since mid-afternoon. Since the Chief Engineer had double-banked the watches at four o'clock the ship had logged just over eighty miles in six hours. At midnight, they would be within 660 miles of the Plate Estuary.

'How come you know all this?' Taggart asked, showing surprise even in his woolly state.

Ben grinned. 'They've been keeping me informed. So that I could tell you when you woke up. Not tomorrow night but the night after, round about now, we should be picking up the pilot.'

'Picking up the pilot,' Taggart repeated. 'Picking up the pilot. . . .' His voice trailed away and his eyes closed. He was sleeping again, breathing shallowly in short panting gasps. Ben sat with him for a further half-hour. Taggart's sleep seemed blessedly peaceful.

Finding it difficult to keep his own eyes open, Ben slipped from the bedroom and eased himself on to the day-room settee. Within seconds, he was fast asleep.

The sound of his name being called seemed to be coming from a long distance away. Ben raised his head from the pillow and, turning his body, slipped off the settee and found himself sitting on the deck of the day-room. It took him a moment to remember where he was and why he should be sitting on the floor. Then the voice came again: a bellow from the next cabin.

'Ben! Ben! The bastards are trying to kill me!'

Ben was off the deck in an instant and ran through to the bedroom. He stopped short at the sight that greeted him. Taggart was sitting cross-legged in the middle of the bed, staring at the wrist-watch which he was holding in two hands in front of him. He seemed mesmerised by the watch.

'Thirty-four, thirty-five, thirty-six . . .' He counted out loud.

'What's wrong?' Ben asked, his voice shrill.

Taggart did not look up but kept counting.

' . . . fifty-three, fifty-four, fifty-five, fifty-six!' He stopped and stared wild-eyed at the American. 'The bastards! They're going to be the death of me!'

Ben stared at him without comprehension.

'Who's trying to kill you? What are you talking about?'

'Those bloody engineers! Haven't you got ears, man? Can't you see what their game is?'

It dawned on Ben that Taggart had been counting the revolutions of the engine. He needed no watch to tell him that the deep persistent beat had slowed to an almost leisurely rhythm. The *Kildare Glen* was no longer vibrating along at midnight's plate-shaking speed.

'There must be something wrong,' Ben said.

'Something wrong?' Taggart echoed the words in a dispirited voice. 'I can't beat them this time. I can't beat them, Ben. Let them have the last laugh.' He was staring into space. Suddenly he screwed up his eyes like a child who was about to burst into tears. He tumbled forward on the bed and curled his great body into a ball, hugging his knees and giving vent to great animal-like sobs.

Ben approached and stretched out a hand to touch a heaving shoulder.

'Let's get you back on the pillow, Captain,' he said gently. 'Is it the pain again?'

Still sobbing, Taggart allowed himself to be rolled over so that his head was on the pillow. As Ben pulled the covering of sheet and single blanket around him, Taggart stared up at him, his eyes filling with tears.

'I've had enough, Ben,' he sobbed. 'I've had enough. I'm too tired to fight any more. Am I dreaming that it's you there or are you really there? Everything's so fuzzy now. Tell me you're real!'

'I'm real, Captain. I'm here, right beside you. Tell me if you're in pain.'

'Pain? Pain? The knife, you mean? The knife in my side? It hurts, Ben. It hurts all the time . . . But I can't pull it out . . . I try and try and try to pull it out but I can't budge it . . . I don't have the strength . . . And every time I move, the blade goes in deeper . . .' He raised himself and seized hold of Ben's shirt-front. 'You pull it out, Ben! You can get your hands on the handle. Pull it out and maybe I'll get some peace!'

He did not have the strength to maintain his frenzied

hold on Ben's shirt and the fingers slackened and fell away. He subsided back on to the pillow.

'I can give you a couple more of those pills, Captain,' Ben murmured. 'If the pain's too much . . .'

'No?' Taggart shouted, and the effort of uttering the word seemed to exhaust him. 'Mind over matter,' he mumbled. 'Mind over matter . . . Leave that damned knife . . . And keep your damned pills! I just want to sleep . . . sleep . . .'

The short panting breaths came again. Sweat ran from his forehead. His eyes closed. He slept uneasily – but he was asleep.

Ben tip-toed from the bedroom, picking up Taggart's wrist-watch on the way. It must have fallen on the deck when he had rearranged the bed-clothes. In the day-room, he was about to put the watch in a desk-drawer when he held it up and watched the second hand sweep through a minute. As he did so, he silently counted off the deep beat of the engine. Fifty-four revs he made it. There *was* something very wrong. The *Kildare Glen* should have been thrashing along at seventy-two or more revs per minute.

The time on the watch was 3.32 a.m. The hour of day had not registered before with Ben. It surprised him to realise he must have been out cold for three hours. It had seemed that he had only spent minutes on the settee before Taggart's shouts had disturbed him. Three thirty-two. That meant Willem Prins was still on the bridge. Fowler would be relieving him in just under half an hour.

Ben made his way to the bridge. In the wheel-house, Prins was talking into the telephone when the American arrived. Ben waited until he had finished his conversation.

'What's the trouble, Mr Prins?'

'We've been losing speed all watch,' the Dutchman

said. 'That's the fourth time I've called the Third Engineer, but all he tells me is that they're having difficulty keeping steam.'

Ben wasted no further time on the bridge. The trouble was down below, so Ferguson was the man to sort it out. Ferguson, however, was not in his cabin. His door was open, on the hook, with the door-curtain flapping gently. With no answer to Ben's knock, the American went into the room, to find the bed-clothes thrown back and no sign of the Chief Engineer. Ben headed for the engine-room. Having climbed down into its depths, he was greeted without warmth by the Third Engineer, who was on the platform.

'I'm looking for Mr Ferguson.' Ben shouted against the machinery noise.

The Third Engineer jerked a thumb in the direction of the stoke-hold.

'He's next door.'

Ben went into the stoke-hold. A furnace-door was open and a half-naked fireman, whom Ben knew only as Goldie, was raking in the furnace depths with a long steel slice. Another fireman looked on and Ferguson seemed to be supervising the operation.

He looked round at Ben's arrival and detached himself from the little group. He did not seem overjoyed to see Ben.

'You'd better stay out of here, Mr Darby. For your own safety. Right now, you're not the most popular man aboard.'

He ushered Ben towards the engine-room.

'I want to know what the hell's happening, Mr Ferguson,' Ben replied. 'Right now, my popularity doesn't matter a goddamn!'

In the passage to the engine-room, Ferguson stopped and faced Ben grimly.

'Look, Mr Darby, we've had a bit of boiler trouble and I'm doing all I can to put things right. It'll be a damned sight easier if you're not looking over my shoulder.'

'Why, for God's sake?'

Ferguson shuffled impatiently.

'Please just take my word for it. The crowd have got it in their heads that you're dishing out the orders and they don't like it. They're being awkward. They're angry at having to work double watches on what they think is your say-so. They were ready to break their backs for young Whitey – but not Taggart. They still blame him for the boy's death.'

'And they're getting back at him by going slow? By not working? Is that what you're telling me?'

'I'm telling you nothing of the kind,' Ferguson said angrily. 'They've been working like dogs . . .' He hesitated. 'It's just that . . . Well, the Third hasn't been able to keep steam up . . . But I'll see to that. And I don't want you interfering. The engine-room's my responsibility. You look after Taggart and leave the engine-room to me. A couple of hours and we'll be licking along fast enough to shake the rivets out of the deckhead.'

Ben trusted the Chief Engineer and had little choice but to accept his advice.

'I'm sorry if it looked like I was interfering,' he said. He told the Chief about being wakened by Taggart and how he had found him sitting up in bed counting the revs. Ben smiled apologetically. 'He seemed to think that you guys down here were slowing the ship down on purpose. If he remembers about it when he wakes up. I'll let him know it was a boiler that was acting up and that you've got things under control.'

'We won't have any more trouble. I'll see to that,' Ferguson promised.

It was a promise that he was unable to keep.

CHAPTER 14

Landfall

Ben woke up with Bourneville licking his face. The chocolate-coloured pup had clambered up on Taggart's settee and made himself at home on the pillow, from which Ben's head had slipped. Ben sat up, gave the pup's head a fondling rub and deposited the playful animal on the deck. It had been seven when Ben had lain down on the settee with the intention of grabbing an hour's shut-eye before breakfast. He was startled, now, to find that it was after eleven. Breakfast was long past.

He looked into Taggart's darkened bedroom. The big man was sleeping, turning restlessly and emitting unintelligible sounds, like a low muttering in a strange language. Taggart had been awake and rambling. He had stayed with him until long after sun-up, when the Captain had lapsed into the same kind of restless sleep as he was now having. Ben crept from the room.

Feeling the stubble on his chin, Ben reckoned that a shave and a shower in his own room were a reasonable priority. Bourneville – who had adopted Ben during the last few days – flopped up on his legs and followed the American across the alleyway to his room. Ben had no sooner reached his bathroom when a knock at the cabin-door and a call brought him out again.

It was the Chief Steward. He laid a mug of creamy coffee and a plate of biscuits on the table.

'I didn't have the heart to wake you for breakfast,

Mr Darby. You were sleeping like a lamb. Will this keep you going till lunch-time?'

'A life-saver you are,' Ben complimented the Chief Steward. 'I was heading for the shower – but the shower can wait. Thank you.'

The Chief Steward did not leave immediately.

'Any idea why we've slowed down?' he asked. 'I thought we were in a hurry to get the Old Man into dock.'

Ben had not given a thought to the ship's speed since waking. Now he cocked his head to one side to listen to the distant throb of the engine. The beat was slow, possibly slower than the fifty-rev tempo in the early hours of the morning.

'We had a bit of boiler trouble during the night,' Ben said. 'Could be it's still acting up.' Inwardly he felt a mixture of bewilderment and anger. Ferguson had promised that it would only take a couple of hours to have the ship belting along at full speed, and by sun-up there had been a noticeable improvement. So, what was wrong now?

Ben waited for the Chief Steward to leave. His instinct was to rush down and find out from Ferguson what was happening, but after what the Chief Engineer had said he realised that some caution might be needed. There was no point in letting the Chief Steward see how agitated he felt. Ferguson had hinted at crew trouble and had clearly been of the opinion that what might be seen as Ben's interference could only make matters worse. Just what had he been hinting at? *What had he been hiding?*

To Ben's relief, the Chief Steward left. He sipped the coffee, needing time to think. He wondered what would happen if he went storming down to the engine-room as he had done during the night. What was Ferguson afraid of? A mutiny? A refusal to work the double watches? What new crisis was he afraid that Ben might provoke?

He was saved the trouble of further speculation. There was a knock at the cabin-door and a head peered round the curtain. It was Ferguson. Ben looked at him with eyebrows raised.

'We got more boiler trouble, Chief?'

'You could say so.' Ferguson had a worried frown. 'I thought I would head you off, Mr Darby. In case you had any notions about chasing me up with the idea you could do something about it. I want you to stay out of the engine-room.'

'Why, Mr Ferguson?'

'For your own good. I've got a tricky situation down there and I'm doing the best I can to sort it out. I want you to leave it that way. If you interfere, somebody is liable to do something stupid.'

'Like what?'

'Like putting sand in the main bearings. Like opening valves that should stay shut. Like accidentally dropping a crow-bar or a Stilson where it would do a hell of a lot of damage.'

'Sabotage?' Ben stared at Ferguson in horror. 'Out here on the ocean! What the hell are you trying to tell me, Chief?'

'I'm trying to tell you that maybe you should forget about us doing twelve or thirteen knots and maybe settle for seven or eight. Because that's a damned sight better than us coming to a dead stop for a couple of days while I have to take the main engine to peices. As long as we're moving, Taggart has a chance – but if we break down, he's a dead man.'

'Has somebody been threatening you, Chief? What makes you think anyone would go to these lengths?'

'Nobody has threatened me,' the Chief denied. 'But I know what's being said. There are a hell of a lot of men on this ship who think that if the Old Man snuffed it before we got to the Plate, it would only be justice – after what happened to the cabin-boy. . . .'

'There's something you're not telling me,' Ben accused. He had a sudden thought. 'This boiler trouble? That's it, isn't it? It's not accidental – and you know it's not accidental!'

Ferguson looked away, guiltily.

'I'm not saying it's not accidental. And I'm not saying it is. I can't prove that what they're doing is deliberate and they know I can't prove it . . . All I know is that they're just waiting for me to accuse them . . . Then we'll really have trouble on our hands. I can't risk that, Mr Darby.'

'Who are *they*, Chief?'

'The firemen . . . Goldie, McQueen . . . The whole damned bunch of them! They're playing silly buggers and they think they're being hell of a clever – but I want you to stay out of it, or things could really turn nasty. They've as good as said so.'

Ben was tense as the anger rose in him.

'What have they as good as said, Chief?'

Ferguson was a genuinely worried man. He stared unhappily at Ben.

'It's not what anybody has said to my face, Mr Darby, but things they know get back to me . . . About Taggart . . . About what will give out first if the ship is pushed too hard – Taggart or the main engine or my blood-pressure . . . About what might happen if I tried to blame the men for a defective boiler when it wasn't their fault . . .'

Ben did not let him finish.

'I don't know exactly what the hell it is you're scared of, Chief – but if it's the men . . .'

'It's not the men!' Ferguson declared hotly. 'What I'm scared of is the damage that one stupid hot-head could do if I push the men too far.'

'And you want me to sit around pretending everything is hunky-dory while they get away with it and I watch the Captain die by inches? Is that what you want?'

'No, no ... That's not what I want.' There was a note of weary pleading in Ferguson's tone. 'You could spread the word that the Old Man isn't as sick as he was ... That he's out of danger ... Maybe I can get them to see sense ... that they're wasting their time trying to slow the ship down.'

Ben's expression hardened.

'Thanks for spelling the situation out, Chief,' he said shortly. 'But there isn't time for making bargains and it's too damned late for telling lies. I'm not your man.'

Ben brushed past Ferguson, heading towards the door.

'What are you going to do?' the Chief cried.

'You said McQueen was in on this. Maybe he won't listen to you – but he'll goddamn listen to me!'

'You don't understand.' Ferguson tried to detain him. 'I could be wrong. I've told you what I think is happening, but I can't be sure the men are responsible. Maybe it's not their fault that we can't make steam. There could be a dozen reasons. All I'm sure of is the mood they're in ... And it's ugly.'

'No uglier than mine,' shouted Ben, and strode off. The engineer made no effort to stop him. He bowed his head, suddenly feeling every day of his fifty-four years.

As he climbed down the fiddley ladders, the rage that had consumed Ben gave way to gnawing uncertainties. It was one thing to go flying off at half-cock with Ferguson but quite another to sail into McQueen with all guns blazing. For a start, what did he use for ammunition? He should have at least quizzed the Chief Engineer on what it was he suspected the firemen of doing to slow the ship's progress. Ferguson had said that he couldn't prove the firemen were to blame and if, with his vast technical knowledge, Ferguson could not be absolutely sure of his ground, what chance did a layman – and an ignorant one at that – have of making any accusations stick?

By the time he had reached the stoke-hold floor, Ben's anger had been replaced by the caution of one who is approaching an unmarked minefield. The first person to see him was a trimmer who was barrowing ash to the disposal hoist. He wheeled his load past Ben, saying nothing but favouring him with a tauntingly contemptuous smile. McQueen, half-naked and dripping with sweat, was firing an open furnace as if his life depended on it. He caught sight of Ben from the corner of his eye and paused briefly.

'Clear off, Yank. This isn't the promenade deck. We carry no passengers down here.' He cocked an eye at Ben. 'Or are you getting your shirt off to give us a hand?'

'Give him a shovel, Mac!' shouted another fireman, at work on the part boiler. 'Maybe he can show us a thing or two.'

McQueen grinned at Ben.

'Well, Yank! Want to give it a go? We've been knocking our pans in for old Crazy Horse with the four rings on his sleeve. Maybe you can do better than us.

Ben unbuttoned his shirt.

'Maybe I can,' he said.

McQueen threw him his shovel. He turned to the fireman at the port boiler.

'Hey, Midge, nip through and tell the Fourth to watch the steam-gauge and let us know if it gets up to a hundred and eighty. We've got an expert on the job now!' The other man laughed uproariously but made no move to follow the suggestion.

Ben ignored McQueen's evident amusement and started firing the furnace. He immediately found a rhythm.

'Hey, not bad,' McQueen applauded. 'I'll say this for you, Yank. You've learned well.'

Ben turned, sweating, to face him.

'Better than you, you son of a bitch.'

McQueen bridled. 'Now, now, Yank,' he growled. 'Just you watch who you're calling a son of a bitch.'

'I'm calling you a son of a bitch, you son of a bitch'' Ben answered vehemently.

McQueen took a menacing pace towards him. Ben half-raised the shovel to indicate that its use as a weapon of defence was not to be taken lightly.

'What brought this on, Yank?' McQueen asked in a less aggressive tone.

'So you're the Number One?' Ben scoffed. 'The best in the business? The best that ever came out of Tyneside? You couldn't fire a piece of toast!'

McQueen took another step nearer Ben.

'I don't like what you're saying, Yank. I've planted men in the ground for a lot less.'

'You're all mouth, Mac. You're one hell of a disappointment to me. I thought you were the salt of the goddamned earth! I was going to tell the world about you ... About the brave and noble breed with a righteous pride in the sweat of their skins and the skills of their hands ... I didn't have you figured for a murdering skunk!'

McQueen moved quickly then. Too quickly for Ben. The shovel – which he had brandished only to deter – was knocked from his hand. A fist, looping at him in a blur, crashed into his face, high on the cheek-bone. Blood splashed in the air from the three-inch cut below Ben's left eye. He staggered back and fell.

'Get up, you bastard,' McQueen roared at him. 'I'm going to bloody murder you.'

Ben got to his feet and hurled himself at the fireman. He had the satisfaction of feeling his knuckles crack against McQueen's jaw, as two hooked punches hit home. McQueen seemed scarcely to notice the blows but came after Ben again, flooring him with a vicious right above the eye and a left to the uninjured cheek.

Ben struggled to his feet again and, half-blind with his own blood and sure that his jaw had become unhooked in the region of his right ear, stormed in once more. This time, his blows were wild and grazed harmlessly past their intended target. A thudding right to Ben's solar plexus sent him scudding backwards across the stoke-hold floor. He lay there, winded.

When Ben finally struggled to his feet and lurched again towards McQueen, it was the fireman who acknowledged the inequality of the struggle.

'No more, Yank,' he decreed, pushing Ben away easily. 'Why, for the love of Jesus, didn't you just stick to your typewriter? Ye've got guts but no more idea than my kid sister.'

At that moment, the Fourth Engineer appeared from the engine-room.

'What the hell's going on?' he demanded, staring at Ben in dismay.

'It's nothing,' Ben answered him, painfully. 'A private matter. Please stay out of it . . .'

The engineer looked questioningly at McQueen.

'Do as he says, Fourth,' the fireman said. When the engineer hesitated, the fireman added: 'He'll be OK. I'll see to him.'

The Fourth Engineer shook his head worriedly, decided that it was none of his business and left.

McQueen led Ben over to a box under a big ventilation shaft and sat him down on it.

'Got a clean hankie, Yank?'

Ben fished a handkerchief from his trouser-pocket. McQueen doused it with water from a canvas bag hanging below the ventilator and gently bathed Ben's face.

'Why did you needle me into that, Yank! I don't want to hurt you.'

'But you want to hurt Taggart'.

'I've never made any secret of what I'd like to do to that bastard.'

'Call it off, Mac.' Ben's face pained whenever he spoke. He persisted nevertheless.

'You didn't hit me when I was down. Don't put the boot into Taggart when he's halfway dead already.'

'He killed young Whitey.'

'He didn't kill Whitey. He gave him a rough time – but he didn't kill him.'

'What makes you so soft on Taggart? You don't owe him anything.'

'He saved my life.'

'There's more to it than that. You'd bat for him anyway.'

'Yes, Mac, I'd bat for him anyway. Because he needs a friend. More than you, more than me . . . More than anyone else I've ever known, he needs a friend.'

'It's his own bloody fault he hasn't a friend in the world.'

'No, Mac – it's not his fault. He's been made bitter. He's been carrying scars on his mind that no man should ever have to bear. I'm the only living soul who knows the black hell he's been in and, just because I know, I'm going to carry a bit of that hell round with me as long as I live . . .'

McQueen was peering at him gravely, disturbed in spite of himself at the unnamed horror to which the American was alluding. His revulsion was somehow communicated by the tone of his voice.

'It's to do with his son,' McQueen guessed. 'The one who died?'

Ben stared up at McQueen, his tortured soul in his eyes.

'It was not just that he died. It was the way he died.'

Ben looked away, unable to expose to McQueen's gaze the naked torment of his feelings of the images imprinted on his brain by his knowledge of Michael Taggart's death.

'Tell me,' whispered McQueen.

'No,' Ben said hoarsely. 'No I can't . . . I won't! It's better that no one knows. I'm asking you, Mac, don't go on with this madness to get your revenge on Taggart. Call it off. Now. There's enough goddamn hate in the world. Don't work off yours on a man who's already nailed to his cross!'

McQueen drew back, visibly shaken by Ben's passion and his words.

'Blimey!' he stammered.

McQueen stumbled a couple of paces away from Ben, his face suddenly angry.

'What makes you so sure I can do anything for Taggart?'

'You taught me to fire a boiler, Mac,' Ben said softly. 'You're the best. I know you're the best. And I saw you a few minutes ago . . . Giving it everything you've got . . . Piling that coal right up the back of the furnace . . . Choking the back end . . . It's a mass of clinker back there, Mac . . . You must be really proud of yourself . . . But you didn't fool Ferguson. He knows why you're not making enough steam to boil a kettle – even if he won't quite admit it to himself. And I know, Mac . . . Don't sell your pride for your hate . . . Call it off. And get your buddies to call it off – before it's too late.'

McQueen stared hard at Ben.

'You're a bastard, Yank,' he said, but the words were devoid of rancour.

'And you've got a reputation to save,' said Ben. 'My money says you still want to be Number One. *Numero Uno.*'

Ben was not witness to what went on in the stoke-hold after his confrontation with McQueen. Nor was he privy to the arguments that raged in the firemen's mess and brought about a change in attitude towards the need to reach the River Plate without further hindrance or delay. What was apparent to him, however, was a definite improvement in the *Kildare Glen*'s performance during the afternoon watch.

Ferguson came to see him. There was a new respect and admiration for the American in him, although his manner was restrained. He made no mention of Ben's cut and bruised face, although his eyes went again and again to the mute injuries, as if they had a special fascination. Nor did he imply that the build-up of clinker at the back of the furnaces, which had caused the reduction of steam pressure, had been deliberately contrived. He had concluded and the firemen themselves had agreed that careless firing was at least partly to blame for the loss of steam. Dirty boilers might also have made a contribution.

The good news from Ferguson was that an assault upon the clinker with slices had cleared the worst, if not all of the blockages, and pressure had been restored. The bad news was that it would not be possible to recapture the same gallop that the *Kildare Glen* had achieved twenty-four hours previously.

Ben did not enlighten the Chief Engineer with details of what had occurred between himself and McQueen. He had no doubt that some version of what had taken place would reach him in due course. Ben's main satisfaction was that he had won back vital time for Taggart, to whom he was now able to give undivided attention.

The Captain's condition continued to give him cause for concern. That the pain had returned was all too obvious, but Taggart resisted all offers of relieving morphine until late evening, when he was literally crying out in agony. Ben gave him six more doses during the course of the following twenty-four hours. The midnight when the *Kildare Glen* should have reached the broad estuary of the Plate came and went with the South American continent still a hundred miles distant. The delays, caused by Fowler's bogus concern for conserving fuel and by the tactics of the firemen, had cost the *Kildare Glen* at least eight precious hours.

Ben sat with Taggart throughout most of that final night at sea. Towards dawn his fatigue got too much for him and he fell asleep in the chair he had placed near the Captain's bed. He was awakened by the ratcheting sound of the bridge telephone and its grinding ring. He blinked in disbelief at the bed. It was empty.

The bathroom was empty. There was no sign of Taggart in the day-room. But the Captain's cap was gone from the top of his desk. Ben raced for the bridge ladder. He was halfway up when he heard Taggart's familiar voice:

'Ring slow ahead, Mister Mate. And stream the ladder for the pilot.'

All the officers were on the bridge: Fowler, Prins and the Third Mate. Taggart was standing in the starboard wing. He had dressed in his high-necked white tunic uniform and his cap was pulled down firmly on his head. Ben could scarcely believe that he had managed to dress and make his way to the bridge unaided, while he had slept.

The Third Mate dodged past Ben to ring the telegraph in the wheel-house, while both Fowler and Prins kept staring uneasily at Taggart. The Captain's appearance on the bridge had clearly taken them by surprise and uncertainty was written on their faces.

The Bosun's voice came up from the fore-deck below:

'Ladder ready for the pilot, sir.'

'Stand by to bring him aboard,' Taggart sang out. He turned and saw Ben, without seeming to recognise him.

'Well, boy, is the ensign hoisted?' he asked briskly.

Ben looked dumbly towards Prins and saw him nod his head anxiously, telling him to assent.

'Yes, sir,' Ben answered Taggart.

Taggart half-smiled his approval, but he seemed to have difficulty focusing his eyes. His knees buckled slowly and he slid to a heap at the American's feet. Ben tried to save him but was almost bowled over by the big man's sudden slump forward.

With the help of Prins, he rolled Taggart on to his back and slackened the tight tunic-neck. Prins had a hand on the Captain's wrist.

'He's alive,' the Dutchman murmured. 'The pulse is beating like a drum.

The pilot took the *Kildare Glen* in towards the long southern breakwater that guards the port of Montevideo and asked for dead-slow speed. The ship made way slowly against the current, marking time while the white motor-launch – which had rounded the western tip of the breakwater moments before – surged across the mile of open water between the freighter and the port entrance.

On the deck, below the bridge, Taggart had already been strapped into a jacket stretcher and a block had been rigged to the companion-way davit, ready to lower him into the launch. Ben stood with the little group on the deck. Into a case he had packed clothes for himself and Taggart and also the identity documents which both would require. In his hand Ben held Taggart's uniform cap.

It had been Fowler's suggestion that Ben accompany Taggart to the hospital. Fowler had seemed to enjoy taking command and dealing with the various officials who had boarded with the pilot – and he had taken his time over it. Now, however, the wrangling had been all sorted out. The *Kildare Glen* was not to berth at Montevideo but to proceed upriver to Buenos Aires, where the bulk of her cargo was waiting. She would stop off at Montevideo when she returned downriver in ten days' time. In the meantime, Taggart was to be hospitalised in Montevideo. If he lived, thought Ben. The Captain had not recovered consciousness but was quietly moaning, his head turning from side to side as he lay in the stretcher. His face and neck were flushed a flaming red and he seemed to be sweating from every pore.

When the launch finally came alongside, the transfer was completed in under five minutes. A white-jacketed doctor supervised Taggart's installation in the tiny cabin of the launch. Ben did not crowd in after him, but waited outside in the narrow waist. Solemn faces looked down at him from the rust-stained freighter's rail as the launch pulled away. He heard the grating ring of the bridge telegraph and the pilot's helm order and the *Kildare Glen* was already swinging away to port as the launch turned sharply towards the breakwater head.

A short distance upriver, Ben could see, protruding from the muddy-grey waters of the Plate, the dark pillar that was the bridge structure of the German pocket battleship *Graf Spee*: a silent memorial to one of the first great naval battles of the war. Her captain had taken his own life, and the rusting bulk was all that remained of his dreams of glory.

An ambulance was waiting on the quayside, near the Aduana. It was a canvas-topped vehicle and all Ben saw of Montevideo as it raced across town was what was visible through the drawn flaps at the back. Taggart lay under a blanket on the bench-bed whilst Ben knelt beside him, preventing him from rolling off as the ambulance – klaxon blaring unceasingly – wove its way through jams of bell-ringing trams, hooting buses and the assortment of ancient trucks, horse-drawn wagons and private cars that thronged the streets of the Uruguayan capital. The journey seemed interminable, but within thirty minutes of leaving the Customs House the ambulance pulled up at the rear of a stark grey building with the forbidding exterior of a barracks or a prison.

A white-clad nun emerged to take charge of the patient and supervise the porters, who carried Taggart into the dim interior. Ben followed the procession through stone-flagged corridors into a high-roofed central hallway. The man signalled to the porters to continue with Taggart down a tunnel-like passageway ending in swing doors, but she barred Ben's way. Beyond understanding that he was permitted to go no further, Ben found the nursing sister's Spanish unintelligible.

The nun made signs as if she were writing on a pad and pointed towards a glass-fronted recess at the far end of the hall. Ben nodded understanding. It was the reception area and particulars were wanted. The nun beamed approval as Ben indicated with signs that he would report to the office.

It was manned by a uniformed janitor who spoke no English. The communication impasse was quickly solved by an internal telephone call. Minutes later, a second nun with a wrinkled face arrived. Ben guessed she must be seventy if she were a day, but she had merry twinkling eyes.

'I'm Sister Theresa,' she announced. 'And you must be the gentleman who came with the English captain.' She was as Irish as the shamrock and her voice still had the lilt of Donegal. She acted as interpreter so that the paper formalities of Taggart's admittance could be completed.

'Sure, you don't want to be waiting around in this dismal place,' she told Ben, and led him out to a cloistered garden of paved walks and tree-shaded seats. She absented herself briefly, then returned carrying a tray with a glass and a jug of iced lemon.

'They've taken the Captain straight to the theatre,' she reported, and left Ben to wait. He could hear the noise of traffic, not far away, but the high stone walls muted the sound. Ben took in his surroundings, feeling a tranquillity he had not known in months. There was relief in it that, in spite of all the setbacks, he had finally delivered Taggart into good hands. It had been a close-run thing but, for better or worse, he had discharged the burden of responsibility that Fate and his own conscience had thrust upon him: a burden of responsibility which he had not willingly sought nor accepted with any degree of confidence in his own fitness to shoulder. There was no self-satisfaction in Ben's relief, no element of self-congratulatory pride — only a profound thankfulness that, somehow, in spite of all the trials and tribulations of the immediate past, he had floundered through darkness and emerged into light.

Here — in the peace of this garden — the travails of the world seemed a million miles away. Here was the end of the long journey through darkness. Here there was only light — and Ben surrendered himself to its serenity.

It seemed that only minutes had passed when he saw Sister Theresa coming towards him. In spite of her years, she held herself very erect and there was grace in her unhurried steps. The eyes gave the lined face a beatific radiance as she stretched out a thin bony hand to rest on Ben's wrist.

'Doctor Ramirez apologises for not coming to you in person,' she said, 'but he does not speak English . . . He asked me to tell you that everything that could be done to save the Captain was done . . . but the Captain is now at peace . . .'

Ben stared at her, strangely empty of feeling.

'Captain Taggart is dead?'

'Only minutes ago. He died on the operating table . . . You know that it was his appendix?'

'Yes.'

'The appendix had ruptured ... The infection of the peritoneum was too great ... Doctor Ramirez did everything he could. I am so sorry ... Doctor Ramirez, poor man, is so upset. He is so sure he could have saved the Captain, if only he had been brought in sooner ... Even three, four hours might have made all the difference ...'

She spoke on in her soft Irish voice, but Ben scarcely heard her. He was counting hours lost at sea, hours lost that could have been saved. He was startled back to the present as Sister Theresa said, with a resigned finality, 'It is the will of God.'

But was it? Was it the will of God or the will of perverse Man?

The emptiness that Ben had felt when Sister Theresa had broken the news of Taggart's death remained with him. He felt empty and lost. For all his fears for Taggart when he had disembarked from the *Kildare Glen*, he had, somehow, never lost hope that the Captain would survive. And he had not stopped to think what the consequences of his death might be. The reality was that he was alone and stranded in an alien place, with no less a responsibility for the dead sea-captain than he had borne for the living man.

Without the kindly help of Sister Theresa, he would not have known which way to turn. It was her inspiration to telephone a compatriot, Father O'Brien, at the St Helen's Club, and ask for help. The club, with its social hall and reading-room, was run by the Apostleship of the Sea – the Roman Catholic Mission to Sailors – and the Irish priest was its guiding light.

Within half an hour of receiving Sister Theresa's call, this bustling cheerful Irishman – whose crooked nose testified to earlier flirations with the pugilistic arts – was at the hospital and taking charge. Ben was only too happy to let him do so and sat, dazed, as the priest enumerated all the things that would have to be done and how he proposed to tackle them.

Did Ben know who the *Kildare Glen*'s shipping agents were, both here and in Buenos Aires? Because they and the ship-owners in Britain would have to be informed of Taggart's death. Ben did not, but the names and addresses were amongst Taggart's documents.

'Leave me to take care of that,' Father O'Brien told Ben. 'I'll also let the British consulate know and I'll pass on the news to the British Patriotic Committee because they'll want to be represented at the funeral. D'ye know what faith the Captain was?'

Ben confessed that he had no idea.

'No matter,' said the priest, 'I'll have a word with me old friend at Holy Trinity – he's of the Anglican persuasion – and the new young fellow at the Emmanuel Church ... That's the Methodist place. We'll come to some arrangement between the three of us. And you'll need a place to stay. D'ye have any money?'

Ben had no money. But he could remedy that by calling at the US consulate.

'That'll take time,' said the priest. 'Ye'll need something to tide you over.' He took a wad of pesos from his pocket and handed it over to Ben without even counting the amount. 'This'll keep you going. Ye can pay me back anytime.'

Ben found himself swept along by the priest's energy and bustling kindness. He was the possessor of a tiny open-topped convertible of venerable years, which he drove with the cheerful abandon of a madman.

He deposited Ben at the Hotel Pyramides on the Calle Ituzaingo.

'It's not the Ritz,' he informed Ben, 'but it's clean and friendly and, for a peso-fifty a day, ye can ask no more. I'll look in again later to see that ye've got fixed up all right. If ye go out for a drink at any of the bars, be sure ye don't pay more than twenty-five centesimos for a big bottle of beer — and ye're being robbed if ye're asked for more than sixty cents for a whisky!'

Before he drove off like a maniac into the afternoon traffic, he had a final word for Ben.

'Uruguay's a grand country and ye should be at home here in Montevideo. The man who made this country the envy of South America was a fellow called José Batlle y Ordóñez. They made him President in 1903. Have ye heard of him?'

'I can't say I have,' Ben replied.

'Well he's God's proof that a fellow like yerself can leave yer mark on history. The pair of you had something in common, ye know. He was a journalist, too.'

With a broad grin on his face, and a roar of the convertible's engine, he surged out into the traffic.

The Church of the Holy Trinity stood on the Calle Reconquista looking out to sea. It was only a block away from the Hotel Pyramides and it was to there that Taggart's body was to be taken for a funeral service. Father O'Brien, who had taken charge of all the arrangements, had come to an amicable agreement with the Anglican clergyman on who should conduct the final rites. He himself would say an early Mass at his Mission for the Captain because he counted all sailors as his flock, but since the Captain's papers said he was Church of England, it was only right that the Anglican should officiate at the interment.

There was to be only the briefest interval between Taggart's death and his funeral: a mere forty-eight hours separating the two events. During the day that intervened, Father O'Brien paid a flying visit to the Pyramides to report to Ben on his activities and brief him for the following day.

'I'm taking it ye'll be the Captain's chief mourner and take the head of the coffin at the burial,' he said.

'Usually, it's the job of the eldest son, but you're the nearest to family the poor man has in this part of the world. Did he have any family?'

'There was a son,' Ben told the priest. 'He was killed ... just over a year ago ... In the desert war. He was an only son.'

'God take pity on the poor grieving widow.' Father O'Brien said sadly. 'To lose both of her nearest and dearest, and at different ends of the earth – it will be a sad day for her.'

Ben did not feel it necessary to tell the priest that Taggart had been separated from his wife for some years. Nor did he voice the fear that not only would he have to fill the role of chief mourner, he would probably be the only mourner.

'Will you manage to find some others ... for the coffin?' he asked the priest.

'Lord save us, we'd be in a bad way if we were stuck for pall-bearers?' The priest was amused by Ben's concern. 'Look, I told you that you could safely leave everything to me. We'll do the Captain proud, I tell you. All you've got to worry about is getting to the church for ten o'clock tomorrow morning – and that should be no problem, since the ship's agent is sending a car to collect you at a quarter to!'

'I'll be ready,' Ben promised.

At quarter to ten the following day, Ben was ready for the big black chauffeur-driven limousine that appeared at the hotel door – but he was totally unprepared for the surprises the day held in store.

The first came when he entered the Church of the Holy Trinity, where he was welcomed at the door by the robed vicar and escorted to a reserved pew before the altar. To Ben's astonishment, the church was packed with people: so many that some had been unable to find seats. There were businessmen in light tropical suits and black ties, most wearing black arm-bands. There were their ladies, with wide black straw hats and elbow-length black gloves. There were two rows of Uruguayan navymen, all smart as paint in their best dress uniforms. There were merchant sailors from the port, stiff-looking and uncomfortable in collars and ties. There were dignitaries from the city, well-scrubbed and important-looking. There were representatives from the Army, the policy, the fire service, the Customs, the Port Authority, the Government.

Before them, in front of the altar, sat the huge casket that contained the mortal remains of Captain William Taggart. Across it was draped the red ensign.

Ben caught a glimpse of Father O'Brien in a side-pew. The priest nodded and gave him a thumbs-up sign. Ben nodded recognition with a tight smile. The priest had promised to do Taggart proud and he certainly had. Ben had expected the Irishman to rustle up maybe a dozen sailors from the ships in harbour. He had not expected the whole city of Montevideo to turn out.

'We are gathered here in the sight of God,' the vicar intoned, and the service began. Ben started at the ensign-draped coffin, his mind filled with memories of the giant whose disintegration he had witnessed. He had been drawn to Taggart from the outset by a strange prescience of tragedy. Now the tragedy had unfolded. It was over.

Words drifted to Ben, catching him almost unawares with their imagery.

'Let us give thanks for the life and works of our departed comrade and all who go down to the sea in ships and occupy their business in greater waters. These men see the works of the Lord and His wonders in the deep. They reel to and fro, and stagger like a drunken man, and are at their wit's end. . . .'

At their wit's end! The words pierced at Ben like a lance.

'... So when they cry out unto the Lord in their trouble ...'

Oh Captain, Captain, was it to the Lord that you cried out?

'... he delivereth them out of their distress ...'

'Is this your deliverance, Captain? Is It?

'... Then they are glad, because they are at rest. And so he bringeth them to the haven where they would be.'

The long rest of death, and the haven — a grave in Montevideo?

'The days of the man are but as grass, for he flourisheth as a flower of the field. For as soon as the wind goeth over it, it is gone. And the place thereof shall know it no more ...

And the place thereof shall know it no more!

'Now let us pray for the means of grace and the hope of glory ...'

But there is no glory. It is a myth, Taggart had said. There is no glory!

'... being mindful that all flesh is grass, and all the glory of man as the flower of grass. The grass withereth and the flower thereof falleth away ...'

All glory is dust! It scatters in the wind and is gone.

The carriage for the coffin was a flat-topped haulier's wagon, draped with black cloth. It was drawn by two black horses with black plumes fastened to their tossing heads. Six Uruguayan sailors carried the great casket from the church, sweating under the burden, and laid it on the wagon. At the church door, a white-shirted piper in a Stewart tartan kilt played a haunting lament.

The horse-drawn bier moved off. It was followed immediately by an open truck, garlanded in black, its back laden with wreaths. Behind the truck with the wreaths marched the Uruguayan Navy, their band striking up the sombre notes of the Dead March from Handel's 'Saul'.

Ben's limousine followed the band. Into it, beside him, crowded the Anglican priest and three others who were briefly introduced to him. They were all British: the chairman of the British Patriotic Committee, a member of the consular staff, and a naval attaché.

Behind Ben's limousine came many more: official cars from the city services departments; private cars from the British business community; and flag-emblazoned sedans from the international diplomatic fraternity.

The cortège proceeded at crawling pace up the Calle Brecma and turned right towards the Square of Independence. At every corner, police had stopped the traffic. The streets were lined with solemn, silent crowds, who crossed themselves as the coffin passed. Ben was bewildered by it all. The citizens of the Uruguayan capital had turned out *en masse* to pay their final respects to an unknown foreigner.

'Not quite unknown, Mr Darby,' Ben was informed by the young naval attaché, who had shared Ben's limousine to the cemetery and returned with him afterwards to the reception in the Victoria Hall, the headquarters of the British Society. A buffet lunch had been laid on and the two men were at the side of the throng milling around tables groaning with platters of sandwiches. 'Didn't you see yesterday's papers?' asked the attaché.

Ben had seen no newspapers, other than a week-old *New York Herald Tribune*.

'Captain Taggart got a huge write-up in the *Buenos Aires Herald*,' the navyman told him. 'All about his magnificent war record. And he lost a son in North Africa, did you know?'

'Yes,' Ben murmured. 'Yes, I knew. How did the Buenos Aires paper get the story? The Captain only died two days ago.'

The naval attaché smiled.

'Our information services have to be on the ball in South America. Anything we can put out that wins a bit of popular sympathy for the Allies is worth a hundred political speeches. And Captain Taggart was quite a hero.'

'Everybody loves a dead hero,' Ben said. His irony was lost on the attaché, who went on seriously:

'The story took a trick, anyway. Most of the BA papers took it up and even the Spanish-language papers in Monte had it by afternoon. There's a lot of rivalry between here and BA and the locals went to town on it because it was really a Monte story. Tomorrow's papers will splash the funeral and that'll be one in the eye for the Germans.'

Ben stared at him. 'Why?'

'There's a sizeable German community here – as there is a British one – and they're now slow in the propaganda stakes. They won tremendous sympathy after the *Graf Spee* fight, with the mass funeral of all those German sailors – and they even got their oar in at Captain Taggart's funeral.'

'How, for God's sake?'

'Didn't you see the wreath? "From the officers and men of the *Tacoma*, to a gallant adversary." The *Tacoma*'s the big German ship interned in the harbour. She supplied the *Graf Spee* and she's been tied up down there since Langdorff scuttled his ship.'

At that moment they were joined by one of the senior members of the British Patriotic Committee, a tall military figure with white hair who walked with the aid of a stick. An array of 1914–18 medals jangled at his chest.

'Well, gentlemen, we gave the gallant captain a fitting send-off, don't you think?' he said.

The naval attaché introduced Ben.

'A wonderful turn-out, eh?' the man said to Ben.

'You must have gone to a lot of trouble,' Ben said politely.

'Got to show the flag, old boy,' the other said fiercely. 'Got to show the flag. He was one of our own, after all. One of our own.'

Ben scarcely recognised the *Kildare Glen* as she glided in past the breakwater and made a full turn towards Montevideo's No. 1 dock. She had been painted from stem to stern in dull battleship grey and her funnel, masts, samson posts and hold ventilators boasted a new coat of light grey: evidence of a job-and-finish bargain that the new captain had struck with the deck-hands within an hour of taking command in Buenos Aires. Beckett, the new captain, had offered the deck sailors indefinite shore liberty on satisfactory completion of the painting job, and the work had been finished in three-and-a-half days flat: giving the crewmen twelve days of freedom in which to enjoy the delights of Buenos Aires.

It must have been a sickening disappointment to Fowler to find that his command of the freighter was to be of only a few days' duration. London, it seemed, had moved with almost lightning speed to replace Taggart, and the chance that an experienced master like Beckett happened to be present and available in BA was so unlikely that Fowler could not have calculated the astronomic odds against its occurrence. He could rightly have concluded that not only Taggart but all the gods in heaven had decreed that he was not destined for command.

With 8,000 tons of cargo in her holds, the *Kildare Glen* now sat low in the water: another reason why she looked quite different to Ben's eyes. When, finally, the ship had berthed, Ben followed the shipping agent up the gangway. Later, he was introduced to the man who now occupied Taggart's rooms.

Beckett, to Ben's surprise, turned out to be a man of

sixty-seven – a grey-haired veteran of the 1914 war, with a permanent reminder of that conflict. He had a metal artificial leg: the consequence of an accident while streaming a paravane. He was one of the calmest men that Ben had ever met: thoughtful, wholly imperturbable, and with a quiet authority and wisdom that was leavened by a droll sense of humour. Ben liked him instantly.

'I've heard a great deal about you, Mr Darby,' Beckett said, shaking Ben's hand. 'A pity about poor Taggart. I knew him years ago.'

'You sailed with him?'

'No, we were both on the grain trade . . . The Great Lakes . . . We seemed to follow each other around for a time and we kept meeting up . . . He was an ambitious young fellow in those days, but I liked him a lot. Always so cheerful and outgoing. Nothing ever got him down.'

Ben was silent. Beckett studied him from below beetled brows.

'They tell me Bill went a bit strange . . . towards the end.'

'Yes, I suppose he did,' Ben said. 'He was under a lot of strain. And he lost his son . . .'

'Yes, yes,' murmured Beckett. 'You don't need to tell me about the pressures. I've seen so many good men crack up. It's the war . . . the strain that goes on and on without end. Human overload. A man can take only so much, you know – then something gives. I've seen it so often. We humans should have Plimsoll lines, like ships – to show when we're carrying more than it's safe to take. But we don't . . . We go quietly mad . . . we stop smiling . . . we turn religious, or nasty . . . Our personalities change . . . We lose our affection for the rest of the human race . . . we begin to wonder if there's any point to the whole stupid struggle of battling on. We begin to despair because we've forgotten how to hope.'

It was Ben's turn to look closely at the other man.

'You're bearing up pretty well yourself, Captain,' he observed.

Beckett laughed. 'Hell, they'll have to take me out and shoot me before I let life get on top of me,' he snorted. 'I don't have the imagination to worry myself into the grave.'

'There's more to you than that,' Ben said, smiling. 'You've been through the mill, I can tell. Seems to me you've worked out a few answers about living.'

Beckett grinned. 'Because I've lived so long?' he asked impishly. 'Well, maybe I have learned a few thing along the way, young feller. If I worry, I try to worry about things that matter – like would my next clean collar get past my wife's inspection? Or will a late frost get at the apple trees in my back garden? The unimportant things, like the political reconstruction of Europe, I'm quite happy to leave to cleverer people – like yourself, or my wife.'

He was teasing Ben. And Ben laughed for the first time in many, many days.

The *Kildare Glen* stayed in Montevideo for four more days. During that time, Beckett experienced a problem which Ben helped him to overcome. It concerned the fate of the pup called Bourneville.

'We can't take it back to the UK,' the Captain confided to Ben, with some unhappiness. 'The damnable thing is that I've become attached to the cute little fellow.'

'Why can't you take him home with you?' Ben asked, surprised.

'The quarantine laws,' Becket said. 'They'd put the poor little blighter down. They're as strict as hell about dogs getting into the country, in case of rabies. There's no chance of you wanting to take the dog when you land in Freetown, is there?'

Ben thought about it, but the encumbrance of a pet was more than he wanted to have in West Africa. It wasn't as if he could offer the dog the security of a home.

'How about finding him a home in Montevideo?' Ben asked brightly. 'Can't we land him here?'

'There's nothing to stop us,' Beckett admitted. 'But I wouldn't like to give him to just anybody. I'd like to be sure he would be looked after.'

Ben thought immediately of Father O'Brien. To everyone's delight, the priest agreed happily to take in Bourneville.

'Sure, a man without a wife needs some sort of companionship. Does the little fellow like travelling around in case, d'ye think?' he asked Ben.

'I'm sure he could get used to it,' Ben said and, remembering the way that Father O'Brien drove, he succeeded in keeping his face solemn as he said it.

The *Kildare Glen* sailed on a Sunday afternoon and it seemed the whole of Montevideo turned out to bid her farewell. There must have been 10,000 men, women and children gathered along the length of the south breakwater as the freighter slipped her moorings and nosed towards the harbour entrance. Tens of thousands more were assembled along the Rambla Sud America on the seaward side of the city.

The cruiser *Uruguay* was moored at the sea-wall. Beckett ordered the *Kildare Glen*'s red ensign to be dipped in salute to the warship. A great roar of approval went up from the crowds as the courtesy was observed, to be followed by another when the ancient cruiser dipped her colours in reply.

Ben watched the scene from the lower bridge, exhilarated by the warmth of the demonstration. As the *Kildare Glen* passed the end of the crowded mole, he picked out a solitary figure at the extreme point. It was Father O'Brien and, on a leash at his feet, was a chocolate-coloured dog with floppy ears. It began to bark and leap up and down excitedly as the ship glided past, so close. The priest picked the dog up in one arm. The other arm he extended and moved in a slow wave.

Ben, his heart strangely full, waved slowly in return. In the broad estuary of the Plate, the pilot was disembarked and the *Kildare Glen*, her engines quickening to full speed, headed for the open sea.

Beckett, parading on the top bridge, caught sight of Ben on the deck below. He called out to him.

'Next stop, Freetown.'

Sierra Leone waited, 4,000 miles away.